# TOWN IN A
# Lobster Stew

**Center Point
Large Print**

**This Large Print Book carries the
Seal of Approval of N.A.V.H.**

# TOWN IN A
# Lobster Stew

# B. B. Haywood

CENTER POINT PUBLISHING
THORNDIKE, MAINE

This Center Point Large Print edition is published in the year 2011 by arrangement with Berkley Books, a member of Penguin Group (USA) Inc.

The text of this Large Print edition is unabridged.
In other aspects, this book may vary
from the original edition.
Printed in the United States of America
on permanent paper.
Set in 16-point Times New Roman type.

ISBN: 978-1-61173-049-4

Library of Congress Cataloging-in-Publication Data

Haywood, B. B.
Town in a lobster stew / B. B. Haywood.
p. cm.
ISBN 978-1-61173-049-4 (library binding : alk. paper)
1. City and town life—Maine—Fiction. 2. Cooking (Lobsters)—Fiction.
  3. Cooking—Competitions—Fiction. 4. Murder—Investigation—Fiction.
  5. Maine—Fiction. 6. Large type books. I. Title.
PS3608.A9874T7 2011
813'.6—dc22

2010053678

For George, Robert E.,
and Barbara (the other B.B.)

And for Verna

# ACKNOWLEDGMENTS

Many thanks to the staff of Thomas Memorial Library, Cape Elizabeth, Maine, for providing years of good company and helping to successfully launch the first book. In particular, thanks to Rachel Davis for her great publicity and to Joyce Lourie for all her support. Special thanks, once again, to Todd Merrill and Jen Dyer at Merrill Blueberry Farms, Ellsworth, Maine, for providing numerous details about blueberry farming. Deep gratitude to the Maine chefs who graciously revealed the secrets of their lobster recipes, which you'll find at the end of the book. Thanks as well to many others who provided help and encouragement during the (sometimes difficult) writing of this novel, including Rock, Diane, Laura Leigh, Maryann, Donna, Chris, Freda, Helen, Gloria and Frank, and everyone at Cypress Gardens RV park in Winter Haven, Florida. Warmest thanks to Sheila Connolly for her supportive words and to Teresa Fasolino for her wonderful cover illustrations. Of course, this book wouldn't exist without the help of Kae and Jon Tienstra, Leis Pederson, and the talented staff at Berkley Prime Crime. Finally, hugs, kisses, and much love for Sarah and Matthew, who both are off on great adventures. (Note for Sarah: No lobsters were harmed during the writing of this novel!) For updates about Candy and Doc Holliday, Holliday's Blueberry Acres, and Cape Willington, Maine, as well as special chapters and details about upcoming books, visit www.hollidaysblueberryacres.com.

# PROLOGUE

Something was wrong. Very wrong.

He knew he had to do something about it.

Crossing to the antique brass umbrella stand by the back door, he removed the wooden walking cane and stepped out onto the small concrete porch behind the house. He took a moment to steady himself, leaning absently on the cane as he gazed across the well-kept yard, where dusk-driven shadows gathered in the silence. With a sharpened gaze he studied the white clapboard house next door.

It stood dark and empty. She was gone, he knew. Earlier in the day he'd watched through the front window as she drove away in her old green sedan. She wore the blue patterned frock he liked so much, one of her prettiest. He could still remember the first time he saw her in it.

She had looked like an angel to him then, her skin pale and clear and almost luminescent, like fine porcelain, her gray eyes giving him that no-nonsense look of hers when he'd gallantly reached out to take her hand. She had hesitated, then acquiesced after a few moments with a gentle *tsk, tsk* of her tongue. She was like that, always keeping everything proper. He could still remember the feel of her hand in his—light and cool to the touch, dry yet soft. He had fallen in love with her all over again.

Yet she had not returned his love, not that day, not ever. Their brief affair so many years ago still shone brightly in his memory. He'd been married in those long-ago days, but told her he'd seek a divorce if only she'd have him. She refused—then and in all the years since.

Life whirled them away from one another, and for decades he watched from afar as she married and lived a life he so desperately wanted to share with her. Only when his own dear Emily passed away nine years ago, a victim of cancer, had he gathered the gumption to buy this house he lived in now, next door to hers.

He'd been uncertain of her reaction to this bold maneuver, but she seemed genuinely glad to reconnect with an old friend, and they began to reestablish their relationship, becoming good next-door neighbors, if nothing else at first. In the years since then she had warmed to him, her own husband dead and buried these past twelve years. It was just the two of them now, living alone in their old homes.

But still she kept him at a distance, always a friend, never a lover. They held hands on occasion, shared a dinner or two over glasses of white wine and candlelight. Every week or so she brought him a warm bowl of homemade soup or a few fresh-baked blueberry muffins. On rare occasions she invited him over to watch an old movie. Romances with Irene Dunne and detective stories with Humphrey Bogart were her favorites. His tastes ran a different direction, toward war movies and John Wayne westerns. But he never let that keep him from sitting next to her on her sofa, her smooth, placid face illuminated by the soft glow of the old Magnavox television set. At those times he had trouble keeping his eyes focused on the TV screen, as his gaze tended to wander to her hands, her knees, her ears, the back of her neck. But he always remained proper, despite his longing. Occasionally she would catch him glancing her way and she'd send him a smile. She never gave him anything more.

But that didn't stop him from loving her, from watching over her from a distance. He felt himself her protector.

He hesitated a few more moments, thumping the cane nervously on the concrete porch as the darkness deepened in the thick stand of trees behind the houses. He tried, but hard as he might he could not see movement in the house again. But it had been there—he was sure of it.

Pulling the back door closed behind him, he carefully stepped down off the porch and began to cross the yard.

The grass was moist and fragrant, wearing the deep, glowing green of midspring. He loved this time of year in Maine. Many his age fled south in their later years, but he held steadfast to this close-knit coastal village, unwilling to abandon it because of something as inconsequential as cold weather, or mist or fog, or the dampness that went right to the bones, or the fierce storms coming in off the deep, cold ocean. For he knew that after winter came the season of growth and renewal, when the foliage around Cape Willington sent out those tight, lime-colored buds, which, during one glorious week in May, burst open as shiny new leaves unfurled from twigs and branches.

He approached her home slowly, his gaze scanning the structure from end to end. He spotted nothing out of the ordinary. That eased his concern some, but he remained determined to investigate.

The three-story house, which included two floors of living space as well as a full attic, loomed dark and silent above him as he approached it. Gingerly he climbed the three wooden steps onto the back porch.

He stooped forward slightly and peered in through the thick glass of the back door, but it took him a few moments to realize something was askew. The door stood ajar, opened an inch or two. That made him uneasy, and he took a step back, steadying himself with his cane as he pondered this incongruity.

Had she left it open by mistake? Or had someone entered the house after she had gone, leaving the door ajar to make good an escape?

His heart quickened its beat as his mind worked.

Something in the heavy silence spooked him, and he nearly turned and fled back to the safety of his own place. Better to call the police and let them handle the matter. They could search the home faster and more effectively than he could.

But he dismissed that idea almost at once. He would not let himself be rattled like a child. He thought of her and pushed at the door.

It hinged open with a faint, elongated squeal. He stayed on the porch for a few moments, his gaze sweeping the gloomy interior. Nothing looked wrong so far as he could see.

He stepped inside, leaving the door open behind him.

The sound of his breathing was raspy in his ears now, but it was the only sound he heard. He took a few more steps, putting out a hand to lean on the scrubbed wooden table at the center of the room. She had set the table for two, with rose-patterned porcelain plates, fine polished silverware, crystal goblets, and a cream-colored candle at the center.

His head swiveled toward the sideboard on his right, where she kept the dinnerware as well as a dozen empty ketchup bottles, lovingly displayed, a small portion of her vast collection. These were some of her most prized bottles, dating back decades, to the early years of the previous century. A warm swell of emotion flowed through him as he fondly recalled what had started her obsession with those bottles so long ago. They were scattered all over the house now, on shelves and in cupboards, arranged carefully in glass cabinets, and many more stashed away in closets and cardboard boxes.

Probing slightly ahead of him with his cane, as if he were looking for soft spots in the floor, he moved forward, through an archway and into the living room. Here the ticking of the ornate grandfather clock in the corner filled the silence in an almost intrusive manner. He was tempted to shush it, to tell it to quiet down. Instead, he pursed his lips in annoyance and looked around. The faded, overstuffed sofa and armchair were carefully brushed, fluffed, spotlessly clean, and decorated with large white doilies, which she had made herself back in the sixties, she'd told him once with not a hint of pride. Photographs in mismatched frames stood on a side table against one wall. Many of them showed her with her husband, a tall, gaunt, dour gentleman who never smiled in the photos and always wore a coat and tie. In the photos, he had noticed years ago, husband and wife stood side by side but rarely held hands or touched.

He shook his head sadly, thinking of what might have been.

There were photos of her as a young woman as well, including one taken up north with the Lodge in the background. But there were no photos of him in her collection. He had checked, many times.

He crossed the room and passed under another archway into the hall, which stretched from the front entry to the kitchen at the back. A formal dining room with a large mahogany table and high-backed chairs was directly in front of him. To his right was the staircase to the second floor, with its polished dark-wood banister.

Sighing, he took a few steps along the hallway, toward the back of the house. The place was empty. There was no one here. He had been mistaken.

He was about to call out, just to make sure, when he heard a noise from above his head. A creak, as if someone had stepped on a loose floorboard.

He froze. His head tilted back slowly as his gaze followed the rise of the stairs. Was someone up there? He swallowed hard. He half expected an attacker to come racing down the stairs toward him. But the landing at the top was shrouded in darkness. He saw no one there.

He heard the footsteps then, as abrupt as gunshots in the stillness. Someone was crossing over his head, walking from the back of the house to the front. *To the spare bedroom,* he thought. He'd been in there a few times. There was another display cabinet in that room for her ketchup bottles, he recalled. And a twin poster bed with a white coverlet. An antique floor lamp with stylized crystal droplets hanging from the edges of its shade. Her trusty old Singer sewing machine, vintage 1960s. And, of course, the magnificent wall-length shelving unit, with its secret document drawer.

He felt a chill go through him. *Could that be what the intruder is looking for? The ledger?*

Determined to find out what was going on, he returned to the foot of the stairs, clamped his hand tightly on the banister, and slowly started up, half pulling himself as he went, coaxing his tired legs to take the steps one at a time.

He'd climbed only a half dozen steps when he started breathing heavily. He stopped midway to catch his breath, and paused again a few steps from the top.

As he climbed, he could hear someone opening a drawer, closing it, opening another, moving things around. *Looking for something,* he thought. His anger grew, propelling him up the last few steps to the top. He stood on the landing, huffing, and clenched his cane tighter in his right hand. At least he had a weapon, and he intended to use it.

He stepped from the landing into the hallway. It was directly above the one below, connecting the bedrooms at front and back. Still breathing heavily, he first looked right, toward the back of the house, then left, toward the front bedroom.

The room was shadowed with the oncoming of night. He squinted into the swirl of grays and blacks, trying to make out anything that looked familiar. He could still hear faint sounds as someone rummaged around in there. He moved his foot a step forward and put his weight on it. Beneath his shoe, a floorboard creaked loudly, amplified by the long narrow hallway.

He looked down, horrified, and when he looked up again a figure stood silhouetted in the doorway at the end of the hall. The figure remained there for a moment, as if appraising him, and then ducked back into the room.

His heart jumped in his chest. "Hey, who are you?" he called, starting toward the room. "What are you doing in there?"

He thumped at the floor with his cane. His anger was becoming physical. He stopped a few steps from the bedroom door, which was half-open. Cautiously he craned his neck forward, trying to peer inside, but he saw nothing. He lifted his cane, placed its tip against the door, and pushed.

As the door swung open the shadowy figure came swiftly toward him. He yelped in terror and fell back, struggling to stay on his feet as the figure came closer, adding substance, becoming something more human, more like . . . *him*.

He stared in disbelief. It was as if he were looking into a mirror. He let out a gasp of surprise. The intruder wore a light gray sweater, just as he did, over a white shirt and baggy brown trousers, just like his. Black shoes. Gray hair.

A wig, he realized with a start. His eyes studied

it in fascination. It was well made and looked almost authentic. Even the part was in the right place. His mouth fell open. *Who would do such a thing?*

"What . . . what's going on here?" he sputtered. "Who are you?"

"Who do I look like? I'm *you!*" the intruder said in a voice he vaguely recognized.

That brought him back to reality. He focused his gaze. It took a few moments but finally his eyes widened in recognition. "Hey, wait a minute. I *know* you," he said emphatically. The anger returned, flashing through him. He poked at the air with his finger. "I know who you are! You don't belong here. This isn't your home. You need to get out of here right now!"

In indignation he lifted his cane, brandishing it at the intruder like a sword. "I'm going to call the police! I'm going to call them right now!" He turned abruptly and started toward the stairs. But a hand on his shoulder pulled him back.

"Wait a minute, old man. You're not going anywhere."

He jerked his shoulder forward, out of the intruder's grasp. "Let go! I'm calling the police."

The hand returned to his shoulder, and having had enough of this nonsense, he turned and lashed out with his cane, swinging it toward the intruder. But there was no power in the attack. The intruder raised an arm and batted away the cane with a grunt, knocking it out of his hand. It clattered to the floor.

The face under the wig hardened. "You shouldn't have done that."

"I'll stop you if I have to. This is her house. You have no right to be here." He swung out with his fists.

But the intruder backed away, out of his reach.

Seeing his chance, he turned and scurried toward the stairs, but the intruder followed, grabbing at his sweater and pulling him off balance. He tumbled toward the banister, his legs going out from underneath him. He grabbed for a handhold, but his aim went high. Unable to restrain or protect himself, he fell forward, slamming his head with a dull *thunk!* into the hard wood banister.

He crumbled, a thousand pinpricks of light shooting into his eyes. His ears were ringing, and his elbows and knees hurt. The side of his head felt numb.

For a few moments he lay there, unmoving, groaning. Hands reached out toward him, taking him by the arms, but he swatted at them furiously, driving them away. Gasping, he reached up for the banister, finally grabbed hold, and tried to pull himself to his feet. He needed to call the police. He needed to get help. He needed to get rid of this intruder and get back home where he was safe.

Safe. In his own home. That's where he needed to be. He needed to get back home!

He got his legs under him and started for the stairs, but the intruder was on him again, and he fell forward awkwardly, over the edge of the top step.

He let out no sound as he fell. The stairs rushed up to meet him too quickly.

*I've failed.* The desperate words flashed in his frantic mind.

He landed once hard and bounced, landed hard a second time, bones twisting and snapping inside, shattering his life. His body broken, he tumbled and slid to the bottom, where he lay in an unmoving heap.

A final thought flicked through his brain. *My lovely Wilma Mae . . .*

Then, only darkness.

From *The Cape Crier*
Cape Willington, Maine
May 20th Edition

## COMMUNITY CORNER
by Candy Holliday
Community Correspondent

### IT'S ICE CREAM TIME!
After a long, wet spring, it's officially summer in Maine! The sun has finally come out from behind the clouds! The tourists are back!! The stores are open! And, of course, ice cream is our top priority! The Ice Cream Shack is now officially open, and owner Lyra Graveton (who did a bang-up job in *Oklahoma!* last year) recently announced her new flavor for the summer. Drumroll, please. It's . . . Fruit Lover's Paradise! To create her chilly concoction, Lyra mixes pieces of peach, blueberry, and watermelon in vanilla ice cream with a delicate dark chocolate swirl throughout. Yum! You can get your three servings of fruit a day in a single scoop! This is the way life should be!

## CAPE OBSERVES MEMORIAL DAY

The town of Cape Willington will host its traditional Memorial Day activities on Monday, May 30. The main event will be the Memorial Day Parade, which starts off at 1 P.M. from the high school parking lot and follows a route that takes it south on River Road to the Coastal Loop, up Main Street, and down Ocean Avenue to Town Cemetery. After a brief ceremony and laying of the wreath on the Veterans' Memorial Bench, the parade will regroup and head north along the Coastal Loop to Stone Hill Cemetery for a second ceremony, speeches, and a twenty-one-gun salute. Everyone is invited to participate. Groups and individuals interested in marching in the parade should meet at the high school parking lot at noon. The event will take place rain or shine.

## LOBSTER LOVERS UNITE

While the Memorial Day Parade is the main event going on in town this coming holiday weekend, there are plenty of other activities taking place, including the world famous and totally scrumptious Lobster Stew Cook-off, now in its twenty-ninth year. This year's culinary event takes place on Saturday, May 28, at the Lightkeeper's Inn, located on the corner of Ocean Avenue and the Coastal Loop (they asked me to put that in there for the out-of-towners). The chefs will begin their crustaceous concoctions around 9 A.M., with judging taking place at noon. The event opens to the public at 11 A.M. and continues throughout the afternoon.

Eleven wonderful chefs will be working their magic this year, including Melody Barnes, Wanda Boyle, William "Bumpy" Brigham, Delilah Daggerstone, Charlotte Depew, Lyra Graveton (taking a break from her ice cream–scooping duties!), Walter Gruthers, Juanita Perez, Burt Ramsay, Tillie Shaw, and Anita Weller. I've heard rumors of a guest judge, so stay tuned for that news—as always, you'll be the first to know!

Emerald Isle, a wonderful Celtic band, will entertain the crowd from 1 to 3 P.M. Other events taking place throughout the day will include children's games, face painting, and a raffle with great prizes. You can browse several craft booths as well. And, of course, be sure to sample the stews, at just $3 a cup. Such a deal! You can purchase tickets at Gumm's, Zeke's, or at the Lightkeeper's Inn on the day of the event. For more information, contact Wanda Boyle at 555-6571.

## PLANTS AND PASTRIES

But wait, there's more! A Plant and Pastry Sale is scheduled for Saturday, May 28, from 10 A.M. to 2 P.M. at Town Park. (I told you there was a lot going on!) The joint operation, sponsored by our local community gardeners and the Cape Young Bakers' Group, will offer an eclectic assortment of perennials and phyllos, plus pies, tarts, cookies, croissants, and other assorted goodies. There's even a rumor (another one!) that Herr Georg Wolfsburger, of the renowned Black Forest Bakery, will prepare a selection of his famous German pastries especially for the event. So if you're looking for that special plant to fill an empty spot in your garden, this is the sale for you. And you get to take home dessert as well!

## LASSO UP SOME SNOW

Sure, it seems like the wrong time of year, but congratulations go out to Cape's hardworking (and often unsung) snowplow drivers, who won second place at the Eighteenth Annual Washington County Snowplow Rodeo. Yee haw! The team was assembled by Gordon Davies, Cape's manager of public works, and consists of Tom Farmington, Francis

Robichaud, Payne Webster, and Pete Barkely.

What's the most difficult maneuver they had to perform? According to Gordon, that would be driving the plow through a twisty course of orange cones that have tennis balls balanced on their tops. Sounds tricky, but our boys came through with flying colors. Great work, gentlemen! The team moves on to the state competition in Augusta next month. Be sure to mark your calendars, and head on over to the state capital on June 22 to cheer on our team.

**HOORAY FOR HULA-HOOPS**
Although she's best known for flossing her teeth while driving, Elsie Lingholt is heading to New Brunswick, Canada, to compete in the Women's International Hula-Hoop Competition. When she gets back to Cape Willington, Elsie plans to start a local women's Hula-hoop group. Hopefully we'll see them marching in the next town parade. Now Elsie has a lot to smile about!

**TASTY TIDBITS**
There's so much love in Cape Willington these days, with seaside weddings galore. We'll list them all in our special Wedding Section, scheduled for early June, so keep an

eye out for that. In the meantime, congrat-ulations to all the happy couples. May all your dreams come true!

The annual Beach Cleanup Weekend was a great success, thanks to Jim Harrison and his organizational skills. Three miles of beach and the docks were cleaned up so they can be fully enjoyed by all this summer.

Official Judicious F. P. Bosworth sightings for the first three weeks of May:

Visible: 7 days
Invisible: 14 days

It seems Judicious has been keeping to himself lately. We hope to see more of you this summer, Judicious! As always, pass on your Judicious sightings to the *Cape Crier* for ongoing publication.

High school seniors, PLEASE send us your postgraduation plans so we can print them in our special Graduation Issue next month. You can mail, e-mail, or text them to us, or just give us a call. See the inside front cover of this issue for contact information. Also, please include any prom photos you would like us to publish in our Keepsake Issue.

Finally, mark your calendars for the Ham

and Bean Supper, scheduled for Saturday, June 4, from 4:30 until 6:30 P.M. at the Chapel by the Sea. The Reverend James P. Daisy will be attending, but he promises no sermons! He does tell us, though, that he cooks a mean baked bean dish. We can't wait. Good food and good company are promised.

# ONE

Wilma Mae Wendell hurried about the kitchen in a tizzy.

While the water rose to a boil in its teakettle on the gas burner, she darted first to the cabinet, where she stood on the toes of her sturdy brown shoes to reach the higher shelves, then to the fridge and the sink before pausing beside a silver serving tray that sat on the oak countertop. With practiced hands she arranged the rose-patterned teacups, matching saucers and bowls, polished silverware, cloth napkins, and cookie plates on the tray.

As she worked, she talked.

"I just can't believe it's gone," she said with a quiver of disbelief in her voice. "It's always been in exactly the same spot, year after year, right up there in the front bedroom on the second floor." She tilted her head toward the ceiling to emphasize her point but kept her eyes on the tray.

"I put it in there myself, in a special place where no one else could find it. And it's been right there, safe and sound, ever since James—well, *Mr.* Sedley, you know; I still tend to call him that after all these years, even though he's always insisted I call him James—ever since he gave it to me for safekeeping. At least that's what he told me at the time—*safekeeping,* he said—but *I* know he was mostly just tired of all the commotion that always seems to follow him and that silly recipe of his around."

She lowered her voice just a bit, as if revealing a secret. "He didn't mind the spotlight too much, I can tell you that. But the truth is it just tired him out after a while." She reached toward a cupboard, took out a box of sugar cubes, and proceeded to fill a crystal container using sterling silver pincers. "I think one day he finally realized he'd simply had enough of the whole celebrity life and decided to return to his own kitchen for a little peace and quiet. It was for the best. He was always more comfortable cooking in front of a stove, you know, than he was standing up in front of a crowd."

Wilma Mae shook her white-haired head and made a clucking sound with her tongue. "But he's a lovely gentleman, he is, my Mr. Sedley. He always has been. I've known him for years, longer than I can remember—or longer than I care to admit, at least." She smiled to herself, but it was a melancholy smile. "I was just a teenager when we met. He was a very handsome young man back then, in his early twenties, with his black hair and lovely gray eyes. The same color as mine! Ooh, all the girls thought he was *so* handsome. We used to talk about him all the time back in the serving station. Some of them . . . well, they couldn't help themselves, now could they?"

She shrugged, as if that was explanation enough. "But he was already married, even then, to a rather plain woman who held on to him real tight. And well she should. She passed away a while ago—more than nine years now, I think. Yes, that's about right—it was a few years after my own Milton left me. It's just me and Mr. Sedley now, just the two of us. Anyway, I told him I'd keep it safe for him, and that's exactly what I've done all these years, right up until now. But it's not there anymore, is it? It's got me *so* worried, I don't know what to do. What will Mr. Sedley think?"

With questioning eyes, she looked over at her guest.

Candy Holliday sat at the kitchen table, perched at the edge of a white wooden chair, trying earnestly to follow the elderly woman's rapidly ricocheting chain of thought. Candy sat politely, listening, greatly impressed with the fact that Wilma Mae had said all she had while barely taking a breath.

Candy had come prepared for an interview and had set out a pen and reporter's notebook on the table before her. But she hadn't written anything down yet. She'd only just arrived when Wilma Mae launched into her soliloquy.

Now, realizing Wilma Mae had stopped talking, Candy cleared her throat. Hesitantly, she began. "Well, I don't know Mr. Sedley myself, but I'm sure he would understand . . . whatever it is he . . .

is supposed to understand about . . . whatever it is you just said." She frowned, uncertain if she'd made any sense at all.

Wilma Mae gave her an indulgent look. "Yes, Candy dear, perhaps he would, but he *trusted* me with it, don't you see? And Lord knows what will happen if it gets out in public. Lord knows! It's fairly valuable, you know. Both Mr. Sedley and I received generous offers for it. *Very* generous offers. But we turned them all down, of course."

"Um . . . of course." Candy thought about that for a moment, then finally shook her head. "Mrs. Wendell, I'm sorry, but I'm a little confused. I'm not sure what we're talking about here. Can we back up a little? What, exactly, have you lost?"

Wilma Mae made a clucking sound with her tongue, as if she thought Candy should pay more attention. "Why, Mr. Sedley's recipe, of course. And it's not lost, dear. It's missing. There's a difference. That's why I called you. I'm hoping you can help me."

"Oh." The word came out quickly. Candy blinked several times. "Oh, I thought I was here for an interview. That's what we talked about, right? On the phone? An interview for next week's issue of the paper? You're an honorary judge for the Lobster Stew Cook-off on Saturday, right? But you . . . you want me to help you find a missing recipe?"

Candy tilted her head as she considered her

words. Suddenly it all started to make sense. "Is this the famous lobster stew recipe you're talking about? The one you used all those years to win the cook-off yourself?"

Wilma Mae seemed pleased Candy remembered. "Oh, aren't you smart! The very one! It made the most delicious lobster stew you've ever tasted in your life. I won the cook-off six years in a row with that recipe." Wilma Mae allowed herself a brief moment to feel just a bit smug. "And Mr. Sedley won *seven* consecutive times with that same recipe—which he created, I should add."

"Wow. That must be some recipe. And now it's missing?"

"That's right, dear. It was taken right out from under my nose. But it shouldn't be too difficult to find. You see, I think I know who stole it."

Another surprise. "You mean someone *stole* the recipe from you?"

Wilma Mae nodded emphatically. "That's the only explanation, dear. Someone stole my lobster stew recipe from its secret hiding place. And I need a detective like you to help me get it back."

# TWO

Candy feebly protested. "Mrs. Wendell, I'm very flattered, but I'm just a blueberry farmer who writes columns for the local newspaper on the side. I'm certainly not a detective."

"Oh, but I think you are," Wilma Mae said with a playful wag of her finger. She picked up the silver serving tray and walked out of the kitchen into the living room, talking as she went. "I'm a good judge of character, Candy dear, and we both know it's true. You're the person I'm looking for. There's no doubt about that. The whole town knows about you and your detecting skills."

Candy sighed. It was true. After tracking down Sapphire Vine's murderer the previous summer, she had quickly developed a reputation around town as a solver of mysteries both large and small. Folks started calling out to the farm to ask for her help in all kinds of situations. Most were simple requests, involving missing pets or misplaced items. But some were more serious. One woman asked her to spy on a wayward husband, while another wanted Candy to find out where her teenage daughter went when she sneaked out of the house late at night. One elderly woman even sought Candy's help in catching a ghost that was haunting her house. It turned out to be a neighborhood kid flashing a light in her window after dark.

Candy turned down most requests—just as she was now trying to turn down Wilma Mae's—but sometimes she found herself reluctantly involved, despite her best intentions to do otherwise. She sensed that's what would happen with Wilma Mae.

And, Candy had to admit, in this particular case, she *was* intrigued. Wilma Mae's lobster stew recipe was the stuff of local legend and highly coveted around town, though Candy herself knew little about the story behind the recipe.

Here was her chance to find out more, especially with Cape Willington's annual Lobster Stew Cook-off only days away.

So she followed Wilma Mae into the living room, which seemed to practically glow in the warm May midmorning sunlight. Wilma Mae set down the tray on an antique coffee table and motioned Candy toward the fifties-era sofa. It might have been purple once, Candy surmised, or perhaps brown, though its color had been washed clean by the sun and the passage of years. Still, it was well cared for and in good shape, with white doilies carefully placed on its rounded armrests.

As she settled onto the sofa, Candy scanned the room. The hardwood floors gleamed, and someone had dusted recently. A dark-paneled grandfather clock in the far corner kept the beat of time. Atop an old Magnavox TV set, an arrangement of fresh flowers in a crystal vase brightened the place, offsetting the dark, aging oil landscapes and family portraits that hung on the walls.

Opposite her, against the interior wall, stood an antique mahogany cabinet with glass panels of artfully engraved glass. No doubt its very talented creator had intended the eventual owner to display fine china dinnerware within, or perhaps crystal goblets or priceless keepsakes, or even trophies of some sort. But Wilma Mae displayed empty ketchup bottles, arranged as proudly and artfully as if they were indeed trophies.

The elderly woman settled into a matching armchair and leaned forward to pour. As they drank their tea, they chatted about Wilma Mae's tidy home, the weather, Candy's job at the newspaper—and the ketchup bottles.

"They're very dear to me," Wilma Mae explained with a wistful smile on her face. "I just think they're so lovely—all those different shapes and colors of glass, not to mention the history behind them. You probably won't believe this, but in many ways my life has been defined by a bottle of ketchup. That one right there."

She pointed to a bottle prominently displayed at the center of the mahogany cabinet. "That was the one that started it all. It dates back to 1947, though I have some bottles that are much older, of course. But that one is special."

The bottle, Candy noticed, was the typical tall, narrow shape, tapering from shoulder to neck, with a metal twist cap and its original label still in place. "Is it valuable?" Candy asked.

"Oh no." Wilma Mae waved a dismissive hand. "Probably worth no more than thirty or forty dollars, though some of my bottles might fetch a few hundred. But that one is special. It has sentimental value. It was used by none other than Cornelius Roberts Pruitt himself when he was vacationing at the Lodge up on Moosehead Lake in the late 1940s."

"Cornelius Roberts Pruitt?" The name sounded familiar to Candy. "Wasn't he the father of Helen?"

"The very same. The Pruitts used to be one of the richest families in New England, which was saying something. They still have a lot of money, of course, and still own a lot of land hereabouts. You've been out to Pruitt Manor, haven't you, and met Helen?" asked Wilma Mae, referring to the Pruitt clan's current matriarch, Helen Ross Pruitt, who often summered at Pruitt Manor, an English Tudor-style mansion located out on the point near Kimball Light.

Candy nodded. "Maggie and I were out there last fall for tea," she said, remembering how exciting that day was, and how thrilled Maggie Tremont, her best friend, had remained for weeks after.

"Well, back in those days—the thirties and the forties—the Pruitts used to visit their summer cottage, as they called it, just about every year. They came up right after Memorial Day and brought the whole extended family with them—grandparents, cousins, nieces and nephews, and of course the dogs—anyone who wanted to come.

They used to drive up in a caravan of vehicles, with the family riding in cars and all their belongings following behind them in trucks. It was quite a spectacle when they rolled into town. They spent the summer exploring the Maine coast and the rest of northern New England, and they had a ball." Wilma Mae slapped her knees for emphasis. "They rode horses with the Rockefellers on Mount Desert Island, sailed down to the islands of Casco Bay, hiked up Mount Katahdin with some of the Roosevelts, drove over to see Franconia Notch and the Old Man of the Mountain—they were just regular tourists who loved the region. Anyway, for one or two weeks every summer, Cornelius would visit the Lodge at Moosehead Lake. Sometimes he brought a few of his children, but most times he came alone. He told the family he needed to get away on his own for a few days to cleanse his soul and commune with nature, but mostly he just wanted to commune with his mistresses."

At this, Wilma Mae giggled softly and blushed so bright red she looked like she might catch fire. She fanned herself with her hand. "Oh my, it's getting warm in here, isn't it? It must be the spring sun—or the hot tea. It's an herbal blend, you know—chamomile, calendula, red clover, that sort of thing. I think it also has lavender in it. I picked it up at Zeke's General Store yesterday, when I was out running errands. I find it very

37

soothing, don't you?" She reached for her cup and held it with both hands as she took a sip, looking over the rim at Candy.

"Oh yes, it's very good, and it is quite hot," Candy said with a knowing smile. "I can see where it would make you quite warm."

Wilma Mae nodded appreciatively, set her cup back down on its saucer, and pressed on, her color lightening just a bit as she continued the story.

"Well, you may not know this," she said, "but I was a waitress at the Lodge for several summers back in the forties, and I used to serve Mr. Pruitt—he was always Mr. Pruitt to us, never Cornelius. He was a very stern man, very proper, with a long face, dark eyes, and unruly brown hair, which he tried to keep slicked down. Even on vacation he dressed for all his meals. One morning at breakfast, he was chatting with his table guests and turned a bottle of ketchup—*that* bottle of ketchup"—for emphasis, Wilma Mae pointed to the bottle in the cabinet—"upside down over a plate of steak and eggs, and slapped the bottom so firmly that ketchup squirted out all over the tablecloth and right onto the morning dress of Mrs. Daisy Porter-Sykes, who was one of his closest friends."

"Was she one of his mistresses?" Candy asked, finding herself drawn into the story.

"Oh yes, for quite a long time. Several years, I think. But the affair ended that morning." Wilma Mae gave Candy a grave expression. "I didn't care

38

much for her. None of us did. She was a snooty socialite up from Boston, and she could be quite cruel and condescending to the help. Her husband made his money in timber and land speculation before and during the war. She traveled without him quite often, which made sense, since she was nearly twenty years younger than he was. And she was probably thirty years younger than Cornelius. She'd been meeting him at the Lodge for several years, or so I heard. But that morning she was so upset at him for ruining her morning dress with the ketchup that she told him off, right then and there, in no uncertain terms, and stomped out of the room in a huff, with her boa flying!"

Candy laughed. "That must have been quite a scene."

"Oh, it was!" Wilma Mae said, her eyes lighting up. "She checked out of the hotel that very morning and, as far as I know, never saw him again. It caused quite a bit of scandal, but more importantly, Cornelius was without a mistress for the rest of the week." Wilma Mae paused and blinked several times. "So . . ."

"So . . . ?" prompted Candy.

Wilma Mae cleared her throat. "So, naturally, Cornelius needed companionship for the rest of his stay." She hesitated, and when she spoke again, her voice was hushed, almost a whisper. "I don't know if I should be telling you this, but I became his companion."

Candy's eyes widened in surprise. "His companion? You don't mean . . ."

"Oh yes, it's true," said Wilma Mae with a firm nod of her head. "I was deflowered by none other than Cornelius Roberts Pruitt!"

# THREE

Wilma Mae's blush returned, but this time she paid it no attention. "I suppose you might think I was some sort of hussy, but I can tell you I was not. I was an innocent girl, still a virgin at the time. I knew nothing of the ways of the world. But Cornelius did. He was a very charismatic man, with an air of confidence and power that was, well, intoxicating to someone like me." She added in a whispery voice, as if sharing a secret, "And he had lots of money!"

She laughed sweetly and pointed to an aged black-and-white photograph in an ornate gold frame that sat among many others on the dark mahogany side table against the wall. "That's him there," she said, then added thoughtfully, "His nose was a bit crooked and his teeth were yellow, but he had lovely hands and beautiful eyes. And he smelled good."

Candy rose from where she sat on the sofa and crossed the room to the table. She stooped and peered intently at the photograph Wilma Mae had pointed out. It showed a tall, dark-featured man standing on a sloping lawn in the midst of a large gathering of people assembled for a group portrait. The women in the photograph wore crisp white dresses and wide-brimmed hats adorned with ribbons. They sat in chairs, while most of the men stood behind them, many with their hands thrust deep in their coat pockets. The man at the center of the photograph wore a casually tailored light-colored linen suit, a wide tie, and a straw hat tilted at a jaunty angle. He was gazing off into the distance, an enigmatic smile frozen on his tanned, leathery face. Behind him rose the columns of an elegant yet rustic structure, with striped awnings and a dark roof, and beyond that a blustery sky. Candy could see several staff members standing on the porch behind the main group or looking out of the building's upper windows, half-hidden in the shadows.

"That's most of the family there, taken on an earlier trip to the Lodge," Wilma Mae continued. "Cornelius, of course, is standing at the center. The young girl to his right with the pretty smile is Helen. I'm standing behind them on the porch. You can just see me there, partially in shadow. I'm the skinny one in the white apron with her hands down at her sides."

Candy looked closer. "There you are. You're very lovely in the picture." She paused, her gaze shifting. "And that's Cornelius Roberts Pruitt."

"That's him. I was just a serving girl and

thought I was invisible to him, but he sought me out the same day his affair ended with Daisy Porter-Sykes." She paused as her gaze drifted out the window to the sun-dappled trees in the front yard. "It wasn't hard to fall for him. He seemed to understand my . . . innocence, I guess. He was very kind to me—for a short while."

She sighed deeply as her gaze shifted back to Candy, who had returned to the sofa. "Our affair was a brief one. It lasted only a few days. He left the Lodge by the end of the week to return to his family, and I was left in tears."

Candy was mesmerized as Wilma Mae paused. She wasn't quite sure what to say. Finally, she asked, "Did you hear from him again?"

"Oh, no, no." Wilma Mae fervently shook her head. "He returned to the Lodge the next summer, of course, but he seemed to barely recognize me. Or perhaps he chose to simply ignore me, since he had a new mistress by then. No, it was Mr. Sedley who saved me."

"Mr. Sedley? From next door?"

"Yes, that's right. . . . Well, he didn't live next door at the time, of course. He was an assistant cook in the Lodge's kitchen. After Cornelius left, I was in such a state, I couldn't bear to look at anyone. I was so humiliated, and mad at myself for being such a foolish girl. So I locked myself in my room and refused to talk to anyone or eat anything. But Mr. Sedley rescued me. He heard I was distraught and brought me a tray with a bowl of lobster stew."

Now Candy was beginning to see the connection. "His own recipe?" she guessed.

"He said he made it just for me. He knew lobster was my favorite. It was such a delicacy at the time." Wilma Mae pushed her shoulders together in a girlish way. "I must tell you, I'd never had anyone do anything so nice for me before. He sat beside me on my bed, wiped away my tears, and fed me spoonfuls of the lobster stew. It was so romantic. Soon we were both giggling like children. I found out later that he had had his eye on me for a while."

"But . . . you said he was a married man."

"We couldn't help it," Wilma Mae continued, undeterred. "Sometimes nature takes its course. But that was the only afternoon we were . . . romantic." She straightened her back and fixed Candy with a solemn gaze. "As I said, I don't want you to think I was a loose woman. I had never done anything like it before—nor since. Cornelius and Mr. Sedley were the only two men I've ever been . . . intimate with . . . other than my own Milton, of course. So I broke it off quickly with Mr. Sedley—much to his dismay, I believe. He followed me around the rest of the summer like a lost puppy, but I held him off. That was his last summer at the Lodge. After he left, our lives took us in different directions. But eventually we both wound up here in Cape Willington. And then he entered the Lobster Stew Cook-off."

"With the recipe he created for you?" Candy asked.

"Yes, that's right. As I said, it makes just a wonderful stew. It's the secret ingredient that makes it special, you know. For years he wouldn't tell me what it was, but eventually I found out. When he first entered the cook-off back in the eighties and won with his stew, it created an instant sensation in town. *Everyone* wanted to make it. Mr. Sedley received a number of offers for the recipe. People wanted to *pay* him for it. I heard even Mr. Duffy, who ran the Main Street Diner back then, before he turned it over to his nephew, offered three hundred dollars for it. Three hundred dollars! But Mr. Sedley refused all offers. He said he would hold on to it for a while, and he continued to enter the cook-off, winning all those times. But eventually he decided to retire from the competition. A few years later he gave the recipe to me for safekeeping. He said it belonged to me anyway, since he made it for me, and I was the first person to taste it."

"You used the recipe yourself to win the cook-off, right?"

"Oh yes, but only with Mr. Sedley's blessing. In fact, it was his suggestion."

"And you won six more times with it?"

Wilma Mae nodded. "As I said, Mr. Sedley won

seven consecutive times. So after I won six, I stopped entering, so I wouldn't win more than he had. When I retired from the cook-off, I carefully hid the recipe away where no one could find it, until either Mr. Sedley or I decided what to do with it. We've talked about passing it on to someone, but we still haven't decided who should receive it."

Candy brought the conversation back to where it had started. "And now the recipe's been stolen?"

The color in Wilma Mae's face faded, and she pursed her lips sadly. "Yes." For a moment she seemed on the verge of tears. Then, abruptly, she slapped her knees and rose. "And we're going to get it back, aren't we?" She pointed toward the ceiling. "Come with me. It's time we investigated the scene of the crime."

# FOUR

Taking Candy by the hand, Wilma Mae led the way out of the living room, into the hallway, and up the staircase. She talked as she went.

"This house was built about eighty-five years ago by an architect named John Patrick Mulroy, who used to work out of Portland with John Calvin Stevens and Francis Fassett before he opened his own office in Bangor around 1890. Later, when he was in his sixties, he retired here to Cape Willington and designed several homes in town, including this one. It's one of his simpler designs, as he built it inexpensively for a friend of his. Still, it has some lovely angles. Like many of his contemporaries, Mulroy had an affinity for the Queen Anne and Colonial Revival styles, and you can see that in certain areas of the home."

At the top of the stairs Wilma Mae headed left and entered the front bedroom. She stopped in the center of the room and turned toward Candy.

"He also," she said dramatically, raising a finger, "had a predilection for creating secret hiding places in the homes he built."

"Ooh." Candy's eyebrows rose in interest. "That sounds like it would make a good story for the newspaper. So there's a secret hiding place up here?"

"There is! Can you guess where it is?"

Candy scanned the room, trying to find a likely spot. To her left was a twin poster bed with a white coverlet, and beside it a forty-year-old sewing machine on an antique table. A fairly new chocolate brown wing chair and an antique floor lamp occupied the far corner, toward the street. In front of Candy, between two tall windows, stood another dark wood and glass cabinet displaying more ketchup bottles.

But the most impressive feature of the room was to Candy's right. Built-in shelves and drawers, bracketed between corner cupboards, occupied the entire wall. Some older books were neatly arranged on a few of the upper shelves, but mostly ketchup bottles of all sizes, shapes, colors, and ages occupied the myriad shelves, nooks, and crannies. *There must be hundreds of them,* Candy realized, impressed with the extensiveness of the collection.

She took one more quick look around the room, then turned back to Wilma Mae. "I'd say it's either in that cabinet or in these shelves over here."

Wilma Mae nodded approvingly and motioned toward the shelves. "You've hit right on it. Mulroy had an affinity for built-in drawers, cupboards, and shelves," she explained. "He worked with one of the local cabinetmakers to create built-ins like these in many of the homes he designed here at Cape. It was one of the things that originally attracted me and Mr. Wendell to this home. When we moved in, some of the shelves needed repair, so we brought in a carpenter. He's the one who discovered the secret hiding spot. There's actually a hidden drawer—a document box it's called, used for hiding wills, contracts, deeds, that sort of thing. Here, I'll show you."

She moved toward the shelves as Candy watched in fascination. Wilma Mae gently removed a long, narrow drawer sandwiched horizontally between rows of shelves and bottles. She set the drawer aside on a small table and reached inside the drawer housing, feeling along the side with her fingertip. When she found a slight depression, she pressed it firmly. A spring-loaded drawer popped out of the bottom of the housing.

"Oh, neat." Candy stepped closer for a better look. The secret drawer was perhaps eighteen inches wide and about two inches in height—not large enough for a thick book, but certainly capable of holding a number of documents. The drawer, Candy saw, was empty.

Wilma Mae took a step back, folding her hands at her waist. "That's where I kept the recipe all these years. I've rarely taken it out of there. Mr. Sedley never cared to see it again, and since I quit entering the cook-off, I haven't had much reason to look at it either. I've taken it out a few times to show a close friend or two. But I always returned it to its proper hiding place right away."

"What did it look like?" Candy asked. "Was it just on a single sheet of paper? Or in a recipe book?"

"Oh no. It was written in an old gray ledger, dear. A ledger of his recipes, or formulas, as Mr. Sedley used to call them many years ago. He listed a general description and precise ingredients for each formula he created. He also noted cooking times, temperatures, special preparation details, and the date he created each one. But he kept other things in his ledger as well—financial information, notes on the weather, his observations of guests and staff, that sort of thing.

I believe he also tried his hand at sketching and writing poetry, but he kept those in a different book."

The next obvious question came to Candy. "When did you notice the ledger was missing?" She looked around for her pen and reporter's notebook and realized she'd left them on the kitchen table. Drat! She always seemed to be without those items when she really needed them. She'd been trying to work on that but still hadn't quite acclimated herself to a reporter's habits.

"Well, that's the interesting part," Wilma Mae said. "Before yesterday, I hadn't checked that drawer in the better part of a year. But lately several people have been coming around the house asking about the recipe. This one woman in particular has been here three or four times, just in the past week or two. She wanted to see the recipe, and she was very adamant about it. I told her I wasn't showing it to anyone at this time and that it was stored away in a safe place. And then she started *grilling* me about it. She wanted to know *everything* about it—who created it, when it was created, what the ingredients were. She even asked me about Mr. Sedley and my relationship with him." Wilma Mae became a little flustered. "She was a very prying woman, and to be honest, she made me quite nervous. She said if I didn't tell her what she wanted to know, she'd find out herself. I started worrying about the recipe, so I checked the secret drawer late yesterday afternoon, when I got home from running my errands. Something about the house just didn't feel right. That's when I discovered it was missing."

"And that's when you called me," Candy confirmed. "So you think this woman might have had something to do with the recipe's disappearance?"

"I think it's certainly possible, don't you?"

Candy thought about that. "Perhaps—but how would she have known where you had it hidden?"

Wilma Mae shook her head. "I'm not sure about that. As far as I know, only myself and Mr. Sedley knew about that compartment—and the carpenter who discovered it, of course."

Candy's mind was working. "What was this woman's name—the one who's been bugging you the past few weeks?" she asked after a few moments.

"Well, I think she said it was Wanda Boyle."

Candy felt a prickling on her arms. "Wanda Boyle? You're sure she said her name was Wanda Boyle?"

Wilma Mae nodded. "Yes, I believe so. Why? Is something wrong?"

Candy's shoulders slumped, and her chin fell to her chest as she let out a long breath. "Oh boy."

# FIVE

At Wilma Mae's invitation, Candy took a few minutes to examine the secret drawer. She could see nothing unusual about it, other than the fact that it was ingeniously designed. She played with the mechanism that released it, pushing the drawer into its hiding spot, then popping it back out a few times.

She leaned in for a closer look. There were no tool or scratch marks, no signs of forced entry, nothing to indicate the drawer had been broken into. Nothing, as far as she could see, to indicate anything had been stolen from it—or that anything had ever been inside, for that matter.

That meant whoever had stolen the recipe— *allegedly* stolen the recipe, Candy reminded herself—must have known how to open the drawer.

Could Wanda Boyle have done such a thing? Would she have broken into Wilma Mae's home, climbed those stairs, found this bedroom, and activated the release mechanism that opened the drawer?

Why would she have wanted the recipe in the first place?

As Candy pondered these questions and continued to study the drawer, she said *hmm* several times, causing Wilma Mae to look at her expectantly. But since she wasn't a forensics expert, she didn't know what to do next. Look for fingerprints? Hair samples? Fibers? Way out of her league. She was hardly an investigator of any sort, even in the broadest definition of the term. She still found it amusing that people around town thought of her as a detective at all—which, of course, she wasn't. She knew that better than anyone.

And here was the proof.

A helpful note from the alleged thief would have solved the problem—perhaps with an address and phone number to make things easier? In the end she had nothing concrete, no theories or suppositions to offer the elderly woman.

As they headed back downstairs, Candy tried to sort out all she had just heard and seen.

Wilma Mae was quite a tale spinner—that much was true. But was anything else?

Candy was torn. The practical part of her couldn't help thinking that maybe Wilma Mae had simply misplaced the ledger that contained the recipe—left it out on another shelf somewhere, or in the back of another drawer, or given it to someone and simply forgotten she'd done so. People forgot where they put things all the time. Even Candy did it, all too often, much to her frustration. And Wilma Mae was well into her eighties. These sorts of things happened.

That was the simplest explanation. But was it the right one?

Maybe Wilma Mae *was* telling the truth. Maybe

someone—Wanda Boyle?—*had* stolen the recipe from the elderly woman . . . but again, Candy asked herself, why?

There seemed to be only one logical explanation: the Lobster Stew Cook-off. Wilma Mae had said the recipe was valuable. It probably was, Candy realized—in more ways than one.

Because, ultimately, it was an *award-winning* recipe.

That could make it very valuable to certain people in town. But was it worth the risk of stealing it from the home of an elderly woman? That was the part that nagged at her the most. Who could, or would, do such a thing? Who would be that desperate?

Candy almost let out a quick laugh. Knowing this town, she could probably think of a half dozen people, and not even break a sweat doing it.

In some strange way, it was all starting to make sense to her. Winning the annual cook-off was a fairly prestigious achievement around town—the newspaper devoted substantial portions of two issues to it. There was no doubt some people were petty enough to steal recipes from one another if it gave them a competitive edge. These sorts of things happened in small towns all the time. Didn't they?

And it certainly could have happened here in Cape Willington, Maine, given its overabundance of unique characters.

Couldn't it?

Candy felt a quick chill go up her spine, a mixture of nervousness and excitement, as she realized she might be onto something. Call it intuition, a sixth sense, or whatever, but she had to admit she was inclined to believe Wilma Mae.

And that made her pulse quicken, knowing what—and who—she faced.

*Wanda Boyle? Why, of all people, does it have to be her?*

Candy shook her head and absently brushed back her honey-colored hair.

She knew what she had to do.

Standing in the kitchen, she told Wilma Mae she'd dig around, ask a few questions in town, and see what she could find out.

Wilma Mae was beside herself with gratitude. "I can't tell you how happy I am," the elderly woman said enthusiastically. "Oh, I can pay you! Mr. Wendell left me a little money. And I know Mr. Sedley and myself would both be so grateful if you could get the recipe back for us. It would be like finding a lost member of the family—that's how much it means to us."

"Mrs. Wendell, I could never take your money," Candy said honestly. "Besides, I don't know if I'll find out anything at all. Just give me a few days to poke around. I'll give you a call over the weekend and we can talk then."

Wilma Mae laid a thin-boned hand on Candy's

arm and gave her a sweet smile. "I knew you were the right person to call. I don't know how to thank you."

Candy felt touched. "I haven't done anything yet . . . but I'm glad to help if I can."

She thanked Wilma Mae for the tea, dropped her pen and reporter's notebook into her purse, and said her good-byes.

Outside, a cool wind blew past her, tossing about her hair and carrying with it the fresh, newborn smell of spring. The chilly breeze pushed her gently along the front walkway, but the midday sun warmed her as she climbed into her old teal-colored Jeep Cherokee, which was starting to show its age. She cranked up the engine, backed out of the driveway, and drove toward the center of town, her mind still occupied with thoughts of Wilma Mae, Wanda Boyle, and the missing lobster stew recipe.

It took her only a few minutes to reach Ocean Avenue, a gently sloping central boulevard lined with quaint shops, restaurants, and other businesses. It ran in length only for a long, stretched-out block, from Main Street at its northerly end to Town Park, the Lightkeeper's Inn, the Coastal Loop road, and the sea at its southerly tip. Its most notable feature was the Pruitt Opera House, which stood in stately fashion halfway down the avenue on the northern side.

Candy glanced at the opera house as she turned

onto Ocean Avenue. It had been there, on the building's high widow's walk, that one of the most harrowing experiences of her life had occurred on a rainy night ten months ago. Even now, the memory of that raw, windy night gave her goose bumps as images of the life-and-death struggle flashed through her mind.

Quickly she shook away those thoughts and turned her attention back to the matter at hand.

Finding a parking spot along Ocean Avenue in July and August, at the height of the busy summer tourist season, could be a tricky business, but she found plenty of spaces today. It was the Thursday before the Memorial Day weekend—the end of spring but not quite summer—and the bulk of the incoming visitors had yet to arrive.

Still, Candy could sense a definite air of excitement around town. Cape Willington nearly doubled in size each summer, as the seasonal people arrived to open up their cabins and camps, and out-of-state cars clogged the streets and took up all the good parking spots. At the height of the summer season, in July and August, Ocean Avenue buzzed with conversations and laughter as the sidewalks, shops, cafés, and rustic seaside inns filled up with families and couples looking to spend a few days or weeks out of the day-to-day rat race of the rest of the world and enjoy some much-needed vacation time right here in Candy's very own cozy coastal village in Downeast Maine.

She pulled the Jeep into a coveted parking spot right in front of the offices of the *Cape Crier* and across the street from Stone & Milbury, the insurance agency where her best friend Maggie Tremont worked. She thought of stopping in briefly to say hi to Maggie but decided she had to check something first. So she pushed through a wood and glass door, identified as number 21B, and dashed up a set of well-worn wooden stairs to the second floor, where she entered the rabbit-warren collection of offices that housed the meager staff of the *Cape Crier*.

She found the editor, Ben Clayton, in his office, sleeves rolled up, hair uncombed, staring intently at a computer screen, and stabbing at the keyboard as he swore softly under his breath.

"Hi, Ben."

"Oh, hi, Candy. I thought you weren't coming in until tomorrow." His eyes flicked to her and back to his computer screen, but he didn't stop typing. His fingers continued to move rapidly over the keys as he got his last few thoughts down before being pulled away into a conversation.

Candy was used to the maneuver. She'd seen it before. It was simply his way of multitasking.

"So how'd the interview with Wilma Mae go?" he asked.

"It was . . . revealing, to say the least. She has plenty of stories to tell, that's for sure. First we had tea, and then we talked about all sorts of things."

"Oh? Like what?"

"Well, her collection of ketchup bottles, for one thing. And Cornelius Roberts Pruitt, Helen's father, who was quite a randy fellow, as it turns out. And Wilma Mae's famous lobster stew recipe. And a secret compartment in the upstairs bedroom of her house, created by some architect named Mulroy. And, oh yeah, it sounds like we might have a recipe thief around town—possibly someone who's trying to rig the Lobster Stew Cook-off." She paused and smiled at him. "Anything else you'd like to know?"

Ben whistled. He stopped typing, leaned back in his chair, crossed his arms, and looked up at her. "Okay, you had me at ketchup. Wow, it sounds like you had a great interview. What's this about a recipe thief? And someone rigging the cook-off? That sounds pretty big. You got a story here?"

"Could be," Candy said, tilting her head thoughtfully to one side, "or maybe it's just a case of a misplaced ledger. I'm not sure which, but I'm going to check it out, see if it leads anywhere. Hey, what have you heard lately about Wanda Boyle?"

"Wanda?" Ben made a face as if he had tasted something particularly nasty, and shrugged. "Just the usual, I guess. She's got her fingers in about every pie in Cape these days. She was doing some political canvassing last week—either for or against global warming, I can't remember which.

Not sure it matters much, as long as she gets her name in the paper. She's been collecting clothes and books for the thrift sale at the Unitarian church—helps put a little shine on her image, I guess. I think she's in charge of the graduation committee at the high school. She's both a comanager and an entrant in the Lobster Stew Cook-off—I'm not quite sure how she's going to pull that one off. Seems like a conflict of interest to me. Why doesn't she just go for the trifecta and judge it too? Then she can make sure she wins the whole kielbasa, which is one of her lifelong goals. And, oh yeah, I think she's trying to get together an all-female version of a barbershop quartet. She's obviously going to sing the low part."

He paused, his brow furrowing in concern. "So what's up? Is she giving you trouble again?"

Candy waved a hand. "Naw, nothing like that. I was just wondering what you'd heard."

Ben shrugged. "It's always the same with her. Wanda this, Wanda that." Another pause. "Are you doing research? Is she going to be in your next column?"

Candy sighed. "She's in *every* column. That's part of the problem, isn't it?"

"You got that right. I guess every town needs a busybody. At least it keeps things interesting."

"That's for sure." Candy indicated the computer screen. "So how's the next issue coming?"

He ran a hand across his rugged face as his gaze

returned to the glowing screen in front of him. "It's coming. The busy season's upon us."

"It sure is." She tapped the doorway with her hand. "Well, I'll let you get back to work."

She had just started down the hall when she heard Ben call after her, "Hey, are we still on for Friday night?"

She stopped, retraced her steps, and popped her head back into his office. "We are, as long as it's something a little more upscale than Duffy's Main Street Diner, please."

He grinned at her, but she saw a tiredness around his eyes. "I've heard there's a new Italian place up on Route 1. They actually have tablecloths. And the antipasto's supposed to be pretty good too. I thought we might try it."

"Mmm, I love Italian. Sounds good to me."

"Who knows," Ben said as his fingers starting moving over the keyboard again, "I might even spring for a bottle of Chianti. Maybe even two."

Candy laughed. "Mr. Moneybags, huh? Okay, you're on."

As she started off again, her smile lingered. After they met last summer, it had taken Ben nearly six months to ask her out. Early on, they had chatted over coffee, rubbed elbows in the office, and occasionally grabbed lunch together, but nothing more than that. Ben had always maintained a respectful professional distance.

Candy didn't mind that he took his time. She

had simply enjoyed having someone else her age, and single like her, to talk to. But eventually his tone had changed. He became more playful, more willing to joke with her, and as he had lightened up she had sensed his interest in her.

She had expected him to ask her out on a date around Christmas or New Year's, but he waited until Valentine's Day. They had a wonderful dinner together that night, and had been going out together ever since, though usually just a few times a month, due to their busy schedules and all.

As they started dating, she began to find out more about him. After graduating from Boston University with a degree in journalism, Ben started working for a newsweekly and spent most of the next decade and a half overseas, primarily in Africa and the Middle East, but also in Europe and Asia, traveling from one assignment—and one conflict—to another. He had been married twice, but both had been brief—three years to a British woman whom he'd met in Africa, less than eighteen months to an American journalist based out of Spain. He had no children. Coming back to the United States, he had sought a less stressful job, one where he could settle in for a while and focus on local news. A college friend of his, whose father owned a few weeklies in New England, suggested the job at the *Cape Crier*. After visiting the town and giving it some thought, he had taken the job, expecting to stay a year or two. He was now in his fourth year as editor.

He was, in many ways, a unique type of a person, Candy thought as she walked along the dark hallway toward her office. Perhaps that's why he fit in so well here in Cape Willington, where *everyone* was a little different. Educated and well traveled, he was also essentially a loner, who preferred to live alone, fish alone, hike alone, and work alone. He had varied interests—William Faulkner was an idol of his, as were Ian Fleming and Max Ernst, the British surrealist. He liked to listen to Texas blues music and watch college football, and he loved English soccer. Manchester United was his team. He apparently knew how to play cricket, though Candy had never witnessed him doing so. But he had talked about it a few times over dinner, trying to explain the complex rules of the game to her. She had always found it too confusing, but she still liked listening to him explain it. He had a few close friends who called or visited him from time to time—mostly college buddies and colleagues from his years overseas. But he hadn't sought out many friends here in Cape—he simply didn't seem to need them. Candy often spotted him alone, sitting at the back of some coffee shop or café along Ocean Avenue or Main Street, eating a pastrami on rye or sipping at a cup of coffee while reading the *Columbia Journalism Review* or *Sports Illustrated.*

Thinking through it all, Candy had a hard time finding much common ground between the two of them. Was he the right fit for her? It was a question she'd asked herself several times over the past few months. But usually, in the end, she decided she was overthinking the whole thing. Better, she decided, to just take it a day at a time and see what developed. In the meantime, Ben was a good guy to hang out with, and they had fun together.

The fact that she was dating again especially pleased her father, Doc, who worried endlessly about his daughter's happiness. And it gave Candy something to talk about with her friend Maggie.

So, at least for the moment, it was a comfortable relationship, for both her and Ben.

She hurried past the offices of Judy Crockett, the newspaper's fortyish part-time sales rep, who floated through the day in a constant state of giggly lightheartedness until she picked up the phone and dialed a client, at which point her steely core of arm-twisting resolve kicked in; and Betty Lynn Spar, the great-granddaughter of a sea captain, who took her name and ancestry seriously. Her shouts of "Ahoy!" and "Full steam ahead!" could be heard periodically throughout the day as she scurried about the office handling phone calls and mail, running errands, brewing coffee, greeting visitors, keeping track of ad accounts and payroll, and generally making sure everything was, according to Betty Lynn, "shipshape."

As Candy passed by the office of Jesse Kidder, the paper's rail-thin, shaggy-haired, lip-pierced graphic designer and on-call photographer, she paused to stick her head in the door.

"Hi, Jesse. Hey, are you covering the cook-off on Saturday? I'm just wondering if I should take a camera with me or if you'll be there to save the world from my horrible photography." As she spoke, she glanced over Jesse's shoulder at his computer screen, where he was working on a mock-up of the upcoming issue's front page.

Jesse swiveled to face her, running a hand over his stubbly face. He smiled indulgently. "Your photos aren't that bad, Candy. You just need to work on your composition. And your light exposure. And your focus. And your depth of field. And your resolution." He paused, considering what he'd just said. "On second thought, I guess I'd better take those shots. What time do you want me there?"

"You're a sweetheart! Thanks so much. I'm showing up about nine, but if you're there by ten or so that should be good. We can get some shots of the contestants preparing their stews, and maybe some close-ups of the ingredients—you know the type of thing I'm looking for."

He nodded. "I'll get some crowd shots too—maybe a photo of a cute little girl eating a bowl of lobster stew—you know, human interest stuff."

"That sounds great. Oh, and you should probably shoot the judges and stay for the awards ceremony if you can, so you can get a few pix of the winner."

"You got it, chief. What time does that take place again?"

"The judging starts at noon, and it should all be over by one or so. After that, you're done. I might even throw in a little free food. Deal?"

"Sounds like an offer I can't refuse. See you there."

Candy's office was next to Jesse's. She blew out a breath of air as she sank into her desk chair and, with mild trepidation, scanned the messages Betty Lynn had left her, all decorated with little drawings of anchors, lighthouses, and life preservers.

*Nothing negative. Good.*

Mostly she saw the typical things—calls from a local historian, Julius Seabury, who was giving a presentation at the library the following week, and from a woman named Cassandra Rockwell, who had just opened a new consignment shop on Main Street. Margaritte Jordan called about a scrap-booking group she was organizing. A PR person from one of the coastal resorts had contacted Candy about a wellness weekend she was promoting. Finn Woodbury, one of Doc's buddies, had called about the upcoming auditions for the Cape Summer Theater's annual summer musical, which would be *Brigadoon* this year.

The last message was from Oliver LaForce, the proprietor of the Lightkeeper's Inn. Candy had met Oliver several times over the past few months. He was a humorless, fastidious man who ran the inn with cold precision. The message, as expected, was businesslike and to the point: *Please call to confirm your attendance on Saturday. A press badge will be waiting for you. I have some news as well. We'll discuss at the event.*

News? That piqued Candy's interest. Could it have anything to do with the rumors she'd heard of a guest judge?

She thought about picking up the phone and calling Oliver right then to find out what was going on. But she quickly decided to put it off until later.

She had something more important to do right now.

Inexorably, her gaze was drawn across the room, to the filing cabinet in the corner. She focused in on the bottom drawer, the one labeled with only two letters: *SV.*

She'd avoided going into that drawer for a long time—but she knew she could avoid it no longer.

It was time to have a look at Sapphire Vine's old files.

# SIX

Sliding out of her chair, she crossed the room and fell into a cross-legged seating position in front of the filing cabinet's bottom drawer.

For the longest time she just sat there, staring at it. She knew she was dredging up old mysteries and unwanted problems. She knew she was delving into the twisted mind of a dead woman. She knew she should probably have followed an earlier instinct and just burned the files, committing them to ashes, which was where they truthfully belonged.

But she hadn't. They were still here, in her possession. And they were here for a reason.

With a great force of will, she moved her hand to the drawer's metal handle. Taking a deep breath, she slid the button aside with her thumb and pulled open the drawer.

She hadn't been in these files for ten months, since she'd inherited them from Sapphire Vine, the newspaper's previous community columnist. Sapphire had been many other things as well, including a gossip, a blackmailer, the reigning Blueberry Queen, a keeper of dark secrets, and ultimately a murder victim. She'd been brutally struck down in her home with a red-handled hammer. Finding her killer and solving the mystery of her death had been Candy's first true case—and it had almost gotten her killed.

Last summer, when Ben had placed the files in Candy's hands, they had helped her track down Sapphire's murderer. But with the mystery solved and the murderer arrested, Candy had brought the files back here to the office, stuffed them in the bottom drawer of the filing cabinet, and left them there, secrets and all.

Some of the folders Candy had opened and perused in an effort to find the murderer. She had not looked at the rest, however, and with good reason. Sapphire had been quietly assembling private, personal, and often damaging information about many of Cape Willington's residents. And the former Blueberry Queen was not averse to using that information for her own gain. That's what led to her death.

So Candy had left the tainted files alone—and had overcome an instinct to burn them and bid them good riddance. She couldn't help feeling, back then, that at some point in the future the files might come in handy.

That time had come.

She leaned forward and started working her way back through the files, carefully checking the labels. She didn't have to flip back too far to find the one she wanted. It was a thick folder labeled *WB*.

Candy pulled it out, glanced around to make sure no one was watching, hesitated just a moment, and opened the cover. Curiously, she started paging through it.

"Just as I thought," she muttered to herself a short while later.

Sapphire had assembled a hefty dossier on Wanda Boyle. Newspaper clippings abounded, covering most of Wanda's activities over the past few years. Sapphire had also included a few grainy black-and-white photos—apparently taken surreptitiously—of Wanda consorting with many of the town's more powerful and wealthier individuals.

That made sense. Wanda did whatever she could to ingratiate herself with the popular folk around town. But after studying the photos, Candy could see nothing inappropriate going on. All the photos had been taken at what looked like public events. No bedroom shots or anyone in a compromising position. It was probably just Sapphire snooping around, looking for dirt that wasn't there—a modus operandi that had, at times, yielded boffo results for the gossip columnist.

Candy pursed her lips as she dug farther back into the folder, where the documents were crisper and starting to turn brown with age. Sapphire had included a few pages about Wanda's husband, who was a building contractor and remodeler, and some brief notes about Wanda's children—their ages, teachers, and classes, mostly.

Candy found the whole thing creepy. Even now,

nearly a year later, Sapphire's level of obsession and attention to detail still horrified yet fascinated her.

She went back and forth through the folder a few more times before finally pulling out the documents she wanted.

One was a year-old newspaper clipping about Wanda's volunteer efforts at the Cape Willington Historical Society, located in the red-roofed Keeper's Quarters out at English Point Lighthouse, just a block or so from here. Dating back to 1857, the lighthouse stood on a point of black rock near the mouth of the English River, which formed the northern boundary of the village of Cape Willington.

The other document, in Sapphire's own flowery handwriting, provided details about Wanda's parents and siblings, including an older brother named Owen, who just happened to be a cabinetmaker and carpenter.

That had caught Candy's attention. Wanda's brother was a carpenter? Could he have been the one who worked on Wilma Mae's shelving unit and discovered the secret document drawer?

It sounded just a little too convenient, though, didn't it? Then again, maybe she'd already discovered her first clue to the mystery.

She was in the process of stuffing the folder back into the filing cabinet when Maggie walked in.

Although Maggie was not a slim woman, neither could she be called full figured. She had a few curves and a few extra pounds, yet she carried herself well, with a certain grace and fluidness of motion. She always dressed well, with discreet makeup that accentuated her best facial features—her prominent cheekbones and her dark, flashing eyes. Her chestnut hair was stylishly cut and naturally curly, resulting in a lush and, Candy often thought, attractive look for her.

Maggie was also incredibly vivacious, a good counter to Candy's more subdued, thoughtful personality.

"Hey stranger," Maggie said, entering the room like a fresh spring breeze. "I saw the Jeep out front and thought I'd stop in to say hello real quick. I haven't seen you all week. What have you been—"

She stopped abruptly when she saw her friend sitting on the floor in front of the filing cabinet instead of at her desk. She gave Candy a mystified look. "Honey, what are you doing down there on the floor? Are you okay?"

As casually as she could, Candy rose to her feet and nonchalantly dusted off her jeans. "Oh, sure, sure, I'm fine."

"Well what were you doing down there?" Maggie repeated.

"Oh, you know." Candy stuck her hands in her back pockets. "I was just . . . you know, relaxing."

71

"Relaxing?" Maggie blinked several times as she looked from Candy to the still-opened drawer. Quickly her mind registered what was going on. She gasped. "You were looking in the bottom filing cabinet, weren't you! You were going through *her* files!"

None too discreetly, Candy reached out with a sneakered foot and slid the bottom drawer closed. "Who, me? Naw, I was just, um, practicing my yoga moves."

But Maggie was having none of it. "Don't give me that. You don't do yoga—though that's not a bad idea, you know. Hey, we could do it together—get us a couple of those cute leotard things, or maybe even capri pants. I'd probably wear black, because of my figure and all, but with your hair color you'd probably look good in a . . ." She paused, catching herself. "Hey, wait a minute. Don't try changing the subject on me, missy." Her gaze narrowed on her friend. "You were looking through Sapphire's old files, weren't you?"

"Um, well, I . . ."

Maggie leveled a finger at her. "Aha! So I was right. And you didn't even call me!"

"I was going to but, well . . . it was a spur-of-the-moment kind of thing."

"But you said you weren't going to look at those files ever again unless it was an extreme emergency. Those were your words: *extreme emergency*."

"Um, well," Candy said hesitantly, "I guess this is sort of an emergency."

"An emergency? But . . ." Maggie's eyes suddenly widened. "Oh my God! You're on a case! You're investigating another mystery, aren't you!"

Candy knew she could never keep anything from her friend. She let out a sigh and flopped back down in her desk chair. With a resigned tone, she said, "Well, if you must know, yes."

Maggie's eyes suddenly brightened. "Oh, thank goodness. Something exciting is finally happening! I've been so stressed lately, what with everything that's been going on with Ed and Amanda and all the drama at work. I need something totally different to do with my life for a while. I need something to occupy my mind. And a good mystery is just the thing. So, tell me," Maggie said as she slid into a folding chair along one wall and tucked her hands expectantly into her knees, "what are you investigating this time? Spill the beans. And don't leave out a single detail." Maggie settled herself again. "So, what have you got?"

"Well, it's not that much, really. Just a small case." Candy held out a hand, with her index finger and thumb slightly apart. "Just an itty-bitty one."

"Okay, so tell me all about it. No, wait! Better yet, let me guess. This'll be fun." Maggie scrunched up her face as she rubbed her chin. "What were you doing today?" She studied Candy with an appraising eye as she pondered her own question. After a moment, her eyebrows rose dramatically. "You interviewed Wilma Mae Wendell, didn't you? About that recipe of hers!" Another pause as she thought it through. "This is about her lobster stew recipe, right? And the cook-off on Saturday?"

"Darn, you're good," Candy admitted.

Maggie shrieked in excitement. "You mean I'm right?"

"Yes, you're right. But I didn't think you'd figure it out that fast. Listen, you can't tell anyone about this, okay? This is just between us for now. But yes, I'm doing something for Wilma Mae."

Maggie's voice was suddenly hushed as she leaned forward. "What is it?"

Candy hesitated, but Maggie had been a big help in tracking down Sapphire's killer last summer. Candy might need her help again. "It's nothing dangerous or anything like that. She just has a little . . . problem."

"What kind of problem? Does it have anything to do with the lobster stew recipe?"

"Well, since you asked, yes."

"Is she giving it to you? Is that it? There are rumors all over town she's giving it away."

"No, that's not it. She's not giving it away."

"Then what?"

Candy leaned close to her friend and said in the lowest whisper she could manage, "The recipe has been stolen."

"Someone stole the lobster stew recipe?" Maggie said loudly before being shushed by Candy. More softly, she repeated, "Someone stole the recipe? Who could have done such a thing?"

"That's what we're trying to find out."

"And she wants you to get it back for her?"

"Yes."

"Ooh, fun. It's the search for the stolen recipe." Maggie's gaze shifted toward the filing cabinet. "That's why you were looking in Sapphire's old files, isn't it? You were looking for clues."

Candy nodded. "Something like that."

Maggie's eyes shifted back to her friend. "What does that mean?"

"It means," Candy said dramatically, "that I'm searching for specific clues, in a specific file. Wilma Mae already has a suspect."

"Who?"

"Don't have a cow, but it's Wanda Boyle."

At the mention of Wanda's name, all the excitement and enthusiasm seem to drain right out of Maggie. The expression on her face instantly deflated to one of total disbelief. For a moment she sat in stunned silence. Then she reached out and took Candy's arm, as if she were comforting a terminally ill friend. "Tell me I heard you wrong. Tell me you're not serious."

"I'm serious."

"Wanda Boyle? Are you crazy? You can't investigate her."

Candy understood her friend's concern. "You think I'm kicking over a hornet's nest?"

"Honey, it's *much* worse than that. She *owns* this town. She knows *everyone*. If she thinks you're investigating her or that you're plotting against her, she'll *ruin* you! She'll turn everyone in this town against you. And she'll ruin me too, because I'm your friend!"

Candy gave a feeble laugh. "You're exaggerating."

But Maggie shook her head adamantly. "No I'm not. You have to stop this investigation right now. Because if you don't, Wanda Boyle will destroy us both!"

# SEVEN

Twenty minutes later, as Candy walked outside and climbed behind the wheel of her Jeep, Maggie's final words echoed in her mind:

*Avoid Wanda at all costs. Stay on her good side. Don't ruffle her feathers. Or we'll both pay for it!*

Candy blew out a long breath of air as she started the engine. She didn't necessarily disagree with Maggie. But she hadn't expected her friend's strong reaction to the news of her latest investigation.

A short time earlier, Maggie had made a quick

exit from the *Cape Crier* offices, saying she had to get back to work. "Something's brewing over there," she told Candy. "I don't know what yet, but I'm going to find out. Whatever it is, it's sure got my boss on edge, so I can't be gone too long."

But before she headed out the door, she pleaded with Candy to abandon the investigation. "You're treading on dangerous territory," she said ominously. "Just tell Wilma Mae you couldn't help her, and let sleeping hornets lie." She left with her final words of advice, her dislike and fear of Wanda Boyle evident.

That fear had caught Candy off-guard, though she completely understood it. She knew well of Wanda's influence around town, and the odd power the woman seemed to wield over its citizens. After talking to Maggie, Candy sensed that going up against a force such as Wanda Boyle, if it came to that, might be difficult and perhaps even disastrous—if Maggie was to be believed. Still, Candy couldn't imagine why her actions would cause any trouble. She was just doing a little poking around. She was no threat to anyone.

She decided, as she sat listening to the Jeep's rumbling engine, that she'd have to be cautious and keep the investigation low-key. But at the same time she told herself that, no matter what happened, she wouldn't let herself be scared off.

She had told Wilma Mae she would look into the

situation. And she was determined to do just that.

So she backed out of her parking spot and headed down Ocean Avenue, past the opera house, which doubled as Town Hall, past the cemetery and Town Park, to the red light at the bottom of the street, where she flicked on her left turn signal.

Just ahead, past a wide expanse of black rocks, low shrubbery, and a narrow, pebble-strewn beach, lay the ocean, bright blue and moderately choppy today. She had rolled down the driver's-side window and could almost feel the ocean's spray on the wind. A seagull rose lazily on an updraft. Candy watched it until the light turned green, then steered the Jeep onto the Coastal Loop headed north.

It didn't take her long to reach her destination. Just a short distance up the road she turned off into a parking lot on her right, which gave her access to the Waterfront Walk and the pathway leading to the English Point Lighthouse and Museum. She pulled out her purse, locked the door, and turned her face into the wind.

A few minutes' walk took her through the low shrubbery and down a slope toward the rugged shore, where the lighthouse rose majestically, a round, white tower gleaming in the early afternoon sun. Around it huddled several buildings, including the Keeper's Quarters and a maintenance shed off to one side.

As many times as she had visited the lighthouse,

she still never ceased to marvel at its stateliness and beauty. It stretched nearly ninety feet into the air, with its iron balcony, or watch deck, at the top accessed by a spiraling cast-iron staircase located inside the tower.

The Keeper's Quarters nestled at the foot of the tower, a two-story Victorian-style home that had housed the lightkeeper and his family until the early 1980s, when the light's operation was modernized. In the mid-1980s, the town took control of both the lighthouse and the buildings surrounding it, turning the Keeper's Quarters into a visitor's center and museum. In the late 1990s, the building became the official home of the Cape Willington Historical Society.

Candy approached the lighthouse with her purse on her shoulder and her hands tucked deep into her pockets. She tilted her head way back and stopped for a few moments to admire it, watching the high clouds scud past its highest point, which made the tower look as if it were dipping to one side. Finally she moved on, turning toward the Keeper's Quarters. She paused to read one of the descriptive plaques posted outside before climbing the gray-painted wooden steps and entering the museum.

Inside, she paused briefly to give her eyes time to adjust to the softer light. She had been in there a couple of times before, to peruse the exhibits, models, and memorabilia. Most impressive were the scaled-down models of the lighthouse station, including one depicting all the buildings and the surrounding landscape that occupied a large table at the center of the main room.

Candy always felt as if she were stepping back in time when she entered the Keeper's Quarters. The place had the smell of an old home, and the bare, worn wooden floor looked much as it must have in the mid-eighteen hundreds. The building's windows were small, yet from here they provided breathtaking views of the sea just outside. Candy could hear the rush and tumble of the ocean just beyond the walls, mingling with the hushed voices of visitors as they toured the exhibits, which were located on both floors of the building.

To her left was a table with pamphlets and brochures on it, and just beyond that a long wooden counter, behind which sat a grizzled old gentleman with a scruffy white beard, wearing a patched cardigan sweater and a battered captain's cap. He gave her a suspicious eye as she walked up to the counter.

"Hello," she said pleasantly.

"Hello yerself, young lady," said the gentleman, not completely unfriendly.

"I'm, um, Candy Holliday. With the *Cape Crier*?" She said it almost as a question. "And, um, I wonder, is the museum director around? I have just a few quick questions for her."

"Candy Holliday, are you?" said the old

gentleman, obviously a volunteer who manned the desk. "Well, I've heard about you. You write that column, don't you? That community column?"

"Yes, that's right."

"Well, I've read it," he said gruffly. "Yup, I've read it. You'll have to sign in."

He pushed an open register book toward her. "Everyone signs the log book. It's the rule around here. Don't matter where you come from—you have to sign it." He slapped a pen down on the counter.

Candy gave him an amused look as she picked up the pen, signed her name, and, beside that, wrote *C. W.* under the *Hometown* column heading. As she added the date at the end of the line, she noticed that other visitors who had signed in today had come from a diverse range of places, including towns in New York, Pennsylvania, Colorado, and even California.

"My name's Mike, by the way," the old gentleman continued. "Captain Mike, they call me around here. I know your dad. We've played poker a few times. I've lost some money to him."

"I'm sorry to hear that. Hopefully you'll win it back someday."

Mike snorted. "Not likely. Doc's a tough player. Merciless, just like that sea out there. He would have made a good lobsterman. I'll tell Charlotte you're here. She's a busy woman, you know. Always in a hurry."

"I'm sure she is. I promise I won't keep her long."

That seemed to appease Mike, and with a grunt he tottered off toward an office at the opposite side of the building.

As Candy waited, she wandered around for a quick look at the museum's facilities and exhibits. Behind and to the left of the reception desk was a long, dark hallway that led to the base of the tower. Nearby, attached to the wall, a TV screen showed a video of the interior of the tower, including the spiral iron staircase and the view from the outside iron watch deck at the top. Hanging on the wall beside the TV was a sign that read VISITORS ARE NOT ALLOWED ENTRY TO THE LIGHTHOUSE TOWER. At the end of the hallway was a white wooden door, apparently the entrance to the tower, and apparently locked.

Candy moved to her right, toward an open doorway, which led to another room at the rear of the cottage, facing the sea. A sign beside the door told her the room re-created the living quarters of the lightkeeper and his family as they might have appeared in the late eighteen hundreds. Candy looked in.

The room was not richly decorated but looked comfortable, with hardwood floors, dark green wainscoting with painted beige walls above, and simple furniture. To one side was a kitchen table next to an old black stove. Dishes, glasses, pots, and pans sat on open shelves. On the right side of the room, a large fireplace was surrounded by several padded chairs, including a rocking chair. A rolltop desk brimming with books, maps, and papers sat in one corner. Victorian lights and decorating accents gave the room a charming appearance.

Adding an even more realistic ambience were the life-size mannequins standing in for the lightkeeper and his family. Dressed in period costumes, the mannequins were arranged around the room as they might have appeared on a cozy afternoon in the Keeper's Quarters. The lightkeeper, complete with beard and moustache, sat in the rocking chair, an open nautical book upside down over his knee and a pipe on a nearby table, while his wife sat across from him mending a garment and two children played a game on the rug in front of the fireplace.

"Hello, Candy," said a voice behind her. She turned. A petite, dark-haired, somewhat disheveled woman wearing a frown and a purple print dress approached from across the room, her thick-heeled shoes rapping solidly on the wooden floor. She extended her hand as she came forward. "I'm Charlotte Depew, the museum's director and advisor to the historical society."

"Hello, Charlotte. Nice to finally meet you."

"And you, Candy." They shook hands in a businesslike manner. Charlotte's hands were small, but her handshake was surprisingly firm, Candy noticed.

"Yes, we've talked on the phone a few times," the director said, "but it's nice to finally put a face to a voice. Your column is very informative. We read it whenever we get a chance. Don't we, Captain Mike?"

"That we do. I've read it," Mike said adamantly as he took his place behind the counter. "Yup, I've read it."

"Mike's a longtime volunteer here," Charlotte said. "He always goes above and beyond the call of duty. Don't you, Captain Mike?"

He gave her a halfhearted wave.

"I just don't know what we'd do without our volunteers," Charlotte continued. "There always seems to be too much to do around here. Without their help, we'd never get anything done. I see you were checking out our new display." She motioned toward the lightkeeper and his family.

"Oh . . . yes. It's very well done."

"You know, I created those costumes and made the wigs myself. Everything is authentic, either originals or replicas based on photographs we have in our archives. It took us nearly six months to assemble all the components for this display."

"You must be very proud of it," Candy said.

"Yes . . . well, of course we are. A lot of people put in a lot of hard work on this. I'm glad you finally have a chance to see it. We've been hoping you would stop by soon so we could show it off. Perhaps you can write up something about it in the paper." She seemed a bit jittery and touched at her somewhat askew hair, trying to tuck a few loose strands back into place.

"Oh, sure, that would be great. In fact, that's why I came around. I wanted to talk to you about your new exhibits and displays, special programs you might have coming up, that sort of thing. Of course," Candy added, seeing Charlotte glance surreptitiously at her watch, "I hope I'm not catching you at a bad time. I probably should have called ahead."

Charlotte was silent for a moment. "Yes, well, we *are* very busy around here today, with the upcoming holiday weekend and all. We have a few special projects going on Saturday and Sunday for our guests."

"She's very busy," Captain Mike called from across the room.

Candy gave him an indulgent smile.

"But as long as you're here," Charlotte continued, "I suppose I could spare a few minutes. And I do have some materials I can give you. A recently printed brochure might be helpful. Why don't we go into my office?"

She motioned the way, and Candy started off, walking past a number of exhibits, including a large diorama showing the various stages in the construction of the lighthouse station, from earliest days to the present. On the walls hung period photographs and drawings of the lighthouse and surrounding buildings. In one corner stood a Fresnel light, its beehive shape rising more than six feet above its platform. Candy stopped to admire it, and Charlotte paused to explain.

"The light's surface is comprised of hundreds of glass prisms arranged in a metal framework," she told Candy, sounding as if she had repeated the words a thousand times. "The prisms are arranged to magnify and bend the light from a source such as a flame into a single concentrated beam. This particular light can be seen more than twenty miles out at sea, all the way to the horizon. And as you can see, it's not only highly effective at what it does, but it's also a work of art."

"It's certainly impressive," Candy said before she turned and followed Charlotte into her small office tucked into a corner of the building.

"Please, have a seat." Charlotte motioned Candy toward a chair and took her own seat behind her tidy desk. "Have you been to our museum before?"

"Oh, sure, a couple of times." As she spoke, Candy reached into her purse for her reporter's notebook and pen. Crossing her legs at the knee, she leaned forward attentively in her chair, brushing back her hair. "But it's been a while, I must confess. Probably a year or two, if I remember correctly. That's why I stopped by today. I'm always looking for stories for my column."

Although she had been the community columnist for the better part of a year now, she still loved saying those words. It always made her feel a little special, and it was a great way to start a conversation.

But Charlotte didn't seem particularly impressed or chatty. Instead, she gave Candy a look that showed annoyance more than anything else, but it quickly slipped away as she turned professional, launching into what sounded like a well-rehearsed speech. "Well, we do have several programs going on throughout the summer. We have a variety of museum workshops coming up for children, teens, and adults. For the third year, we're offering an internship program here at the Keeper's Quarters for our local high school seniors and college students. We're very excited about that. We'll host three weekend sessions in June and July for prospective volunteers. We're currently sending out announcements for that. And the historical society is sponsoring an art and architecture camp this summer for middle schoolers, which is being spearheaded by Wanda Boyle."

"Ahh." Candy's eyes brightened as she tapped her bottom lip with the end of her pen. "Now that sounds very exciting. Can you tell me more about that particular program?"

Charlotte checked her watch again and forced a smile intended to demonstrate her patience. "Of course. As you may know, we've had a number of famous architects design homes here in Cape Willington. John Calvin Stevens is probably the most well-known. He designed two homes in town and did some work out at Pruitt Manor. Charles Bulfinch, who designed the state capitol, also designed our original Town Hall, though that's burned down, of course, but we still have many images of it in our historical archives. William Hatch Wharff, who was born up in Guilford but spent most of his time on the West Coast—he designed more than a hundred buildings in Berkeley and around San Francisco in the early part of the twentieth century—was involved in designing a couple of buildings along Ocean Avenue during the early part of his career. And, of course, several homes in town were designed by John Patrick Mulroy. So we have quite an architectural history here."

"Fascinating. Just fascinating." Candy propped her elbow on her knee and planted her chin in the palm of her hand. "I'd love to hear more about that—perhaps something about Wanda's involvement in putting the program together?"

"Well, I can show you an outline of the program, and I'll see if I can get Wanda's input. I think I have that file right here."

As Charlotte reached toward a short stack of

papers in a mahogany wood tray on a corner of her desk, she looked up and past Candy's shoulder. "Oh, well, better yet, you can talk to her yourself. Here she is."

Charlotte rose and motioned to a woman standing in the office doorway.

"Candy, you know Wanda Boyle, don't you?"

# EIGHT

Candy felt a sudden knot in her stomach as she turned to face the woman behind her. This was the moment she'd been hoping to avoid for at least a while longer—well, forever, if truth be told. But this was a small town. It was next to impossible to avoid someone you wanted to avoid. Now she'd just have to make the best of it.

Tentatively she rose. "Oh, hi."

She stood uneasily, not sure what to say or do next. She still held the notebook in one hand and the pen in the other, so she wiggled the pen rapidly between her fingers and forced a smile.

Wanda studied her with a disapproving expression pasted on her hard-edged face, as if she'd just discovered Candy doing something she shouldn't. She was a tall woman, with broad shoulders and a big frame she carried fairly well. Her body flared around the bust, waist, and hips, but then narrowed to rather petite legs, which were ensconced in form-fitting dark gray slacks.

She wore bright yellow pumps, open at the toes to show off her neatly clipped nails, painted bright red. They matched her flaming red shoulder-length hair, which was savagely tossed back, as if she had been swatting at it for hours. Her waist-length beige jacket, worn over a white blouse, looked somewhat rumpled, Candy noticed, with heavy creases at the elbows. The slacks were heavily creased around the upper thighs and knees as well. *She must have been sitting all morning and afternoon, doing . . . something or other,* Candy thought.

Wanda held a sheaf of papers in one hand and had tucked a folder under an arm. On her chest, she wore a large, bright blue button that read CAPE WILLINGTON WELCOMING COMMITTEE and WANDA BOYLE, CHAIRWOMAN around the edges, circling a big, bold-lettered WELCOME TO CAPE! in the center.

She looked very busy.

For several long moments she stood silently in the doorway. Obviously she'd been unaware that Charlotte had a visitor, and she didn't seem at all pleased when that visitor turned out to be Candy Holliday.

Candy waited cautiously, letting out a breath, her gaze fixed on the other woman. She noticed that Wanda had a thin, barely visible scar on her upper lip. And puffy skin around her jowls. And big hands—*like sides of beef,* Candy thought.

For an instant an image raced through her mind of another pair of thick hands wrapped around her neck, attempting to crush the life from her as the storm raged around them. But she pushed that disturbing thought aside, knowing that was in the past, and this was the present, and Wanda would never attack her like that.

*Would she?*

Finally Wanda spoke, her voice low and husky. "We've met. Haven't we, Candy?" She sounded completely unemotional, as if she were ordering a hamburger and fries at a takeout window.

"Yes, well, that's true, we have." *Several times,* Candy recollected, *and most of them were not pleasant encounters.*

Their first meeting, at a school-related bake sale shortly after Candy had become the community correspondent, was cordial enough, though she'd overheard Wanda taking some verbal potshots at her even then. Candy was "from away," Wanda had none-too-discreetly told one of the members of her close-knit group of friends, a woman named Carol McKaskie. Wanda had drawn a few other women into their conversation and chattered in low tones, often glancing Candy's way and often stifling laughter, making her feel uncomfortable. Candy had heard other words drifting her way that day from Wanda's group—words like *unqualified* and *undeserving.* She had even heard one of them call her a nobody.

Candy had just been trying to do her job, to meet people in town and cover the event, and she had been hurt and confused until she told Maggie about it.

"Oh, they're just jealous old biddies," Maggie said that evening when Candy had cried on her shoulder. "Don't listen to them, honey. They're just frustrated with their small, boring lives. They think they run this town, but most people just ignore them."

That had made Candy feel a little better, but the negative vibes from Wanda had not ceased. In the months since, they had run into each other a few more times, at public events around town, and the meetings had always been uncomfortable for Candy, as Wanda continued to throw evil looks and snarky comments her way.

Candy had had no real explanation for Wanda's hostile behavior, until Ben finally explained it to her.

"She wanted your job," he had told her just a few months ago, on a wintry day in late February when she was up in the office following her most recent disastrous encounter with Wanda at a town meeting. "She called me right after I offered the job to you last summer. She told me, quite seriously, that she thought she was the best-qualified person in town to take over for Sapphire, but I said I'd already made a decision." He'd shaken his head and chuckled. "To be honest, she was pretty peeved. She thought I should have held an open call for the job, posted the opening, that sort of thing. She told me she thought I'd mishandled the whole situation. Well, of course, I disagreed with her and told her I'd hired the right person, which didn't help the situation much. She was even more upset when she found out who got the job."

"So that's why she's been so mad at me," Candy had said dejectedly to Ben at the time.

"She's mad at both of us. But I wouldn't worry about her. She's harmless."

"Harmless?" Candy had felt a little peeved herself. "Why didn't you tell me this before?"

"To be honest, it never came up—and you never asked."

That was true. And at least she finally knew the reason behind Wanda's rude and resentful behavior. "Just give it a little time," Ben had told her that day. "She'll eventually cool off."

But his prediction had not come true, and the situation actually worsened, due to an oversight on Candy's part. In one of her articles about a local fishing tournament for kids, written hastily to meet a tight deadline, Candy had inadvertently left out the name of Wanda's son, Bryan. On the day the paper came out, all hell had broken loose around the office, and Candy found herself at the middle of a firestorm, accused of purposely leaving out Bryan's name and publicly embarrassing the Boyle family. Wanda had called her personally to complain and then had called Ben, asking him to fire Candy, destroy all remaining copies of the paper, and reprint the issue with the corrected text.

Ben had told her, quite politely, that he'd consider her recommendations, and then completely ignored them. Instead, he had run a correction in the next issue, but Wanda had not been appeased. From then on, she had taken it as her patriotic and community duty to scrutinize every word in the paper, particularly in Candy's columns, and proceeded to let everyone know when she found even the slightest error. An e-mail or letter to the editor arrived at the *Cape Crier*'s office just about every week now, taking the paper to task for one issue or another, many of them unfounded, in Ben's opinion. "She's just picking at us. Don't worry about it. Just ignore her," was Ben's simple solution.

But Candy found it unnerving and soon feared to look through her mail and messages, worried that she'd find another accusing missive from Wanda. There had been some nights, after she'd received a particularly barbed message, when Candy lost sleep over it. But she was more concerned for the paper's reputation than her own job.

Ben, however, just shrugged off Candy's concerns and Wanda's rantings. "It comes with the territory," he told her in his laid-back, somewhat disinterested tone. "If you're a writer, sooner or later you're gonna piss someone off. That's just the way it is. You just have to get used to it. Don't let it bother you so much." He had laughed a little to himself. "Well, it helps to have a thick skin, I guess. And I've probably developed a pretty thick one over the years. But just remember this: mistakes happen. Our job is to do the best we can, minimize the errors, correct the ones we make, and move on to the next story."

And Candy had resolved to do just that. She worked hard to make sure the columns and feature articles she wrote were as accurate and as comprehensive as possible. At the same time, she began to realize that she was taking Wanda much too seriously. Finally, she decided to follow Ben's advice, and simply started ignoring her.

But it appeared she couldn't ignore Wanda forever—not when the woman was standing right in front of her.

"Well, isn't that nice?" Charlotte said into the silence, seemingly unaware of the tension between the two. "Wanda, I was just telling Candy about your art and architecture educational project for middle schoolers this summer. She's interested in writing about it for the paper. Perhaps you could take her upstairs and show her some of your research. It would be a wonderful way to promote the program—and be sure to give yourself some credit for all the hard work you've been doing."

"Yes," Candy added, seeing an opportunity to offer a peace flag, and perhaps still get what she came for. "Charlotte was just telling me about some of the architects who've designed houses in town. It'd make a great story. I'd love to hear more about what you've been up to—if you're not too busy, that is." Her smile was more genuine this time.

Wanda cast a dark look at Charlotte and an even more venomous one at Candy. Her lips were moving strangely, as if she wanted to spit a particularly caustic remark in Candy's direction— perhaps something along the lines of, *Not over my dead body, you cheap imitation of a community columnist!* But she held back, apparently with great effort, for her face began to flush red, approaching the shade of her hair. She squared her shoulders as she straightened and took a long, deep breath, calming herself.

"I'm not ready to show it to anyone just yet," she said finally in an oddly hushed tone. "I still have a lot of work to do on it."

Charlotte's gaze focused in on her. "Oh, well, Wanda, you'll forgive me if I'm a little confused, because I was under the impression you were making good progress," she said with a noticeable edge in her voice. "Didn't you tell me just the other day you were nearly finished with it?"

The museum director turned toward Candy, with

an odd glint in her eyes. "Wanda is such a perfectionist," she said in an attempt to be pleasant. "I don't know how she does it! She has to have everything just perfectly right. I guess that's why she's put *so* much time into this latest project of hers. She's been up in those archives for *weeks!*"

There was no mistaking the veiled sarcasm in her words.

"Really?" Candy eyed Wanda, intrigued. *And just what have you been doing up in those archives for weeks, Wanda?* she wanted to ask. Instead, she said, "I don't mean to intrude on your work, but perhaps you could just show me . . . some of the preliminary research you've been doing. I'm particularly interested in any information you might have on John Patrick Mulroy. I've heard he's designed several houses in town—and that he built secret hiding compartments in many of the homes he created."

She watched Wanda closely for any sign of a reaction, but Wanda stood stone-faced, giving nothing away. Her eyes, however, shifted back and forth after a few moments, as if she were contemplating her next move. Candy could practically hear the gears in her head whirring.

The scowl that eventually emerged onto Wanda's face was not a pleasant thing to behold. She apparently knew she'd been backed into a corner, and she seemed none too pleased about it.

"If it's that important, I guess I can show you. It's the least I can do to help you get your facts straight."

"That's very generous of you, Wanda," Candy said with a mild air of triumph.

Charlotte looked from one to the other, then to her watch. "Well, this is very exciting, isn't it? I'm glad you two have a chance to talk, since it appears you're both interested in the same thing. Candy, let me know if there's anything else I can help you with. And I know Wanda will be a wonderful guide for you here at the historical society. She's one of our most knowledgeable volunteers."

"I'm sure she is," Candy said without a hint of sarcasm.

Wanda gave her a nasty look, then, sensing she was being dismissed, stepped into the room, around Candy, and approached Charlotte's desk. "Before we get to that," she said, "I wanted to show you a couple of things."

She flourished the papers she held. "Those records of land deeds from the eighteenth century we were looking for? Here they are. They were buried in a cabinet with the register of voters. I think Edna put them there—she's not always as cautious as she should be when she's filing. And I found the original sketches of the opera house made by Horace Roberts Pruitt himself. I've been looking for those for more than a week. They include details of the widow's walk." Here she glanced at Candy before returning her gaze to Charlotte. "Those were stuck in with the cemetery records. Unfortunately some of our ladies working up there aren't paying attention. You really need to do a better job training them. But I've managed to sort everything out."

Charlotte stiffened a bit when challenged directly by Wanda but otherwise kept her composure. "Well, thank you for your thoroughness, Wanda," she said stiffly as her appraising eyes flicked across the documents Wanda had laid before her on the desk. "Yes, this is very helpful. It's always important to keep our archives accurate and up-to-date. Congratulations on the good work you're doing up there."

"Yeah, well, someone has to do it," Wanda said under her breath as she pulled out the folder from under her arm. "You might want to see these as well. I found them in a battered envelope that must have been sixty or seventy years old. They're architectural notes from Charles Bulfinch himself. In his own handwriting."

"Oh my." Charlotte looked truly impressed as she slid on her reading glasses and examined the papers Wanda handed her. "Well, isn't that wonderful. I don't know how you do it."

"It just takes hard work and determination," Wanda said smugly as she looked Candy's way again. "And a willingness to go the extra mile. I simply refuse to fail. Life's too short to settle for second best."

"That is so true, isn't it?" Charlotte said absently as she continued to examine the documents. Finally she looked up. "Well, thank you so much for showing these to me, Wanda. I'll read them over later this afternoon." She gathered the papers, clipped them together, and dropped them into the mahogany wood tray.

Without another word, Wanda turned on her heels and headed back the way she had come, motioning with a hand for Candy to follow.

She crossed the main display room, waving to Captain Mike as she went, and headed into another section of the Keeper's Quarters, which housed additional exhibits, including displays on navigational equipment, log books, clocks, and uniforms. She turned through a doorway along the left wall marked ADDITIONAL EXHIBITS and headed up a narrow wooden staircase. Candy followed at a respectable distance.

The staircase took them to the second floor of the Keeper's Quarters, located under the building's angled roofline. Here, two rooms were devoted to the museum—one a map room, the other displaying exhibits of the lightkeepers' families and domestic life. Three other rooms farther back on the second floor housed part of the historical society's archives.

Wanda walked straight into one of the archive

rooms. Candy followed her in curiously, surveying the place.

Shelves and drawers occupied just about every spare space along the walls, while a long conference-style table with a number of captain-style chairs provided a place to sit and work. Wanda had obviously made herself comfortable. She'd set herself up at one end of the table, with notepads, her laptop, and a cup of coffee close at hand. Battered folders, aged documents, yellowed drawings, and black-and-white photographs were strewn across the tabletop. Sunlight angled in a small south-facing window. The place felt warm and welcoming.

"What a nice cozy spot," Candy observed.

Wanda gave her a contemptuous look and crossed her arms. "Well, look who finally showed up at the historical society—our very own community columnist. I'm surprised you finally found the time to make it out here. I would think this would be one of the first stops a community columnist would make."

Candy made a wide-open gesture with her hands. "I'm here now."

"Yes, you are." Wanda took a seat in one of the padded wooden chairs. "Now I just have to figure out what you're up to."

Candy gave her a puzzled look. "I'm not quite sure what you mean by that."

"Don't act so innocent. You know exactly what I

mean." She hardened her gaze on Candy. "I suppose you've been getting my e-mails and letters."

Candy nodded, trying to maintain a calm expression as her heart beat a little faster. "We've been getting them. And we've read every one of them. We appreciate your input."

Wanda snorted. "I'm sure you do. Lord knows you could use it, considering that operation you've got going on over there, working with your boyfriend and all."

"What?" Candy felt a jolt of anger shoot through her. She could think of several choice things to say, but instead she forced her emotions back down. This wasn't the time for a confrontation with Wanda Boyle.

"Look," Candy said in as honest a tone as she could muster, "I know we got off on the wrong foot a while back, and I'm sorry about that. I know I left your son's name out of the column, and I'm sorry about that too. I know you wanted the job as community correspondent, and I'm sorry it didn't happen the way you wanted it to. But I'm not your—"

Wanda cut her off. "I know what you are," she said haughtily, her eyes showing something other than anger. "You think you can just walk into this town and take it over. You think you can throw around your pretty looks and get whatever you want. I've been living in this town for more than thirty years, I'll have you know. My husband was born in the next town over. I'm originally from New Hampshire. I've been a New Englander all my life, and I've seen your kind come and go. And let me tell you something, Miss Community Correspondent. You don't impress me. Maybe you've solved a couple of mysteries around here, and maybe the people of Cape Willington are fooled by your perky attitude and your tight jeans, but I'm not. I know what you're up to."

That took Candy aback. "What do you think I'm up to?"

Wanda gave her a hard look. "Don't be coy with me. You wouldn't be here unless you wanted something from me. So what is it? Are you trying to horn in on my territory? Because if you are, you'll lose. I'll crush you. I'll have you run out of town so fast you won't know what happened—and your father too. I *own* this town. Just you remember that. And there's no way you're going to take it away from me!"

# NINE

Candy was still shaking as she headed back to the parking lot. Her encounter with Wanda had not gone well, and she blamed herself for it. She'd walked right into the hornet's nest Maggie had warned her about and got stung. She should have been more cautious. Next time, she vowed, she wouldn't let herself get sideswiped like that.

Wanda was a forceful person, no doubt about that. And Candy took her threats seriously—at least some of them. But she also wondered what motivated Wanda. Did she have such a deep need to feel accepted around town that she was willing to do anything she could to gain recognition—and threaten those who failed to buy into her carefully cultivated reputation as a wonderful human being, when in truth she was anything but?

It was a question Candy didn't have an answer for.

One thing was certain—Wanda, at least for now, was the key suspect in the theft of Wilma Mae's lobster stew recipe, especially given her research of John Patrick Mulroy. But Candy had been unable to determine if Wanda had actually stolen the recipe—not that she hadn't tried.

After Wanda's initial threats, Candy had attempted to cool things off by steering the conversation back to more neutral ground. She was intrigued by Wanda's research and wanted to find out what she knew about Mulroy and his tendency to build secret hiding places into the homes he designed. She also wanted to ask a few questions about Wanda's brother, the carpenter. Was he the one who had worked on Wilma Mae's shelving unit in the upstairs bedroom? That could be a critical piece of the puzzle.

But Wanda had been frustratingly uncooperative. She sat back in her chair, crossed her arms, and glared at Candy, refusing to say anything about her research or anything else relating to the historical society. "You won't get any information out of me," she'd said. "If you want to know something, you'll have to find out yourself."

Candy remained as polite as possible, asking about the architects who had designed some of the historical houses in town. In response, Wanda handed her a few brochures that explained the upcoming summer programs, but she was of no more help.

Candy had been tempted to ask Wanda about her visits to Wilma Mae's house. And she wanted to ask about Wanda's involvement with the cook-off itself. But in the end, she thought she should leave well enough alone. So she had finally shaken her head and left.

Downstairs, Charlotte had disappeared, and Captain Mike was engrossed in a mystery novel, so Candy headed out of the building without another word to anyone.

As she started up the path toward the parking lot, she felt a strange itching on the back of her neck, as if someone were watching her. She turned quickly, eyes searching, but saw nothing suspicious, no one lurking behind her. Off to the right of the Keeper's Quarters stood a maintenance shed, and inside she saw a large, burly man with sandy-colored hair, wearing a dark green shirt and jeans, fiddling with the engine of an industrial-size lawn mower. Her gaze shifted. She spotted a few tourists lingering around the tower, but they all seemed preoccupied, staring up at the lighthouse or out toward the deep blue sea.

She looked up next, at the windows on the second floor of the Keeper's Quarters, and thought she saw a white curtain swaying, as if someone had pulled it aside and had just let it fall back into place. But she saw nothing beyond the curtain other than dusty shadows.

*Is Wanda watching me? Or Charlotte?*

*And if so, why? Do they have something to hide?*

As she'd discovered last summer, there were plenty of people around Cape Willington with secrets they desperately wanted to keep hidden.

*What kinds of secrets are hidden inside the lighthouse museum?* she wondered. *Or up in the historical society's archives?*

Deep in thought, she walked the rest of the way to the Jeep. Despite her clash with Wanda—or perhaps because of it—she sensed she was on the right track. The fact that Wanda was digging around the archives, researching John Patrick Mulroy and the homes he built, was an important discovery, she knew, and could indicate a definite link between Wanda and the missing recipe.

*I actually might be onto something,* she thought as she reached the Jeep and pulled the keys from her purse.

Before she climbed into the front seat, she pulled out her cell phone and keyed down through the list of calls she had recently received. When she found Wilma Mae's number, she pushed the call button.

The elderly woman picked up on the third ring. "Hello?"

"Hi, Wilma Mae, it's Candy Holliday."

"Oh, hello Candy dear. I didn't expect your call so quickly. Have you found my recipe?"

"No, not yet. But I'm working on it. And I have a quick question for you. When I was at your place this morning, you mentioned you had some work done on the shelving unit in the upstairs bedroom. You said you brought in a carpenter to do some repairs to the unit. Do you remember the carpenter's name?"

"Well, let me think. It was a local fellow, I can tell you that. A tall man. Fairly young. Good with his hands. But I'm embarrassed to say his name escapes me at the moment. Isn't that funny? And we were just talking about him."

"Do you have any records or receipts with his name on them? It would certainly help with the case."

"Well, yes, there might be something like that. My Milton took very good care of all the paperwork, you know. He was wonderful at that sort of thing. Very neat and tidy."

"That's nice to hear, Mrs. Wendell. Could you

look around and see if you could find something like that? With his name on it?"

"Of course. I'll look today. I'll call you right away if I find something."

As she keyed the off button, Candy looked out toward the ocean. Maybe she should stop by Wilma Mae's house again in the morning and help her look. But Candy quickly nixed the idea. She was scheduled to work with Herr Georg at the Black Forest Bakery for a few hours in the morning, and in the afternoon she had to run some errands before getting ready for her date with Ben.

It seemed she'd just have to wait until she heard back from Wilma Mae.

She had just pulled onto Ocean Avenue when she saw the police cars parked halfway up the street. Several of them had their lights flashing. A crowd had gathered on the street, the onlookers milling about, talking to each other, trying to figure out what was going on.

Candy approached cautiously, searching for a parking spot, until an officer of the Cape Willington Police Department waved her on.

"What's going on?" Candy called out her rolled-down window as she drove past.

"Just keep moving, ma'am. We have to keep this area clear."

As she passed by the commotion at a crawl, she noticed most of the attention seemed to be focused on the Stone & Milbury office. Through the front windows, Candy could see several officers inside.

She also could see Maggie talking frantically to one of the policemen, her arms waving dramatically in the air.

"Oh my heavens," Candy said to herself as the car behind her honked its horn and the officer waved again for her to drive on past. She glanced up at her rearview mirror, giving the driver behind her a dirty look. "Okay, I'm going, I'm going."

There were no open parking spots along Ocean Avenue, but she found one once she turned onto Main Street, across from Duffy's Main Street Diner. She scooted into the spot, slapped the gearshift into park, pulled heavily on the emergency brake, and unlocked her seat belt, then jumped out of the Jeep, pulling her purse with her. She ran along the sidewalk on Main Street, turned left at the corner, and headed down Ocean Avenue to see if Maggie needed her help.

Halfway down the street, several officers were trying to keep the crowd back, but Candy flashed her business card. "I'm with the *Cape Crier*! I'm a reporter!" she told one of the officers. A moment later she realized she knew him. "Officer Martin. It's me, Candy Holliday. You have to let me in there."

He gave her a skeptical look. "Can't right now, Candy, unless you have business inside."

"My friend's in there! Maggie! You know her!" she added frantically, pointing at Stone &

Milbury's window front. "She . . . she needs her medicine. She asked me to bring it to her." To prove her point, she started digging into her purse. "I've got it right here somewhere. She really needs it."

Officer Martin studied her for a few more moments before skeptically waving her through. "All right. But make it quick. And try not to get in the way."

"Oh, thank you, thank you so much!" She patted him on the shoulder as she raced past and through the office's front door.

Inside, it was strangely quiet, compared to the noisy activity on the street. Three men in dark suits stood to one side, talking softly to each other. A few employees meandered around, shocked looks on their faces. "Where's Maggie?" Candy asked. "Is she hurt? What's going on?"

An older male employee, wearing a white shirt and a tie, pointed to one of the interior offices. "She's in there. She's pretty upset."

"Why? What's wrong?" Candy asked again, but she didn't wait for an answer. She dashed into the office.

Maggie was sitting in an office chair, sobbing. Another man in a dark suit was sitting beside her, talking quietly to her.

Candy crossed the room. "Maggie, are you okay?"

Her best friend looked up. Her eyes were watery,

and her mascara had run. She sat with her head and shoulders slumped forward, and her arms and legs folded together, as if she were a schoolkid waiting to see the principal. "Oh, Candy," she said, her voice quavering.

"Maggie." Candy knelt in front of her and took one of her hands. "What's wrong? Are you hurt? Did something happen?"

Maggie wiped at her tears and nodded. "Uh-huh."

"Are you okay?"

Maggie shook her head and started crying again.

"For heaven's sake, tell me what's going on."

Maggie blubbered, her lips trembling, but finally she got the words out. "Oh, it's . . . it's Mr. Milbury," she said as she looked over at the man in the suit seated next to her.

The man gave her a questioning look. After a moment, he nodded. "All right. I'll let you two alone for a couple of minutes. But I need your statement, Mrs. Tremont. I'll be right over here when you're ready to talk." He rose and walked out of the room.

Candy dropped into his vacated seat. "Maggie, tell me what's going on. Are you in trouble?"

"I don't know," Maggie wailed, the tears flowing again.

"Why, what's happened? Please tell me."

It took Maggie a few moments, but finally she was able to get the words out. "It's . . . it's Mr.

Milbury," she repeated. "They say . . . they say he was embezzling from the company. They say he stole hundreds of thousands of dollars."

She paused as another deep sob swept through her, and her shoulders shuddered.

"They say . . . they say they're going to close the company down. Oh, Candy," she blubbered as the tears started flowing again, "I'm out of a job!"

# TEN

Henry "Doc" Holliday snapped the morning edition of the *Bangor Daily News* and expertly folded it back on itself, so he could continue reading the front-page story, which ran over to the inside.

"It's a mess, all right," he said with a shake of his head. "It looks like old Milbury was pocketing all the money paid to his company by individuals and companies for their insurance premiums." He paused, his eyes running down the columns of copy in the paper. "In some cases he even issued fake policies. It's actually a pretty clever scheme. That's how he bought himself that boat, I guess. And made that addition to his house. And paid for all those vacations to Africa and the South Pacific." He paused again, still reading. "They're saying it's a federal crime."

"Dad, that's terrible." Candy stood by the stove, waiting for the last batch of pies to finish baking.

She'd been up since six that morning, making pies for Melody's Café, as she'd been doing for the better part of a year, to make extra money. So far today she'd baked four—two cherry and two pecan. In a few months, when the crops started ripening in late summer, and the trees grew heavy with fruit in the fall, she'd switch to making fresh blueberry and apple pies.

"Looks like the state and federal attorney general offices are all over it," Doc continued, his nose still buried in the paper. "Apparently, though, it was a local postal inspector who figured out what was going on."

Candy shook her head in amazement. "How did he ever think he'd get away with it?"

Doc folded the paper back together, tossed it on the table, and took a sip of his coffee. He was looking a little better lately, Candy thought absently as she glanced at him. His face wasn't so thin anymore, and his eyes seemed brighter than last summer. He'd been more active lately too. He even appeared to walk with a bit of a bounce in his step on some days, his limp almost completely disappearing.

*It's the spring . . . warmer weather,* Candy thought, watching him. *It lifts the spirits of everyone in town.*

*Well . . . just about everyone.*

"That's the thing about criminals," Doc said, leaning back in his chair and interlocking his hands behind his head, as if he were some great pontificate offering sage wisdom for the masses. "They always think about the benefits but never the consequences. Milbury's been living high on the hog for a lot of years. Now he's got to pay for it. He'll go to jail for a long time."

"And what happens to Maggie?" Candy asked, genuinely worried.

Doc shrugged. "She'll just have to look around for another job, I guess."

Candy grabbed a couple of pot holders and opened the oven door. "It couldn't come at a worse time for her. Amanda graduates in a couple of weeks, property taxes are due next month, and Ed . . . well, she's having a rough time with Ed too. I'm worried about her, Dad."

"Yeah, I know, me too," Doc said with a sigh. "But we've all got our burdens to bear. At least she doesn't have to worry about mummy berry destroying her crops and whether the bees will disappear overnight." He rose and looked out the kitchen window at the blueberry fields behind the house. "It's getting tough for all of us, pumpkin. There's a lot to worry about these days."

"You got that right," Candy said as she started placing the pies on cooling racks she had set out on the counter. "But we're making it okay, Dad, aren't we?"

He shrugged. "For now. But this gentleman-farmer thing is a bit tougher than I originally anticipated—especially at my advanced age. It's starting to wear me out."

"What do you mean? I thought you loved the healthy lifestyle—being outdoors and all that."

"Yeah, I do," Doc admitted, "but I'm not getting any younger. We both know we can't go on like this forever. Sooner or later we'll have to move on."

"Dad, I wish you'd stop talking like that."

"No, I mean it," Doc said firmly. "I've been thinking maybe I should retire to a condo somewhere in Florida, something like that, start taking it easy."

Candy laughed. "Yeah, right. I can picture you down there in Florida, drinking cocktails with little umbrellas in them and playing shuffleboard with all the old geezers."

She closed the oven door with a knee and tossed the pot holders on the counter. "You'd go stir-crazy down there and you know it. Besides, you love this place, don't you? It's what you always wanted. You'd miss it if you sold it, wouldn't you?"

Doc turned toward her. "Sure I'd miss it. But I don't know how much longer I can keep up with it."

"Well, you've got help, don't you?"

Doc gave her a fatherly look. "Of course I do, pumpkin, and you've been doing all you can around here. But you've also been kinda busy these days, what with the newspaper job and the pies and the bakery and everything else you've got going on. You've got a life of your own to live. You've got things to do. You don't want to be stuck on this farm forever, do you?"

He gave her a serious look. "Do you?"

"Dad." Candy let out a breath and put her hands on her hips. "We've had this conversation before, remember? Several times, in fact. You know how I feel about this place, and this town. I'm not going anywhere—at least not for a while. So we'll just have to do the best we can. We got a good start with the vegetable gardens, and we'll finish them up next week. And the fields are in pretty good shape. If we need more help, maybe we should hire someone."

"Hire someone? Like who? And how would we pay for it?"

"I don't know. I'm just saying. We have options. So if you're worrying about the farm, we'll talk about it and see what we can figure out. We'll be fine. You'll see. But right now," she said, picking up her purse and car keys, which had been sitting on the kitchen table, "I have to go. I'll be at the bakery 'til noon, then I gotta swing back by the house and pick up the pies so I can drop them off at Melody's. After that, I'm going to stop by Maggie's to check on her. And then I have to get ready for my date with Ben tonight."

"How's that going?" Doc asked as she headed for the door.

She paused halfway out. "With Ben? It's going fine, Dad. Are you playing poker with the boys tonight?"

That made Doc brighten. "Sure am. Looking forward to it. Robbie's sitting in with us again. That's always fun."

"The teenager?"

"He's college age," Doc corrected, "and he knows what he's doing. He's been playing in some high-stakes games up near Bangor but says he's trying to hone his skills, so he sits in on our game with us old guys to see if he can pick up anything. And we've probably taught him a thing or two."

"Well, you boys have fun. Try to go easy on the kid." She headed out the door and walked to the Jeep.

Traffic on the Coastal Loop seemed heavier today as she drove into town. Tourists and seasonal folks were flooding in for the holiday weekend, which would be good for local businesses like Herr Georg's Black Forest Bakery. Candy had been helping out periodically at the bakery for the past few years, but Herr Georg had recently hired her on as a regular part-time seasonal employee. She worked at the bakery Tuesday, Wednesday, and Friday mornings, and usually helped out on Saturdays as well, though she'd taken off tomorrow so she could cover the Lobster Stew Cook-off at the Lightkeeper's Inn.

As she drove, the conversation with Doc lingered in her mind. She had to admit, he was right. A lot had happened over the past year, and her life was becoming busy. And to be honest, she wasn't sure how she felt about that. She loved being a blueberry farmer, working in the fields and taking care of the gardens. And she loved living in Maine. But she had to admit there were times she felt she needed something else.

In her previous life, working for a successful marketing firm that served the top high-tech companies in Boston, she'd been constantly on the go—until everything had come crashing down around her. By retreating here to Blueberry Acres and Cape Willington in Downeast Maine, she'd been able to start putting the pieces of her life back together.

She'd been happy with her simple life as a farmer. But that all changed last summer, when two murders had rocked the town, and she'd found herself deeply involved in solving them.

At the same time, several opportunities had come her way, and now she seemed to be spending less and less time on the farm. That's what had Doc worried, she knew. For the past few years, they had run the farm together. Though he had originally bought Blueberry Acres for himself, Doc had grown used to sharing the work with her. Now, most of the workload was once again falling on Doc's shoulders—at a time when most men had retired and spent their days fishing and playing with their grandchildren . . .

Candy sighed.

She was still trying to figure it out as she pulled into the last open parking spot on Main Street, got out, and walked into Herr Georg's bakery.

The German baker was thrilled to see her, as always. "Candy, *meine liebchen*!" he called out to her as she came through the door—and almost reeled as the redolent aromas of Herr Georg's concoctions overwhelmed her senses.

"Herr Georg, it smells wonderful in here. What are you baking today?" she asked as she placed her purse and keys behind the counter and reached for an apron that hung on a nearby hook.

The German baker twitched his white moustache and raised a finger as his eyes glistened. "Ah! Today I am making *bienenstich*. Do you know what that is?"

"Um"—Candy thought a moment; they'd gone over this—"that's bee sting cake, right? Filled with custard and topped with honey-glazed sliced almonds, I think. And if I remember correctly it has a very buttery dough, which is probably what I'm smelling right now."

Herr Georg beamed, his white teeth shining out from beneath his moustache. "Very good! You are correct! And Candy, you will get to sample the first piece!"

The morning passed quickly, as hungry tourists

and townspeople descended on the bakery to sample the German baker's luscious pastries and other baked goods, sweets, and imported items. Two towering wedding cakes went out the door, their transport carefully monitored by Herr Georg in his white baker's hat. Candy barely had time for a tea break as she continually bagged pastries and rang up sales on the old register.

By one in the afternoon she was back home, boxing up the pies, which she promptly dropped off at Melody's Café. She was on her way to Maggie's house when her cell phone rang.

Candy had to pull over and dig in her purse to find the phone, which by then had stopped ringing. But the readout told her the call had come from Wilma Mae. She keyed through the phone's contact list and called Wilma Mae's number.

The elderly woman answered on the fourth ring. "Hello?"

"Wilma Mae? It's Candy. You called?"

"Oh, yes, Candy. Thank you for calling me back so quickly. I hope I'm not being too much of a bother but I need your help again. Could you possibly stop by the house this afternoon?"

Candy checked her watch. It was just after two. She was supposed to meet Ben at seven, she wanted to check in on Maggie, and she still had a few errands to run. But Wilma Mae sounded worried. Something must be up. "Sure, I can do that. Is everything okay?"

"I don't know. I'm worried about Mr. Sedley. There's something . . . strange going on."

"Strange? In what way?"

"Well, Mr. Sedley seems to have completely disappeared. When can you come over?"

"I'm on my way. I'll be there shortly."

Candy keyed off the phone and slid it back into her purse. If she hurried she could still run her errands, drop in briefly on Maggie, and make her date with Ben. She gunned the Jeep and headed toward Wilma Mae's house on Rose Hip Lane.

Wilma Mae was standing on the front porch waiting to greet her as she drove into the driveway. The elderly woman hurried down the steps and across the lawn as Candy climbed out of the Jeep.

"Thank you for coming so quickly. I don't know what to do." Her face was drawn, and she was rubbing her hands rapidly together.

"Why, what's up?"

"It's Mr. Sedley. I haven't seen him in several days. I've tried calling him, but he doesn't answer his phone. I think something must be wrong with him. Maybe he's hurt or needs help."

"Should we call the police?" Candy asked.

Wilma Mae shook her head. "I want you to help me check his house. I have a key."

Candy's eyes were drawn to the neat, taupe-colored two-story home next to Wilma Mae's. It was a fairly plain-looking place, with a small covered porch, a single small gabled window pushing out from the front of the low-sloped roof, and white shutters surrounding the four front symmetrical windows. Those windows looked dark now, even in the daylight.

Candy blinked uncertainly. "Do you think that's the right thing to do? Maybe he's just visiting someone else, or maybe he's just keeping to himself?"

Wilma Mae gave Candy a distinctive harrumph. "His car is still in the garage behind the house—I checked. And he would answer if I called." She nodded sharply, as if that settled that. "We need to check his house, and I don't want to do it alone."

"I see." Still, Candy hesitated, but by the look on Wilma Mae's face, she knew there was no other option. "Okay, let's check his house."

Wilma Mae nodded approvingly. "I'll get the key."

# ELEVEN

Wilma Mae followed Candy around the side of the house to the small concrete porch at the rear. As Candy climbed the few steps, Wilma Mae handed her the key. But she didn't need it.

Candy knocked first and called Mr. Sedley's name. When he didn't respond, she turned the knob.

The door opened freely. It was unlocked.

"Maybe he's just resting upstairs and didn't hear me," Candy said softly to Wilma Mae. She pushed the door open farther and stepped inside.

She entered a dark hallway that led straight through to the front of the house. Candy took a couple of steps forward and nearly tripped over an antique brass umbrella stand that stood just inside the back door. She cursed as she held out her hand to steady the stand, which wobbled a little, its contents clattering. It held several old umbrellas as well as a couple of wood and metal walking canes.

"Is everything okay in there?" Wilma Mae called out. She was still outside, standing on the grass beyond the porch, her hands clenched tightly in front of her, watching Candy intently.

"Yup, fine, just fine," Candy called back over her shoulder. "I just tripped over something."

"Be careful," Wilma Mae urged.

"I'll try." Candy took a few more steps and turned to look through an archway that led to the kitchen, but she saw no one there.

"Mr. Sedley!" she called loudly. "Yoo-hoo! Anyone home?"

The place was eerily quiet. Candy looked around. Washed dishes were still in a drying rack beside the sink, waiting to be put away. A stack of opened bills, flyers, and junk mail lay at the end of the counter near her. A folded up newspaper and half-empty cup of tea sat on the kitchen table.

Candy stepped toward the table. Gingerly, she dipped the tip of her pinky into the cup, just breaking the liquid's surface. The tea was cold. It had been here for a while.

She looked around. *Nothing looks out of the ordinary,* she thought.

She walked through another archway into the living room at the front of the house. The TV set was on, though the volume was turned down. The drapes were open. A reading lamp on a corner table was switched on. An open hardback book lay upside down on the sofa, its spine bent back.

But no Mr. Sedley.

Candy looked back into the kitchen, then surveyed the living room again. Something didn't feel right. At first she didn't know what it was, but after a few moments she figured it out.

It was as if Mr. Sedley had left suddenly in the middle of whatever he was doing and hadn't returned.

Pondering what this might mean, she walked out of the living room and into the front hallway. "Mr. Sedley!" she called out again, louder this time. "It's Candy Holliday. Are you here?"

She turned right and almost walked right into Wilma Mae, who had come into the house and along the dark hallway. Candy let out a yelp of surprise, and Wilma Mae squeaked and backed away quickly, her hands flying up in front of her.

Candy put her hand on the elderly woman's

shoulder. "Sorry, I didn't know you were in here," she said, her heart beating just a bit faster.

"Have you found Mr. Sedley yet?" Wilma Mae asked in a loud whisper.

"Not yet. It doesn't look like he's home."

Wilma Mae's gaze shifted to the open staircase that led from the front hallway to the second floor. "You'd better check upstairs."

"Yeah, I guess you're right."

"Just be careful."

Candy nodded and started up the stairs, calling out Mr. Sedley's name. But again, there was no response. And once she checked the second floor, she knew why—no one was home. The place was vacant. "He must have gone somewhere," Candy said to Wilma Mae as she came back down the stairs.

"But his car is in the driveway. And he doesn't walk so well these days. So where could he have gone?"

Candy shook her head as she started along the hallway to another door. "I'd better check the basement, just to make sure."

She found the unfinished basement cold, damp, and full of spiderwebs. It was illuminated only by a single naked lightbulb hanging on a cord from the ceiling, but it was enough for her to see by. An old hot water boiler, which provided heat for the home, sat along one wall. An unused coal bin occupied a dark corner. A few items had been stored down here—an old Schwinn bike, some boxes filled with moldy books and magazines, rusted paint cans, discarded tools and appliances—nothing very valuable or interesting. Candy poked around a little, then switched off the light and climbed back up the stairs. "Nope, he's not down there."

"Well, I'm worried," Wilma Mae announced. She still stood in the hallway looking about her, as if expecting to see Mr. Sedley appear at any moment. "It's just not like him. He's never disappeared like this before."

"Maybe we should call the police."

Wilma Mae nodded in agreement. "Maybe we should."

"Let's call from your place," Candy suggested.

They closed and locked the back door and crossed the yard to Wilma Mae's house. Since Wilma Mae said she was too nervous to make the call, Candy took out her cell phone and dialed the Cape Willington Police Department. As the phone rang, she sniffed the air. Something smelled peculiar.

"Cape Willington Police Department."

"Hi, I'd like to report a missing person."

Candy was connected to a police officer, who asked her several questions—the name and age of the missing individual, and whether the person had any chemical dependency or mental health issues. After also inquiring if there was a history of disappearing and reappearing, the police officer asked, "Are there any signs of foul play?"

"What? No, I don't think so."

"Is he suicidal?"

To the best of her knowledge, Candy said, he was not.

After explaining that Mr. Sedley was an adult who had the right to roam about as he pleased, the officer promised to keep an eye out for him, and asked Candy to check back with the department in forty-eight hours if Mr. Sedley was still missing.

"Forty-eight hours?" Wilma Mae said when Candy had keyed off the phone. "But what if he needs us now? What if he's hurt somewhere and needs our help?"

Candy sighed. "There's not much more we can do right now." She sniffed the air again. That peculiar smell was back. "Do you smell something strange?" she asked, looking around the house.

Wilma Mae seemed distracted. "No, dear."

"Did you leave the gas on?"

"I don't think so." Wilma Mae checked the stove. "No, everything's off. I just can't figure out what happened to Mr. Sedley."

"Well, he'll probably turn up just fine. I wouldn't worry too much about him." Candy checked her watch again. "Wilma Mae, I have to run. Are you going to be okay?"

The elderly woman looked very worried, but finally she nodded.

"Why don't you make yourself a nice cup of tea and relax for a while," Candy suggested. "It'll make you feel better."

Wilma Mae seemed to consider that. "Maybe you're right," she said after a few moments, then checked the clock on the wall. "*Judge Judy*'s on in twenty minutes. Maybe I'll watch a little TV."

"That's a good idea. I have to run now, but you keep in touch, okay? Give me a call if Mr. Sedley turns up. And I'll see you tomorrow at the cook-off, right?"

Wilma Mae brightened. "Oh yes, I'll be there!" But just as quickly her face twisted with concern. "I do hope Mr. Sedley's there too. We're supposed to be honorary judges together, you know. We've been looking forward to it for such a long time."

"I'm sure he'll turn up," Candy said reassuringly.

"I just couldn't imagine being there without Mr. Sedley," Wilma Mae continued. "It wouldn't be right. Oh, I do so hope he's okay."

"I hope so too."

She'd planned to ask Wilma Mae about the carpenter who had made the repairs to the shelving unit upstairs, but the elderly woman seemed too flustered, too worried about Mr. Sedley, and Candy didn't want to upset her any further. So she decided to leave the question for another day. But as she walked outside to the Jeep, she couldn't help feeling that something was definitely amiss—and that she was overlooking important clues that would tell her exactly what it was.

# TWELVE

"Something's going on in this town," Candy said, sitting on the sofa with her legs curled up underneath her. "I know it. I can feel it."

Maggie removed the cork from a bottle of white wine, their second this evening, though it was still early. She sniffed its bouquet thoughtfully. "What, you mean with Ben?"

"Ben? Why would you think something's going on with Ben?"

Maggie took her friend's question in stride. "Well, you're here, aren't you?" she said lightly, indicating her living room as she freshened their glasses. "On a Friday night. When you're supposed to be out on a romantic date with your boyfriend, sipping Chianti and nibbling antipasto at some fancy Italian restaurant up on Route 1. With real tablecloths. Don't get me wrong, I'm glad you're here, but if it were me, I'd rather be out on a date."

"No offense, but me too."

"None taken."

They clinked glasses and sipped. A Michael

Bublé CD played on the stereo, and Maggie had lit a couple of scented candles to create a relaxing atmosphere, which they both desperately needed, given the events of the past few days.

"So," Maggie pressed on, appraising her friend over the rim of her wine glass, "just how *are* things going with you and Ben?"

Candy considered the question. "You know, you're the second person who's asked me about Ben today. Why all the sudden interest?"

"Oh, I don't know. Maybe it's just because we all care about you, honey, and want you to be happy. Or maybe we're just nosy. Or maybe it's a little bit of both. You know, there are all sorts of people around town who are interested in you two. They're always asking about you."

"Really? Like who?"

Maggie waved a hand. "Oh, like everybody. They're always asking me, 'So how are Candy and Ben doing? Are they dating? Has he proposed? Are they getting married?'"

"Married?"

"Well, I wouldn't worry about it, honey. It's just people talking."

Candy gave her friend a look of incomprehension. "But I don't get it. Why would anyone care?"

Maggie shrugged. "I don't know, really. I think we're all just looking for a little bit of romance in our lives, you know? Even if it's vicarious. It makes us hopeful—and happy. And Lord knows, happiness is in short supply around our little town lately, in case you hadn't noticed. Just look at what's happened to me. Six weeks ago my husband tells me he wants a divorce. He needs to find himself, he says, although I have no idea what *that* means. Now my boss absconds with all the company's loot. There's a rumor he ran off to South America with some woman thirty years younger than he is. I don't know what they put in the drinking water lately, but it's making some of the men around here a little squirrelly. I'm just hoping we don't have to put Ben in that category."

"You and me both," Candy admitted, "but if you must know, he was very apologetic when he called to cancel. And he has a perfectly legitimate excuse. Some friend of his came up from Boston at the last minute. They're old buddies. They just wanted to hang out together."

"So he canceled your date to spend time with his buddy? What's that all about?"

Candy gave her a look. "This is only the second time he's canceled on me, missy. He's been pretty good about keeping our dates. And we've had a good time."

"So you think he's your Prince Charming?" Maggie asked boldly. She had no trepidation treading on delicate territory with her best friend.

Candy took another sip of wine as she pondered the question. "Well, no, I'm not sure I'd call him that. He's wonderful and all, but he's certainly not the most romantic person I've ever gone out with. He's usually too preoccupied with other things, especially the paper. He's been a pretty good friend, though."

"Until some old buddy of his comes up from Boston for the weekend. Then you have to fend for yourself on a Friday night."

Candy raised her wineglass. "To Friday nights."

"To Friday nights."

They both drank, and Maggie continued, "If it's any consolation, I'm happy he canceled on you. Otherwise you wouldn't be here. And Lord knows I need a friend tonight."

"Been a tough week, huh?"

"That's putting a mild spin on it. Honey, it's been hell."

"Well, you seem to be holding up okay. You've been a trooper."

Maggie raised an eyebrow. "Hey, you know, that's not a bad idea," she said with a lopsided grin. "I wonder if the state troopers are hiring?"

"Yeah, that's all we need. You with a gun and a badge."

"Hey, I resent that. I'm pretty good with a gun."

"I know. That's what worries me."

They both laughed and sipped more wine. After a few moments, Candy said, "Amanda's not around this weekend?"

"She went off camping with the Zimmermans."

"So you're all alone."

Maggie spread her arms wide. "Welcome to my world."

"Obviously mine too."

"Hey, at least you're living with Doc. You've got someone to talk to. A couple of months ago this place was filled with a husband and a couple of teenagers with raging hormones. Now I'm queen of the castle, and the place is empty."

"You should get a cat."

"You know, I've been thinking about that. It's been six months since I lost Mr. Biggles. A new kitty's just what I need."

"Maybe a Siamese. Or a Maine coon cat. You know—someone who speaks the local language."

"Do Maine coon cats speak with a Maine accent?"

"Ah-yuh," Candy said, and they both laughed again.

Maggie leaned way back in her chair and wiggled her toes. She was going barefoot tonight, and had freshly painted toenails. "So . . . you think something's up?"

"Huh?"

"You just said *something's going on*—like what?"

Candy took a few moments to answer. "Just a bunch of weird things," she said finally, still trying to work it all out. "Too many strange little events that don't seem to be connected. But it's too coincidental that they're all happening at the same time."

"Yeah, life can be strange like that. So tell me

the details. Maybe I can help you figure it out."

"Well, there's this whole thing with Wilma Mae's missing recipe. And Wanda Boyle digging around in the archives at the historical society, supposedly looking for information on architects and historical homes. And I still haven't found out anything about Wanda's brother, the carpenter, who might have repaired the shelving unit in Wilma Mae's upstairs bedroom and discovered the hidden document drawer. And then there's Mr. Sedley's disappearance, which could turn out to be nothing." She paused. "Everything seems to be connected to the Lobster Stew Cook-off for some reason, which just about everyone around town has entered except you and me."

"Like who?"

"Well, Wanda of course."

"Of course."

"And Melody from Melody's Café. And Burt Ramsay from the Lobster Shack."

"That makes sense. He sounds like a ringer, though."

"Yup, he's got a big following. There's always a line stretching around the block to get into his place. You can't go near there in the summer. Then, let's see—Juanita from the diner has entered. And Bumpy Brigham."

"Doc's buddy?"

"Yup, it's got the whole posse in a frenzy. Apparently Bumpy cooks a pretty mean stew.

He's some sort of quasi-gourmet chef or something or other."

"Hmm. I thought all he did was eat, drink, and polish his antique cars."

"Well there you go—you just never know. And then just a whole bunch of regular folks are entering, like Lyra Graveton, Anita Weller, Walter Gruthers, Delilah Daggerstone, and Tillie Shaw. There's even a rumor Solomon Hatch is going to enter, though he'll probably make his stew with nuts and berries. Oh yeah, and Charlotte Depew is on the list."

"Charlotte Depew? From the museum?"

"That's the one. I finally met her yesterday. Did I tell you that?"

"No, but I figured you probably ran into her, since you said you went out to the museum."

"Yes, I did. I think I caught her at a bad time, though. She seemed pretty happy to hand me over to Wanda."

"You saw Wanda?"

"Yeah."

"How'd that go?"

Candy shook her head. "Not good."

"Does she still hate you?"

"Yeah."

"Did she get nasty?"

"A little."

"Are you okay?"

"Yeah. It was my own fault. I encroached on her

territory at the lighthouse, I guess, so that got her feathers all ruffled up. It was like backing a bull into a corner."

"You gotta steer clear of her. I told you. Don't make her madder than she already is."

"I don't know if that's possible. Plus, I still feel she's up to something. I wish I knew what she was really doing. She's been working up in those archives a lot."

"Then let her work. It keeps her out of your hair."

"Yeah, I guess that's true. I don't have much time to follow up with her anyway. I've got so much to do, what with the paper and Herr Georg's bakery and Melody's pies and the farm."

"You're a busy woman." Maggie paused, then sighed. "And I guess I've got to get busy too. I have to look for a new job."

Candy reached over and patted her on her ankle. "Give yourself a couple of days to recoup, okay? You've been through a lot. You deserve some time off. Why don't you take the weekend to relax and enjoy yourself? You can start looking for work next week, and I'll help."

"Really?"

"Sure. Tell you what. Why don't you go to the cook-off tomorrow with me? It'll give you a chance to get out in the air a little bit, enjoy the scenery, and sample the wares."

"Mmm. I wouldn't miss it. Are you working tomorrow?"

Candy nodded. "I have some interviews to do, but we'll have plenty of time to walk around together. And who knows? Maybe something really interesting will happen."

"Are you making a prediction?"

"No, I just have this . . . feeling."

Maggie's brow fell dramatically. "You're not getting psychic on me, are you?"

"No, we've already got plenty of those in town. Just call it intuition. I think tomorrow is going to be a very interesting day."

# THIRTEEN

The day dawned fine and bright, with a light, fresh wind and air as crisp as a just-plucked apple. Early morning dew made the well-manicured lawn at the Lightkeeper's Inn glisten like a tinseled tree on Christmas morning, and moistened the shoes of the first contestants as they arrived to set up their booths and start their stews. Birds chirped in the branches of the maple, oak, ash, and sycamore trees surrounding the inn's pristine front and side yards, accentuated by classical music piped into the property through discreetly placed exterior speakers. The inn's staff had festooned the posts and railings of the building's front and side porches with red, white, and blue streamers, and hung baskets overflowing with red and white petunias and impatiens from every available spot, adding to the morning's myriad colors.

Candy and Maggie arrived on the grounds just before nine and headed first to the food tables, where they each grabbed a cup of steaming coffee and a blueberry muffin. Then they walked over to check in at the registration table, where Candy received a press badge and a few printouts with updates on the contestants, judges, and the day's schedule, plus a hand-drawn map of the property, marking the locations of all the booths, tents, tables, and services.

"I was right," Candy said as she scanned the printouts she'd received.

Maggie took a large bite of her blueberry muffin. "About what?"

"It looks like there's been a change with the judges. I mentioned it in my column last week. They're bringing in some new guy. That should ruffle a few feathers around here, don't you think?"

Maggie wasn't paying attention. She was scrutinizing Candy's press badge, obviously impressed. "Where's mine?" she asked, pointing with a pinky at the badge hanging on a lanyard around Candy's neck.

Candy glanced down at it, smiling. It wasn't her first badge, but she still got a thrill every time she put one on. "You don't get one. You're not press."

"But I'm still important."

"Then we'll get you a badge for important people. I'm sure we'll find something."

"Okay, as long as I get a badge. I really want one. It'll make me feel better."

"Then we'll get you one. Don't worry."

That seemed to appease Maggie, and they began to make their rounds of the booths, checking on all the stews being prepared.

The booths were arranged in two crescent-shaped rows on opposite sides of the lawn. On the left were the booths of Melody Barnes, Burt Ramsay, Lyra Graveton, Tillie Shaw, and Anita Weller, while on the right were those of Bumpy Brigham, Walter Gruthers, Delilah Daggerstone, Juanita Perez, Charlotte Depew, and at the far end of the row, Wanda Boyle. The food services tent was located beyond Wanda's booth beneath a grove of trees, while the judges' tent occupied a centralized position in front of the inn's side porch.

They spotted Wanda Boyle setting up in her booth on the right side of the lawn, so they meandered off in the opposite direction, stopping first to say hello to Melody Barnes, owner of Melody's Café, for which Candy had been baking pies for nearly a year. Melody had brought lobster meat with her in several large Tupperware containers and was peeling and seeding tomatoes when Candy and Maggie walked up.

"I spent more than two hundred dollars on

lobster meat alone," Melody told them as she worked. "I hope enough folks show up so I can make my money back!"

"Oh, I wouldn't worry," Maggie said as she wiped away a few muffin crumbs that had fallen on her blouse. "Your lobster rolls are the talk of the town. I'm sure you'll have long lines of folks at your booth all day waiting to try out your stew."

Melody shook her head. She had started dicing the tomatoes, moving quickly with experienced hands. "I don't know. It looks like I've got some stiff competition out there. Burt Ramsay's got me worried."

Candy half turned to survey the stocky, broad-faced owner of the popular Lobster Shack restaurant, who was working in the booth next door. His restaurant, which was located quite literally in a white shack, occupied a primo spot along the shoreline just off the Coastal Loop. Guests ordered at a window and then sat at picnic tables strewn across a lawn that edged right up to the waterfront's black rocks.

Today Burt wore a floppy chef's hat, a bright orange Hawaiian shirt, and a large white apron, tied tightly around his ample belly. He was humming happily to himself as he monitored the progress of his stew. He waved when he glanced up and saw them looking his way.

"Friendly fellow, isn't he?" Maggie said, waving back.

Candy gave him a pleasant smile, appraising his operation. "He certainly looks festive—and confident," she observed after a few moments.

"Oh, he doesn't look so tough." Maggie continued to wave at Burt as she leaned in close so only the three of them could hear. She glanced at Melody. "You can beat him easily, can't you?"

"I sure hope so," Melody said, though she didn't sound overly confident.

Candy turned to scan Melody's ingredients. "It's all in the recipe, right? Or at least that's what I've heard. Are you using one of your grandmother's recipes, like you do at the restaurant?"

Melody nodded. "I sure am. That's the main reason I'm doing this in the first place. My grandmother's been pretty generous with some of her recipes, but this one was special to her, so she held on to it for a while. She finally gave it to me at Christmastime, after years of coaxing. It's authentic, too. Back in the forties and fifties, she collected recipes from the wives of lobstermen working along the coast. It was a hobby of hers. She and my grandfather had their own seafood restaurant out near Coney Island, you know. They used to visit Maine every fall to look for new recipes."

Maggie sniffed at the mouthwatering aromas drifting out of the stockpots boiling atop several industrial-size burners inside Melody's booth. "I guess good cooking runs in the family."

"That's for sure," Candy said. "You've mentioned

your grandmother and your grandfather before. Sometime I should write that story up for the paper. I'm sure people would love to read about them. But right now," she added, taking Maggie by the elbow, "we'd better let you get on with your work. We'll stop in a little later and taste a few samples."

"The first batch should be ready in an hour or so," Melody told them. "I'll save some for you!"

As Melody turned away, pulling big bunches of leeks and carrots out of produce boxes, Candy and Maggie wandered off to visit the other booths. They chatted briefly with Burt Ramsay and stopped to talk to Lyra Graveton, the quiet, long-haired owner of the Ice Cream Shack, and Tillie Shaw, a plump, red-faced farmer's wife, before they headed the other direction and ran into Doc and the boys.

Doc regularly hung out with his trio of buddies—Finn Woodbury, Artie Groves, and William "Bumpy" Brigham. They were golfing and poker pals who held court nearly every weekday morning in the corner booth at Duffy's Main Street Diner. But today they were like old hens, hovering and cackling around Bumpy, who was already breaking a sweat, even though it was still cool outside, with the temperature struggling to reach the midsixties. This was Bumpy's first year in the competition, and he already seemed to be feeling the pressure.

The other members of the posse were attempting to help him along. Artie was chopping vegetables while Finn monitored the lobster stock boiling in battered old pots on makeshift burners. But he wasn't paying too much attention to his work. Instead, he was wielding a wooden stirring spoon like a golf club, showing Doc how to correct his grip.

"Ya gotta grip it like you're holding an egg," Finn was saying as Candy and Maggie walked up. "Real light, ya know. Ya don't wanna hold it too tight. Don't wanna break that egg. And ya gotta keep your thumb tucked over the side of the shaft, like this."

"Hell, I know all that, Finn," Doc was saying irritably. "I got the grip down. I just gotta figure out how to keep the ball going straight. It keeps shanking off into the rough. With these old legs I get tired tramping around the course looking for that little white goose egg."

He looked up as his daughter stopped in front of the booth. "Well, hello there, pumpkin. And hello Maggie. You're looking particularly lovely this morning. How are you doing?"

"I'm hanging in there, Doc," Maggie said, unmoved by the compliment. "It's been a rough week."

"Yeah, so I've heard. Sorry about the mess over at the insurance agency."

"Old Milbury's got himself in a world of

trouble, that's for sure," Finn put in. A former cop himself, Finn had a friend connected with the Cape Willington Police Department and often heard inside information before it got out to the public. "They're still looking for him. Word is he's trying to skip the country. But when they catch up with him he's gonna put a lot of time in the ol' pokey."

"I hope they put him away for the rest of his life! He deserves everything he gets for ruining my life," Maggie said in a rare flash of anger, though she quickly got her raw emotions under control. "But I'm not going to worry about that today. I'm just going to hang out here, have some fun with my friends, and eat my fill of lobster stew."

"That's the spirit!" Finn said with a hearty laugh.

"We got some good stew coming here soon," Doc said, pointing with a gnarled finger at Bumpy's operation. "I've been keeping an eye on him. He's doing a good job so far. And he's got a secret ingredient."

Bumpy looked up. "White wine and mustard," he whispered loudly to Candy and Maggie. "It came to me in a dream one night. This giant lobster walked right into my living room and told me what to put in the stew. So I listened to it. I mean, who's gonna argue with a talking lobster in a dream? I cooked some up the next day and it turned out pretty good!"

144

"A . . . talking lobster?" Maggie said hesitantly. "But why would it tell you how to cook it? Wouldn't it have said, *Don't eat me?*"

Bumpy gave her a quizzical look, but Doc jumped in to rescue his friend. "Don't worry, he knows what he's doing. He just might win this competition and surprise everyone."

"Well, good luck Bumpy," Candy said, amused by Doc's defense of his friend. "Looks like you've got plenty of helpers—or at least *two* good helpers."

"Hey, you always gotta worry about having too many cooks in the kitchen," Doc said quickly in his own defense.

"I guess that explains why you're standing around observing while everyone else is working."

Doc didn't miss a beat. "There's a lot of truth behind those old sayings, you know. Aristotle once said, *Pleasure in the job puts perfection in the work*. And you know I don't get much pleasure out of cooking. So if I want Bumpy to make a perfect stew, it's best if I stay out of it. Otherwise, I'll just ruin it for him."

"Hmm." Candy gave her father a skeptical look. "Dad, that's the best explanation for not working I've heard from you in a long time."

Doc grinned widely. "What can I say? I'm improving with age. Hey, look, there's Robbie Bridges." He pointed off past her, obviously eager to change the subject.

Candy and Maggie turned to look where he was pointing. After a moment, Candy spotted a thin, gangly dark-haired boy in his late teens, wearing a white shirt and khaki pants, with a clipboard in one hand and a pen in the other, hurrying alongside Oliver LaForce, the inn's proprietor. Oliver was talking rapidly, and Robbie was studiously writing down everything he could, as fast as he could. On Oliver's other side, wearing a blue shirt and purple tie, and strolling along quietly with his hands clasped behind his back, was Alben "Alby" Alcott, the assistant innkeeper, who essentially served as the establishment's general manager and ran the day-to-day operations. Candy noticed the trace of an amused smile on Alby's bearded face.

"Oliver just promoted Robbie from bellman to assistant clerk," Doc said quietly to Candy and Maggie, "though basically Oliver's just been using the boy as a glorified gopher."

"It's good for him," Finn cut in. "Helps the boy learn the business."

"He's running the kid into the ground," Bumpy muttered as he drizzled a handful of herbs into the simmering lobster stock.

"He's young. He'll be fine," Artie said, sliding his glasses up on his nose with a long index finger. "Experience is the best teacher, and he's getting plenty of experience around here."

Candy was intrigued as she watched the trio

146

cross the lawn toward Bumpy's booth. She turned back to Doc and the boys. "You all seem to know an awful lot about Robbie. Why the interest?"

Doc pointed none too discreetly. "Well, that's him—that's the teenager."

It took Candy a few moments to figure out what Doc meant. "Oh, the *teenager*. It's *that* Robbie— your poker-playing buddy. The one I told you to go easy on."

"No need to go easy on that kid," Artie said with more than a hint of jealously. "He's a better poker player than all of us put together."

"You got that right," Finn added. "The boy's got a head for numbers, that's for sure."

Doc leaned in toward Candy. "He took some money from Finn and Artie last night. A pretty big wad of cash. The kid's good."

As she watched the young man approach, Candy was struck by how young he looked. "You guys aren't contributing to the delinquency of a minor, are you?"

"He's hardly a minor," Finn said defensively. "He's nineteen."

Candy raised an eyebrow. "Just so you guys don't turn him into a nineteen-year-old convict."

Doc waved a dismissive hand. "Naw, he's fine. He's just an adventurous kid."

Candy's gaze shifted from Robbie to Oliver, and she realized the inn's proprietor was looking right at her. He nodded as he approached and stopped in front of them. "Good morning, Candy. I see you got my message. I'm glad you could make it today." He held out a smooth hand with well-manicured nails.

"Well, good morning to you too, Oliver." They shook hands, though Candy noticed that Oliver's grip was a bit light, and he withdrew his hand quickly, as if stung in the fingertip. "I wouldn't have missed this for the world," Candy continued. "You know my dad, Henry Holliday, right?"

Oliver's gaze shifted toward Doc. "Yes, we've met a few times. Hello, Henry."

Doc nodded his head. "Oliver. Good to see you again."

"I've heard you're writing a book about the history of Cape Willington."

Doc crossed his arms and put on one of his best professorial looks. "Yes, that's one of the projects I'm working on, though I've just started my research."

"Well, I'm glad to help any way I can. You know, the inn has quite a history. It dates back to 1791, which was also the year the town was incorporated, though of course it was founded decades earlier. In those days there were only a few settlers in this area, along with a sawmill, a school, and a store. So the inn was one of the town's original buildings."

"That's right," Doc said, "until it burned down in 1811, after which it was rebuilt."

"Actually, it was rebuilt three times," Oliver corrected him. "The current building dates back to 1902."

"That would've been when Elias Whitby took over the place," Doc said without skipping a beat.

Oliver paused, studying Doc. He pursed his thin lips. "You've done your homework."

"I've had lots of practice."

"I'm surprised you haven't been over to see me."

"Strangely enough, you were next on my list." Doc had a twinkle in his eye. Candy knew he loved exchanges like this. No one could ever get the better of him when he was on his game.

"Well." Oliver drew out the word as he looked at Candy, then at Maggie, and finally at Finn before turning his gaze back to Doc. "I'll look forward to exchanging notes. I hope you'll call soon to set up a meeting. You know Alby Alcott, my right-hand man?"

"Sure. Hi, Alby." Doc shook hands with the assistant innkeeper.

"Hello, Doc."

Oliver turned to his other side. "And this is my assistant, Robbie Bridges."

Doc nodded at Robbie, who hadn't said a word. "We've met. Hi, Robbie."

"Hi, Doc," the teenager said softly.

"And, of course," Doc said, indicating the others, "you know my friends—Finn Woodbury, Artie

Groves, and our chef for today, Bumpy Brigham."

"Of course." Oliver glanced at the three of them. "Good morning, gentlemen."

The three of them waved and said hello, nearly in unison.

"Well, good!" Oliver clapped his hands together a single time, studied them all for a few moments, and abruptly turned back to Candy. "I wonder if I might have a word with you. There's something I'd like to discuss . . . privately."

Candy had been sipping at her coffee. Caught off-guard, she swallowed quickly and lowered her cup. "Oh, well, um, sure, Oliver." She glanced at Doc, Maggie, and the boys. "I guess I'll . . . be right back."

None of them said a word as they watched her walk away, but Candy thought she heard Maggie whisper to Doc, "I wonder what *that's* all about."

Candy wondered the same thing herself.

Oliver led her a short distance away from the booths, to a small sitting area with wrought-iron furniture arranged around a circular grass-and-brick ground pattern beside a small grove of birch trees. There he stopped and turned toward her. "I apologize for being so mysterious, but I have a favor to ask of you."

It seemed to Candy he was trying to be as pleasant as possible, though it was clear he was finding it difficult. She tilted her head, curious. "And what would that be, Oliver?"

"Well, it seems we've lost one of our judges." He cleared his throat, and she thought she saw a flicker of embarrassment skitter across his eyes. "Well, two, actually, but we've been able to replace one. We don't have a replacement for the second."

"Who's missing?" Candy asked, and almost immediately the answer came to her. "It's Mr. Sedley, isn't it?"

"Unfortunately, yes. We've called his house, but there's no answer. And he hasn't arrived here at the inn this morning. We're forced to go on without him."

Candy was suddenly very worried. "I called the police about it yesterday. Wilma Mae hasn't seen him in several days. She's worried about him."

Oliver pursed his lips. "Yes, I understand that. I've called the police myself and filed a report. We're all concerned about him. But the truth is, I have an event to run here, and I'm short a judge."

Candy looked at him with a confused expression on her face. "What are you saying?"

Oliver took a breath. "You're the community correspondent. You have some sort of status in town. I'd like you to serve as the third judge."

"Me?"

"Yes, I'm hoping you'll consider it. It would certainly solve a problem for us—in more ways than one, since Wilma Mae's thinking of backing out of the judging without Mr. Sedley here, and quite frankly, I'm hoping you might be able to encourage her to remain part of the event."

Candy thought about that a moment. "Is she here yet?"

"She's on her way. She sounds very worried, though."

Candy thought a little more. "What would I have to do? I've never been a judge before."

"We'll introduce you to the public, of course. You'll sit down at a table with the stews in front of them. You taste them. It's a blind test, so you won't know whose stew you're tasting. You confer with Wilma Mae and our other judge—his name is Roger Sykes, by the way."

"Roger . . . Sykes?" Candy repeated. The name sounded familiar.

"He's a restaurateur up from Boston. I met him at a hospitality industry convention a few years ago and we've kept in touch. Anyway, once you've finished the tastings, the three of you reach a consensus. I'll announce third, second, and first places. I award the trophies and ribbons. We're all done."

Candy mulled it over. That didn't sound too hard. "So what time would I have to be over at the judges' table?"

"No later than eleven forty-five. You'll be done in an hour or so."

Candy shook her head. "I still don't know. I don't feel I'm qualified to judge something like this."

Oliver looked at her without blinking. "You eat, right?"

Candy couldn't help but smile. "Of course I eat."

"Well, when you eat there are some foods you like and some you don't. This is just like that. Pick the stew you like. It's that simple. It's just a taste test. Besides, you'll be an honorary judge, which means you don't need expert qualifications."

"Really?"

Completely straight-faced, Oliver LaForce said, "I would not kid you, Candy."

Candy watched him for a moment. "No, I don't suppose you would. But isn't there someone more qualified around? What about Herr Georg?"

"Wolfsburger?" Oliver snorted. "I called him. He's too busy today with something he's doing over at the Plant and Pastry event in Town Park. Besides, he says he's given up the judging business."

That wasn't a surprise, after what happened at the Blueberry Queen Pageant the previous summer. "Well, what about someone else . . . like Ben Clayton?"

"I asked him. He recommended you."

"Oh." Candy had exhausted all her excuses. "Well, in that case, I guess I have no choice. I'll do it."

Oliver gave her the closest thing he could manage to a smile. It was a rather pitiful affair. "Splendid. I'll take care of all the details. And I'll let Wilma Mae know when she arrives that you'll be standing in for Mr. Sedley."

"Okay." Candy let out a breath and checked her watch, wondering what she'd gotten herself into. "I have a few things to take care of first. I still have to conduct several interviews for the paper."

Oliver made a face. "Yes, about that—I'd prefer if you conducted your official interviews after the awards ceremony, so we don't confuse the contestants. We want them to think of you as a judge, not a reporter—for this morning, at least. That also was Ben's suggestion, by the way, not mine, but I think it's a good one. Before the judging begins, you can visit the contestants' booths to watch their preparations and ask general questions, although we ask judges to refrain from inquiring about specific ingredients, so as not to influence your decisions. Let's see, what else? I'll send Robbie over with a judge's badge. You should wear it prominently this morning. Don't eat too much, since you'll be tasting quite a number of stews at noon. If there's anything else, just let me or Alby or Robbie know. We're here to help, though of course we will be quite busy. There's a lot to do. This is an important event for us, you know."

"I'm sure it is," Candy said.

"We're hoping to grow it quite a bit over the next few years. It seems to be quite a popular event around town."

"Everyone's talking about it," Candy confirmed.

Oliver straightened and clasped his hands behind his back. "That's very gratifying to hear. Well, we both have much to do this morning. Again, I appreciate your help with this, Candy. I'll check on you in a little while."

And with that, Oliver moved off across the lawn, motioning for Alby and Robbie to join him.

As Candy wandered back over toward Bumpy's booth, Maggie intercepted her. "So? What did he want? You guys powwowed for quite a while over there."

"Oliver wants me to be a judge."

"A judge? For the cook-off?"

"Yes."

"Wow."

"I know. I'm still in shock."

"So you're going to do it?" Maggie asked as they started walking back toward Bumpy's booth together.

"I guess so. I'm supposed to be at the judges' tent at eleven forty-five. And, oh yeah, I get a badge."

"Another badge? Two of them?"

"Two of them. And you know what?" She pushed a finger at Maggie's shoulder. "*You* can have one of them."

"Oh goody! Which one?"

"The press badge, of course. I won't need it this morning. So you can wear it for me. See, I told you we'd find a badge."

Maggie beamed and winked at Candy. "You're a good friend."

"Hey, what's going on?" Doc asked as they reached the booth.

"Candy's going to be a judge!" Maggie said, unable to contain her excitement.

"For the cook-off?" Doc looked taken aback.

"For the cook-off," Candy confirmed.

"Well, that . . . that's great, pumpkin," said Doc, not sounding completely supportive.

The rest of the boys were excited, though. "Congrats," said Finn, while Artie piped in with, "Way to go, Candy!"

"Wow," said Bumpy as he looked up from his stew, eyes widening. "How about that!"

Candy made a face at him. "Now don't get any ideas, Bumpy. I'm going to be as impartial as possible. Besides, it's a blind test. I won't know which stew is yours—or at least I'm not supposed to know."

"Well," said Bumpy, picking up a towel to wipe the sweat from his brow, "if you happen to taste a stew made with mustard and white wine as its secret ingredients, just remember where it came from. I sure could use some help."

Candy sighed as she turned and surveyed the field. Her shoulders sagged just a bit as she realized she had a long day ahead of her. "You're not the only one."

# FOURTEEN

She ditched her purse in Bumpy's booth, after removing her reporter's notebook, a couple of pens, and her cell phone, and received a sworn promise from Finn that he'd keep an eagle eye on it for her. He saluted her. "Consider it under lock and key, your judgeship."

She left Maggie at the booth as well, stepping in for Artie, who joined Doc in strolling off in search of donuts and coffee for the crew.

Turning to survey the lawn, Candy was trying to figure out her next move when Robbie came running up to her. "Here you go, Candy," he said, handing her a gold badge with red and gold streamers and the word *JUDGE* emblazoned across the center in capital letters. "Good luck!" And he was off again, dashing across the lawn toward the inn.

"Thanks," she said to his disappearing back. "I have a feeling I'll need it."

She felt oddly conspicuous as she put on the badge, which looked somewhat gaudy once she'd attached it to her blouse. She glanced around—and had a strange sensation that she'd just become the center of attention.

She hadn't realized it, but she'd taken a few steps out in front Bumpy's booth, in clear eyesight of most of the contestants. Some were staring directly at her, while others were trying to be more discreet, but they all knew there was a new judge in town.

*Wow, word must have gotten around fast,* Candy thought.

She also realized with a mild jolt of surprise that her status with all of them had just changed. She was no longer the folksy community correspondent. She was now the dreaded cook-off judge. A barrier of officialdom had been inexorably erected between her and the contestants, some of them her friends.

Of course, some of them *weren't* her friends, and this new promotion probably just made things worse. She didn't even want to look in Wanda's direction right now. She knew she'd be slain with daggers. So she turned to her left and let out a breath.

"Oh boy. What have I done?" she asked herself aloud.

She reminded herself that Oliver had pressed this upon her, and she was doing it to help him out. But she decided she was also doing it to help out the town—a sort of civic duty. And that made her feel a little better about it.

*A few hours,* she told herself, *and it'll be all over. Then I can get back to normal.*

*Well, as normal as things get around here,* she amended.

In the meantime, she might as well enjoy her newfound power.

That made her feel even better.

Her first stop, again, was at Melody's booth, but this time Melody greeted her with a pleasant yet wary smile, and wasn't nearly as chatty as she'd been earlier in the day. Burt Ramsay gave her a tip of the spatula as she walked past. Lyra Graveton appeared too busy to talk, humming a show tune to herself as she studied her stew pots, while Tillie Shaw chattered and giggled nervously when Candy stopped to say hello. At the end of the row, Anita Weller, who taught elementary school in a neighboring town, busied herself by cleaning around the cooking area, as if she thought she was being judged on her cleanliness as well as on her culinary skills.

Finally, she met someone who wasn't intimidated by her. As she reached the end of the row of booths she saw Jesse Kidder, the paper's photographer, who was taking pictures of the inn, lawn, and contestants' booths with a wide-angle lens. He was heavily laden down with three cameras and all the accompanying bags and accessories. He wore a floppy khaki hat and a photographer's vest, pockets bulging.

"I thought I'd start wide and then go in close on the booths," he told her as he walked toward her. Then he noticed her badge. "Hey, you're a judge! That's really cool, Candy." He backed away and lifted one of the cameras to his eye. "Here, let me get a few shots. Smile!"

Candy did her best as he snapped off a few quick images of her from different angles. "I'll get more shots of you later on with the other judges at the awards ceremony. Good luck!"

"Thanks, Jesse." The words came out with an edge of melancholy, but he missed any signal she might have been trying to send him about her uncertainty over her new role, and with a quick farewell he wandered off toward the inn, a camera glued to his face, studying the building's facade through the lens.

Candy crossed her arms loosely as she lingered in the shade of a wild cherry tree, which still held its last few white blossoms, and turned to survey the lawn. She was trying to gather the courage to visit the booths on the opposite side of the lawn, and wondering again if she should have given in to Oliver's request, when a soft voice spoke up. "Having second thoughts?"

Candy turned.

Judicious F. P. Bosworth stood beside her.

"Oh, hi, Judicious. I didn't see you there." She paused a moment, trying to register his question. "What was that?"

"Are you having second thoughts about what you've agreed to do?" he repeated quietly.

He was about forty, the son and grandson of judges. A world traveler, Judicious had skipped out on his senior year in high school, much to his family's dismay, and embarked on a journey of self-discovery, backpacking his way through Europe and Asia before winding up on a mountaintop in Tibet, where he spent the better part of two decades at a Buddhist monastery. Now he was back in Cape Willington, living by himself in a small log cabin on a forested patch of land at the edge of town.

Apparently, during his many years at the monastery, Judicious had learned to make himself invisible at will, and most around town let him think it, and even indulged him in his firm belief. Today, though, he was clearly visible. He looked lean and healthy, with bright blue eyes and black uncombed hair. He wore dark green trousers, a khaki long-sleeved shirt, and black Converse sneakers.

"Oh, well, I . . . I don't know," Candy said hesitantly. "About what? Oh, you mean the whole judging thing?"

At moments like this, Judicious always confused her a little. She wondered how he knew what she was thinking, but then realized her body language probably gave her away.

When he didn't respond, she realized he was still waiting for an answer to his question. "Well, yes, to be honest, I guess maybe I am. Just a little."

"You'll be fine," Judicious said reassuringly. "Oliver made a good choice. Just remember to keep a close eye on everything that happens today. There's a lot going on."

"I can see that," Candy said, her gaze sweeping the lawn, which was becoming more crowded as the morning passed.

"No." Judicious turned his whole body to face her, to emphasize his point. He touched her elbow. "You need to keep a close eye on everything. There's a lot happening today, and you'll need to remember it all later on."

"Oh. Okay." Candy felt a little uneasy under his odd gaze. "I'll be sure to do that, Judicious."

"Can you see what's going on over there?" he continued, pointing with his eyes across the lawn.

Candy turned casually, letting her gaze drift right, so she could surreptitiously glance at the booth on the far side of the lawn, where Wanda was working.

Wanda had several helpers who seemed to be doing most of the cooking for her, while she stood off to one side, talking animatedly to a small group of her friends. They had their heads close together and were obviously discussing something important—probably her, Candy thought.

When one of them saw Candy looking their way, she nudged Wanda, who turned her head almost imperceptibly to glance toward Candy.

After a moment, their heads moved closer together as they all turned their backs to her.

Candy shook her head. "They're quite a group, aren't they?" she muttered.

When she looked around, expecting a reply to her comment, Judicious was gone.

She searched the grounds for him, spinning around in a complete circle, but he was nowhere in sight. "Well, that was strange," she said to herself. "Maybe he made himself invisible."

It wasn't the first time she'd thought he might actually have that skill.

She turned back to the lawn, trying to plan her next move. The booths of Bumpy Brigham, Walter Gruthers, Delilah Daggerstone, Juanita Perez, and Charlotte Depew were located on the far side, in a line that arced from a small parking lot toward the inn's south wing and the food services tent.

Of course, Wanda's booth lay in that direction as well.

Candy supposed she should head over there, but her feet just wouldn't go that way.

Instead, they took her off in another direction, toward the judges' tent. She passed by families and couples who strolled the lawn, headed toward the booths to watch the contestants work. The day had turned out beautiful, with a pale blue sky and high wispy clouds drifting over the bright green lawn and freshly leafed trees. The temperature was steadily warming. A light wind tossed Candy's hair.

As she approached the inn she saw Ben, who was walking past, chatting with another man Candy didn't recognize.

"Oh, Candy, there you are," Ben said when he saw her. "I've been looking for you." Before she could say anything, he added, "Hey, I'm sorry about last night. I hated to cancel on you. But, as I said, I had a friend come into town at the last minute. Candy, I'd like you to meet Roger Sykes."

Candy turned toward the man at Ben's side. He wasn't quite as tall as Ben, nor quite as good-looking, but he had a pleasant, tanned face, framed by black hair and a black, well-trimmed goatee, all of which made his teeth look blazing white. He was probably in his early to midthirties, and wore a charcoal gray suit and expensive-looking black shoes, which seemed out of place among the other more casual outfits on the lawn.

He held out a hand toward her. "Hello, Candy."

"Hello." She reached out to shake his hand. "So you're Roger Sykes. I didn't know you were Ben's friend. I just heard from Oliver that you're going to be a judge today."

"And I've heard we're going to be working together. I'm honored. Ben's told me quite a lot about you. If you're half as wonderful as he says, you must be quite a catch."

"Oh, he's just being polite," Candy said with a smile.

"I'm glad Oliver took my suggestion," Ben said, pointing at the judge's badge. "It looks good on you."

Candy glanced down at the fancy badge and its

ribbons. "Well, thank you . . . I guess. It's not exactly what I'd planned on doing today. To be honest, I'm feeling a little stressed about it."

"Oh, it won't be so bad," Roger said, patting her arm. "I'll help you any way I can. I'm just glad I don't have to judge this whole thing by myself."

"Besides," Ben added, "it's good publicity for the paper. And you can write about it in your next column. Sort of an insider's look at what it's like to be a judge."

"Yeah, I suppose so," Candy said halfheartedly. She looked over at Roger. "So do you have experience doing these sorts of events?"

"I've done a few of them. It's something I sort of fell into."

"Roger came up at the last minute to fill in for one of the judges who couldn't make it today," Ben explained. "He called me yesterday afternoon. It was all pretty sudden. But it's great to see him. We went to BU together. I used to hang out with him and his brother back in our college days."

Roger filled in some of the details. "Brant Wisely had a last-minute emergency," he explained, "so he called me and asked if I could fill in for him. I've known Oliver for a few years, and of course Ben and I go way back. I've been meaning to visit Cape Willington for some time. It just worked out for the benefit of everyone. And I get to meet wonderful people like you."

Brant Wisely, Candy knew, was the well-regarded food critic for the *Boston Globe*. He maintained a summer cottage in Harpswell, down the coast a ways toward Portland, and had served as one of the event's judges a few times over the years. Many around town had been looking forward to his visit.

"Roger owns a couple of seafood restaurants in Boston," Ben continued, "so he's well qualified to serve as a judge—though Oliver's a bit put out by the last-minute substitution."

"And now he's had to replace another judge," Candy said.

Ben shrugged. "You know what they say about the best-laid plans. Oliver's always been a bit of a perfectionist."

"I'm sure he'll get over it," Roger said with a chuckle. "Brant promised to make it up to him somehow. I think they're talking about some sort of culinary event later in the summer."

"Hey, it all worked out for the best," Ben said, slapping Roger on the shoulder. He turned to Candy. "I'm going to introduce Roger to a couple of folks, and then we're going to head over to the judges' booth. Want to come along?"

Candy shook her head. "I'll meet up with you later. I still have to visit the rest of the booths, and I want to make some notes for my column."

Ben nodded, serious again. "Okay. I just spotted Robbie Bridges making the rounds of the booths, telling the contestants they have one hour to get their stews over to the judges' table for tasting. Things will be heating up here pretty soon."

"At least I know what they're serving for lunch," Roger said, flashing his dazzling smile. "I'm looking forward to it, actually. It'll give me a chance to sharpen my taste buds. It was nice to meet you, Candy. We'll have fun working together. I'll see you shortly."

As Ben and Roger moved away, Candy felt a nudge in her back. "So, you got a new boyfriend?"

"Huh?" Candy turned around.

Maggie stood behind her, grinning like the Cheshire cat. "Who's Mr. Handsome?" She pointed with her eyebrows at the disappearing backs of Ben and Roger.

"The guy with the goatee? That's Roger Sykes. He's the new judge today—well, the *other* new judge. He's a friend of Ben's."

"Well, he can be my friend too. He reminds me of a young Burt Reynolds. I've always had a thing for guys who look like that. Do you think he'd ever go for a gal like me?"

Candy considered that. "Maybe. Of course, he's probably married with four kids."

Maggie looked dejected. "You're probably right. Just my luck." She paused, and they both noticed Roger turn around to glance in their direction. He waved.

"Isn't that cute?" Maggie waved back. "I don't

think he was looking at me, though. If I didn't know better, I'd say he has eyes for you."

"Aw, go on, you're kidding."

"No, I'm not. I saw the way he was ogling you."

"He wasn't ogling me," Candy said with a laugh.

"Well, that's what it looked like to me. If I didn't know better, I'd say Ben has some competition."

Candy scoffed at the remark. "They're friends. Nothing like that could ever happen."

"Things like that happen *all the time,*" Maggie said dramatically.

Candy laughed again, though it was a bit forced this time, as she pulled her notebook and pen out of her back pocket. Quickly she jotted down a few things while they were fresh in her memory. *Brant Wisely out. Roger Sykes in. Owns restaurants in Boston. Ben's friend.* She paused a moment, then added, *Ask Oliver about his views on the last-minute change in judges. Interview Roger about the winner.*

"Oh, here comes Wilma Mae," Maggie said.

Candy looked up. The elderly woman was walking across the crowded lawn, looking totally disoriented. She didn't seem to know where she was. Then she saw Candy, and recognition dawned. She hurried over to them.

"Oh, Candy, I'm so glad you're here," Wilma Mae said, her voice trembling. "I still can't seem to find Mr. Sedley. He never returned home, and

I'm incredibly worried about him. Where could he be?"

"We've alerted the police," Candy said. "I'm sure he'll turn up soon. I really wouldn't worry about him too much. I'm sure there's a logical explanation and he's fine." Deep inside, she hoped she was right.

"Oliver told me you're going to serve as a judge in Mr. Sedley's place."

Candy nodded. "I've agreed to do that, yes. I hope it's okay with you."

"Oh, it's fine, dear, fine. I just wish Mr. Sedley was here. He does love this event so much."

Candy pointed toward the judges' tent. "Look, Wilma Mae, why don't we take you over to the judges' table and get you something to drink? We'll find you a comfortable chair, and you can sit and wait there until the judging begins."

"Oh, Candy dear, that would be wonderful. I don't know what I'd do without you. To be honest, I could do with a nice warm bowl of lobster stew."

"I know just where to get one for you. Come on."

Taking Wilma Mae by the arm, Candy and Maggie escorted the elderly woman across the lawn to the blue and white striped tent. Candy set Wilma Mae down in a padded wicker chair, while Maggie ran off to find her a bottle of water.

Candy had planned to visit the other booths, but instead she was pulled into a series of conversations with people who wanted to meet the new judge. Maggie returned with several bottles of water, handing one to Candy, and sat down with Wilma Mae as the day warmed. Before Candy knew it, an hour had passed, and when she looked around, covered bowls of lobster stew, in groups of three, were being set out on a long table adorned with neatly pressed white tablecloths.

In front of each group of bowls was a numbered placard but no other identifying information; this would, presumably, ensure the judges' objectivity. Only Oliver and Robbie knew who had created each of the sample stews. There was a bowl of each stew for each of the three judges.

As Candy took the seat next to Wilma Mae, Oliver appeared from inside the inn. He had changed his clothes for the judging and presentations. He now wore sharply pressed gray slacks, a light blue shirt with a yellow bow tie, a navy blue blazer, and a stylish wide-brimmed hat.

He walked down several steps to the lawn and crossed to a microphone set up on a podium to one side of the judges' table. He flicked on the mic, tapped it a few times to make sure it was hot, and then said, "Welcome, everyone, to the Twenty-Ninth Annual Cape Willington Lobster Stew Cook-off!"

The crowd gathered around the tent and podium, as well as others across the lawn, responded with a warm round of applause. Oliver put on his reading glasses, looked down at a sheaf of papers in front of him, and launched into his opening remarks.

"As you know, our little event has traditionally served as the kickoff of the summer season here in Cape Willington. We have the good fortune of a beautiful day, and we have eleven very talented contestants who have made some wonderful stews for us to sample today."

As she was listening to him speak, Candy spotted Roger Sykes, who stood near Oliver, along with Alby, Robbie, and Wanda. He must have sensed her looking at him, for he glanced her way and gave her a warm smile before turning his attention back to Oliver.

Wanda, however, ignored her completely.

"As you might have heard," Oliver told the crowd, "we've had to make some last-minute changes to our lineup of judges this morning. Brant Wisely, who has been a good friend of this event, sent his regrets earlier in the week. Stepping in for him today is a highly qualified individual who owns two award-winning restaurants down in Boston—Harbor Seafood on the waterfront, and the Captain's Table at Copley Square. Ladies and gentlemen, would you please give a warm welcome to today's primary judge, Mr. Roger Sykes!"

Roger raised his hand slightly and turned this way and that as the crowd applauded politely.

Oliver pulled him toward the podium, and after a few moments, Roger acquiesced and leaned toward the mic.

"First, I'd like to apologize for not being as handsome nor as talented as Brant Wisely," he said charmingly, drawing a few chuckles from the audience. "I know how much all of you were looking forward to meeting Brant and having him serve as a judge for today's event. However, I promise you, I'll do my very best to fill his sizable shoes. I'm looking forward to meeting the contestants today and to tasting all your wonderful stews."

As the audience applauded again, Oliver referred to his notes before he continued.

"Our next judge," he said, "needs no introduction. She has been a mainstay of this event almost since its inception and has won it herself six consecutive times. Please welcome back to our event Mrs. Wilma Mae Wendell!"

Candy and Maggie helped Wilma Mae stand as the crowd applauded. The elderly woman did her best to smile. But she seemed preoccupied and quickly sank back down into her seat.

"Are you okay, Wilma Mae?" Candy asked, leaning close to her.

The elderly woman smiled bravely. "I'll be alright."

"We'll get you something to eat in just a few minutes."

Candy turned back to the podium as Oliver glanced her way. "Finally," he said, "we have a last-minute fill-in for one of our honorary judges who couldn't make it today. I'm sure you've all read her wonderful columns in the *Cape Crier* newspaper. She has graciously agreed to serve as our third judge today. Ladies and gentlemen, would you please welcome our community correspondent and the co-owner of Holliday's Blueberry Acres, Ms. Candy Holliday."

Candy rose briefly, flashed a smile at the crowd, waved, and sat back down, all in the space of three seconds.

Maggie, who was sitting nearby, patted her shoulder. "Well at least no one can accuse you of hogging the spotlight."

"I'm trying to keep a low profile," Candy whispered as she noticed several disapproving looks peppered throughout the crowd. Obviously Wanda's friends.

Speaking of which . . .

"And now," Oliver said, looking around, "I'd like to turn the microphone over to a woman who has been invaluable to this event. In fact, without her help, we never could have pulled it off. I'd like to invite Wanda Boyle to make a few comments."

"Oh, great," Maggie said. "I wonder what she has to say."

"I'm sure she'll be delightful," Candy added with a touch of sarcasm.

"Hmm, this one is very good," Wilma Mae said.

Candy looked around. "What?"

Wilma Mae had taken a bowl of stew that sat nearby, removed the plastic wrapping covering it, located a spoon, and was dipping into it.

"Wilma Mae! You're not supposed to eat that yet!"

The elderly woman seemed not to hear her as she shoved a spoonful into her mouth. "But . . . I'm so hungry," she said apologetically after she swallowed. "And this stew is so—"

She stopped abruptly as her face changed in an instant, first to an expression of shock and then to one of horror.

"Oh my!" she squeaked, and tumbled out of her chair in a dead faint, falling heavily onto the well-manicured lawn of the Lightkeeper's Inn.

# FIFTEEN

"Oh my God!"

As Candy dropped to one knee beside the unconscious Wilma Mae, several others swarmed around to help, and a small pocket of chaos enveloped them. Maggie jumped up, calling out loudly for a doctor, interrupting the ceremony taking place at the podium.

Wanda stopped in midsentence, her words trailing off as she looked around with a confused expression on her face. Oliver studied the situation for a moment, seemed to quickly grasp what was going on, and snapped his fingers at Robbie, who dashed off to summon an on-call nurse Oliver had hired for the event.

Candy checked Wilma Mae's pulse, which was faint but steady, and tapped the elderly woman gently on the cheeks. "Wilma Mae! Wilma Mae! Can you hear me?"

Wilma Mae let out several quick breaths as her eyelids fluttered.

Alby Alcott arrived and knelt on the other side of Wilma Mae. "Here, let me have a look at her."

"She just fainted dead away," Candy said. "She was eating the stew—"

Even as the words left her mouth something clicked inside her brain.

*The stew? Is that what caused Wilma Mae to faint?*

She twisted toward the table, where the cup of stew still sat, barely touched, growing cooler.

"She's coming around," Alby said. "Could every-one just back away, please? Give us some air."

Candy felt a wave of relief going through her as she turned back toward the elderly woman. "Wilma Mae, what happened?" she asked breathlessly.

The elderly woman looked up at her with blinking, unfocused eyes. "Oh . . . oh . . . Candy dear." She put a hand to her forehead, looking dazed. "Where am I?"

"I think she just needs a few minutes to recover," Alby said reassuringly. "I'll go see where the nurse is, though." He rose and dashed off.

Wilma Mae's gaze shifted through the faces around her, then settled back on Candy's. "Why is everyone looking at me so strangely?"

"You fainted," Candy told her. "You gave us quite a scare."

"Oh, oh." Wilma Mae's mouth worked a little, and the tip of her tongue flicked out, tasting her lips. Suddenly her gaze sharpened. "It was the stew!" she said in a harsh whisper.

Candy leaned closer. "The stew? Was something wrong with it?"

"Oh no, no. It was . . . delicious."

"Delicious?"

Wilma Mae's gray eyes stared deep into her. Reaching up with an unsteady hand, she took Candy by the shoulder and pulled her closer. "It was made with *Mr. Sedley's recipe!*"

"What?" Candy's head popped up again. She turned back toward the table, searching for the cup of stew Wilma Mae had eaten from. But someone had already whisked it away. "Where'd it go?" she asked no one in particular.

She never got an answer. Oliver was back at the microphone. "There's nothing to worry about, folks. We've just had a small interruption. Mrs. Wendell fainted, but it appears she's going to be okay. Just give us a couple of minutes to attend to her and we'll begin again. The judging will commence shortly."

The nurse arrived and quickly took control of the situation. "Let's get her inside," she said. "She can rest in there, out of this crowd, and I'll give her a quick checkup."

With the nurse's help, Candy and Maggie were able to get Wilma Mae on her feet. They escorted the dazed woman into the inn, to a quiet side lounge, where they placed her on a sofa. While Candy and the nurse helped Wilma Mae lie down, propping pillows around her to make her comfortable, Maggie ran off to find more water and a cool cloth.

"I'm so embarrassed," Wilma Mae said weakly, holding on to Candy's hand. "I didn't mean to cause so much trouble, but that stew just took me by surprise."

As the nurse busied herself taking off Wilma Mae's shoes, Candy leaned close. "Are you sure it was Mr. Sedley's recipe?" she whispered. "Maybe you were mistaken, or maybe it just tasted similar."

"Oh no, that was definitely his recipe," Wilma Mae whispered back. "There's no mistaking it. It's the secret ingredient, you know." She glanced at the nurse, then said softly into Candy's ear, "It's a pinch of cinnamon, though it has to be added in a special way. It adds a subtle sweetness to the flavor. Mr. Sedley always said someone sprinkled cinnamon on me the day I was born, so that's why he put it in the stew."

At the mention of her longtime friend, she paused and her eyes began to water. "I *do* hope he's all right. I just don't know what I'd do without him."

Candy patted her hand. "We're going to find out where he is. Don't you worry about that. You just need to stay here for a while and rest. I'll be right back." She rose and started toward the door.

"Where're you going?" Maggie asked, coming back into the room.

"To look for something. Keep an eye on Wilma Mae for me, will you?"

"Sure." Maggie studied her. "Is everything all right?"

"I don't know yet."

"Need any help?"

"If I do, I know where to look."

"I've always got your back, you know."

Candy nodded. "I know."

Outside, Oliver had quickly put the day's events back on track. The old cups of stew for the judges had been cleared away, and Alby, Robbie, and a few other staff members were bringing in newer, warmer cups, which they were again placing in front of placards with large black numerals. Roger Sykes was leaning over the table, checking out the samples with a studious eye, while Wanda Boyle was just concluding her remarks.

Standing nearby, Alby saw Candy and motioned. "We're ready for the judges," he said, crossing quickly to her. In a lower voice, he asked, "How's Wilma Mae? Is she going to be able to participate?"

Candy shook her head. "I don't think so. She's a little shaken up."

"Is she going to be all right?"

"She'll be okay. The nurse is with her."

Alby thought for a moment. "Well, we'll have to move on without her. Hopefully you and Roger will be able to agree on a winner. If you wouldn't mind, would you please take the chair next to his? He's taking his seat now."

"Okay, sure."

Alby headed off in a different direction, and as she moved toward the table, Robbie walked past. She grabbed his arm. "What happened to the cups of stew that were just here?"

Robbie looked at her, uncertain at first. Then he seemed to understand what she was asking. "Oh, you mean the old cups? They got jostled around when that old woman fainted, and we weren't sure who they belonged to, so Mr. LaForce had us clear them off and get new cups from all the contestants."

"Where'd you take the old cups?"

Robbie shrugged. "To the kitchen. We dumped them in the trash."

Candy groaned. "Are there any left?"

He shook his head. "I don't think so. Why?"

She sighed in resignation. "Nothing."

Robbie looked uncomfortable. "I gotta go."

As he hurried off, Candy crossed to the judges' table, pulled out a chair, and sat down next to Roger. "Okay, what do I have to do?"

# SIXTEEN

Thirty minutes later she was done.

She had tasted eleven stews, then retasted several of them to determine her favorites, pausing between each tasting to nibble on a saltine cracker and drink from a bottle of water to cleanse her palate. She had to admit, as she made her way through the samples spoonful by spoonful, she was impressed by the range of colors, consistencies, textures, and flavors.

About halfway through the tasting she came across a stew that was a little sweeter than the others, and detected a hint of cinnamon. The lobster meat was delectable, and the broth had a chunky consistency, thanks to perfectly sized pieces of potatoes, onions, and even a few carrots. She studied the lobster meat for the longest time, wondering if the brown spice flecks covering it were indeed cinnamon. She thought of Wilma Mae and wished she knew who had made that stew. But there was no way of telling—at least, not for the moment.

She tried a second spoonful and had to admit it was excellent. But by the time she reached the end and had tasted the final stew, she knew there were others she'd enjoyed almost as much.

One stew in particular intrigued her, with its huge chunks of lobster meat and generously cut tomato wedges seasoned with dill and sea salt. It made a wonderful combination, and she truly enjoyed the presentation, with its corn-colored broth accentuated by the red and white lobster meat and fresh green parsley.

Another stew was topped with several slices of lemon and had a wonderful citrusy flavor, while a fourth one consisted of shelled lobster claws swimming in a beautiful milky orange broth seasoned with a trace of cayenne pepper.

There were others that stood out as well, including one with beet red chunks of lobster swimming in a tasty broth sharpened by undertones of red wine, and another with paper-thin slices of green and red peppers immersed in a light broth flavored with a trace of garlic.

She also, she thought, detected Bumpy's stew. She had to admit, it was very good—perhaps not an award winner, but very good indeed. She'd have to compliment Bumpy on it later.

After much consideration, she narrowed her favorites down to six, and then to five, and finally to three. The most difficult part was ranking her final choices.

Once she puzzled out the order of the top three, she couldn't help wondering again who had made them. It was an intriguing game to play. She thought one could be Burt Ramsay's stew, and another seemed to have Melody's touch. But which one was Wanda's?

In the end, she felt she'd done her job fairly, choosing the stews she honestly thought were the best, and not based on who might have made them. That was the way it should be. Now, like the rest of the crowd, she'd just have to wait for the names of the winners to be announced.

She looked up. Wanda stood perhaps twenty-five feet away, next to Oliver, who had a tight smile on his face as she chatted with him. She wore a businesslike outfit, with a red jacket and beige slacks, accented by gold jewelry and shiny gold shoes. Her flaming red hair was neatly arranged. Candy had to admit, the woman knew how to stand out in a crowd, and she certainly looked like she knew what she was doing. Maybe that's why certain people were attracted to her. They admired her confidence. And the woman had that in spades.

Roger leaned close. "I think I'm ready. How about you?"

They compared their lists and discovered some agreement between the two of them. For the next ten minutes, they sorted through their notes, discussing back and forth, trying to reach a consensus. Roger had selected as his top two stews ones that had been on Candy's narrowed-down list of three, but in a reverse order. Candy's top pick was farther down his list, which surprised her. As they negotiated, he wouldn't even consider her top choice, for reasons he had a hard time explaining. "It's too gimmicky. It just doesn't work for me," was all he said.

Finally, with much compromise on Candy's part and somewhat less on Roger's, they came to an agreement and handed their final list to Oliver. He studied it as he walked over to one side of the tent, where he checked a sheet on the clipboard held by Robbie to confirm the identity of each contestant. He jotted down several names, hesitating almost imperceptibly as he wrote one or two of them, then walked toward to the podium, waving the sheet of paper high in the air, flashing it for the crowd. "We have our winners!" he announced as he walked, his smile almost genuine.

The crowd applauded enthusiastically as Oliver reached the podium, switched on the microphone, and put on his reading glasses. "May I have your attention please?" He waited a few moments for the crowd to quiet, then said again, "May I have your attention—I'm going to announce the winners of today's cook-off competition!"

"Who do you think will win?" a voice behind Candy asked.

She turned. Doc, Bumpy, and the boys had come

up on the back side of the judges' table. Bumpy looked nervous, and Finn seemed distracted. Artie was chewing on a fingernail. Only Doc appeared calm.

"I have no idea, Dad." She rose and joined them at one end of the tent, edging up close to her father and crossing her arms in front of her to watch the proceedings. "I just chose the stews I thought were the best. At this point, anyone could win this thing."

"I probably didn't win," Bumpy said dejectedly.

Finn patted him on the back. "Hang in there, buddy. You ain't out of this yet."

"You have as good a shot as anyone," Artie told him encouragingly.

Candy held her comments until the winners were announced.

"First," Oliver said, his amplified voice carrying out over the lawn, "I would like to thank all the contestants who participated in today's event, and congratulate them on their wonderful stews. It's inspiring to know we have so many excellent cooks in our little coastal community. I'm sure the judges had a very difficult time making their selections."

"He's got that right," Candy said softly to her father.

"I'd also like to thank all of our guests and visitors for coming out today and enjoying this lovely spring weather," Oliver continued. "Of course, we couldn't have pulled all this together without the help of our dear friend, Wanda Boyle, her talented assistants, and our top-notch staff here at the Lightkeeper's Inn. Finally, I'd like to remind all of you that Emerald Isle, a wonderful Celtic band, will start playing shortly. We have some activities planned for the children a little later this afternoon. And I invite all of you to stick around and sample the excellent stews available today. As far as I'm concerned, all of our contestants are award winners. However, there can be only one champion. And now, if the judges would please join me here at the podium, I'll read the names of the third-, second-, and first-place winners."

"I guess that's my cue," Candy said, and to a smattering of applause she walked to the podium with Roger. Oliver shook both their hands, and then she and Roger stood together on the proprietor's right. Wanda Boyle stood on his left, looking smug and confident, as if she'd just won the lottery.

*She thinks she's already got this thing wrapped up,* Candy realized with a start. *What is she up to?*

The words of Judicious came back to her at that moment: *Keep a close eye on everything that happens today.*

Candy was doing her best.

"Here we go," Oliver said dramatically. He checked his sheet, adjusted his reading glasses, then continued, "And our third runner-up is . . . Melody Barnes from Melody's Café!"

Upon hearing her name, Melody beamed, waved her hand high in the air so everyone would know where she was, and worked her way through the crowd to the podium. She shook hands with Oliver, Wanda, and the two judges, and Oliver proudly awarded her a small trophy in the shape of a golden lobster, along with a white ribbon, as Jesse Kidder snapped a few photos of her.

Candy applauded warmly along with the crowd, pleased her friend had made the final cut. That meant Melody's stew had been the corn-colored one with the huge chunks of lobster meat. She should have guessed. She had it as number two on her list, while Roger had it as number three on his.

"Next," Oliver said, "our second-place winner is"—again he paused as he checked the name—"Tillie Shaw!"

The endlessly enthusiastic farmer's wife gave a quick shout of joy, jumped up and down, and applauded herself as she trotted to the podium and shook hands with everyone, then collected her trophy and red ribbon. She stood next to Melody at one side of the podium, barely able to contain herself. Candy again applauded with the others. That had been one of Roger's choices, a stew Candy had found a little bland and under-whelming. It hadn't been in her top six. Nevertheless, he had insisted.

"Finally," Oliver said, waving the paper in his hand, "we've come to the moment you've been waiting for all morning. Here we go. The winner of the Twenty-Ninth Annual Cape Willington Lobster Stew Cook-off is"—another dramatic pause as the crowd waited in hushed antici-pation—"Juanita Perez from Duffy's Main Street Diner!"

A few in the crowd gasped as others burst into applause. Candy heard Doc and the boys join in, adding a few whistles and cheers of congrat-ulations to the warm ovation, which grew louder as Juanita emerged from a group of friends and made her way to the podium. She wore an ankle-length denim skirt and a stylish white blouse with silver jewelry. Straight black hair tumbled down her back. She smiled sweetly, dark eyes gleaming as she shook hands with Oliver, Wanda, Roger, and then Candy.

"Nice job, Juanita!" Candy congratulated her as they shook hands. "You made a wonderful stew."

"Oh, thank you. Thank you!" She seemed on the verge of speechlessness.

It had been a fairly simple stew, Candy knew, with few ingredients other than cream, butter, beautifully cooked lobster, and carefully chosen spices, including cayenne. It had been one of Candy's top three choices. After much contem-plation, she had placed it as number three on her own list. But Roger's enthusiasm, which he credited to that bite of heat provided by the cayenne, had elevated Juanita's stew to the top of their combined list.

So Candy knew who had cooked two of the stews on her list. She had placed Melody second and Juanita third in her own ranking.

But, she wondered as Juanita received a trophy and blue ribbon, who had made her personal favorite stew—the one at the top of her list, the one with the sweet hint of cinnamon? She had to admit, of all the very good stews she had tasted today, it had emerged a winner, clearly the best one. Even now, as she thought about it, her mouth watered.

But then she shuddered as a particularly distasteful thought ran through her mind.

What if it was Wanda Boyle's stew?

If Wilma Mae was right and Wanda had stolen Mr. Sedley's recipe, then Candy had indeed put Wanda Boyle's stew at the top of her own list, even though Roger had been less than impressed by it.

Suddenly, she realized, she had to know who had made it. If she could find that out, it would either prove or disprove Wilma Mae's accusation once and for all.

Her gaze shifted back and forth across the tent. The easiest way to find out, she thought, would be to get a quick look at the clipboard in Robbie's hands, for it held the sheet Oliver had reviewed to determine the names of the winning contestants.

She looked around and finally spotted the teenager off to one side, talking to a large, burly man with sandy-colored hair, wearing a dark green shirt and jeans. He looked vaguely familiar, and Candy wondered where she'd seen him before. Then she remembered. He had been working in the maintenance shed out at the lighthouse when she had visited on Thursday.

They were talking in low tones, rather intensely, she thought. Robbie looked upset.

Roger leaned in close to her again, so their shoulders touched. "I think we chose the right one," he said, breaking into her thoughts.

Candy looked around. Juanita stood at the podium, holding up her trophy and ribbon, a huge smile on her face as Jesse shot a few photos and the crowd continued to applaud.

"Oh, absolutely," Candy agreed. She glanced toward Roger and found herself gazing straight into his shining dark eyes. In that moment she found them oddly compelling. What was she reading in those eyes? she wondered. Was he just being friendly, or was there more to that look of his? Was Maggie right? Was he ogling her?

And, if so, was that such a bad thing?

She had to force herself to shift her gaze back toward the podium. "Um, yeah, she seems overjoyed. And she deserves to be—her stew was very good."

"It certainly was." Together they watched as Juanita accepted congratulations from others, including many of the contestants. Burt Ramsay, Lyra Graveton, Delilah Daggerstone, Walter Gruthers, and Anita Weller were gathered around her, shaking her hand and congratulating her and the other winners. Jesse remained in the midst of the pandemonium, snapping photos. Juanita's close friend Dolores, who also worked at the diner, gave her a tight hug, and Doc, Bumpy, and the boys were standing in line to congratulate her, since they knew her well from the diner.

But where had Wanda gone? She was curiously absent from the conclusion of the proceedings, Candy realized, when she should rightfully be deep in the thick of it, given her position as comanager.

Candy searched the tent but could see no sign of the woman.

Had she hightailed it out of there when she found out she wasn't the winner? Could she be that sore of a loser?

*No doubt,* Candy thought.

As the crowd began to disperse, Roger turned to face her and casually reached out to take her hand. His touch felt warm and oddly sensual. "Well, it's been great working with you today, Candy," he said in smooth tones, holding her hand lightly. "I've really enjoyed your company."

Candy resisted an urge to remove her hand from

his, thinking it might appear rude. Instead, she smiled in a pleasant, noncommittal sort of way. "It was nice working with you too, Roger. That was a lot of fun. And thanks for all your help. Without your advice, I probably would have looked like an idiot today."

Roger gave her a doubtful look. "You? Never. You did great, stepping in at the last minute like that. You should be proud. It's too bad about your friend Mrs. Wendell, though. I hope she isn't too banged up."

"Oh, I think she'll be fine. She's resting right now."

"That's good to hear. And what a shame about Mr. Sedley. It's too bad he couldn't join us either."

"Yeah, it is. I think he was really looking forward to it."

"I'm sure he was. I hope he turns up soon." He glinted up at the sun, then looked around, his gaze focusing in the distance. Abruptly he released her hand. "Well, I think it's time for me to push on. I'm sure we'll get a chance to meet again soon. Ah, look, here comes Ben." He pointed across the lawn.

Candy turned to watch Ben walk toward them with long, athletic strides. He was looking particularly handsome today, his hair tussled, his face sun kissed, evidence of the many hours he spent outdoors.

Roger's move had been clearly calculated, she knew. What was he up to?

"So," Candy said curiously, turning back to him, "what have you two got planned for this afternoon?"

Roger grinned. "There's a Red Sox game on at one," he said in a tone that told her it was time to get away from this boring event and into some real fun. "Ben and I are headed to this sports bar he's told me about. We thought we'd eat some salty bar peanuts and open up a few cold ones."

"Oh, it's that new place up on Route 1, right? What's it called? The Rocky Coast Alehouse?"

"That's the one." Roger paused, then asked slyly, "So, would you like to join us? I'm sure Ben would enjoy your company, and I know I certainly would."

The question came so quickly that Candy wasn't prepared for it. "Oh, no, thanks. Well, I'd like to, but I have too much to do this afternoon. I have to track down the winners and interview them, and at least say hello to the other contestants, and then do a few quick follow-ups. And I have to check on Wilma Mae and Maggie. Another time, okay?"

"Another time," Roger said quietly as Ben finally reached them.

"Hello you two. What a beautiful day, huh?"

"It sure is," Candy said, looking at him fondly.

He smiled at her. "Hey, you did a great job today."

"Well, thanks. I had some help, though." She indicated Roger, who stood silently beside her.

Ben continued. "I knew you'd be fine. And everyone's buzzing about Juanita. She's on cloud nine. What a great choice. She'll make a great story for the paper."

He checked his watch and looked over at Roger. "If we hurry we can catch the third inning." He turned back to Candy. "Hey, you want to come along? I think Jesse's coming with us. But we still have plenty of room, no waiting." He raised an eyebrow in a boyish, almost irresistible way.

But Candy resisted—for now. She laughed and patted him on the shoulder, then pushed him gently away. "Thanks, but it sounds like a guys' day out to me. Go ahead and have some fun. I'll catch up with you later."

"You sure? Okay." He leaned forward and gave her a quick, unexpected kiss on the cheek. "I'll call you and we can reschedule that date. Remember, Italian."

Candy smiled. "Italian. And a bottle of Chianti."

"You got it."

They said their good-byes, and as Ben and Roger headed toward the parking lot, corralling Jesse as they went, Candy touched her cheek.

Ben was rarely so affectionate, especially in public, and especially at an event like this, where anyone could be watching.

"What was that all about?" she said to herself.

Finally she shook her head. "Men," she muttered.

With a certain amount of effort, she pushed all thoughts of Ben and Roger from her mind. Right now, she had other things to do.

She was eager to relocate Robbie, who was no longer in view, and get a quick look at the cook-off contestant list on his clipboard. First, though, she wanted to find out what had happened to Wilma Mae.

She turned, crossed the tent, and walked up onto the porch, where some guests lounged in rocking chairs, sipping on glasses of iced tea or white wine. But just before she went inside, she stopped and looked out across the lawn one more time, wondering what had become of Wanda.

Most of the contestants had returned to their booths. It was time to start selling their stews to the public. But Candy saw only Wanda's helpers in her booth.

From her elevated position on the porch, she scanned the crowd one more time and thought she saw Wanda in her red jacket stomping off toward the parking lot. But she couldn't be sure.

Giving up, she entered the inn and turned into the side lounge, where she'd left Wilma Mae, Maggie, and the nurse a while earlier.

All three of them were gone.

Candy looked around, surprised, wondering what had become of them. She stepped back out of the room, looked both ways along the hall, and saw the nurse at the opposite end, near the main lobby. Candy started toward her, flagging her down.

"Hello!" she called as she approached the nurse. "Do you have any idea what happened to Wilma Mae—the elderly woman who fainted outside?"

"Yes," the nurse answered, seeming preoccupied. "She said she wanted to go home, so your friend took her. She said she'd call you later."

Candy gave her a wave. "Okay, thanks."

As the nurse walked away, Candy checked her watch. She knew she had to get back outside to start her interviews, but first she wanted to find out who had made the stew at the top of her list. Of course, by visiting all of the booths outside and tasting every stew, she could eventually find out what she wanted to know. But that would take up a good part of the afternoon, and she wasn't sure she'd be able to identify all the stews exactly, now that she was away from the judges' table. Besides, she wasn't sure she could eat another spoonful of lobster stew right now. She'd had enough to last her for a while.

That left Robbie's clipboard. It was the quickest way to find out who had made the cinnamon-flavored stew. In just a few seconds she'd have her answer. But first, she had to find Robbie.

So where was he?

She had just turned, planning to head back outside to search for him, when he magically appeared right in front of her, almost as if conjured from thin air. Clipboard in hand, he had entered the hall from the porch, and now walked quickly toward her with his head bowed low, studying the carpet, as if he had a million things on his mind. But halfway along the hall he jigged to his right, entered a doorway, and disappeared from view. *Must be some sort of office,* Candy thought. She waited. Half a minute later he emerged from the door without the clipboard and walked in the opposite direction from her, back toward the porch and the lawn outside. He exited the building through the doorway, turned a corner, and was gone.

*Well, that's just a little too convenient, isn't it?* Candy thought, biting her lip. *Should I really do this?*

But she already knew the answer. She'd never have a better opportunity than right now to get a look at that clipboard.

As nonchalantly as possible, she strolled along the hall toward the office door Robbie had entered. She stopped once or twice to admire a painting hanging on the wall, pretending to be just another hotel guest. When she finally reached the door midway along the hall, she stuck her head around the corner.

It was a small suite of offices, with a receptionist's desk in the main area and two more offices branching off on either side, both with their doors open.

Nobody was home.

She checked the nameplates on the main office door: OLIVER LAFORCE, INNKEEPER, read one sign, and beneath that, ALBEN ALCOTT, ASSISTANT INNKEEPER.

Lingering as casually as possible at the doorway, she quickly scanned the reception area, then looked through the open doors to the interior offices.

She thought she saw the clipboard on the desk in the office to the left.

Before she could talk herself out of it, she slipped in the door, crossed the receptionist's area in a half dozen quick steps, and entered Oliver LaForce's office, checking it carefully again to make sure it was empty.

It was nicely decorated with antique furniture and plush plum-colored carpeting. A handsome oak cupboard stood along one wall, a small white brick fireplace occupied another, and a large window looked out over the lawn.

She made a beeline for the desk.

Sure enough, Robbie had set down the clipboard right in the center of the leather-trimmed blotter pad. She scooted around the desk to get a better look at the documents attached to the clipboard.

The top sheet was a schedule, with Robbie's scribbled notes all over it. The sheet she needed must be underneath it.

As she reached toward the clipboard, she heard

voices in the hallway. Her heart jumped in her chest as she backed away from the desk, her eyes darting to the main doorway, ready to bolt if necessary. But it was just a couple walking past. They never peered into the offices.

She waited until they had moved on down the hall, took a quick, deep breath to steady herself, and stepped back toward the desk. "Do it now and get out of here," she told herself.

She glanced up once more to make sure she was still alone, then reached down and began to page back through the sheets attached to the clipboard, her fingers moving quickly. The fourth one in was the one she sought.

As soon as she saw it, her brow furrowed.

Someone had used a felt-tip pen to draw a big black *X* across the page and written the words *Do not use—fake list* across the top.

The handwritten words were in a tight, neat script, different from Robbie's more scribbled handwriting on the clipboard's top page. That meant either Oliver or Alby had drawn the *X* across this page and written the words at the top.

Candy quickly flicked back through the other sheets on the clipboard, looking for another listing of contestants, but she couldn't find one.

She returned to the sheet with the black *X* on it. The placards on the judges' table, one in front of each group of stews, had had numbers on them. On the sheet in front of her, the contestants' names were listed alphabetically, with handwritten black numerals prior to each name. She simply had to match a number to a name to find the information she needed.

The top stew on her list had been number nine. She traced down the column with her finger but didn't have to look too far. The name she sought was the second one on the list, directly beneath *Barnes, Melody* and just above *Brigham, William*.

Next to the numeral nine was the name of Wanda Boyle.

Candy groaned. Her worst fears were confirmed.

Wanda had made the stew with the hint of cinnamon in it. That meant she must have had Mr. Sedley's recipe. And she must have stolen it from Wilma Mae's house. The elderly woman had been right.

But Candy hesitated. What about the black *X*? What about the words *Do not use—fake list* written at the top?

What did it all mean?

As she pondered this question, she started checking the list for some of the other names and their assigned numbers, but before she could focus in on it, she heard voices just outside the door.

One of them was Alby's.

He was talking to someone in the hall.

Candy's heart thumped. Moving quicker than

she ever had in her life, she let the sheets on the clipboard fall back into place and darted into the reception area. She paused for a moment to look around nonchalantly, then started out, running into Alby as he was coming in.

"Oh! Hi!" she said to a surprised Alby. "There you are. I've been looking for you!"

Alby had stopped dead in his tracks and was staring at her with a confused look on his face. "Candy?"

She stuck out her hand. "I . . . um . . . I just wanted to say thank you for asking me to be a judge today. I was looking for Oliver to thank him as well, but he's not in his office."

"Um, no," Alby said, still off balance as he glanced into Oliver's empty office. "He's outside, touring the booths."

"Then I guess I'll look for him out there. Thanks again, Alby!"

And before he could say another word, she dashed out the door and hurried along the hall. In a few moments she was out the door, onto the porch, and down the steps into the sunlight.

She didn't stop until she was halfway across the lawn. Finally she slowed and looked back.

Alby was nowhere to be seen. He must have bought her explanation.

She rolled her eyes into her head, dropped her shoulders, and let out a long breath. "Whew, that was close."

She was safely away, but she was uncertain of what she had found. The evidence was confusing. She stopped, raising her hand to her brow to shield her eyes from the sunlight, and surveyed the booths arrayed around the edge of the lawn. "I guess I'll just have to do this the hard way," she said to herself and sighed.

There was only one logical place to start: Wanda Boyle's booth. One taste of her stew and she'd know for sure whether it had been made using Mr. Sedley's recipe.

"Okay, I guess you have to do it, just to make sure," she said, encouraging herself.

She had just started off across the lawn, determination in every step, when her cell phone rang. She pulled it out of her pocket and checked the front display screen.

It was Maggie.

She flipped open the phone and held it up to her ear. "Maggie? Where are you?"

"Candy?"

"Yes, what's up? Did you take Wilma Mae home?"

A pause. Then, in a voice that gave Candy a chill, Maggie said, "You'd better get over here right away."

"Where are you?"

"I'm at Wilma Mae's house. And something's wrong. Something's very, very wrong."

# SEVENTEEN

Feeling a sense of urgency, Candy pulled the Jeep into the driveway at Wilma Mae's house and slammed on the brakes. She slipped the transmission into park, unhooked her seat belt, flicked off the engine, and withdrew the key from the ignition, all in one fluid motion.

She jumped out and, in a dozen steps, was across the yard and up on the front porch. In a couple more steps she was at the front door, which stood wide open.

"Hello?" she called through the screen door. Without waiting for an answer, she opened it and walked inside.

She was halfway along the hallway when something particularly offensive, a smell like rotten eggs, assailed her nostrils. She made a face. "Mrs. Wendell? Maggie? What's that smell?"

"We're up here!" Maggie called from the second floor.

Candy retreated back along the hall and turned up the stairs, taking them two at a time. On the second floor she found the two of them in Wilma Mae's back bedroom.

The elderly woman was stretched out on an antique four-poster bed, which had a white frilled coverlet on it. Her eyes were closed, and she was holding a cold cloth to her head. Maggie turned toward Candy as she walked in. "Thank goodness you're here."

"Why, what's wrong?"

"Didn't you smell it downstairs? You can't breathe down there."

"So what do you think it is?"

Maggie looked around at Wilma Mae, then took Candy's arm and led her out into the hallway, well clear of Wilma Mae's room. "I don't know," she said in a worried whisper, "and I'm not sure I want to find out."

"You don't think . . . ?" Candy let the sentence trail off, unable to finish it.

"I don't know what to think," Maggie said. "I just know that something's wrong. That smell isn't . . . normal, if you know what I mean. It smells . . . well, it smells like something died."

Candy suddenly felt all cold inside. "I guess we have to check the house. I'll do it—but you have to come with me."

"Should we call the police?"

Candy thought about that. "Let's find out what it is first. Maybe we're just overreacting. Maybe it's just a dead critter in the walls. Maybe a cat crawled in the basement window and couldn't crawl out again."

"Or maybe it's something else."

"Or maybe it's something else," Candy echoed. "That's what we've got to find out. So . . . are you with me?"

Maggie looked doubtful. "I don't know if I can do this."

"I don't know if I can either. But we have to find out what's going on. And I can't do it alone. I need your help. Okay?"

Maggie chewed her lip for a few moments. Finally she gave an almost imperceptible nod. "Okay. I'll do my best. But you lead. I'll follow."

"That's good. Just stay right behind me, so I know where you are."

"Trust me—I'm not going anywhere on my own."

"Good. So where should we start? Did you look upstairs here?"

Maggie shook her head. "I've only been in Wilma Mae's bedroom and downstairs in the kitchen. But the smell is stronger down there."

"Have you been in the living room? Or the dining room?"

"Not yet."

"Okay. That's where we'll start."

They checked on Wilma Mae, but she had fallen into an uneasy sleep, so they let her be as they started back down the stairs.

The putrid smell grew stronger as they reached the bottom and turned into the hall.

"Let's look in there first," Candy said, pointing to the living room. She had been here just a couple of days ago, interviewing Wilma Mae, but now the place looked foreign to her, and for a moment her head spun. She stopped to orient herself.

"Are you okay?" Maggie asked, touching her lightly on the shoulder.

Candy jumped involuntarily. "Yeah, I'm just . . . nervous."

"Me too." Maggie sniffed. "The smell's pretty strong in here."

Candy nodded. "Come on."

She made a quick tour of the living room, checking under and behind the sofa, in the corners behind the tables, underneath the cabinets, and even behind the grandfather clock.

"Look in there," Maggie said, pointing to a coat closet tucked into a back corner of the living room.

Candy nodded and took cautious steps toward it. Closing her eyes, she reached out, grabbed the doorknob, turned it, and flung open the door. She opened one eye and peered into the darkness as Maggie looked over her shoulder. "See anything?"

A musty smell came from the closet. Candy opened the other eye and leaned in for a closer look. She saw some old coats hanging on a wooden rail, boxes stuffed on a shelf above that, and well-worn boots, galoshes, and sneakers on the floor. A broom and dust mop stood in one corner, while a few more boxes were stacked on the floor to the left of the door.

"Nothing," Candy said. She turned, surveying the room. "Whatever it is, it's not in here. Let's check the dining room next."

The formal dining room occupied the right front corner of the home's first floor. They found an antique mahogany table with a half dozen chairs, an oak hutch with dinner plates and more ketchup bottles arranged neatly on shelves, and an old cabinet-style stereo that probably dated back to the sixties. Again, Candy checked in the corners and under the furniture, as well as another closet stuffed with tablecloths, linens, and other soft goods, but found nothing.

They moved back out into the hallway and stood for a few moments eyeing the kitchen at the rear of the home. "I guess that's next," Maggie said, obviously not really wanting to move at all.

"I guess," Candy said, her voice sounding a little hoarse.

Reluctantly they both started along the hall. As they moved toward the back of the house, the smell grew worse, more potent, like rotten trash that'd been left out in the sun too long. Maggie made a little sound of disgust in the back of her throat, and Candy had to swallow several times to settle her stomach. But they kept moving forward.

When they reached the kitchen, Candy immediately crossed it and opened the back door, letting in a cool breath of air. They both lingered by the door as they looked around the kitchen.

"I should check the cupboards and cabinets," Candy said finally.

Maggie nodded. "I'll check the pantry."

They moved in different directions, opening doors and peering into the dark recesses inside. A few minutes later they rejoined by the back door. "Nothing," Candy said.

Maggie looked back out into the hallway and pointed at a door halfway along, underneath the staircase. "Where does that lead?"

Candy shrugged. "A storage area? Or the basement?"

"The basement?"

They both looked at each other.

"I guess we have to look down there too, don't we?" Maggie asked finally.

Candy nodded, feeling chilled. "I guess we do."

"Okay." Maggie paused, breathing hard. "You go first."

Candy clenched her jaw tightly, pushing down her fear. She'd just checked out a basement yesterday, over at Mr. Sedley's house. That had been creepy enough. Now she had to go down into another one. For some reason, the basements of these old homes always gave her the willies. For the most part they were dark, silent, cold places, full of spiderwebs, shadows, and secrets. She didn't relish the idea of what she'd find down there. But she knew it had to be done.

Gathering her courage, she walked along the hall to the door, with Maggie right behind her. Gingerly she turned the knob and pushed open the door. Instantly they were assaulted by a smell that reminded her of decaying meat, only a hundred times worse. Candy held her hand to her nose and started breathing through her mouth, while Maggie coughed violently.

"It's coming from down there," Candy said, stating the obvious.

Maggie trembled in fear but managed to put her hand on Candy's shoulder. "I'm with you," was all she could say.

Her hand still holding shut her nose, Candy reached out to flick on the light switch, then stepped through the door onto a landing. With only a moment's hesitation she started down the wooden steps, which creaked loudly as they descended. She had a fleeting concern that one of the steps would break on her, like she'd often seen in the movies, plunging her down into a dark abyss. So she held tightly to the railing, while Maggie held tightly to the back of her blouse, whimpering softly.

Fortunately none of the steps broke, and they reached the bottom safely. Here, the smell was partially consumed by the dankness of the basement, resulting in a sickening miasma of odors. Candy had to fight down a sudden urge to gag. Her eyes began to water.

"This is crazy," Maggie whispered in a high voice behind her. "We should go back up and call the police."

"Just give me a minute," Candy told her. "I have to find out what's causing it."

"We know what's causing it," Maggie said, finally giving words to what they both were thinking. Her voice crackled in anguish.

"Then where is he?" Candy's eyes swept the room.

Finally Maggie pointed. "There."

Candy studied the area of the basement Maggie had indicated. She saw it then: a bulging blue tarpaulin, wrapped around something thick and heavy, stuffed into a far corner.

Slowly Candy approached the tarpaulin, feeling numb, as if she were outside of her own body and someone else was doing what she was about to do. Maggie didn't follow her now; she stayed behind at the foot of the stairs, unable to move any farther. Candy didn't blame her. She couldn't believe she was doing what she was doing. Only thoughts of Wilma Mae and Mr. Sedley, and the love they shared, drove her on.

When she reached the tarp, she knelt on the cold, dusty cement floor. Holding her breath, she held out a hand and placed it delicately on the bulky wrapped mass in front of her. Whatever was inside felt cold and stiff.

She quickly removed her hand and looked for a seam, a way to unwrap it. But she could see nothing.

Uncertain of what to do next, if she should even disturb the macabre bundle in front of her, if it indeed turned out to be a crime scene, she did the only thing she could think of.

She started to roll it toward her.

Slowly she unspun the bundle across the floor, and slowly the tarpaulin began to unwrap, the leading edge falling away. She rose and stepped over it, so she could push the bulk of it along across the cement floor. It was a large tarpaulin, perhaps eight feet square, and it took her several seconds to unroll it fully, as Maggie watched in silent, horrified fascination.

And when Candy was done, when she had fully unrolled the tarpaulin, the dead, stiff body of James Sedley rolled out across the cold cement floor of Wilma Mae Wendell's basement.

# EIGHTEEN

The flashing lights of four squad cars and an ambulance danced across Candy's eyes, making her blink rapidly before she turned away. The sun was sinking toward the western horizon, casting long slants of yellow sunlight along Wilma Mae's tidy front yard. Blackbirds chattered noisily in the high branches of a tall, sparsely limbed pine tree, angry about something. Candy looked up at them, wondering what had got them so upset and thinking how wonderful it would be to become a bird right now, and just fly away into that sun-paled blue sky, out over the trees into the far distance, to disappear forever. . . .

She was still dazed and disturbed by what she

and Maggie had discovered in the basement. Her breathing had returned to normal, but her chest still felt empty, like someone had plucked out her heart.

When an officer led her out here to sit on the front porch steps, she had felt ill, probably from the smell, which still clung to her. But as she sat here in the sun and breathed deeply of the cool Maine air, she began to feel better, and the nausea receded.

Still, she didn't want to risk standing at the moment, afraid her legs might be too weak to hold her, or the nausea might return, or her head might start spinning. So she sat—though she stayed well off to one side of the steps to avoid getting tramped on by the police officers and EMTs, who were moving rapidly but carefully in and out of the house.

Daryl Durr, Cape Willington's chief of police, had showed up half an hour ago, shortly after she had called the station and reported the finding of Mr. Sedley. He had talked to her briefly before he headed down into the basement, sending her outside to recover. "Stay close, though," he told her gruffly. "I want to talk to you."

And so Candy sat on the porch as the afternoon light died, trying to keep the scene in her head from playing over and over.

When Mr. Sedley's body had rolled out onto the basement floor, Candy and Maggie had both screamed. It had been a surreal, terrifying moment, though in their hearts they both had known what was coming. But that hadn't lessened the shock of seeing poor Mr. Sedley so absolutely, completely, unbelievably dead.

Once past the initial shock, Candy had reluctantly taken a step toward the body to check for a pulse but decided there was no need. The body had started to bloat and the eyes bulged. The sickening smell permeated everything. There was no doubt Mr. Sedley had been dead several days.

Ignoring Maggie's stifled sobs, Candy had quickly scanned the body. The hair was slicked and matted, as if he'd been bleeding from a head wound, though the blood had congealed into a misshapen reddish black mass. Candy had also noticed dark bruising on his forehead and neck. She'd seen no evidence, though, of a more violent death—no blood on his clothes, nothing that looked like a stab or bullet wound.

He wore a light gray sweater, rumpled brown pants, and black shoes.

*What was he doing here?* she'd asked herself. *What happened to him?*

She'd considered wrapping the body back up in the tarpaulin but decided against it almost immediately. She'd already contaminated a crime scene, and she thought it best to leave the rest for the experts.

They hadn't lingered any longer. Back upstairs,

Maggie leaned against a wall, held a hand to her chest, and coughed uncontrollably, trying to get the smell out of her nose and the images out of mind. Candy was coughing as well and her eyes were watering, though whether from the air in the basement or for other reasons, she didn't know.

"Who did that to him?" Maggie asked as she waved a hand rapidly in front of her face, trying to clear the air. "Who would wrap him up like that? Did he suffocate? Was it an accident?"

"It was no accident," Candy assured her, though she had no other answers.

"How long do you think he's been down there?"

"I don't know," Candy said thoughtfully. "But we can't worry about him anymore. We have someone else to worry about."

"Who?"

"Wilma Mae. What are we going to tell her?"

As it turned out, neither had the heart to say anything to her right away, so while Candy hovered in the living room, waiting for the police to arrive, Maggie agreed to go up and sit with Wilma Mae while she slept.

Now a half dozen police officers quietly but diligently searched the house, while a photographer took pictures down in the basement and the EMTs waited to remove the body. Most of them wore face masks because of the smell, and they talked in low voices.

Sitting on the porch, Candy could hear them

speaking to each other inside, though their words were indistinct. But she didn't have to hear them clearly to know what they were talking about. Despite what had happened the previous summer, murder was rare in Cape Willington, as it was in most of Maine's rural villages and towns. Any time it happened, it caused shock and surprise.

That, Candy thought, was probably the best description of how she felt, and more. She was devastated. She hadn't known Mr. Sedley, except through what Wilma Mae had told her, but she felt as if she had lost a close friend. She couldn't even begin to grasp what Wilma Mae must be feeling.

She heard footsteps behind her and turned to look back at the house. Maggie walked out onto the porch and sat down beside her.

"How's Wilma Mae?" Candy asked, propping up one side of her head with the palm of her hand, to steady herself while she talked.

Maggie shrugged. "She took it surprisingly well. I expected tears. I got denial."

"Did Chief Durr explain everything to her?"

Maggie nodded. "He did. He was very professional and very personable."

"Does she understand?"

Maggie considered that a few moments, then nodded again. "I think so. She heard him. She's just not ready to acknowledge it yet."

Candy nodded. "That makes sense, I guess. We all have to handle things in our own way."

Maggie shrugged. "I guess. She's dealing with it as best she can. But right now I think she'd rather just not talk about it. She's worried about one thing, though."

"What's that?"

"She doesn't know where she's going to sleep tonight. She doesn't want to stay in her house anymore."

"Yeah, that would be kinda tough to do. Does she have any friends around town? Relatives?"

"I think she has a sister out in California. And maybe a nephew or something like that up in Machias."

Candy said, "Hmm," and stared out at the lawn for a few long moments. Finally she looked back at her friend. "She can always stay with me and Doc. We've got plenty of room out at the farm. She might like hanging around Blueberry Acres for a few days."

"I was thinking the same thing," Maggie said, her eyes twinkling, "but I have a better idea."

"What's that?"

"Well, she can stay with me."

"With you?"

"Sure! I've got plenty of room, and I'm not busy right now. Amanda's away camping with Cameron and the Zimmermans, and Ed's—well, Ed's gone, isn't he? The house has been kind of lonely lately. It wouldn't be so bad to have someone around for a few days. And I think it'd be good for Wilma Mae too. I can help keep her mind off things. We'll drink a few cups of tea, or maybe a few glasses of wine. Watch some TV. Make some popcorn. You know, normal stuff."

Candy nodded her approval. "That might be just the thing she needs."

She turned at the sound of footsteps again. Chief Daryl Durr walked out onto the porch.

He nodded at Maggie. "She's asking for you," he said.

Maggie put her hands on her knees and rose. "Guess I should get back. I'll help her pack," she said to the two of them. To Chief Durr, she added, "I'm going to take her home with me for a few days."

"That's a good idea. Thanks."

He waited until Maggie had disappeared into the house, then dropped down beside Candy, sitting next to her on the porch steps. "So," he began slowly, staring out toward the fading sun, "how come every time there's a murder in this town, you seem to be stuck right in the middle of it?"

Candy didn't answer. She couldn't tell if he was joking or serious, so she thought it best not to say anything.

He leaned back, turning his head to eye her, squinting slightly as he did so. "So you want to tell me what happened?"

He waited patiently, his gaze focused on the trees over the rooftops, while Candy explained how Wilma Mae had fainted at the cook-off, and how Maggie had driven the elderly woman back to her home, and about the call from Maggie, and how she and Maggie had found the body in the basement. She stuck to the facts but left out details about the missing recipe and her suspicions about Wanda Boyle.

When she was done, Chief Durr turned his appraising gaze back toward her. "Sounds good so far. Anything else you'd like to tell me?"

Candy looked at him, giving him her best uncomprehending look. "Like what?"

He sighed. "Why do I have this strange suspicion you know more than you're telling me—again?"

Candy gulped, but she kept her mouth shut. She wasn't ready to say anything else—not yet, anyway.

Daryl Durr swiped at the knees of his sharply pressed khaki trousers, as if brushing away a layer of dust, and rose to his feet. He stepped down off the steps onto the pathway and turned to look her in the eye. "I would like to remind you, Ms. Holliday, that any information you have must be shared with us. Withholding information of any kind is a serious crime."

Candy brushed absently at her hair and squinted back at him. "What makes you think I'm withholding information?"

"I'm not making any insinuations. I'm just letting you know."

"I called the station yesterday afternoon," Candy said, surprised to hear an edge of anger in her voice. "I told the person I talked to that Mr. Sedley was missing. I did my best to notify you and your staff yesterday that something was wrong. Oliver LaForce said he called you too."

Chief Durr seemed taken aback by that bit of information. "The innkeeper?"

"He said he called the station this morning."

The police chief thought about that a moment. "I don't seem to remember hearing anything about that, but I'll check on it when I get back to the station. Now, again, just to make my point clear. We're the town police. You're not. When you first suspected the body might be in the house, that's when you should have called us."

"I was going to, but I had to check it out first. I was just being thorough."

The chief nodded his head. "I understand that, Ms. Holliday. And fortunately, we think we were able to get what we needed from the scene. The crime lab van from Augusta will be here shortly, and they'll follow up. But by disturbing the body like you did, you could have destroyed crucial evidence. You need to learn to leave the detecting to the detectives. Amateur sleuthing is frowned upon in this town. Besides, I thought you learned your lesson after the last time something like this happened. You could have gotten both yourself and your friend killed. Next time, call us first."

Feeling he had made himself perfectly clear, he nodded sharply and started up the steps, heading back into the house.

But as he passed her, Candy looked up at him. "Next time?"

The chief stopped and stared down at her for a moment. He gave her a pained smile, not completely unlike something she'd see from Doc. "Somehow I get the impression you're not going to listen to me and that this won't be the last time you and I meet like this. Isn't that right, Ms. Holliday?"

Candy batted her eyes and smiled sweetly at him. "Why, Chief Durr, I haven't the foggiest idea what you're talking about."

# NINETEEN

*Whoever stole the lobster stew recipe must have murdered Mr. Sedley.*

Candy couldn't get that thought out of her head. It was the one crucial point she kept coming back to, when everything else that had happened over the past few days still seemed fuzzy. There was so much she couldn't figure out—and most of it had to do with Wanda.

Had she really cooked the stew with the cinnamon in it, as the list on Robbie's clipboard seemed to indicate? And if she had, did that mean she'd also stolen the recipe from Wilma Mae's house?

Did it mean—and this was the point that kept sticking in Candy's mind—Wanda murdered Mr. Sedley?

Or did the black *X* on Robbie's clipboard indicate the list was not to be believed? In which case, maybe Wanda *hadn't* stolen the recipe. Maybe she *hadn't* made the cinnamon-flavored lobster stew.

And maybe she *hadn't* murdered Mr. Sedley.

Candy knew that was why she'd kept certain bits of information to herself yesterday when she talked to Chief Durr on the front porch steps of Wilma Mae's house. She worried about it afterwards, wondering if she'd done the right thing. But after thinking it through, she was convinced she had. She didn't have a firm enough grasp on all the facts yet, and she didn't want to go around incriminating folks in town—even Wanda Boyle—if she didn't know the truth herself.

*Whoever stole the lobster stew recipe must have murdered Mr. Sedley.*

But who had it been? That was the most confusing part. Candy could think of a bunch of people who might have wanted that recipe, starting with the eleven cook-off contestants. Certainly someone like Burt Ramsay would have coveted the recipe for his business. The same could be said for Melody Barnes. And what about Juanita? Candy recalled Wilma Mae telling her that, years ago, Mr. Duffy, who ran the diner back then, had offered to buy the recipe from Mr. Sedley. Juanita had worked at the diner for years. Could she be mixed up in the recipe's theft?

But it didn't make any sense. The cinnamon-flavored recipe had been at the top of Candy's list, but not Roger's. Juanita had won with a different recipe.

*Whoever stole the lobster stew recipe must have murdered Mr. Sedley.*

No matter how hard she tried, Candy couldn't get that thought out of her head.

It was Sunday morning, and Candy was working in the vegetable garden with Doc, planting carrots, cucumber, pumpkin, squash, and sunflower seeds, and putting in green pepper and tomato plants she'd bought at Hatch's Garden Center and Farm Stand a few miles up the Coastal Loop. After the wet spring, the soil in the garden was moist and rich underneath and slightly dry on top. They'd been putting compost, straw, and even grass clippings on the garden patches for years to build up the nutrients. The dirt dug easily with a shovel now, airy and as dark as used coffee grinds— which Candy admitted she also occasionally threw on the garden, though she knew they worked better if she tossed them into the composter along with eggshells, potato skins, and other kitchen detritus.

They got most of the seeds and all of the plants in before they decided to take a break late in the morning. Doc's leg was acting up again, and he was complaining about his back as well. He wore a white cotton shirt, opened several buttons at the neck, and beat-up khaki pants he used only for gardening and working in the fields—and occasionally for running to the hardware store. They were torn at the knees and threadbare in the rear, and the shirt was as thin as onion skin at the elbows, but he refused to toss the old clothes out. "They've still got plenty of good years in them," he told her when she pointed out his sartorial shortcomings.

He also wore a floppy Australian-style hat, aviator-style sunglasses, and his scuffed Timberland boots, which he'd had for as long as she could remember. Add a pipe, Candy thought, and he might have looked like some nineteenth-century explorer or an archaeologist overseeing a dig in Egypt.

As she watched him work, she wondered, not for the first time, if he ever thought of getting married again. He seemed comfortable enough with the bachelor life, but she detected moments of loneliness in him, when he thought she wasn't watching him and let his guard down. Whenever she asked him about it, he would just wave his hand, give her an indulgent smile, and tell her not to worry about him.

"But I do worry about you, Dad," she would say.

"And I worry about you too, pumpkin," he'd

reply. "But for the most part, we're both doing okay, right? So what else is there to worry about?"

And, strangely enough, when he put it like that, she had trouble arguing with him. Ten years ago, she'd never envisioned herself here, living with her father on a blueberry farm in Downeast Maine, and she couldn't say it was exactly where she'd hoped to be at this stage of her life, at her age. But she also couldn't say it bothered her too much. She had, she knew, learned to simply accept it. Life was what it was, she'd decided one day. The harder you pushed against it, the harder it pushed back. So all you could do was learn to live with it, make the best you could of it, and try to be happy.

Until something happened that shook your life in a way you'd never expected.

That had happened to her several times before. Now it was happening again.

*Whoever stole the lobster stew recipe must have murdered Mr. Sedley.*

She went inside around noon, showered, and changed. It was her third hot shower since discovering Mr. Sedley's body the previous day. Most of the smell was gone from her hair and body, but it still seemed to linger in her nostrils and on her fingertips. She had hoped the garden dirt would erase some of that smell, and it had. The remnants were faint now, but the images still lurked in her mind.

Doc had had the TV on that morning when she awoke, and news of the murder was being reported on all the local channels. But she did her best to ignore watching it. Sensing her distress, Doc had flicked off the TV as they drank their coffee before heading outside.

Now, feeling fresh and strangely cleansed by the earth, she called Maggie to see how Wilma Mae was doing and then settled herself in a chair on the front porch with the sun in her face, her notebooks within easy reach, and her laptop balanced on her knees. It was time to write.

She'd planned to work on her column and an article for the paper, but half an hour later she found herself staring at a blank screen, wondering where her mind had gone.

She'd been thinking about the body in the basement again. And the missing recipe. And the secret drawer in the front bedroom. And the cook-off, and the contestants. And Judicious's odd comment: *Just remember to keep a close eye on everything that happens today.* And the sheet of paper with the *X* through it. And the booths she hadn't visited, where the answers she sought might have been found.

*Whoever stole—and made—the lobster stew recipe must have murdered Mr. Sedley.*

Candy's thoughts returned again to the cook-off contestants, for they were the most likely suspects in Mr. Sedley's murder. Who could have done it? she wondered. Wanda? Quite possibly. Burt Ramsay? Again, possibly yes. But who else?

As Candy thought about it, she realized there were some contestants she could eliminate. Melody Barnes for one—Candy had been at her booth and knew the woman well. She had no real motive for stealing the recipe, as far as Candy could tell. She had come in third in the competition using her grandmother's recipe. So why would she need Mr. Sedley's? Plus, Melody had used tomatoes in her stew, which had been absent from the cinnamon-flavored one.

And she thought she could probably eliminate Bumpy Brigham. Bumpy, Candy decided, just didn't have murder in him. Besides, she knew his secret stew ingredients. He had told her. So she could tick him off the list.

Who else?

Tillie Shaw? Doubtful. The woman didn't seem to have a mean bone in her. Anita Weller? Delilah Daggerstone? Charlotte Depew? Lyra Graveton? Walter Gruthers?

Juanita Perez?

Candy shook her head. None of them seemed like murderers to her. Mr. Sedley was just a kindly old gentleman. She found it difficult to imagine any of them doing to him what she'd witnessed in the basement.

*How had he wound up down there, rolled up in*

*the tarpaulin like that?* she wondered. *Who put him there?*

Again, she asked herself, *Who?*

She kept coming back to two names: Wanda Boyle and Burt Ramsay.

She had walked by Burt's booth yesterday morning at the cook-off. Had she seen a bottle of cinnamon among his supplies? She couldn't remember—she hadn't looked that closely.

If only she had had the time to visit Wanda's booth and taste her stew. That would've given her the answers she needed.

Doc passed right by her, whistling and blocking the sun for an instant as he headed toward the barn, and on the spur of the moment she asked him, "Dad, how many stews did you sample yesterday at the cook-off?"

"Huh? Stews?" He stopped, looking at her with a slight grin, and thought about it for a moment. "Four, maybe five. Why?"

"Which ones? Which were your favorites?"

"Well, let's see. I tried Bumpy's, of course, which wasn't too bad. I walked over and had some of Melody's. And Burt Ramsay's . . ."

"What did you think of his stew?" she cut in.

"It was okay—a pretty typical lobster stew. About what I expected. Kind of a thick, almost gritty texture. Why?"

"Did you taste any cinnamon in it?"

Doc gave her a funny look. "Cinnamon?"

She waited.

His grin twitched as he considered the question. "I don't know. I can't say it jumped out at me. Why?"

"Just wondering."

He sharpened his gaze on her. "Are you on the case?"

Candy shook her head. "I don't know. I've been politely warned off by Chief Durr."

"And it's a good thing," Doc said, his voice suddenly turning stern. "These aren't games being played out there, pumpkin. People are getting themselves killed. Look what happened last summer with you and Maggie up on that widow's walk. These are dangerous times. It's best to just walk away and leave the investigations to the police."

Candy made a face at him. "You sound like Chief Durr."

"Well, I guess we think alike. We're just trying to keep you out of trouble."

"Trouble," Candy insisted as her cell phone rang, "seems to keep finding me."

She glanced at the name on the phone's readout, then flipped it open. "Hi, Ben."

"Hello, Candy. I just called to see how you're doing. I heard what happened yesterday. That must have been quite a shock for you."

"Yeah, it was pretty awful. But I'm glad we found him when we did. The poor old guy."

"You got that right. It's a real shame. Do they know what happened to him yet?"

"If they do, they haven't told me."

"Look," Ben said, and she could almost hear him leaning forward, as he did sometimes when he was moving to a more intense topic of conversation. He was probably also rubbing his forehead in a thoughtful way. "You have some connections over at the police department, right?"

"Connections?" Candy had to think about that. "You mean Finn?"

"Yeah. He knows someone inside, right?"

"I guess so—at least, that's what he's said."

"Do you think you could give him a call, see if you can find out what's going on with this murder?"

Candy was surprised. "Me?"

"Well, sure. On behalf of the newspaper, I mean."

She sat up straighter in her chair. "But, Ben, I'm not a news reporter. I'm the community correspondent."

"You've just been promoted," Ben told her. "I'm putting you in charge of this story."

"You're putting me in charge?" she said in disbelief.

"Sure, you're the best person to write this story. Think about it, Candy. You're already inside—you've been talking to Wilma Mae, and you discovered the body. You've practically got a front-row seat for this whole deal."

He actually sounded excited about this idea, she realized, as she felt her heart suddenly tighten in her chest.

"I think you're ready for something meatier than the typical community story," he told her.

"Meatier?"

"Candy," Ben said, his voice controlled yet burgeoning, "people have won Pulitzers for this type of reporting."

"Pulitzers?" The word came out as a sort of croak. Candy had momentarily lost her voice.

"This could be big. And it's fallen right into your lap."

"But . . . but I'm not a crime reporter," Candy repeated, finding her voice again. "I don't know . . . the jargon or the writing style or how any of those crime things work. I certainly don't know all the people over at the police station."

"You know the chief, right? You've talked to some of the officers. Besides, there's not a lot of heavy lifting involved. You make a few phone calls, talk to the chief, maybe interview a few people. Who knows what you'll come across."

Candy blinked several times.

"Think about it," Ben coaxed.

So Candy thought about it. She wanted to hate the idea. She wanted to hate the idea that he wanted her to do it. And she wanted to hate the fact that, right now, it sounded like he wanted a story a lot more than he wanted her.

But strange as it sounded, and much to her surprise, she realized she actually agreed with him.

She was sitting on a pretty big story. So why not make the best of it?

*My God,* she thought. *I'm starting to think like a reporter.*

She cleared her throat. "Well . . . I suppose I could do that—make a few phone calls, see what I can find out."

"Super. I know you'll do a great job. By the way, I need the story by Tuesday afternoon."

"Tuesday?" She couldn't keep the shock out of her voice.

Ben must have noticed her concern. "If it helps, I'll give you an extra day for your community column. You can turn it in on Wednesday. But no later than noon. I need to get this issue on the street by Friday, okay? This is a big one for us."

Candy blew out a breath. It sounded like a lot of work, but something in her didn't want to let Ben down. She knew this was important to him. And she still cared about the guy. "Okay, I'll see what I can do."

"Great. Oh, there's one other thing. I received a really strange e-mail this morning. It came into the office's account, but it was addressed to you. Something like, 'For Candy Holliday's eyes only.' It just looks like another complaint—something about the cook-off probably—but I forwarded it to your home account. Did you get it?"

Candy looked down at the laptop's screen. She used the touchpad to move the cursor to her e-mail account's icon. "I haven't opened it yet, but I'm doing it now." She waited a few moments while the program launched, then checked her new e-mails. She saw the one forwarded by Ben. "Yeah, I got it."

"Okay. Just let me know if you need anything else. Are you going to the parade tomorrow?"

"I think so."

"Good. At least one of us will be there."

"You're not going?"

"I'm not sure yet. Roger and I are talking about going fishing. But we'll see."

"Did you guys have fun yesterday? I heard the Red Sox won."

"Yeah, it was okay."

"By the way," Candy said, her mind already working ahead, "you wouldn't happen to have Roger's phone number, would you?"

"Roger? Sure. Why?"

"Just in case I have any questions for him about the cook-off." As he gave it to her, she wrote it down in her notebook, so she could key it into her cell phone's contact list. "How long is he going to be in town?" she asked, setting the notebook aside.

"He's here for the rest of this coming week. We're supposed to have dinner together tomorrow night. Want to come along?"

Candy thought about that. "I don't know yet. I have a lot of work to do. I have this tough editor who just called me out of the blue, put me on a criminal case, assigned a news story, and told me he needs it in two days. I mean, the *nerve* of some people."

Ben laughed. "Yeah, you've got to watch out for guys like that. Let me know, okay?"

"I will." She hit the end button and quickly keyed Roger's number into her cell phone's contact list.

Maybe it was time to give him a call to see what he remembered about the stews he had sampled yesterday.

It was a good idea, she thought, and she planned to do just that—as soon as she read the presumably nasty e-mail Ben had forwarded to her. She might as well get the bad news out of the way first.

# TWENTY

The subject line at the top of the e-mail read, *Fwd: For Candy Holliday's Eyes Only.*

Just as Ben had said.

She'd seen these types of e-mails before. Usually they were complaints. But it didn't look like Wanda's handiwork this time. She usually wanted anyone and everyone to read her letters and e-mails—as many people as possible. Never before had she labeled one of her messages this way.

Candy took a few moments to mentally prepare herself. When she felt she was ready for whatever she might read, she positioned the mouse and tapped the laptop's touchpad. The e-mail opened. She dropped her gaze to the text in the lower pane.

It was short and to the point: *The wrong person won the cook-off. Contact me if you want to know what really happened.*

It was signed *Cinnamon Girl.*

Candy felt goose bumps rise on her arm as a cool breeze blew down from the blueberry fields and across the porch. She rubbed at her arms and leaned back.

The wrong person won the cook-off? At first glance, she'd say Ben was right—it did sound like a complaint, at least on its surface.

But it was the sign-off that gave her pause.

*Cinnamon Girl.*

Was that a coincidence? Or was someone trying to tell her something? Was there a hidden meaning in the name?

There was only one way to find out.

Still, she hesitated, knowing she should think carefully before taking a step deeper into the mystery. Sometimes when you stepped in too far, it became impossible to step back out, as she had found out. The last time she'd taken such a step, she had put herself and others in danger. Was she certain she wanted to put herself in possible danger again?

This had all started with a stolen lobster stew recipe, she reminded herself—a fairly non-threatening mystery. Now someone had died. That changed the situation completely, and it made her pause, as any person with a dab of common sense would.

In the end, though, she knew she had to do it. But she resolved to be smarter about it this time.

She clicked the reply button, which opened a new window, and looked at the name in the address field's *To* line. It was addressed to *CinnamonGirl,* followed by a series of five numbers, at a Gmail account.

Candy typed, *Okay, I'm interested. What do you know?* and before she could think about it any more, she hit the send button in the upper left corner of the screen.

She waited.

Doc walked past again, still whistling and carrying a glass of iced tea. She hadn't even noticed him going into the house. He walked off the porch and headed across the gravel driveway, past the Jeep and his old Ford pickup, to the barn again.

Candy decided to follow him—at least partway. A little walk would help clear her mind, so she could focus on her article. She rose, set the laptop on a nearby wooden bench, and started after her father, though she angled off behind the barn, where she kept her chickens.

Ray Hutchins had built the coop for her a year and a half ago, and had expanded it for her last fall, in partial payment for all she had done to help him out of a tight spot, he'd told her at the time. She'd had fifteen chickens last year but had lost two of them over the winter, so she was down to thirteen, which always seemed to be tempting fate—not that she was a superstitious person, she always reminded herself. She planned to expand her flock again this year when she and Doc drove to the annual Common Ground Country Fair up in Unity.

She'd had foxes try to get into the coop several times, so she and Doc had reinforced the chicken wire around the sides and lower edges of the coop. She also made sure the chickens were in their roosts and closed up every night. And she always kept Doc's shotgun close at hand, in the kitchen closet, just in case.

Today the chickens were happy and chattering away as usual, oblivious to the cares and worries of those in the world around them. They pecked and scratched eagerly as she threw a few handfuls of feed onto the ground in the coop. She checked their water and looked around for eggs, though there were only a few. She'd already collected a bunch earlier in the day and decided to leave these until evening.

When she got back to the porch, she checked her e-mail and found another message from Cinnamon Girl. This one was equally short:

*I can't tell you this way. We have to meet.*

Candy puzzled over that. Was security an issue? Or was she being drawn out somewhere for a reason?

Again, she thought, there's only one way to find out.

She hit reply again and typed, *When do you want to meet?*

It took less than a minute to get an answer. *This afternoon. 4 p.m.*

*Where?* Candy sent back.

*Backstage at the Pruitt Opera House,* came the reply.

Candy hesitated briefly. She had a history with that place. Finally she typed, *How will I find you?*

*I'll find you.*

Candy thought a few moments before sending her next message. *It's Sunday afternoon. The place is probably locked up. How will I get in?*

She waited a long time for a reply. *Back basement door. Come alone.*

Candy groaned.

She knew which door Cinnamon Girl meant. She had used it before, on a rainy night the previous summer, when she'd entered the opera house after hours to hunt for a murderer.

The Pruitt Opera House on Ocean Avenue also

doubled as Town Hall, since the town's offices were located in the building's basement, where they'd been since the late 1970s. Candy knew the layout, and she knew how to get from the back basement door to the auditorium's backstage area.

At this time of year, the auditorium was used mostly for movies on Friday and Saturday nights. Earlier in the spring, a regional Shakespeare group had staged its annual production on the opera house's stage—*The Tempest* this year. And the high school would hold its graduation ceremonies in the auditorium in mid-June. In early July, a series of performances by local folk musicians would take place on the stage, after which the auditorium would come into heavy usage for the second half of the summer, as the town's thespians geared up for the annual musical production in August.

Candy's uneasiness returned as she pondered the last message from Cinnamon Girl. Why the anonymous e-mail? And why the secretive meeting at a public yet relatively inaccessible place? Why not meet in a coffee shop or in Town Park or in a parking lot somewhere? Why all the subterfuge?

For a fleeting moment she thought about skipping the meeting. Why put herself in harm's way? For all she knew, Cinnamon Girl could be a psycho.

And yet, her instincts told her the opposite.

It was that moniker that eventually decided her. It was a subtle clue, designed to let her know that whoever this person was, she (Candy assumed it was a she, though she supposed it could be a he) knew certain details about Wilma Mae's recipe— and might know a lot more.

Candy checked her watch. It was a quarter to three.

If she was going to do this, she had to get moving.

She rose again, set her laptop aside, and crossed to the barn. Doc was fiddling around on a workbench, listening to a game on the radio. He looked around when Candy walked in. "What's up, pumpkin?"

"Do you have Finn's number? I need to give him a call."

"Finn?"

"Yeah, I . . . have a question for him about the opera house."

Doc gave her a quizzical look. "What are you up to?"

She crossed her arms. "Just my job, Dad. So, Finn's number?"

After a few moments he shrugged. "It's somewhere on my desk. Check the Rolodex on the right-hand side. I think I put his old business card in there."

She started back toward the house. "I'm going to give him a call, then I'm going out for a while.

I have some research to do."

"Just be careful, pumpkin. It's a tough world out there."

"Don't I know it, Dad."

# TWENTY-ONE

Finn Woodbury lived with his wife Marti in one of the newer condos along the English River. It was a small community of buildings known as Water's Edge, upriver from the older neighborhood of Fowler's Corner, where Maggie lived. Finn and Marti spent a good bit of time there, from late April through late December, but when the coldest weather set in at the beginning of each new year, they usually hitched up the fifth-wheeler they kept in the backyard and headed down Interstate 95, making a beeline for an RV park in Central Florida, about an hour south of Orlando, where they waited out the winter season in warmer weather. And every spring, when they made the trip back up I-95 and returned to Cape Willington, they usually brought a few crates of oranges, a big bag of Spanish moss, and some pretty good suntans.

Finn opened the door when she rang the bell. He was eating a ham and cheese sandwich. While he chewed, he motioned her inside, closing the door behind her.

"Come on back," he said, waving a hand. "I'm

just having a snack. Want something? A Coke? A beer?"

"No thanks, I'm fine," Candy said as she followed him back to the kitchen.

"Go ahead, have a seat," Finn said as he sat himself. "Marti's out shopping. She wanted me to go with her, but she was headed to some of those discount stores over near Ellsworth. Treasure hunting, she calls it. We got a house full of treasures, I told her. We don't have room for any more. But that never stops her. She says it makes her happy, and who am I to stand in the way of her happiness?"

He paused, took a bite of his sandwich, and looked at her as he chewed. He wore cargo shorts and a green golf shirt today; his tweed jacket, which he always had on when he went out, was slung over the back of his chair. He was only a little taller than Candy, and broad, though he didn't seem overweight. His stomach was still tight, and his toned legs indicated he kept himself active. His salt-and-pepper beard was neatly trimmed. He looked at her with studious brown eyes. "So, you need my help with something?"

"Yeah, thanks for taking the time to see me. I . . . have this meeting in a little while, and I wanted to talk to you about it first."

He sat back in his chair. "What kind of meeting?"

"Well, I suppose you could say it's with some sort of informant."

"I see." Absently he took another bite of the sandwich, followed by a pull from a can of Coke, as he thought this over. "So what's the name of your informant?"

"I don't know."

"Uh-huh. And how did this informant contact you?"

"E-mail."

"No way to identify the sender?"

"It was a Gmail account. Someone named Cinnamon Girl."

"Cinnamon Girl, huh? Just like the old Neil Young song. Interesting." He stared down at a nondescript spot on the floor for a few moments, then asked, "So, where are you meeting this person, and when is it going down?"

She told him. "That's why I wanted to talk to you first—to find out what I'm walking into."

"Why, are you worried?"

She had to admit she was.

"Think it's a scam?"

"I don't know. I just know someone who insists on staying anonymous wants to meet me in a very odd place."

"It can get pretty dark in that backstage area," Finn said thoughtfully, "even in the middle of the day. That's the point, of course. No windows, little light. It's probably a good place to meet if you wanted to remain anonymous. This person can just stay in the shadows if she or he wants to, and talk to you from there—or come up on you from behind."

"I know." She gave him a long look.

He seemed to understand. "So you need a little backup." It was a statement, not a question.

"I was thinking about something like that, yes."

"Where's Maggie? Doesn't she usually help you out with this sort of thing?"

"She's keeping an eye on Wilma Mae." Candy hesitated before she added, "Besides, I put her in a lot of danger last time. This time . . ." Her voice trailed off.

He smiled. "This time you'd rather put *me* in danger."

"Well"—Candy raised her eyebrows—"when you put it that way . . ."

He took a contemplative bite of the sandwich. "Did this informant tell you to come alone?"

"Yes."

"Okay, at least we know the ground rules. But nothing says we can't bend them a little." His eyes suddenly widened as he held up a thick finger. "You know what? I have just the thing."

He set down his sandwich, got up from the table, and crossed to a drawer at the far end of the kitchen counter. He pulled it open and started digging through it, burrowing under various tools, seed packets, menus, bulbs, candles, batteries, matchbooks, plastic boxes of screws and nails, user guides, pens and pencils, and other assorted and sundry items. He finally found what he was looking for near the back, pulled it out, slammed the drawer closed with his hip, and returned to the table.

"Here you go," he said, holding it up for her to see.

It was an earpiece with a thin wire that connected it to a small black box with a skinny six-inch antenna. He also held up a small black button about the size of a penny with a clip on the back of it, also attached to a small black box by a thin wire.

"What's that?" Candy asked, peering at the devices.

Finn displayed it proudly. "It's an audio bug and receiver. I pieced it together myself with parts I bought at Radio Shack. It's got a range of about fifty feet or so, so I'll have to stay close by."

"Close by?"

"Sure, like in the parking lot maybe. Here." He leaned forward and attached the small black button to the collar of Candy's blouse. He slipped the black box in her left front pocket. "It helps if we can get the miniature mic as close to your mouth as possible. It should be concealed, of course. It would've helped if you'd worn something like a turtleneck, so we could just hide it under the fold, but we'll figure it out. We'll have to hide the transmitter too, but that can go anywhere. And we'll string the wire inside your clothes."

He held up the earpiece connected to the black box with the antenna. "I'll be outside in the car. I can even lie down in the backseat if that would help, so no one will see me—especially your informant. Don't want to scare them away. Then I just pop this earpiece in, and I can hear everything you say. If you get into trouble, just holler. I'll be there in two shakes."

Candy eyed the device skeptically. "You think this'll work? I'll be backstage at the Pruitt. Even if I need your help, it would take you a few minutes to get in there from the parking lot if you entered by the back basement door."

Finn shook his head. "That's the best part. There's a stage door the actors and crew use. It opens from the backstage area right into the side parking lot. I can jump out of the car and be there to help you out in less than thirty seconds."

"But isn't that door locked?"

Finn grinned. "Sure it is. It's got a new security keypad on it. I know, because I asked to have it installed. I'm a show producer, you know. I've got a little clout around this town."

Candy smiled with him. "And because you're the producer, you know the combination to the keypad, don't you?"

He raised his arms in an exaggerated shrug. "What can I say? I'm good at what I do." His expression turned serious again as he set the gear on the table and sat back down. "Listen, Candy, this doesn't have anything to do with Mr. Sedley's death, does it?"

Candy had anticipated the question and had formulated her answer on the drive over. "It might, but I'm just trying to help out a friend. Wilma Mae asked me to do a little digging around."

He didn't seem convinced. He leaned forward, putting his elbows on the table. "Look, I've been hearing some buzz from the station. They're saying Mr. Sedley had serious trauma to the head. He probably had a few other broken bones too, and maybe a broken neck. Someone beat him up pretty good. But there's something else. They're saying he didn't die where you found him. They think his body was moved. Somebody probably killed him somewhere else in the house—upstairs maybe, either accidentally or on purpose—and dragged or carried his body down into the basement. At least, that's what they've figured out so far."

"Do they have any suspects?"

"I don't know yet. And there's one more thing— the tarp."

"The one he was wrapped in?"

"That's right. They're saying it's not Wilma Mae's—it came from somewhere else."

"You mean . . . what? The murderer brought it with him?"

Finn shrugged. "Who knows what's going on? But my point is this: you're walking into very murky territory here. This is serious business, Candy. I wouldn't take any chances if I were you. If there's any indication—anything whatsoever—that you're in danger, just yell out my name—don't hesitate—and I'll be on my way. I don't want you to get yourself hurt."

She reached across the table and clapped her hand on his wrist. "Finn, thanks for doing this for me."

He patted her hand and gave her a guarded smile. "Hey, no problem. It's the least I can do. You know, I could probably get in trouble for helping you, but what the hell. It'll be fun. Just like the old days. Besides, Doc would never forgive me if I let something happen to you."

"Finn Woodbury," Candy said, her voice suddenly stern, "you are under no circumstances to tell my dad about this. Is that understood?"

He nodded silently, as if chastised.

"This is just between you and me," she continued. "At least for now. Or unless we find a killer. In that case, I'll share the credit with you."

He held out his hand to shake. "It's a deal."

# TWENTY-TWO

Thirty minutes later, she stood at the back basement door of the Pruitt Opera House.

Candy reached out and tentatively turned the door handle. It was unlocked, just as Cinnamon

Girl said it would be. She pushed open the door, peered inside, and couldn't help giving a last look back over her shoulder, just to make sure.

She'd parked the Jeep on the far side of the lot, near the stage door. Finn was crouched down in the backseat, hidden from view. She absently touched the black button mic attached to a bra strap and, with the other hand, tapped the transmitter tucked into her back pocket. The wire snaked around her body inside her blouse. She just hoped the little spy gadget worked the way Finn said it would.

They had tested it out a few times around Finn's place before they left. Finn had gone upstairs and outside to determine its range. It seemed to work fine.

Still, Candy was nervous. She knew she might be overreacting, creating villains when there were none, but after what had happened the last time, she didn't want to take any chances. She just hoped she wouldn't need Finn's help at all—that whoever this Cinnamon Girl was, she (or he) was legit, and nonthreatening.

Taking a deep breath, she walked inside, letting the door close behind her. She entered a darkened hallway, illuminated by dim off-hours lighting. Still, she could see the way ahead clearly enough. The long hallway was deserted.

Before she took a step forward, she instinctively looked down.

She'd visited Town Hall several times in the past year or so but always entered by the main door upstairs. The last time she'd been in this hallway, on a stormy night ten months ago, she'd seen wet footprints tracked across the floor—a tip-off she should have paid more attention to. But today there were no footprints of any kind, no sound, no movements—nothing to indicate anyone had been this way recently.

She'd brought a flashlight with her, just in case, in a black canvas shoulder bag she used sometimes for work. She liked it because she could flip the bag back behind her when she didn't need it, so it stayed out of the way, and it was large enough to carry all the notepads, files, pens, business cards, water bottles, and other work-related items she needed, plus a digital tape recorder, an address book, and her cell phone. Today, it also carried a flashlight.

She pulled out the flashlight and held it low, though she didn't flick it on yet, and started forward, walking as quietly as possible. She wore tennis shoes, and at times they squeaked on the tiled floor. But she found she could minimize the squeaks by walking on the sides of her feet. Cautiously, and a bit awkwardly, she crept forward and soon reached the end of the corridor.

Just as she'd done on that night ten months ago, she turned right into another long corridor. It too was dimly lit. At the far end, she knew, was a stairwell that led to the upper floor. That's where she was headed.

She moved more quickly now, not wanting to linger any longer than she had to, passing by the closed doors of a number of offices, many of them leased by the town. Near the end of the hall, on the left, was the town council's office, reserved for the use of the council chairman and selectmen. Since last November's election, the office had had a new occupant, Mason Flint, a retired schoolteacher who'd been a selectman and chairman of the finance committee before becoming council chairman. He'd won the position not only because of his experience in local politics, but also because he promised to improve tourism and bring stability to the town. Candy had met him a couple of times. He seemed like a nice fellow, and so far his tenure had been uneventful.

Still, the office also held unwanted memories for Candy, so she hurried past the closed door without stopping.

As she reached the end of the hall, she turned left and pushed through a door to a dark staircase. The last time she'd been here, she'd dashed up these stairs two at a time in near panic, but now she started up them more cautiously, one at a time, peering upward as she went. But the stairwell, like the hallways, was empty.

At the top of the stairs she turned left, pushing

through another set of doors, and entered a long hallway with faded red carpeting that ran along the entire right side of the auditorium. It sloped gently downward to her right and eventually led through another door to the backstage area. Candy briefly considered heading along the hall in that direction but decided against it. Instead, she stepped straight across the hall and pulled open another door, which led into the auditorium itself.

The elaborately decorated auditorium of the Pruitt Opera House seated three hundred and fifty people in cloth-upholstered seats, but tonight it was empty, like the rest of the building. It was a great, oddly hushed space that held its own special memories for her. A few lights had been left on high in the ceiling and under the balcony, which loomed above her on her left. The stage was down to her right. The main house curtain, she noticed, was open.

*That's good,* she thought. *At least it won't be too dark backstage.*

She hesitated before she moved on. She thought of checking the audio device to make sure it was working but realized it made no difference, since she had no earpiece and couldn't hear Finn. It was only one-way audio. *Well,* she thought, *I'm not in the FBI or anything like that. I don't have access to the latest high-tech gear. This is just amateur detecting. So,* she told herself, *go ahead and detect. Get on with it.*

She turned right and headed down the side aisle, which sloped downward toward the front of the auditorium.

As she walked, she listened, but she could hear nothing except her own soft footsteps and her own breathing. Even the traffic outside on Ocean Avenue and the Coastal Loop was almost inaudible in here. Horace Roberts Pruitt, the grandfather of Cornelius, had built the opera house well, with thick walls and architectural techniques designed to insulate the building against exterior noise.

Candy slowed, her gaze moving back and forth, as she approached the stage. An eight-foot pit area stretched before the first-row seats, and steps led up to the stage itself. She hesitated only briefly before climbing the steps.

Slowly she crossed toward center stage, feeling strangely vulnerable. Hearing an errant creak from the auditorium, she turned on her heels and looked out over the sea of seats, then up toward the balcony, then back to the wings on either side of her, where she saw nothing but shadows among the side curtains.

She turned to face the rear of the stage, where a long, closed curtain hid the backstage area from her view. She took a few tentative steps toward the rear curtain, still looking back and forth, her eyes watching for any sign of movement. "Hello? Anyone here?" she called softly. She paused and listened for a reply but heard nothing.

"Hello?" she called again. "Cinnamon Girl?"

As she reached the rear curtain, she turned to look into the shadows in the right and left wings.

Did something move there?

She saw it then, to her left—a flickering light, briefly, as if signaling to her.

"Hello?" she called a third time, though now her voice was more of a whisper. She took a few steps in that direction.

A light flashed in her eyes. She stopped abruptly.

Just as quickly as it had come, the light disappeared. A low, indistinct voice spoke from the shadows. "Over here."

"Is that you?"

No response.

Hesitantly, Candy took a few steps toward the shadows of the left wing, where the voice had come from. As she drew closer, the voice spoke again. "Back here."

This time, she decided it definitely sounded like a woman's voice.

She let out a breath. She hadn't realized she'd been holding it in.

Candy reached the wing and peered deeper into the shadows, but she could see nothing. "Where are you?"

"Back here."

The voice, low and muffled, had come from her right. She thought of flicking on the flashlight she still held but hesitated. She didn't want to spook Cinnamon Girl, so for the moment she left it off. But she tightened her grip on it, her thumb resting on the switch, ready to flick it on at the first sign of trouble.

But she didn't need it. The other light flicked on at that moment, shining at her feet. "This way," the voice said, drawing her on.

Candy took a step or two forward. "Who are you? What information do you have?"

"Closer." The voice sounded mysterious but not menacing.

So Candy moved closer. The light still shone on the floor at her feet, creating a path for her, guiding her along. She stepped around a few pieces of scenery, a pile of stacked chairs, a wooden table behind the rear curtain.

She could make out the shape of the person now, standing about twelve feet in front of her, though she could see no distinct features. The tall, thick stage curtains on either side of them muffled most sounds, but she thought she could hear the other person breathing.

As she approached, the flashlight's beam swung away and then flicked off. The two of them stood silently for a moment, facing each other in semidarkness.

Candy squinted, waiting for her eyes to adjust to the dim light. She cleared her throat. "Okay, so here I am. What did you want to tell me?"

"It's simple," the shadow said. "There's something fishy going on in this town, and it has nothing to do with lobster stew."

Candy considered that. "So what do you think is going on?"

"I think," the shadowy figure said in a low voice, "that one of the cooks yesterday was using a recipe stolen from Wilma Mae Wendell."

"What makes you say that?" Candy asked, immediately suspicious. She had told only a few people about the stolen recipe, though it was possible Wilma Mae herself had let her guard down and mentioned it to someone at the cook-off. Still, Candy didn't want to give anything away—at least not yet.

The shadow was silent for a few moments. Then the voice said gruffly, "She asked you to find it for her, didn't she?"

"Find what?"

A sound of exasperation leaked out of the shadow. "The lobster stew recipe. The one Mr. Sedley used to win the cook-off all those years. He gave it to Wilma Mae, and she's been keeping it for him. But someone stole it from her place— sometime this week, is my guess. So now she's got you looking for it, right?"

Candy took a small step forward, her thumb still resting on the flashlight's switch. "How do you know all this?"

"Ha!" the shadow said, ignoring Candy's

question. "I knew it! I was right!" After a moment of gloating, the shadow continued. "There's something else. Yesterday, at the cook-off, someone interfered with the judging."

That gave Candy a jolt. She felt her uneasiness return as she recalled a similar episode that had occurred ten months earlier—an episode that ended in murder.

"So who interfered?" she asked.

"Me," the shadow answered.

Candy crept forward another step, her senses sharpening. "What's going on? Is this some sort of joke?"

"It's no joke. It's deadly serious."

Considering what she had discovered yesterday, Candy couldn't disagree. She took another step forward. "How do you know so much?"

"Because I was there yesterday, at the cook-off. I saw what went on. But it turned out all wrong. That's the problem. And now Mr. Sedley's dead. That's an even bigger problem. And I've been trying to figure out the connection between the two. I've unraveled some of it, but I can't do it all on my own. You have the answers I need. That's why I contacted you."

Candy's curiosity surged. She inched forward another step as she squinted into the darkness, trying to get a better look at Cinnamon Girl's face. She thought she could dimly make out some of the features. "Who *are* you?" she asked again, this time drawing out the words.

When the figure didn't answer, Candy decided she'd had enough. In a quick, precise movement, she raised her flashlight, flicked on the switch, and aimed the beam directly in Cinnamon Girl's face.

It looked oddly grotesque in the harsh light, all sharp angles and unflattering lines. But there was no mistaking the identity of the person standing in the shadows backstage at the Pruitt Opera House.

Just as she'd suspected. "Wanda Boyle."

# TWENTY-THREE

"Who were you expecting? Elmer Fudd?" Wanda made a smug sound in the back of her throat. "Surprised?"

Candy had to admit she was, even though she'd started to figure it out when she first heard the shadow's low voice. "Yes, actually, I am."

"Well good. I didn't think you'd be so easy to fool, not with your reputation as a hotshot detective." She held up a hand to shield her eyes from the flashlight's beam. "Now could you get that light out of my eyes before you give me a headache?"

Candy did as the other woman asked, turning the beam down toward the heavily varnished floor. The shadowy grays returned, engulfing them. It was eerily quiet backstage, where the curtains muffled most sounds, and Candy let her voice grow a little louder. "What kind of game are you playing, Wanda?"

"Is that what you think? This is a game?" Wanda's tone became defensive, and her words turned hard-edged. "Well it's not. I'm sitting on some hot information, and I think it could be tied to Mr. Sedley's death."

Candy's annoyance at Wanda quickly fell away. "What kind of information?"

"First, I have to know a few things. Consider it a little information sharing. You tell me what you know, and I'll tell you what I know. But you have to go first. That day you came to the museum. Were you there to see Charlotte . . . or me?"

When Candy hesitated to answer, Wanda went on. "Let me guess. You were there because you were looking for me, right?"

Candy considered her answer but could see no point in acting coy any longer. "Yes."

"I thought so. I knew something was up when you came snooping around that day. So let's figure this out. The recipe was stolen from Wilma Mae. She asked you to find it for her. And you must have come right out to the museum. So what can we deduce from that?"

"I don't know," Candy said with a slight smile. "What can we deduce?"

Wanda leveled a finger at her. "I'll tell you what.

You came out to the museum because you thought *I* was the one who stole the recipe. Isn't that right?"

Candy pursed her lips. "I suppose that could be true."

"You suppose?"

"Okay, Wanda, what do you want me to say? Yes, if you must know, I thought you could be involved. And yes, that's why I was out at the museum. You were the most likely suspect, and Wilma Mae's convinced you took the recipe from her." She paused, looking hard at Wanda. "So, as long as we're making confessions . . . did you?"

"Did I what? Steal the recipe?" Wanda snorted, though it might have been a laugh. It was hard to tell. "I won't lie to you. I've thought about it for a long time. I've been trying to get my hands on that recipe for years. Those two old coots didn't need it anymore. What good was it to them? They'd both retired from the competition. It was a total waste. So yeah, I've been after it for a while. It's time Wilma Mae passed it on to someone else who can use it. I even offered to pay her for it. I offered him money too . . . back when he was alive. But it didn't work. For whatever reason, they just couldn't seem to part with it."

"Maybe that's because it has sentimental value to them," Candy said, irritation creeping into her tone. "You'd know that if you talked to her. But I guess you did talk to her, didn't you? You just didn't *listen* to her."

An uncomfortable silence hovered for a few moments between the two of them. Eventually Wanda broke the silence by letting out a breath of air through her nose. "I suppose Wilma Mae told you I visited her recently."

"She mentioned that, yes," Candy confirmed. "She said you visited her several times over the past few weeks. You know you scared the poor woman half to death."

Wanda's body shifted uneasily. "That was never my intention. But I was getting impatient. I was trying to push her a little. But mostly I just wanted to know more about that recipe."

"Why? What's so important about it?"

Again, Wanda snorted. "I wouldn't expect you to understand. You're still new around here, aren't you? You have no idea how much some folks want to win that contest."

"But why?" Candy asked again, trying to understand.

"Because of the trophy," Wanda snapped, "and the prestige that goes with it. You don't know this, because you haven't lived here long enough, but if you have that cook-off trophy sitting on a shelf in your home, you can write your own ticket in this town. Suddenly you know all the best people. You get invited to all the right parties. You're someone people look up to. Winning that trophy means a lot in this little town. A *lot*. There are people who would do *anything* to get their hands on it."

"Anything?" Candy asked, her voice suddenly quiet. "Even murder?"

"Even murder," Wanda confirmed, and then she shut her mouth abruptly, as if she fully realized what she'd just said. She also seemed to realize where they were. Her head twisted left, toward the auditorium, as if she could see through the curtains and out toward the balcony. She appeared to be listening for something. After a few moments, she turned back toward Candy. "Did anyone see you as you came in here?"

"No. The place is empty."

"And you came alone, right?"

Candy swallowed and a moment later hoped Wanda had missed that little giveaway. "I came in here alone," she said, knowing it wasn't a complete lie. She'd left Finn in the parking lot and had walked into the building by herself.

Wanda gave her a suspicious look but finally shrugged. "We can't stand out here in the open talking. This way."

She flicked on her flashlight and, pointing it toward the floor, headed off through an opening in another curtain, then along the building's rear wall, to a storage room at the very back of the stage area. She walked in, keeping the flashlight pointed low. "We can talk privately in here." She stopped at the center of the room, turned, and waved to Candy. "Come on in. Shut the door."

Candy paused just outside the doorway, peering

inside. She flicked on her own flashlight and shined it around the room. It was just an old storage area, perhaps eight by ten feet in size. The place looked dusty, cold, and largely unused. White swaybacked shelves along the left wall were stacked with dusty props. Moldy boxes were piled in a back corner, and a table and two metal chairs were pushed up against the right wall. Old posters hung on the bare plastered walls, with peeling paint up along the ceiling and in the corners.

She entered the room cautiously, taking only a few steps inside, and somewhat reluctantly reached around to close the door behind her. She crossed her arms, leaving the flashlight on, so its beam illuminated the shelves on her left and gave them some light. "So what's this all about? Why all the secrecy?"

"Because," Wanda said, "in case you hadn't noticed, someone's been killed. That's pretty serious business. It means there's a murderer in this town. And I have no intention of getting murdered myself."

"Why would someone want to murder you?"

Wanda let out an annoying sound to indicate her impatience. "I *told* you. I saw someone using Mr. Sedley's recipe yesterday. And that means I might know who stole the recipe from Wilma Mae's house."

Candy felt a chill.

*Whoever stole the lobster stew recipe must have murdered Mr. Sedley.*

"You think that person had something to do with Mr. Sedley's death?"

"Do you?" Wanda asked, volleying the words back to her.

Candy shook her head thoughtfully. "I don't know. It's possible, I guess."

"Exactly. That's why I have to be cautious."

"So who is it?" Candy asked point-blank, uncrossing her arms. She was suddenly very curious to hear Wanda's revelation.

"You have to promise first," Wanda said quietly, "to keep this to yourself."

Again, Candy found herself becoming irritated. "There you go again, playing games."

"And I told you, I'm not playing games." Wanda's tone was hard and unyielding. "I came to you for a reason. I could have gone to the cops."

"Why didn't you?"

Wanda hesitated for a moment, as if reluctant to say the next few words. "If you must know, it's because you're the only person around here who seems to know what's going on. And, well, you're the only person I thought I could trust."

That caught Candy off-guard. She rocked a little bit, as if lightly slapped on the shoulder. "Really. You trust me? After all those e-mails and letters you've been sending to the paper, after all the accusations and threats to get me fired? You trust *me?*"

"I know. Strange, isn't it?" An uncompromising smile crossed Wanda's face, disappearing as quickly as it had come. "I hate to admit it, but it's true. I had to tell someone about this. I thought of everyone I know. But there's no one else I could completely trust. I know I disagree with you a lot. I still think you're too new in town to do what you've been doing at the paper. You don't deserve that job." She paused, composing herself, letting her rising anger pass. "But I'm not going to hold that against you right now. The truth is, you *do* have experience with this sort of thing. And that's what I need right now. I need a detective. I need someone who knows what they're doing. And I need someone to help me figure out what's going on in this town."

Wanda paused as she took in a deep breath. "If it's who I think it is, it'll cause a huge stink. So I have to make absolutely sure that if I accuse someone, they're one-hundred-percent guilty. I don't want to get caught with egg on my face. I can't afford to look like a fool. But someone's been up to no good, and I think I know who it is."

"Is it someone we both know?"

"It is. The last thing I want to do is accuse an innocent person. So you have to agree to keep this between us until we get to the bottom of it."

Candy considered that. After a moment, she

nodded slightly. "Okay, we'll keep this just between you and me—at least for now. So, who is your suspect?"

"I'll tell you," Wanda said slyly, "but before that, I have another question for you: what do *you* think happened to Mr. Sedley?"

Candy had been puzzling it out, and she had a theory. She decided there was no harm in sharing it with Wanda. "My guess? He saw someone breaking into Wilma Mae's house—probably the same person who stole the recipe. He tried to stop them—and got himself killed."

Wanda's face dropped into a frown as she listened. "I thought you'd say something like that. And you know what that means, don't you?"

"No. What?"

"If you thought *I* was the one who stole the recipe, it means you also thought *I* killed Mr. Sedley, right?" Her gaze locked onto Candy's, demanding an answer.

Candy was silent for a tense moment as the two women faced each other across the dimly lit room. Finally Candy nodded. "Something like that, yeah. But it's like you said. Nothing makes much sense right now, does it?"

"No, it doesn't. But just so you know, I didn't do it. I didn't steal Wilma Mae's recipe, and I didn't kill Mr. Sedley. Okay?"

Candy watched Wanda's face as she spoke, and had to admit she believed the other woman.

"Okay. I'm glad we cleared the air about that. But it still leaves a lot of unanswered questions."

"It sure does. And I have another one for you: what was the secret ingredient in Mr. Sedley's recipe?"

Candy's gaze narrowed. Her suspicions returned. "Why don't you tell me? It sounds like you already know, given the name on your e-mails."

"Yeah, I thought that would get your attention." Wanda gave her a smug look. "It was cinnamon, right?"

"And how would you know that," Candy asked, "unless you actually *did* steal the recipe?"

"Because *I* do my research," Wanda said sarcastically. "I know how to dig around when I need to find out something."

"And where do you do your digging?"

Wanda answered quickly. "At the historical society."

Candy's brow fell as she thought about that. "In the archives? But Charlotte said you were up there doing research on architects in Cape Willington, for the summer program."

"That's where I started, yes, but I couldn't find what I wanted. I managed to locate the original plans for a few of the historic homes in the area, including one or two designed by John Patrick Mulroy. But I didn't find the plans I was looking for."

"Let me guess. You were looking for details

about Wilma Mae's house. You heard she'd stashed the recipe in a secret hiding spot, and you were trying to find out where it was."

Wanda studied her for a moment. "You know about that?"

"I know about lots of things. For instance, I know a carpenter who worked on renovations at Wilma Mae's house discovered a secret drawer in a shelving unit upstairs. And I know your brother Owen is a carpenter. Is he the one who found that drawer and tipped you off?"

Wanda almost laughed. "Owen? A carpenter? Hardly. He did some carpentry when he was a kid but he hasn't worked in the field for years. He works at the post office in Blue Hill now. But you're right about the secret drawer. I've heard rumors about it."

"And you were looking for Mulroy's plans to see if you could figure out where it was located. Did you find anything?"

"No," Wanda said promptly, "so I had to take a different route. I knew Wilma Mae and Mr. Sedley won that competition a total of thirteen times back in the seventies, eighties, and nineties. So I figured *someone* must have tasted that stew. And *someone* must have written about it."

When Candy considered that, it made perfect sense. "Ahh. So you went looking for articles in old issues of the *Cape Crier*."

Wanda nodded. "The historical society has

issues going back to the 1940s. It took a lot of digging around. Most of those old issues are still on microfiche. I spent weeks up in that stuffy old attic, looking for what I wanted. I had to search through dozens of issues going back thirty years."

Candy had to admit, she admired Wanda's tenaciousness. "And what did you find?"

"Several references to cinnamon as the secret ingredient. I can give you the issue dates if you want to check them out yourself. It makes for some very interesting reading."

"So," Candy said, jumping ahead, "if you knew cinnamon was the secret ingredient in Wilma Mae's recipe, and you wanted to win the cook-off so badly, why didn't you just make your own stew using cinnamon?"

"Good point, Sherlock," Wanda said sarcastically, "because that's exactly what I planned to do. Until someone beat me to it."

"Really? Who?"

Wanda gave Candy a crooked grin, relishing the moment. "You're the detective. Think about it. I spent some time researching lobster stew recipes that used cinnamon as an ingredient, so I had a pretty good idea what to do when I made my stew. I gathered all the ingredients, including the best cinnamon I could find between here and Boston, and I showed up Saturday morning ready to go. But then what should I spy? I'll tell you—I spotted *someone else* using cinnamon as an ingredient."

"Someone else? But I only tasted one stew with cinnamon."

"That's right," Wanda said mysteriously, "but whose stew was it?"

Candy knew the answer. She had seen the list on Robbie Bridges' clipboard. "It was yours."

Wanda looked impressed. "What do you know? The detective is right—or at least partially right. It *should* have been mine. I *should* have won that contest. But something went wrong. That's why I'm here talking to you now."

"But you made that stew, right? You're the one who used cinnamon as your secret ingredient?"

Wanda looked at her as if she were a teacher correcting a student in school. "No, dummy, that's what I'm trying to tell you. I didn't have Wilma Mae's recipe. I didn't make that stew. But I know who did."

"Who?"

Wanda paused dramatically, then said with a flourish, "It was Charlotte Depew."

# TWENTY-FOUR

"Charlotte?" Candy scoffed at that idea. "That can't be right. You must be mistaken."

"I'm not mistaken. I saw it with my own two eyes."

"And I saw something with my own eyes too that proves you wrong," Candy said adamantly.

"What did you see?"

"Well what did you see?"

In a temporary standoff, they stared fiercely at each other, silent again. Finally Wanda spoke, though she kept her mouth tight, as if holding in her irritation. "It's like I said. There's something fishy going on in this town."

"Then we'd better figure out what it is before someone else gets killed."

Wanda nodded a single time in agreement. "You got that right."

Silence again. Candy decided it was her turn to break the ice. "I'll tell you what—I'll explain what I saw, and you explain what you saw, and we'll see how our stories match up, and maybe it will all start to make sense."

Wanda smirked. "Okay, Sherlock. Sounds like a good idea." She pointed at Candy with her chin. "So go ahead."

"Well, okay." Candy looked down at the floor, taking a moment to organize her thoughts. "Okay, so—the cook-off. Roger and I were judging the stews, and yes, I thought I tasted one made with cinnamon. It was very good. Of course, there were a lot of good stews there yesterday, but when I made up my final list, I put the cinnamon-flavored one right at the top. I thought it was the best stew there."

"Of course it was," Wanda agreed. "It was made with Mr. Sedley's recipe."

"Well, that's the thing. When Wilma Mae fainted, it was because she tasted that stew, and she recognized it. So I knew someone there had made a stew with that recipe."

Wanda grunted. "I figured it was something like that."

Candy continued. "The stews made by Juanita Perez and Melody Barnes were both in my top three, but I didn't know who made my number one stew—the cinnamon one."

"And you figured if you knew who made it," Wanda put in, "you'd know who stole it."

Candy nodded. "Exactly."

Wanda gazed at her. "You know, if you suspected me, you could have just walked over to my booth and tasted my stew yourself."

"I could have, but I never made it over there."

"I noticed."

Candy ignored the comment and went on. "Instead, I got a look at the list of contestants on Robbie Bridges' clipboard. I checked names and numbers, and your name matched up with the cinnamon-flavored stew. But," Candy added, "there was a big black $X$ across the list for some reason. And someone had written a note up in the corner, saying the list was a fake."

"A fake?" Wanda's face scrunched up. "Who wrote that?"

Candy shrugged. "I don't know. Oliver LaForce, is my guess."

A flash of anger flitted across Wanda's eyes. "Oliver!" She practically spat out the word. "I knew he had something to do with it. That at least explains part of it."

"Part of what?"

"What happened yesterday."

Still confused, Candy motioned toward Wanda. "Okay. I've told you what I saw. Now it's your turn. Tell me what's going on."

"It's simple," Wanda said a little haughtily. "I thought I'd be smart and pull a switcheroo. But obviously it backfired."

Candy shook her head. "What are you talking about?"

"I'm talking about the cook-off. You saw where my booth was located, over on the far side of the lawn. When I got there yesterday morning I had everything I needed, and I was all set to make a stew using cinnamon. But when I looked over at the booth next to me, what do you think I saw?"

"Ahh." Candy finally realized what she was hinting at. "You saw Charlotte using cinnamon in her stew too."

Wanda pointed at her with a finger. "You got it, Sherlock."

"So what did you do?"

"Naturally I was shocked. I thought she had

spied on me somehow, found out what I'd been doing up in the archives, and stolen my idea. But then I realized I had it all wrong. And you were the key to the whole thing."

"Me?"

"Yeah, you. Like I said, when you showed up at the museum that day, I knew right away it was no coincidence. I'd heard you were interviewing Wilma Mae for the paper, and there'd been rumors going around town that something had happened to that recipe. Just so you know, Wilma Mae's not great at keeping secrets. So I figured when you showed up at the museum that day, it must be true."

Candy could see where this was going. "So yesterday, when you looked over at Charlotte's booth and saw her using cinnamon . . ."

Wanda snapped her fingers. "It popped into my head just like that. I realized Charlotte really *did* have Mr. Sedley's recipe. I figured she must have stolen it or got her hands on it somehow, and she was making it for the cook-off. I even remembered her looking through an old ledger a few days ago."

That caught Candy's attention. "You saw Charlotte with a ledger? What did it look like?"

"Just some beat-up old gray thing. I'd never seen it before around the archives. I tend to notice things like that."

"Where was she when you saw her reading it?"

"In her office. I popped in to say hello, and she was hunched over it. But when I walked in, she closed it real discreetly and slid it in the top drawer of her desk." Wanda paused. "That was it, wasn't it? That ledger belonged to Mr. Sedley, it had the recipe in it, and somehow Charlotte got her hands on it."

Candy gave a noncommittal shrug, although her mind was racing. Still, she had a hard time believing it was true. "But Charlotte? She's the last person I'd suspect of being a thief."

"If you knew her like I know her," Wanda said, "you wouldn't be so surprised. She's wanted to win that contest for years. But more importantly, she didn't want *me* to win it. So that must have driven her to a life of crime."

"But I thought you two were good friends."

Wanda shifted her position. "Appearances can be deceiving," was all she would say.

"You two sure had me fooled," Candy admitted. "So Wilma Mae was right. She really did taste Mr. Sedley's stew yesterday. And Charlotte was the one who made it."

Wanda nodded. "When I saw what she was doing, and figured it out, I couldn't decide what to do with my own stew. If I made my recipe with cinnamon, and Charlotte made hers, there'd be two similar stews, and I figured they'd cancel each other out, and neither of us would win. So I decided I'd let her finish the recipe she was making, and I'd make something else. I went back to my original recipe. I used lemons."

"Ohh." Candy smiled. "So *you're* the one who made that lemony stew."

"That was mine."

"It actually wasn't half bad. I kind of liked it."

"Well, thanks." Wanda seemed gratified, and the beginnings of a smile worked across her lips.

"But Roger didn't," Candy continued, as the smile dropped away quickly from Wanda's face. "He thought it was too citrusy, and he nixed it right off the list."

Wanda frowned.

A thought crossed Candy's mind. "But it still doesn't make any sense. If you made the stew with the lemon, and Charlotte made the one with cinnamon, how come your name matched up with the cinnamon-flavored stew?"

Wanda's sly smile returned. "It was simple. I swapped the lists."

"What do you mean, you swapped the lists?"

"Just what I said. Robbie wasn't the only one there yesterday with a list of the contestants, you know. There were a few other lists floating around the event. I had one. Alby had one somewhere. I think Oliver kept one in his office. That morning, before the whole thing began, I got a look at Robbie's list. I remembered my number, and Charlotte's. So when I figured out what Charlotte was doing, I created a new list of names and numbers, using the one I had with me. I handwrote the numbers so they matched the originals. I just switched the numbers for myself and Charlotte."

"Clever," Candy said. She had to admire Wanda's plan. "It also means you cheated."

Wanda shrugged her broad shoulders. "Maybe. But so did Charlotte. I figured I was just righting a wrong. But Oliver must have figured out what happened."

"So *that's* why he put an *X* across the sheet on Robbie's clipboard."

"Looks that way," Wanda said. "He must have also had a talk with Roger and told him what was going on. Or maybe something else happened. I don't know."

"And as it turned out," Candy said thoughtfully, "neither of you won."

"Sure surprised the heck out of both of us," Wanda agreed. "I was shocked when Juanita won. But so was Charlotte. I saw her stomp across the lawn toward the parking lot, so I followed her. I thought she was leaving. But she came back and said something to Oliver. What, I don't know. He just gave her the brush-off. He told her the judges' decision was final—or something like that. I couldn't hear everything they said."

Wanda gave her an odd look then. "So tell me— how did Juanita win anyway? I know she had a pretty good stew, but it wasn't the best one there, was it?"

"No, it wasn't," Candy admitted.

"Then what happened?"

"Roger happened," Candy said. "He made the final decision. I had Juanita's stew highly rated, and so did he, so we reached a consensus. He didn't seem to like your stew—or Charlotte's—or Mr. Sedley's, I guess."

"Why not?"

"I don't know. He kept saying everything was too gimmicky. I'm not sure what he meant by that."

Wanda rubbed her chin with her fingers and looked over at Candy. "So what do we do now? Do we go to the police?"

Candy thought for a long time, her mind working furiously. But there was only one good option she could see. She sighed. "I think I have to talk to Charlotte."

# TWENTY-FIVE

As she climbed back into the Jeep, Candy heard snoring. She turned around and saw Finn stretched out on the backseat, asleep.

She reached around, grabbed his ankle, and gave it a good shake. "Hey, partner. Wake up. I thought you were watching my back."

Finn gave a snort and woke with a sputtering

jolt. His head jerked up, and he twisted it back and forth, obviously completely clueless about where he was or what he was doing there. Then he saw Candy. "Oh! Hi."

"Hi yourself. Have a good nap?"

His face immediately turned red. "Um, yeah." He looked around again, then sat up with a grunt and looked out the passenger-side window. "Guess I fell asleep."

"Guess you did."

He rubbed his eyes. "What time is it?"

Candy checked her watch. "It's about four thirty-five. You gotta be somewhere?"

"Marti's due back at the house any minute. We're headed out to dinner at the Legion. It's taco night."

"Mmm," Candy said as she started the engine. "I guess we'd better get you home then."

He looked over sheepishly. "Hey, sorry about falling asleep. I know I was supposed to be there for you. How'd the meeting go with Cinnamon Girl? Any problems?"

Candy checked her rearview mirror, put the transmission into reverse, and looked back over her shoulder. "Depends on your definition of *problems*. But basically no, everything went okay."

"So who was it?"

Candy tilted her head at the listening device still stuck in his ear. "Couldn't you hear us?"

"Oh, this?" Finn reached up and plucked the device out of his ear. "Damn thing isn't worth a lick. I couldn't hear a word. Just static from the time you entered the building."

"Static? But we tested it at your place. It worked fine."

Finn shrugged. "There must be some sort of interference around here. I was planning to check out the building and make sure you were okay, but I thought I'd give you a few more minutes and see what happened."

Candy's eyes shifted toward him. "And then you fell asleep."

"Yeah, I guess so." He sounded contrite. "It was just so warm in here, and I didn't sleep well last night. Might have been that chili I had for dinner. I think Marti put too much pepper in it."

"Well," Candy said with a slight smile, "that'll do it. You've got to watch for stuff like that. Doc avoids onions like they were radioactive."

"They don't agree with me either." Finn patted his stomach. "So, what's the next step in the investigation?"

"The next step," Candy said, "is to return your spy gear to you and drop you off at home so you have time to make it to taco night with Marti. Then I'm headed out to the lighthouse. I have a little business to take care of with Charlotte Depew."

"Charlotte Depew? Does she have anything to do with Cinnamon Girl?"

"That's what I'm going to try to find out."

Finn shifted in his seat. "Hey, who is Cinnamon Girl anyway? You never did say."

"Nope," Candy answered, focusing her gaze on the road in front of her, "I never did."

By the time she dropped Finn off at his home, Candy had told him a little bit of the story, but she kept a lot back, including the identity of Wanda Boyle. She still wasn't completely sure who was guilty and who was innocent, and had to think it through herself before she could begin to explain to others exactly what was going on.

She was still mentally sorting through all the pieces as she pulled into the public parking area at the English Point Lighthouse.

The place was nearly full, packed with tourists and seasonal people in town for the long Memorial Day weekend. They were out in droves on Waterfront Walk and the pathways leading to the lighthouse.

After circling the parking lot several times, Candy finally managed to snag a spot. A Mercury sedan with an older couple from New Jersey was just backing out. Candy whipped the Jeep into the spot, just to make sure another car lingering nearby didn't get it before she did. She switched off the engine, grabbed her black canvas bag, and jumped out. Throwing the bag over her shoulder, she slammed the door shut and headed off toward the lighthouse at a brisk pace.

The ocean was choppy in a stiff onshore breeze, and the waves crashed loudly with the incoming tide, but she barely noticed today. She checked her watch again as she walked. It was closing in on five o'clock, and she wasn't sure how late the museum stayed open. It was listed in the paper every week, but she rarely paid attention to the dates and times. She wasn't even sure Charlotte worked on Sundays. *Come to think of it, probably not,* she guessed. But she didn't know where Charlotte lived, so this was her best bet if she wanted to talk to the woman before Tuesday morning.

As she came over the rise, she saw a crowd milling around the base of the tower and the door to the Keeper's Quarters. She hurried down the path, taking the time to glance up at the lighthouse. It seemed to gleam today in the sunlight, tall and majestic. It never ceased to impress her.

Coming down off the slope, she angled to her right, toward the museum, and weaved her way through the meandering tourists—singles and couples and families huddled together, staring up the exterior face of the lighthouse. Soon she was climbing the gray-painted wooden steps and pushing her way through the glass door into the museum.

She saw no one behind the long desk to her left, but a few visitors lingered in the main room, gazing at the exhibits. She looked around quickly and started toward Charlotte's office, but a voice from her left, on the other side of the counter, stopped her.

"Sorry, museum's closed," a male's voice said gruffly.

She'd seen no one there a moment ago, but now she looked farther behind the counter, to the dark hallway beyond, which led to the tower door. The same burly man she'd seen before, with sandy-colored hair, wearing a dark green shirt and jeans, was standing near the door at the end of the hallway, checking the knob to make sure it was locked. Satisfied, he walked toward her, emerging from the shadows of the hall. He bounced a set of keys in one hand.

"I was just looking for Charlotte Depew," Candy said, glancing toward the door to Charlotte's office. It was closed.

"She's gone," the man in the green shirt informed her. "She usually doesn't work on Sundays, but she came in for a couple of hours to help out today. She left a while ago."

"Do you where she went? Where she lives?"

"Sorry, can't divulge that information." The man dropped the keys in a desk drawer behind the counter and walked around into the room, motioning to a group of guests on his left. "Folks, we're closed. We're open tomorrow morning at nine o'clock. You're welcome to stop by then."

As he herded the rest of the visitors out the door, Candy stood rooted to a spot on the floor, trying to figure out a way to have a quick look around up in the archives, and perhaps even in Charlotte's office.

That's when she noticed the name tag attached to the man's green shirt: B. Bridges.

She looked up at his face and smiled. "Hey, I think I saw you yesterday at the cook-off, talking to Robbie Bridges. Any relation?"

He looked at her skeptically. "I'm his father."

"Oh, well, you must be very proud. He's a fine young man." And before he could say anything, she held out her hand. "I'm Candy Holliday. I write a column for the *Cape Crier*."

"Yup, I know who you are." He shook her hand somewhat reluctantly.

"So . . . you're Robbie's dad."

"That's right. Name's Bob." He said the words slowly, as if hesitant to engage her in conversation.

"Well, Bob . . . listen, I have a little favor to ask you. I was out here last Thursday—actually, I think I saw you working in your maintenance shed—and guess what? I left my notebook here by mistake. Silly me! I don't suppose you've seen it? It's long and thin, with a spiral wire at the top, and it's got a green cover. Sound familiar?"

Bob thought a long moment, watching her skeptically, and finally shook his head. "Don't think I've seen anything like that. But you can check the lost and found. It's that cardboard box behind the counter." He pointed.

Candy's head swiveled toward the counter. "Okay, I'll do that. Thanks, Bob."

She headed toward the counter as the maintenance man started off in the opposite direction, toward the front exhibit rooms. A few moments later, she heard him climbing the wooden stairs to the second floor. The aged steps creaked as he made his way upward.

She lingered by the counter, waiting until she heard him moving around upstairs. She took one glance around, to make sure she was alone, then dashed across the room toward the door to Charlotte's office. When she reached it, she tried the doorknob. It was locked.

She swore under her breath. She wanted to get a look inside to see if she could find Mr. Sedley's ledger. Wanda had seen Charlotte slip it into her top desk drawer. Candy knew it was a long shot, but she had to try.

Then she remembered the keys Bob had tossed into a desk drawer behind the counter.

She hurried back across the room. She was just opening the desk drawer when she heard Bob coming down the stairs.

"Dang," she said under her breath.

Softly she closed the drawer and took a few steps sideways. Looking around, she spotted a battered cardboard box on the floor behind the counter. She dipped toward it, pretending to dig through the odd assortment of mittens, scarves, toys, hats, handkerchiefs, paperback books, and other items.

Bob called to her as he came through an archway. "Find it?"

Candy straightened. "No. Come to think of it, I might have left it in Charlotte's office. I don't suppose I could have a look around in there."

"I don't suppose you could," Bob said with a frown.

Candy persisted. "I really need that notebook this weekend so I can write my column. Isn't there any way I can get a quick look around inside?"

" 'Fraid not. I don't let anyone in there when Charlotte's not around."

"I don't suppose you could give her a call? Tell her it's urgent."

"I have instructions to call Charlotte only in emergencies."

"But this *is* an emergency," Candy persisted.

But Bob would have none of it. He waved his arms at her, as if herding her out the door. "Whatever it is, it'll wait until tomorrow or Tuesday. Right now, I gotta close up and get home. It's Sunday, you know. On a holiday weekend," he reminded her.

In the end, no amount of pleading could make him change his mind. Candy finally relented, stepping back outside into the late afternoon sunlight.

Bob stepped through after her. He pulled the door closed with a *click* and tested the doorknob to make sure it was locked.

As she turned to face Bob, Candy repositioned the strap of the black canvas bag on her shoulder. "Well, it was nice to finally meet you. Robbie seems like he's doing pretty well at the inn."

"Yup, he's got a good deal going on over there," Bob said, looking distracted. "I just hope he doesn't screw things up."

"Why? Is something wrong?"

Bob waved a hand. "No, nothing like that. He's basically a good kid. He just needs a little guidance now and then."

"He's young," Candy said, giving Bob an understanding look. "He'll learn."

"That he will." Bob stared out toward the ocean. "That he will."

Candy was going to ask him another question when she heard her cell phone buzz. She'd set it on vibrate when she'd dropped it in the bag at home, so it wouldn't ring when she was in the middle of her meeting with Cinnamon Girl, alias Wanda Boyle. Now it made a little whirring sound, like a bee buzzing nearby. She pulled the bag off her shoulder and fished in it for the phone.

She glanced at the front screen. It was Maggie.

She looked up to say her good-byes to Bob, but

he was gone. She turned both ways and saw him walking off toward the maintenance shed with a determined gait, his arms swinging loosely as his sides. He hadn't said another word to her. He'd just walked off.

Candy shook her head. "Men." She flipped open the phone. "Hi, what's up?"

"I hate to keep doing this to you," Maggie said, sounding worried, "but you have to get over here right away."

"Why, what's wrong? Where are you?"

"I'm at my house," Maggie said, "and Wilma Mae's gone."

# TWENTY-SIX

Twelve minutes later she wheeled into the driveway at Maggie's house and pulled the Jeep to a stop. Maggie was outside on the front steps waiting for her, dressed in stonewashed jeans and a persimmon-colored cardigan with a navy blue anchor appliqué over the lower left pocket. The air had cooled as the sun set, and the breeze off the ocean tousled her already windswept dark brown hair.

Candy jumped out of the Jeep, leaving the door open behind her. "What happened?" she asked as she and Maggie walked toward each other.

Maggie's face was hard with concern. "She pulled a fast one on me. The old goat stole my keys right off the counter and took the car. She was all bundled up. She told me she was going for a walk."

"Why would she do that?"

"I guess she needed to be somewhere."

Candy looked around, up and down the street, as if hoping Wilma Mae would suddenly drive up. "Do you have any idea where she went?"

Maggie nodded. "I've got a couple of ideas. You?"

"Same." She pointed toward the Jeep. "Hop in. We'll find her."

As Maggie climbed into the passenger seat and closed the door, Candy gave her a sideways look. "Where've you been? You look like you got caught in a hurricane."

"I've been frantic, out looking for Wilma Mae. It's getting windy out there."

"And chilly too."

As she backed out of the driveway and headed toward town, Candy checked the sky. Here in this part of Maine, at this time of year, so far east in the time zone, the sun rose early, at around five A.M., and set relatively early in the evening, at around eight fifteen P.M. They still had a few hours of light left until dusk, but a bank of thickening clouds coming in from the southeast was beginning to filter the sun's warmth and light, cooling the air and stealing the brightness from the late afternoon. Candy had put on a long-sleeved shirt when she'd left the house to meet Cinnamon Girl, but her jacket was still on a hook by the back kitchen door. She shivered as she reached for the Jeep's heater, turning the fan on low to warm them.

"How has she been?" Candy asked as she drove.

"Eerily peaceful. It's as if she's completely forgotten about Mr. Sedley's murder. She's been chatting all day about all sorts of inconsequential stuff but never mentions him. If I didn't know better, I'd say she's completely forgotten about him."

"She's probably just having a hard time dealing with it."

Maggie tried to arrange her hair, brushing it back and forth with her hand in an effort to tame it. "That's my guess. I was getting worried about her. So when she said she was going for a walk, I thought it sounded like a good idea."

"Guess it wasn't all fun and games for you two, huh?"

Maggie sighed wistfully. "No. And I was *so* looking forward to our pillow fight tonight."

They drove through the light at the Coastal Loop and soon turned right onto Rose Hip Lane. At the second house from the end on the right, she turned into the empty driveway at Wilma Mae's house. Police tape still crisscrossed the front door, and the place looked dark inside.

They both climbed out as soon as Candy shut off

the engine, and they walked into the front yard. They stood looking up at the house, studying the windows.

"You see anyone?" Candy asked after a few moments.

"No. My car's not here either. Should we check inside?"

Candy shook her head. "I doubt she would've gone in. It'd be too traumatic for her. I'll check the garage to see if your car's there, but my guess is she's not here."

"Where then?"

"I don't know. Let's cruise down Ocean Avenue and then head out on the Loop and see if we spot her."

Twenty minutes later, they still hadn't found Wilma Mae, and Candy was beginning to worry. Then Maggie had a thought. "You know, tomorrow's Memorial Day."

Candy gave her a look. "Yeah? And?"

"Do you suppose Mr. Wendell was in the military?"

Candy gave her a smile. "Good idea, Watson. Let's check it out. By the way, have I told you about Cinnamon Girl?"

Maggie twisted in her seat. "No. But do tell. I love a good story."

"Then this one will blow your socks off." As they drove out the Loop, Candy proceeded to tell her best friend about the meeting at the Pruitt

Opera House with Wanda, and about her conversation with Ben.

She'd just about finished, and Maggie was listening rapturously, as they drove through the gate at Stone Hill Cemetery.

Suddenly they both grew quiet. Neither of them had been here since the previous summer, when they'd laid Susan Jane Vincent to rest. The memories of that day, and the harrowing week before it, came back to them both. But Maggie broke the spell fairly quickly as she pointed into the dimming light and said, "There's my car."

It was parked along one of the dirt roads that wound through the hilly cemetery, which occupied a windswept bluff overlooking the English River. Candy angled toward the car, creeping slowly ahead as they scanned the landscape for any sign of Wilma Mae.

They both spotted her at about the same time, standing at a grave site off to the left, in the shadows of a tall pine tree. "There she is," Candy said.

She pulled the Jeep to a stop behind Maggie's car, and they both climbed out. The wind was fiercer out here, on open land along the river, tossing their hair and pulling at their clothes. Candy wrapped her arms tightly around herself while Maggie lowered her head, and together they trudged up the slope toward Wilma Mae.

She must have heard them as they approached,

for she turned her head slightly their direction. She held a small bouquet of flowers in her hands and stood silently as they walked up to her.

"Wilma Mae, here you are. We were worried about you," Maggie said.

"We've been looking all over town," Candy added. "We were afraid you'd gotten yourself lost."

"Oh no, dear, I'm not lost," said Wilma Mae softly. "I've been here the whole time. It's Sunday afternoon. I always come out to visit my Milton on Sunday afternoons. It's a tradition with us. He was expecting me."

"Well, that's fine," Candy said. "We just wish you would have told us where you were going."

"Oh, I know I should have," said Wilma Mae with a soft clucking of her tongue, "and I *am* sorry for stealing your car, Maggie. I hope you're not *too* mad at me. But I just wanted a few minutes alone with him."

Maggie patted the elderly woman on the shoulder. "Don't worry, Wilma Mae, I'm not mad. I understand completely."

"It's just," Wilma Mae continued, her chest welling, "well, things are changing, aren't they? You see, even though Milton left me all those years ago, I've always had Mr. Sedley to keep me company. That made it easier for me, you know? Having someone like him around to talk to was, well, it was wonderful. Just wonderful. And I don't know if I ever told him that—how special he was to me. And now that he's gone too . . ." her voice trailed off. "Well, I feel so alone now."

She leaned forward and placed the flowers on her husband's grave. "Now I guess I'll have two graves to visit on Sunday afternoons, won't I?"

Candy and Maggie stood at her side as the wind calmed and Wilma Mae cried.

# TWENTY-SEVEN

Wilma Mae was in better spirits the following morning when Candy stopped by Maggie's house around ten o'clock. They had agreed to go together to the Memorial Day Parade, which started at one.

Cape Willington's Memorial Day Parade was a town tradition dating back to the early 1940s, and had long been both a celebration of the beginning of the summer season as well as a solemn and patriotic event commemorating those who had served their country.

From nine until one, the police blocked off Ocean Avenue for a townwide flea market, sponsored by the local American Legion post. Over the past few years, Finn had become involved in organizing the event, and he relied on Doc and the boys, as well as Marti and the ladies of the Women's Auxiliary, to help him with the details.

Candy had planned to make only a few brief

appearances at the day's events. She hoped to grab some quick quotes and jot down a few notes for her column, but her plan was to spend most of the afternoon at the farm, working on the gardens with Doc and writing her articles, which were due the following day. But he'd taken off early in the morning to help Finn with the flea market, telling Candy he'd catch up with her later in the day. Shortly after, Maggie had called to coax Candy into attending the parade with her and Wilma Mae.

"Come on, it'll be fun," Maggie told her over the phone. "Just us three girls, out for the afternoon. Who knows, maybe we can pick up a few cute sailors."

Candy laughed. "Well, that does sound tempting. But in case you hadn't noticed, most of the sailors around here are marching in the parade today and they're pushing eighty."

"Hey, those senior citizens can boogie. Have you seen them at the VFW hall on Saturday night? And they'll be out in droves today. It'll be easy pickin's for us girls. Besides, we need to cheer up Wilma Mae. Come on, it'll be fun."

Candy finally relented, and so just after ten in the morning, the three of them climbed into Candy's Jeep and headed toward town.

Wilma Mae had dressed for the occasion. She wore a navy blue knee-length dress with a red, white, and blue scarf tied around her neck for an accent. A large American flag broach and sensible walking shoes completed her ensemble.

Maggie had opted for gray slacks, a sage green cotton sweater over a cream-colored blouse, and stylish loafers, while Candy wore her best blue jeans and a butter-colored fleece pullover. The weather had cooled off, with the warmer temperatures of the past few days retreating southward, allowing chillier Canadian air to filter in. Still, the weatherman had promised a shift in the wind later in the day and a gradual warming into the high sixties by late afternoon. A gentle breeze out of the northwest brought with it a bit of a late spring nip. Still, few Mainers who were out and about today would notice, since they were well accustomed to climate vagaries at this time of year and knew true summer would probably not arrive in its fullness until mid-June or later—if it arrived at all.

Traffic was heavy as they turned onto the Loop. As they approached the center of town a policeman directed their vehicle toward a parking area located between the opera house and Town Park. They snatched one of the last spots, grabbed their purses, locked up the Jeep, and headed toward Ocean Avenue.

They made a quick tour of the booths and grabbed some hot dogs at a cart set up just outside Town Park. As they settled onto a park bench to eat, Candy watched Wilma Mae and noticed a definite improvement in her demeanor. She was almost chipper today, quipping away with Maggie about knickknacks they'd seen at the flea market and a small silver broach she'd bought at one of the tables. The elderly woman even smiled once or twice. Candy admired her ability to recover so quickly from the gruesome death of her longtime friend and onetime lover.

Abruptly, Wilma Mae turned. "Oh look, here comes that nice baker man," she said, straightening her back and folding her hands neatly in her lap as Herr Georg walked up to them.

"Ahh, ladies, hello, hello! How are all of you on this fine New England day?"

They spent the next ten minutes chatting with Herr Georg, who regaled them with stories of his latest creations, including a wedding cake he was baking for a wealthy family up from Rhode Island. "Eight tiers!" Herr Georg explained. "It will *tower* over the wedding party at the reception. It just may be my greatest creation yet!"

After Herr Georg bid them an adieu and walked on, Wilma Mae leaned in close to Candy. "He's very handsome, isn't he?"

"Who, Herr Georg? Well, yes, I suppose so."

"His moustache is particularly elegant," Wilma Mae said. "Do you know if he's married?"

"What?" Candy was surprised by Wilma Mae's questions. "Well, no, I don't think so. I mean, no, he isn't."

Wilma Mae clucked her tongue. "A nice man like that, living alone. Such a shame."

They were just starting back up Ocean Avenue toward Main Street when Candy's cell phone rang. She pulled it out of her purse and checked the readout, then flipped the phone open and held it up to her ear. "Hi, Dad. What's up?"

"Candy," he said, an urgency in his voice. "Where are you?"

She told him.

"I'm over at the diner with the boys," he said. "You'd better get up here right away. Something big is happening. You need to hear this."

Suddenly she felt very worried. "What's going on, Dad?"

"I don't know if I should say anything over the phone." His voice had fallen to a whisper.

"Oh, for heaven's sake. No one's listening on our line. Just say it."

"Well . . ." He seemed to think it over, then said secretively, "Finn just got word. There's been a huge discovery, and the police are trying to keep it all hushed up for the moment, but it's about to break all over town."

"Dad." Candy had stopped along the sidewalk, and Maggie and Wilma Mae were staring at her with questioning looks on their face. "Just tell me what's going on."

"It's Charlotte Depew," Doc said finally. "She's been murdered."

# TWENTY-EIGHT

Juanita Perez set a steaming cup of hot coffee and a thick slice of fresh-baked apple pie down in front of Candy. "This one's on the house," she said quietly, leaning in toward her. "Just let me know if you need anything else."

She winked, patted Candy on the shoulder, and turned away, practically floating on air as she set off to tend to her other customers.

"Hey, where'd that come from? How'd you rate that?" Doc asked hungrily, nudging her in the side. He was sitting beside her in the corner booth at Duffy's Main Street Diner. Wilma Mae and Maggie had squeezed into the booth on the opposite side, next to Artie and Bumpy. Finn was off in a corner by the counter, talking quietly to someone on his cell phone.

Mystified, Candy shook her head, staring down at the cup of coffee and the slice of pie on the table before her. "I really don't know, Dad. I haven't ordered anything yet."

"It's simple," Bumpy told her as if it were the most obvious thing in the world. "You were a judge at the cook-off. She's letting you know she's grateful she won."

"Well, yes, but I wasn't the only one who made the final decision. And I certainly didn't expect a free cup of coffee."

Artie grinned at her. "Hey, enjoy it. It's probably not your last one. Who knows—maybe there *is* such a thing as a free lunch."

He elbowed Bumpy, who gave Candy a wink as Finn walked over to their table, slapping shut his cell phone. "They're keeping it low-key until today's events are over," he informed everyone at the table in a quiet voice meant just for them, "but they're moving quickly on it. The crime van's already at the scene."

"Where did it happen?" Doc asked.

"Upriver. It's that picnic area about a mile or two from town, with the boat dock."

"Oh yeah, I know the place," Artie said. "There's good fishing from that dock."

"Yeah, been there a few times myself." Finn scratched his head. "Caught a pretty-good-sized striped bass there last year. Anyway, some fisherman almost tripped over her body this morning just after dawn. Apparently he thought it was a dead animal at first. Got quite a shock when he realized what it was. According to early reports, she'd been dead several hours."

"So it happened sometime overnight," Doc said thoughtfully.

Candy scrunched up her face. "What was she doing out there in the middle of the night?"

Finn shrugged. "That's what they're trying to figure out."

"Meeting someone," Bumpy surmised.

"Makes sense," Artie added. "A midnight rendezvous. They argued. Things got out of control. It happens, you know."

"I know," Candy said, remembering a similar incident up at Mount Desert Island the previous year.

"A crime of passion, huh?" Finn considered that. "Could be."

"Except," Candy said, "she just doesn't seem like the outdoorsy, midnight-rendezvous type. I had her pegged for a more cerebral, museum-loving, wine-and-cheese, sitting-in-front-of-the-fireplace-reading-a-good-book type."

"Sometimes love knows no bounds." Wilma Mae spoke up in a high, clear voice, surprising all of them. "If she found someone she fell for, she would follow him wherever he went, to the highest mountain or the lowest valley, or even to a riverbank. I've found love in the strangest of places."

Everyone sitting around the table fell silent for a moment. It was, Candy thought as she glanced at the faces around her, a somewhat awkward silence. Obviously the conversation had taken a turn the boys were unaccustomed to, and they didn't know how to respond.

Candy decided it was up to her to get the conversation moving again. And she knew just how to do it. For better or worse, it was time to reveal a few cards in her hand.

She cleared her throat. "Well, I suppose it's possible she was there for some romantic rendezvous. Or," she said, trying not to sound too ominous, "maybe she was just involved in something she shouldn't have been involved in."

*Now that caught everyone's attention,* she thought, slightly amused, as all heads turned in her direction. Maggie's head had tilted quizzically, while Finn's expression was stern and Doc's was concerned. But Bumpy was grinning. "Ooh. Now what's *that* supposed to mean?"

"You're not hiding something from us, are you?" Finn added suspiciously. "Remember, we've had two murders in this town in the past few days. If you've got something to say, you'd better tell us."

"And you've got to go to the police," Artie added, looking nervous.

"I know all that," Candy said, "and yes, I am going to go to the police."

"Today," Doc said, emphasizing the word.

Candy turned to him. "Yes, Dad, today. I promise."

"They've got a lot going on right now," Finn said, "but I've got a number you can call."

Candy thought about it a moment, then nodded, and Finn and the boys dug in their pockets to find a piece of paper he could write on. Artie turned up a business card he didn't need, so Finn scratched a number on the back of that. He handed the card to Candy.

"So," he said, "before you give them a call, anything you'd care to share with us?" Almost as an afterthought, he added, "Does this have anything to do with that Cinnamon Girl character—the person you met up with yesterday at the opera house?"

"It does."

"Who's Cinnamon Girl?" Doc asked.

Finn ignored him, his eyes holding steady on Candy. "Did she give you a few clues?"

"She did."

His gaze sharpened. "Come to think of it, you never did tell me who Cinnamon Girl was."

"No, I didn't," she agreed, and found herself strangely hesitant to share her information with him. *Why is that?* she wondered curiously. *Could it be that I really do enjoy detective work, and I want to solve this mystery all by myself?*

She had to admit, there was some truth to that. Then she reminded herself that two people were dead, and this was no time for games. Lives were at stake.

"It's Wanda Boyle," she finally said out loud, before she could change her mind.

That revelation drew gasps from around the table, but Wilma Mae's was the loudest. "You met with that horrid woman?"

Candy looked around at the elderly woman. "Yes, I did—twice in fact. But yesterday's meeting was the most recent." And, briefly, she told everyone at the table about her meeting with Wanda at the opera house the previous day, although she left out certain parts, including a few small details concerning Charlotte Depew. She'd decided to save those tidbits for the police.

"I didn't know who she was at first," she added, referring to Cinnamon Girl. "She sent me an anonymous e-mail. I could have been meeting up with just about anyone."

"You went alone?" Doc asked, concerned.

"No. Finn backed me up."

"Finn!" The word erupted from several mouths at once, as all eyes turned toward the retired cop.

He sat stoically with his arms crossed, looking from one to the other. "Well, someone had to do it," he said finally. "I couldn't let her go in there alone."

Artie leveled a long finger at him. "You been holding out on us," he accused.

Doc studied both his daughter and Finn with an appraising eye. "It seems they've *both* been holding out on us."

"It's like it's a conspiracy or something," Bumpy said in a hushed voice, and after a moment they all smiled, breaking the small amount of tension that had built around the table. They were, after all, friends, which trumped everything else.

"So what does Wanda Boyle have to do with all this?" Doc asked after a few moments, bringing the conversation back on track.

Wilma Mae put a hand on the table and leaned toward Candy. "Did she steal my recipe?" the elderly woman asked.

Candy shook her head. "I don't think so." But before she could say anything else, her cell phone rang. She checked the number but didn't recognize it. Turning away from the others momentarily, she flipped open the phone. "Hello."

"Is this Candy Holliday?"

"Yes. Who's this?" She had to stick a finger in her other ear, as Doc and the boys were chattering again, discussing the latest developments.

"It's Captain Mike," the voice at the other end of the line said. "You remember me?"

"Yes, of course. From the museum." As she spoke, she rose and walked away from the booth, to a quieter spot at the rear of the diner.

"That's right. I work there Tuesday and Thursday afternoons. And sometimes Sundays. I saw you come in the other day."

"Yes, I remember meeting you," Candy said.

"Well, I want to talk to you."

"About what?"

"I'll tell you when you get here."

"Get here? Where am I going?"

"I'm over at the Rusty Moose Tavern. You know where that's at?"

"Sure, Doc and the boys go there all the time. I'm just around the corner at the diner."

"Well, this time," Captain Mike said, "tell Doc

and the boys to stay right where they are and have another round of donuts and coffee. I want to talk to you only. In private. I'll be in the back booth. How soon can you get here?"

# TWENTY-NINE

Deep in thought, Candy keyed off the phone and turned slightly, so she could eye the corner booth at Duffy's. Doc and the boys were still giving Finn a hard time, though he seemed to be taking it fairly easily, while Wilma Mae was watching her intently. Obviously she had more questions for Candy. But they'd have to wait.

With Doc and the boys so riled up, she knew she'd have a tough time slipping away from them. It'd be best if she could get away unnoticed. But how?

*Maybe Maggie can help,* Candy thought as she stepped back to the table.

As she approached the booth, she walked past Doc to the other side of the table and batted a hand at Maggie's shoulder. "Scoot over, would you?"

Maggie gave her a curious look. "Hello, stranger. I thought you were sitting over there."

"I was. I'm sitting over here now."

"And why is that?"

"Because I have to talk to you."

"Oh. Okay." Sensing something was up, Maggie

moved over to make room for her friend. "So who was that on the phone?"

"Someone I need to talk to—in person," Candy said softly, turning her head aside and casually hiding her mouth behind a hand, so she could speak unnoticed.

"Part of the investigation?"

"I think so, yeah."

"So . . . I take it you need my help with something."

Candy smiled. "You must be reading my mind."

"I'm getting pretty good at that, aren't I? So, what do you need?"

"I have to get out of here right now, without Doc and the boys noticing. I don't want them asking lots of questions. And I don't want them following me. Can you provide a little distraction so I can slip away?"

Maggie shifted her head slightly, glanced surreptitiously around at the boys, and then looked back at Candy with a mischievous smile on her face. "You got it, honey."

Immediately she reached across the table, stretching out her hand. "Hey, Doc, would you give me that bottle of ketchup over there? That one right there?" She jabbed her finger toward it to get his attention.

Interrupted in midsentence, Doc turned toward her. "What?"

"The ketchup? Please?"

He gave her an odd look. "Ketchup? But you haven't ordered anything yet."

"I know, but Wilma Mae wants to see it. She collects ketchup bottles. We were talking about it the other day. She just loves them—don't you, Wilma Mae?"

The elderly woman gave her a confused look. "I do?" She clutched the purse in her lap just a bit tighter.

Maggie wiggled her fingers impatiently at Doc. "Come on, let's have a look at it."

Doc studied her for another few moments, then raised his eyebrows in resignation. "Well . . . okay." He reached for the well-used red plastic bottle of restaurant ketchup, which sat in front of him in a black wire rack, and held it out to her. "Here you go."

Maggie grabbed it out of his hand and angled the bottle toward Wilma Mae, as if she were showing off a fine chardonnay. "Here, have a look, Wilma Mae. It's a nice bottle, don't you think? It's a little beat-up, and it's probably got germs all over it—influenza or something like that—but it's not so bad, is it? And it has a nice red color to it."

"But I . . . I . . ." Wilma Mae stammered, unsure of how to respond.

Doc watched the both of them for a moment, then shook his head and turned back to Finn. Bumpy and Artie were deep in a conversation about the pitching rotation for the Red Sox. Wilma Mae sat perfectly still, giving Maggie a look of total bewilderment. "I don't know what to say, dear."

"Well, that's okay, I just thought . . ."

Before anyone knew what was happening, Maggie fumbled the bottle, which fell to the table and rolled. She reached out and snatched it up, squeezing the bottle as she did so. A thin stream of red ketchup shot out and covered the front of Artie's blue shirt.

"Hey, what the . . . !" He jumped up in his seat as Maggie fumbled the bottle again, turning it toward Bumpy, who howled in surprise and laughter as the thin red stream of ketchup squirted out toward him, up his shirt to his chin. "Watch out with that thing!"

"Duck!" Artie shouted. "She's got a loose weapon!"

Several folks in nearby booths looked up in alarm but were laughing a few moments later as Maggie's fingers slipped again and the bottle bounced. When she grabbed it a third time Doc held out his napkin as a matador would hold a cape for a bull, yelling at her, "Don't point that at me!"

Finn had slipped out of the booth and was laughing heartily, darting out of range, and even Wilma Mae was chuckling as Artie and Bumpy sputtered and wiped napkins down the fronts of their shirts, trying to remove some of the ketchup, which only made the stains worse.

Maggie turned toward Candy. "Quick! We need some paper towels."

"Right! You got it! Keep an eye on my purse!"

Candy jumped out of her seat and hurried toward the counter, where Juanita was already reaching for a thick roll of paper towels. She held it out toward Candy, who pointed toward the corner table. "Would you mind helping them out, Juanita? As a favor to me? I'll be right back."

Juanita nodded enthusiastically. "You got it, Candy!"

And before anyone noticed what she was doing, she had managed to slip out the door and was headed down the sidewalk, walking briskly, threading her way through the spectators lined up for the Memorial Day Parade.

The Rusty Moose was literally just around the corner from the diner, but Candy headed in the opposite direction, knowing she couldn't walk in front of the diner's large corner window, where she'd be easily spotted by the boys in the corner booth. Instead, she headed down Main Street toward the Black Forest Bakery. But before she reached it, she turned into a narrow alley just past the coffee shop. From there, she worked her way across the back parking lots, now crammed with cars, toward the Rusty Moose's rear door.

The usual tavern detritus greeted her as she approached the building—empty liquor boxes, bundles of trash awaiting transport to the Dumpster, an abandoned ice machine, coffee cans filled with coagulated grease. Barely noticing the junk, Candy hurried past, pulled at the old screen door, and entered a dark hallway that led past the restrooms before depositing her in the tavern's main public room.

It was a typical coastal bar, dimly lit, smelling of stale beer, sweat, and the sea, since it was located right across the street from the docks and warehouses along the English River. Candy had to pause a moment to allow her eyes to adjust to the light. She noticed a few grizzled heads swiveling in her direction, but most of the tavern's inhabitants seemed to know who she was—Doc and the boys hung out here often—and turned back to their drinks and conversations with brief nods or a tip of an index finger. Candy nodded a brief acknowledgment to them and, looking around quickly, spotted Captain Mike in the dark booth on her left.

She slid into the booth across from him. "Hi," she said.

"Hello there, young lady." Captain Mike reached up to touch the brim of his battered cap. "You got here pretty fast."

"I was in the neighborhood. It was a cinch. So, what's this all about?"

"Well, like I said on the phone, I got something to tell ya."

"About what?"

Captain Mike pointed with his chin out toward the English River, and it was clear he was indicating upriver. "About that whole business."

Candy knew instantly what he meant. She leaned over the table toward him, dropping her voice into a low whisper. "Charlotte?"

He lifted his beer mug and took a long pull. He set it back down on the table with a thud before he replied. "That's right. Charlotte."

"What do you know about her? Did you overhear something when you were working at the museum?"

"Well now, you're pretty quick, aren't you?" Captain Mike scratched at the side of his beard, up near his ear. "I might have. I just might have." He leaned forward a little, lowering his voice to a gravely growl. "The police came to see me a little while ago, down on my boat."

"What did they want?"

Captain Mike's left shoulder nudged upward in the barest of movements. Candy supposed it was a maritimer's attempt at a nonchalant shrug. "Guess they wanted to find out if I knew anything. Guess they're talking to everyone who's seen Charlotte over the past few days. That includes me—and you." He gave her a squinty look, probably well practiced over the years with his crew.

"But I haven't heard anything from them lately."

"You will, missy, you will. They'll be coming around soon enough, asking lots of questions about Charlotte's whereabouts over the past few days, and what she was doing with herself—and who was visitin' her. You and me, we got some answers, don't we? But you and me, we gotta stick together."

Candy wasn't sure what he meant. "Why?"

"Because we know things, don't we?"

"Well, maybe." She paused. "What kinds of things are we talking about exactly?"

"Well, Wanda, for instance."

"Wanda?" Candy's voice rose, and she immediately looked around. No one in the tavern seemed to be paying them any attention. Still, Candy felt as if ears were listening. She lowered her voice again. "Is this a good place for us to talk about this?"

"It's the best place in town to talk about this," Captain Mike told her, and he lifted a finger to point around the room. "These men know how to keep secrets. And if you need them, they'll be there to watch your back."

Candy wasn't sure whether that was a good thing or not, and she flinched slightly as she felt a strange tingle dance up her spine, as if someone had just drawn a fingernail along it. "Well, that's . . . reassuring to know."

"Yup, those policemen came by and asked me

all sorts of questions," Captain Mike continued, unaware of her reaction. "I told them what I know—but I didn't tell them *everything* I know."

"You mean about Wanda?"

"Yessir. That's why I called you." He was about to say more, but a redheaded waitress in jeans and a black T-shirt approached the table. "Hey there, Captain Mike. How're you doing with that beer of yours?"

In response, he picked it up, drained it in one gulp, and slapped it back down on the table. "I could use another, Rosie. And bring one for my pretty friend here."

"You got it." Rosie smiled at Candy. "You want anything else, honey?"

"No, that's it, thanks."

After the waitress had gone, Candy said, "I don't really drink beer that much."

Captain Mike waved a hand. "Ahh, it'll be good for you. Put some hair on your chest. Now, what was I saying? Oh yeah, that's right. Now, I don't really know what that woman was up to, but she definitely had it in for Charlotte."

"You mean Wanda?"

"What?"

"Wanda—she had it in for Charlotte?"

Captain Mike made a face at her. "Well, that's what I said, wasn't it? Anyways, this Wanda, I found out she's been complaining to the folks on the museum board about Charlotte. She sent them a letter, so I heard. Told them she didn't think Charlotte was doing a very good job. Wanted her fired. Well, Charlotte finds out and she's angry as a wasp. She was like that for three, four days, buzzing around the place. Couldn't even talk to her—she'd bite your head right off."

Candy folded her arms on the table, suddenly very interested. "When did all this happen?"

"Oh, I don't know." Captain Mike scratched at his beard again. "Sometime in the past few weeks. Two, maybe three weeks ago. Something like that. So anyway, after that, Charlotte started being real sweet to Wanda on the surface, but behind her back she was watching Wanda like a hawk. Charlotte was trying to find out what she was doing up there in the archives."

"And you think this has something to do with Charlotte's death?"

Captain Mike shook his head emphatically. "I didn't say that. Nope, I didn't say that at all." He leaned in even closer, just inches from her. "I heard what happened to her. They're keeping it all hush-hush, but I got my sources. She was strangled, you know. They said she had fishing line wrapped around her neck so many times they couldn't count the strands. Cut right through her windpipe. I bet it wasn't a pretty scene."

At this new bit of information, Candy had to hold back a gasp as Rosie returned with two mugs of beer, which she set down on the tabletop with graceful ease, so not a drop was lost.

"Thank ye kindly, my dear." Captain Mike grinned widely at the redheaded waitress as he took one of the mugs by the handle and raised it to his lips. He drank deeply and smacked his lips. "Good as always."

She gave him a warm smile. "Let me know if you two need anything else."

After Rosie had walked off again, Captain Mike turned his eagle eyes on Candy. "Someone done her in real good, that's for sure. Why, I don't know. Maybe someone was just trying to keep her quiet. But I'm not saying it was Wanda. Nope, I don't know nothing 'bout that. I'm just telling you what I've heard. Charlotte's dead, and Wanda was up to something, that's for sure."

Candy thought through what he'd said. In some ways it fit with everything else she'd learned so far. Wanda had been trying to get Charlotte fired, so Charlotte was fighting back. Was that why she'd entered the cook-off? To keep Wanda from winning? And did it mean Charlotte had stolen the recipe, as Wanda claimed?

But it still didn't answer the critical question: who had murdered two people in town?

Candy thought about Charlotte with fishing line wrapped around her neck. What was she doing up at that landing in the middle of the night, in the middle of nowhere?

Who had she been there to meet?

She looked back at Captain Mike. "Why are you telling me all this?"

He gave her that almost nonexistent maritimer's shrug again. "Well, because you're a detective, ain't you? And you're trying to figure out what's going on in this town. So I'm just trying to help you out."

"But I'm not a detective!" Candy insisted.

Captain Mike grinned. "Well of course you are. You're *our* detective. And we're glad to have you." He took a swig of his beer. "I've read your column, you know. Yup, I've read it."

# THIRTY

A short while later, Candy was back outside. She'd found a couple of dollars in her pocket, which she left on the table to help Captain Mike with the tab, and after thanking him for the information, she headed past the tavern's denizens to the front door. She exited onto Coastal Loop road, which was thick with people waiting for the parade to arrive.

Even though she'd taken only a few sips of beer, leaving the rest in the mug, she felt a little light-headed. Was it the beer, or was it what Captain Mike had told her about Charlotte's death? She wasn't sure, but she figured it wasn't a good thing either way.

Still, she knew she was making some progress. She'd learned another valuable piece of information, which she added to all the other pieces she'd gathered. She wished she had her pen and notebook with her, so she could make a list. But as she started down the crowded sidewalk, headed toward Main Street, she tried to organize all the random bits of information into some sort of pattern in her head, hoping to see where it all led.

This much she knew:

Someone had stolen Mr. Sedley's lobster stew recipe from a hidden drawer in Wilma Mae's house—presumably Charlotte Depew. She had used it to make a stew at the cook-off on Saturday, and should have won, because she used an award-winning recipe. But she had lost.

Now she was dead. She'd been found upriver at a secluded picnic area with a boat dock frequented by fishermen. She had fishing line wrapped around her neck, strangling her.

She'd been battling Wanda Boyle, who wanted her fired. Wanda had been searching the historical society's archives for information about Mr. Sedley's recipe. And Charlotte had been very curious to find out what Wanda was doing up there. The mutual distrust between the two of them, and possibly even growing hatred, seemed evident.

Mr. Sedley was dead too, apparently beaten

and wrapped up in a tarpaulin in Wilma Mae's basement. According to Finn, he'd been killed elsewhere in the house and dragged there. And, apparently, the tarp didn't belong to Wilma Mae. Someone—most likely the murderer—had brought it from somewhere else.

And then there was the strange issue of the cook-off contestants' list with the black *X* across it, and the equally strange admonition from Judicious to watch everything going on that day at the cook-off. She'd done her best to do as he'd suggested. But she still thought she was missing something. What was it?

As her mind worked over myriad unanswered questions, she could hear, in the distance at the opposite end of Main Street, sirens and a band playing. The parade was on its way. The crowd was becoming tense with anticipation. Children craned their necks excitedly down the street, waiting for the parade's arrival.

Someone hurried past, jostling her, but she barely noticed. Her thoughts were focused on the fishing line around Charlotte's neck.

*Fishing line.*

No doubt the police were following up on that clue at this very moment. That's probably why they'd talked to Captain Mike—no doubt he was an avid angler and probably kept fishing line in his boat. But the same could be said for lots of people around town. Finn and the boys fished all the time. Doc went out with them often. Finn had said he frequented that picnic area upriver. They all probably did. And they all probably had fishing line in their garages or toolsheds.

Even Ben fished.

Ben.

He was out fishing right now, wasn't he? Wasn't that what he'd told her yesterday when he called? He was going fishing today with Roger?

She thought about calling Ben to compare notes. He could probably give her some insight into the mystery. He might have even heard something she hadn't.

She had other calls to make as well. She needed to contact the police department. And she wanted to call Maggie to see how things were going at the diner.

Jostled again, she looked up. Lost in her thoughts, she'd wandered all the way down the Coastal Loop road, past the Unitarian church and the cemetery, to Town Park, which was aswarm with people waiting for the parade's arrival. It had reached the top of Ocean Avenue now and was headed down toward the sea, led by three police squad cars with sirens blaring.

Candy's head turned. Directly across from her stood the Lightkeeper's Inn.

As she studied the inn's facade and lawn, she realized there were too many pieces of this puzzle that still weren't fitting together, too many loose ends. And it was time to start tying up some of those loose ends. It was time to talk to Oliver LaForce.

Heading off again, she cut a path through the crowd and crossed Ocean Avenue, hurrying her pace just ahead of the squad cars. All around her onlookers were angling for better views of the oncoming parade. A police officer blew his whistle at her, motioning for her to clear off the street, so she quickened her pace to a trot, with the Lightkeeper's Inn squarely in her sights.

As she'd expected, Oliver was busy—very busy. She found him in the front lobby, greeting guests and directing staff members. Robbie was behind the check-in counter, dealing with a heavily bejeweled woman who held a small white-haired dog loosely in her left arm. Alby hurried past with a handful of papers, seeming to barely recognize her. The place was hopping.

Candy walked right up to Oliver and tapped him on the shoulder. "Hi. We need to talk."

He turned to look at her. It took him a few moments for his face to register recognition. "Candy? What are you doing here?"

"I need a few minutes of your time."

He frowned. "I'm sorry, but as you can see, that's quite impossible today. We're very busy."

"Oliver, we need to talk now."

He gave her an annoyed look. "If you call the office and make an appointment, I'll be glad to see you tomorrow or Wednesday afternoon."

"This can't wait. It's about"—she leaned forward and whispered—"Charlotte Depew."

At the mention of Charlotte's name, his face pulled down into a deep frown. "What makes you think I know anything about her?"

"I don't know if you do," Candy said, her voice still low, "but I know the judging at the cook-off on Saturday was tainted, and I know Charlotte should have won."

"Won?" Oliver scrutinized her with his small, dark eyes. "I didn't have anything to do with that. You and Roger Sykes were the judges."

"You're right, we were." She paused. "But I saw your contestants' sheet with the $X$ across it. You obviously saw it too. Something's going on here, Oliver. I need to figure out what it is. And I need your help. Of course," she added, "I could always just go to the police and tell them what I know."

"Hmm." He considered that, his eyes darting back and forth across the lobby. After a few moments he pointed down the hallway. "Perhaps we should talk privately in my office."

"Perhaps we should."

She let him take the lead, since she didn't want to appear as if she knew the way. Halfway down the hall, he headed through the door into the office suite, angled across the receptionist's area, and entered his office. His loafers brushed across the thick carpeting as he walked to his desk, moving around it as he glanced down at several messages left for him. Standing behind the desk, he quickly sorted through them with elegant, manicured fingers. "Sit down," he said without looking up. "But close the door first."

She did as he requested. When she had settled into one of the dark red leather-upholstered chairs in front of his desk, he sat himself, folded his fingers together in front of his chin, and looked up at her. "Now, what's this all about?"

Candy came right to the point. "The cook-off contest."

"What about it?"

"Someone tried to rig the results."

Oliver's brow fell. "That's a serious charge—especially since you were one of the judges. How exactly were the results to be . . . rigged, as you call it?"

"By changing the order of numbers assigned to the contestants. There was a sheet on Robbie's clipboard—"

"Ah yes, the sheet."

"So you know about it?"

"Of course I know about it."

Candy nodded. It was time to show her cards. "So *you* were the one who put that big black *X* across the sheet and wrote the words *fake list* at the top? Right?"

Oliver took the longest time to respond. He appeared to be running a number of scenarios through his head, searching for the best way to answer. Finally he leaned back in his chair and took a deep breath. "Yes, in fact, I did."

Candy wasn't surprised he'd done it, but she *was* surprised he confessed to it so readily. Finally she was starting to get some answers. "So, you *x*-ed out the sheet because you suspected the list had been tampered with," she said, more as a statement than a question.

"Yes."

"You didn't create a new sheet and change the numbers back to their original order?"

He shook his head. "There was no time. When I discovered there was a problem, it was too late in the morning and too close to the judging."

"What made you realize something was wrong with the list?"

Oliver motioned dismissively with his hand. "Simple. It wasn't my handwriting. I assigned those numbers to the names myself, though Wanda helped me distribute the lists." He stopped and eyed her closely, as if he suspected that's where she was getting her information. But he let his suspicions pass for the moment and continued. "It was a fairly close re-creation, of course. No one else would have noticed it. But I did. The numbers weren't shaped properly. It was plainly obvious to me. But it caught me off-guard. As I studied the numbers more closely, I realized the arrangement was off. Two of them had been switched."

"Let me guess. The numbers for Charlotte Depew and Wanda Boyle."

Oliver looked impressed. "Well, well, well. Now how would you know something like that?"

"I keep my eyes open."

"Yes," he said slowly. "I bet you do."

Candy pressed forward. "So, you knew the numbers had been switched. How did you handle it?"

"Well, as I said, there was no time to create a new physical list. But it didn't really matter. Since only those two numbers had been transposed, I simply had to remind myself to reverse those numbers mentally if required later. Hence the $X$ across the sheet and the note to myself. But in the end it didn't make any difference, did it, since none of the contestants in the top three was involved in the . . . rigging? When you and Roger chose your top three, I double-checked the names and numbers on Robbie's sheet to make sure I was right. There was no crossover, or tainting, as you call it, to affect the outcome."

"I don't believe it," Candy said.

"What?"

"You said something to Roger about it, didn't you?"

That's the part that had taken her a while to figure out—Roger's odd behavior at the cook-off. Why had he purposely steered away from the cinnamon-flavored stew? Everyone else who had tasted it had considered it good enough to win awards. So why hadn't Roger?

In the end, after talking to Wanda, Candy had come to agree with her. Charlotte Depew's cinnamon-flavored recipe *should* have won that contest, just as it had done the previous thirteen times it had been entered. *That* was the point of the whole thing, wasn't it? It's why Charlotte—or whoever had stolen that recipe, and more than likely murdered Mr. Sedley—had done it. For the silly recipe, as Wilma Mae had called it.

What had the elderly woman said? Candy thought back to the morning she had interviewed Wilma Mae, which had been just a few days ago, but seemed on the other side of a chasm of time now, separated by the deaths of two people.

*. . . he was mostly just tired of all the commotion that always seems to follow him and that silly recipe of his around.*

That was it.

Candy felt cold. That silly recipe was indeed causing all sorts of commotion.

Oliver must have told Roger about the switched numbers, she'd realized after much consideration. That's why Roger avoided the stews cooked by Wanda and Charlotte, calling them *gimmicky*. Somehow he must have known which stews were theirs, and he'd refused to consider either of them for the top three. So, in a way, the results *had* been tainted. The stew that should have won had not.

She turned back to Oliver, not realizing she'd turned away. Her musings had overtaken her for a few moments. He appeared to have spoken, but she had missed it. "I'm sorry, could you repeat that?"

Again, Oliver gave her an annoyed look. "I *said,* why would you say something like that?"

Candy looked at him, and this time there was nothing but honesty on her face. "Because Charlotte's recipe should have won."

Oliver sighed impatiently as he straightened in his chair, as if ready to rise, bringing the meeting to a halt. He checked his watch. "Candy, I'm a busy man. I don't have time for games. If you have something to ask me, then ask. Otherwise, I have an inn full of guests and an overworked staff to deal with."

He gave Candy a hard look as she bit her lip. Her mind raced. There was something else. What was she missing?

Suddenly she remembered. She sat forward and returned his look. "Okay, Oliver, one last question and then I'll get out of your hair. What did Charlotte say to you when she approached you after the contest?"

"After the contest?"

"That's right. She came up to you on the lawn, didn't she? She had something to say to you."

Oliver stiffened as he recalled the incident. "Oh yes. I know what you're referring to. Yes, she did approach me, in a very angered state. I thought she was just upset because she'd lost the contest. I said a few words to try to calm her down, but she obviously wasn't listening to me. I told her I'd be happy to discuss the situation with her at a later date . . ." His voice trailed off for a moment as the memory of the episode took full shape in his mind. "And then . . . and then she said something very strange to me."

He was silent as he considered the words, his gaze distant. Then his eyes darted back and met Candy's. "She said, *He promised, he promised.* She repeated it several times, with great conviction. It was, to be honest, somewhat . . . disturbing."

"What do you think she meant by that?" Candy asked, intrigued.

Oliver shook his head. "I honestly have no idea."

"Did she say anything else?"

He thought about it but quickly shook his head. "Not that I can recall." He stopped, his eyes darting again, his lips working. "There was . . . one other thing, though."

She watched him, enthralled. "And what would that be, Oliver?"

"Well, it was something else I noticed that day— something very strange. Right before Wilma Mae fainted."

"Yes?" Candy said, coaxing him on.

"Well, I was quite cautious with the samples that day. I supervised Robbie, Alby, and the other staff members as they collected the bowls of stew from the contestants, and I double- and triple-checked with Robbie to make sure each sample was correctly positioned next to the proper placard. I didn't want any mix-ups, and everything was correct the final time I checked. And then"—he blinked several times—"and then I looked over, and I saw one of the bowls of stew sitting right in front of Mrs. Wendell."

"What do you mean?"

"Well, it was the oddest thing. Someone had moved one of the bowls of stew—and placed it directly in front of her."

Candy's eyes turned away, and she felt her heart quicken as she considered the ramifications of that. Had someone placed Charlotte's bowl of stew in front of Wilma Mae on purpose, knowing she would recognize it as Mr. Sedley's recipe? And if so, why?

It also meant . . .

Her gaze snapped back to Oliver. "It means someone else was trying to sabotage the results."

He sighed wearily and checked his watch again. "Honestly, I don't know what it means. But I don't have time to figure it out right now." He stood. "Candy, this has been enlightening, but I hope we don't have to talk about it again. And I hope you're discreet about what you've learned. Juanita Perez cooked a great stew. She deserved to win. As I've said, I'm confident in our judges' final decision. I'd like to leave it at that, if it's all the same to you."

# THIRTY-ONE

Her cell phone rang the moment she walked out of the inn. She fished it out of her pocket as she trotted down the stairs. Stepping onto the lawn, she angled to her left, back toward Ocean Avenue, moving at a quick pace. "Hello?"

"Where are you?"

"Hey, Mags. Sorry, I got delayed. I had to make another stop."

"Everything go okay? You find that person you were looking for?"

"I did. Nice work getting me out of there."

Maggie laughed softly. "Hey, it was a cinch, thanks to that disgusting old bottle of ketchup. And it was actually kind of fun. They never even noticed you were gone."

"Were they upset?"

"Naw, they're fine. Juanita got them some soda water and we got most of the stains out. It livened up the place for a few minutes, and then they got to talking about some golf trip they're planning and disappeared into that little world of theirs."

"Are they still there?"

"No, they headed out to see the parade."

"They left you alone?"

"We told them to go ahead."

"You and Wilma Mae didn't go along?"

Maggie lowered her voice over the phone. "We talked about it. Wilma Mae wanted to watch the ceremony out at the cemetery. But we're getting a little . . . tired. I'm thinking maybe we should take her home."

Candy put a hand to her forehead. She'd been so busy, she hadn't considered how Wilma Mae must be feeling, what with all that had happened in her life lately. "You're right. The poor thing's been through a lot. Okay, I'm on my way. I'll be there in a few minutes."

She keyed off the phone and was just about to close it when she noticed an alert telling her she had a new text message. Curious, she thumbed through the menus and read the subject line on the top message.

It was from an unidentified number.

She pressed the middle button, displaying the message:

*Hi there cinnamon girl again we have to talk your place two thirty be there you want to see this.*

Candy's mouth tightened.

Cinnamon Girl. Wanda.

Candy read the message again, her eyes lingering on the last few words: *you want to see this.*

See what? Had Wanda found the ledger?

Candy checked the time on her phone. It was a few minutes before two o'clock. She flipped the phone closed and slid it into the front pocket of her jeans. If she wanted to make it back to her place in time to meet Wanda, she'd have to hurry.

Now that the parade had passed, Ocean Avenue was jammed with people hurrying off in every direction as the first cars allowed back onto the road started inching their way up along the Loop. She could hear the sounds of the band and sirens fading into the distance as the parade marched northwest toward Stone Hill Cemetery.

She quickened her pace, but immediately the dispersing crowd slowed her up, making her move in starts and stops. *At this pace I'll never make it home in time to meet Wanda,* she thought.

On a sudden impulse she reached into her pocket for the phone and called Maggie again. "Can you meet me at the Jeep? I have to hurry."

"Sure. What's up?"

"I'll tell you in the car."

A short time later, feeling a bit bedraggled after rushing about and fighting her way through the crowds, she saw Maggie standing beside the Jeep, and waved.

"Who's your hairdresser?" her best friend asked as she walked up.

Candy gave her a half smile. "Why?"

Maggie discreetly indicated her hair. "You might want to make an appointment."

Candy's hand instantly went to her hair. "Does it look that bad?" she asked in an exaggerated whisper.

"Nothing a good comb-through won't fix." Maggie reached up to brush back several loose strands of Candy's hair and arrange it a bit. "There, that helps. Oh, here. You probably need this." She handed over Candy's purse, which she'd been carrying. "I found your keys and opened it up. I hope that's okay."

She pointed through the window. Wilma Mae was sitting in the backseat, wrapped in a shawl. When she saw Candy, the elderly woman waved with her fingers and smiled weakly.

Candy opened the driver's-side door and climbed in. "How's she doing?"

"She's hanging in there. Aren't you, Wilma Mae?" Maggie flashed a wave at the elderly woman as she scooted around the front of the Jeep and climbed into the passenger seat. "We had fun with the boys, but then they took off and left us girls sitting in the booth alone, so we sort of watched the parade from there." She looked over at Candy as she snapped her seat belt closed. "So, it sounds like you've been busy."

"I have, and I found out some interesting things."

"Like what?"

Candy started up the Jeep, checked the rearview mirror, and looked behind her as she backed out. "Like Wanda was trying to get Charlotte fired."

"Really?"

"Yup, and I got some interesting news from Oliver about the cook-off and that stew Wilma Mae tasted."

"My, my."

"And, oh yeah, Captain Mike's watching my back."

Maggie laughed. "Captain Mike? That old geezer?"

"The very one. If I'm ever in trouble, and you need to get help, he's definitely the one you should call." And as they sat in a long line of cars waiting to exit the parking lot, Candy told Maggie everything she'd found out about Charlotte and Wanda and the contestants' sheet on Robbie's clipboard and the mysteriously mobile bowl of lobster stew that had somehow showed up in front of Wilma Mae.

"Who could have put it there?" Maggie asked.

"I can think of several people right off the bat." Candy flicked on her signal and finally made a left-hand turn out of the parking lot onto the Loop, aided by a uniformed police officer, who held the traffic back for them. Maggie waved politely at the nice officer. "Like Robbie Bridges."

"Or Roger Sykes."

"Yup, there's him. Alby could have done it too, I suppose. Even Wanda, though I don't recall seeing her around the judges' table. Or maybe there's someone else we don't know about yet."

"Of course, that's the stew Wilma Mae ate," Maggie said softly, turning around and giving the elderly woman a smile. But Wilma Mae was staring out the window in silence. She seemed oblivious to their conversation.

"Of course." Candy glanced down at her watch again. It was nearly two twenty. She had to be back at the farm in less than ten minutes to meet Cinnamon Girl, alias Wanda, and they were still stuck in postparade traffic.

"So this mystery stew just happens to show up right in front of her? Doesn't that sound awfully suspicious to you?"

"It does."

Maggie leaned close and lowered her voice. "Do you think someone put it there on purpose, so Wilma Mae would see it?"

"That's my guess."

"But why?"

"I don't know. That's what I'm trying to figure out. I can't see where there's anything to be gained by it. Unless . . ." Candy's voice trailed off as a sudden thought came to her.

"Unless what?"

Candy glanced back over her shoulder, then said in a whisper only Maggie could hear, "Unless someone wanted to get rid of Wilma Mae. Maybe someone didn't want her judging the cook-off. And they figured the best way to disrupt things was to put that stew in front of her and create a ruckus."

"I guess it worked, didn't it?"

"It certainly did."

The traffic thickened as the minutes ticked by all too quickly, and Candy soon realized there wasn't enough time to take Maggie and Wilma Mae back to Maggie's home in Fowler's Corner and still make it to the farm by two thirty to catch Wanda.

So at the intersection of River Road, Candy flicked on her signal again and turned left instead of right. "I know you're going to hate this," she told Maggie, "but you're going to have to indulge me on something."

"What's that? We're not going home?"

"We're going to Blueberry Acres. I have to meet someone at the farm at two thirty, and I'm late. So you'll just have to come along for the ride, okay?"

"Well, sure, but . . . who are you meeting?"

Candy looked as apologetic as possible, as if she were delivering some really bad news. "It's Wanda Boyle."

Maggie's shocked expression and silence told her everything she needed to know, but the situation couldn't be helped.

Ten minutes later they turned into the long dirt driveway that led to the farm. As Candy drove toward the house, she spotted Wanda's SUV parked in front of the barn.

She pulled the Jeep to a halt beside Wanda's vehicle and turned toward her friend. "Look, you don't even have to get out of the car," she told Maggie. "Just sit tight and let me talk to her."

"What about Wilma Mae?"

Candy looked around. The elderly woman was nodding off. "On second thought, maybe you should take her inside and let her lie down." She handed the keys to Maggie. "As soon as I'm done here we'll take her back to your place."

"Well, okay." Maggie sounded uncertain as she looked over. "Just be careful. Whatever you do, don't turn your back on her. I don't trust her."

"Neither do I," Candy said as she opened the driver's-side door and climbed out.

She found Wanda behind the barn looking at the chickens.

"Hello, Wanda," Candy said as she walked up behind her nemesis.

Wanda turned, surveying her imperiously. "You're late."

"I got stuck in traffic."

"I was just about to leave."

"Well, I'm here now. So what's this all about?"

Wanda stood with her body tense and her lips tightly pursed, displaying her disapproval at having been kept waiting. When she thought she had sufficiently communicated that fact, she nodded just slightly. "I'll show you. It's in the SUV."

Together they started around the side of the barn. Wanda walked just a little ahead of Candy, taking determined steps, as if she were a prizefighter about to enter the ring. She came around the end of the barn at full steam, crossed the driveway toward her vehicle, and practically walked right into Maggie, who was coming around the side of the Jeep.

Both women froze in their tracks. After a few moments, their heads dropped and they took aggressive stances, like two stags on a mountain-top squaring off, antlers lowered. Candy could practically see the steam coming out of their nostrils.

"What are you doing here?" Wanda growled.

"I was *invited*," Maggie responded roughly, giving no ground.

"This is a private meeting," Wanda insisted.

"Fine by me. I want nothing to do with it, or with you. I just have to get Wilma Mae in the house. She's worn out."

"Wilma Mae?" Wanda's head swung toward the Jeep. She spotted the elderly woman sitting in the backseat.

At the same time, Wilma Mae saw Wanda. Her eyes grew wide with fright as she recalled the times Wanda had come to her house, demanding to see Mr. Sedley's recipe.

Seeing her reaction, Maggie opened the rear door and spoke softly to Wilma Mae, motioning for her to step out. But the elderly woman refused, clutching her purse tightly and shaking her head in fear.

"What's wrong?" Maggie asked.

Wilma Mae could only shake her head and point.

Maggie spun on Wanda. "See what you've done? Now you've scared her."

Wanda took a step forward, but before she could say anything, Candy interceded. "Wanda, what did you want to show me? Let's get this over with."

It took a few moments for Wanda to register the words, but finally she wheeled away. "Fine," she huffed.

She crossed to her vehicle, opened the back door, and pulled out a large manila envelope, which she held tightly. It was clear she had no intention of handing it over to Candy just yet. "Is there someplace we can look at this . . . in private?"

Candy and Maggie exchanged a brief, knowing look before Candy waved her hand. "Come on, we can talk in Doc's office."

Taking the keys back from Maggie, she walked to the house and unlocked the door. She walked through first, with Wanda right behind her. As she entered the kitchen, Candy took a quick glance at the Jeep and saw that Maggie had managed to coax Wilma Mae out of the backseat. The elderly woman stood uncertainly, looking about her.

Candy turned back to Wanda. "This way."

Doc had taken one of the rooms at the back of the house for his office. Its hardwood floors were covered with dark area rugs, bookshelves lined the walls, and a large wooden desk, piled high with books, folders, and papers, occupied one end of the room.

After glancing around, Wanda crossed to a table underneath a large window that looked out over the blueberry barrens behind the house. She cleared a spot on the table, opened the manila envelope's flap, and withdrew an aged, folded document from inside. Delicately she unfolded the document, laid it out on the table in the space she had cleared, and flattened it carefully with her hands to smooth the creases. When she was done, she stepped back so Candy could get a better look at it. "Have any idea what this is?" she asked smugly.

Candy switched on a light and stepped closer. She knew right away what it was. "Some type of blueprint."

"That's right, but a blueprint for what?"

Candy held Wanda's gaze for a moment, then leaned closer for a better look.

It was a single sheet, perhaps three feet long and two feet wide, with several design sketches on it, drawn in thin, precise lines and annotated with an architect's hand. The sketches showed different angles of a carpentry project. *A shelving unit,* Candy realized as she leaned in even closer.

It hit her quickly, and she couldn't help gasping. "They're the plans for the shelving unit in Wilma Mae's upstairs bedroom."

"That's right." Wanda jabbed a finger at the

blueprints. "And if you look right here, you can see the design for the secret drawer."

Candy studied the drawings for several moments. Wanda was right. She looked up. "These are Mulroy's plans?"

"A copy of his original, as far as I can tell," Wanda confirmed.

"But that means . . ." Candy's mind worked quickly as the ramifications quickly became apparent. Slowly she straightened. "Whoever had these plans would have known exactly where Wilma Mae had hidden the recipe for Mr. Sedley's lobster stew."

"That's right, Sherlock."

Candy took a step back as her gaze narrowed on Wanda. "Where did you get these?"

Wanda squared her shoulders back proudly, well aware that she had once again scooped the town's amateur detective. "I found them in Charlotte Depew's office."

# THIRTY-TWO

"Charlotte." The word left Candy in a long breath. She'd been reluctant to believe it was true, but here was more proof. All evidence pointed to Charlotte as the one who had stolen the recipe from Wilma Mae's house.

One mystery, it appeared, had been solved. But larger, deadlier questions loomed.

If Charlotte had stolen the recipe, had she also murdered Mr. Sedley?

And who had killed Charlotte?

Candy stood with her arms crossed, staring down at the plans. So Charlotte had managed to get her hands on exactly what she needed to win the Lobster Stew Cook-off—details about the document drawer secreted away in the shelving unit designed by James Patrick Mulroy. The architect's plans showed the exact location of the drawer, as well as the device that activated it.

But had Charlotte used that information to steal the recipe herself, or had she conspired with someone else, who stole the ledger for her?

It was an interesting question, but either way, Charlotte was still implicated in the crime.

So where had Charlotte found the plans? Probably in the museum's archives, Candy surmised. It would have been easy enough for Charlotte to dig around up there for hours after work, when the place had emptied out and she could go through the file cabinets undisturbed. She'd probably discovered the plans in the back of some forgotten drawer located in an ancient cabinet secreted away in a dark corner of the archives, some place only she knew about, where no one else looked.

Not even Wanda.

*Or,* Candy thought, *maybe she got them somewhere else.*

340

Her gaze was drawn to the upper left-hand corner of the blueprints. Someone had written a message there. She leaned forward again, her eyes squinting so she could see a little clearer. Uncrossing her arms, she put her hands on the table and leaned forward even more, her head twisting around to match the slope of the lines.

The writing was clearly in a different hand than the original architect's—cursive, slanted, and scribbled hastily, as opposed to Mulroy's neatly printed block letters. Still, the message was easy enough to read:

*Here are the plans. PS Make sure no one else sees this.*

She read it again. So. That answered the question of where Charlotte had found the blueprints.

She hadn't *found* them. They'd been given to her.

But by whom?

*Perhaps by the same person who killed Charlotte,* Candy realized with a start.

But that didn't make sense. Why would someone give Charlotte the plans and then kill her?

Candy studied the scribbled lines again. There was no signature, no way to determine who had written those sentences.

Wanda broke into her reverie. "Raises all sorts of questions, doesn't it?" she asked, her voice seeming out of place in the serenity of Doc's office.

"Yes, it does." Candy looked up. "But it also answers a few." She tapped at the blueprints with her index finger. "This is the missing link. We know the recipe was stolen, right? We know Charlotte used it to create her stew for the cook-off. You told me that yourself. And now we know how she got her hands on the recipe. She took it from Wilma Mae's house, using these blueprints, which showed the exact location of the document drawer—and the ledger."

"Right." Wanda gave Candy a smug look. "Just like I said, Sherlock."

Candy stiffened as something clicked inside her, and a long-suppressed knot of irritation suddenly unraveled. She could hold it back no longer as she straightened and turned to face the larger woman. "Wanda, what's up with you?" she asked angrily.

The smugness abruptly disappeared from Wanda's face. "What?"

"I mean, come on, what's with the attitude?"

Wanda's face settled into a cold mask. "I'm sure I don't know what you're referring to."

But Candy was having none of it. "You know exactly what I'm referring to. It's these smug comments you've been making over the past few days. Calling me Sherlock. My name is Candy. You can call me either that or ma'am. We're done with the Sherlock thing. You got it?"

Now Wanda looked offended. "Well!" she said. If she had had a feather boa, Candy thought, she probably would have flipped it back over her shoulder and stormed off.

"And while we're on the subject," Candy continued, "did you use this same attitude with Charlotte?"

Wanda's expression changed again, to one of wariness. "What do you mean by that?"

"You've been after Charlotte for a while, haven't you, like a dog nipping at her heels. Why, I don't know. Maybe you wanted her job too, just like you wanted mine. Or maybe you just like to throw your weight around. It really doesn't matter much to me. But whatever it was, it drove Charlotte to desperate measures."

There was silence for a few moments. When Wanda responded, her tone was icy. "If you must know, yes, I thought the woman was incompetent, and I let her and others know it. She was good at PR and in playing Little Miss Director. But the archives were a mess, and she was often rude to her volunteers."

Candy read between the lines. "Like you?"

"Yes, like me. I offered her lots of suggestions for improvement. But do you think she listened to me? *Noooo*." Wanda mimicked Charlotte's voice, which sounded a bit eerie to Candy. Wanda continued, her voice growing angrier. "I watched her file all my suggestions away in some drawer in her office, and that was that. She had no intention of following through on any of my ideas."

"So you went over her head."

"Of course I did. Someone had to know what was going on around that place."

"You sent a letter to the board, which got Charlotte in hot water."

"I was just trying to improve the archives."

"You were trying to get her fired."

"I was tired of being ignored."

"Well, I guess she stopped ignoring you, didn't she? I suppose she tried to reason with you."

"She tried, yes."

"And I suppose you told her to go take a hike."

Wanda nodded, her face still hard. "Something like that."

"And I suppose she didn't take that well."

A pause. "No, she did not."

"So she started trying to figure out ways to beat you, didn't she? She went to great lengths to get that recipe so she could win the cook-off—breaking and entering, at the very least. And possibly murder. And she did it all to prevent you from winning."

Wanda shrugged, unimpressed. "I suppose so."

"You created an enemy."

"I have plenty of enemies. What's another one?"

At that moment, Maggie poked her head into the room. "Did someone say *enemies?*"

Wanda completely ignored the interruption, but Candy glanced at her friend. "Hi, Maggie."

"Having a nice chat?" Maggie smiled sweetly.

Candy's eyes shifted back to Wanda. "I suppose you could say that."

"Well, I know you kids are having fun in here, and I hate to break up the party, but I just got a call from Amanda and Cameron. They came back a little early, and I'd sure love to head back home to see them. So whenever you're ready, we'll be waiting in the kitchen."

"Is Wilma Mae doing okay?"

"She's fine. A little tired, but she's a trooper."

"Okay," Candy said. "We just need a couple more minutes in here."

"Sounds good." Maggie looked at Candy and mouthed something that looked like *Be careful* and then wiggled her fingers at them. "So, um, carry on, you two. Try not to break anything."

When she was gone, Wanda abruptly turned toward the table and began to fold up the blueprints. "This was a bad idea," she announced. "I shouldn't have come to you. I'm leaving."

Candy was mildly amused. "What's the matter? Did I get too close to the truth?"

"It's nothing like that. I thought you could help." She stuffed the document back into its envelope. "Pretend you never saw this."

"But I have seen it."

"Then *forget it,*" Wanda said, her voice rising.

"I can't." Candy was surprised to find herself strangely calm. "Let me ask you something, Wanda. You said you found these plans in Charlotte's office. You went in to look for the ledger, didn't you? So did you find it?"

Wanda hesitated only briefly before she answered. "No. She must have hidden it well. But I'm sure it's there somewhere. I ran out of time. I only had a couple of minutes. I found this instead and hightailed it out of there."

"So you just went into her office and removed evidence without telling anyone?"

Wanda looked at her blankly. "Evidence?"

Candy pointed at the manila envelope in Wanda's hands. "*That* is evidence. The police will certainly search her office, if they haven't done so already. They'll be looking for clues to her death. And you've got an important one right there. You should take it to the police." Candy paused, as her own words struck her. "We *both* have clues that will help them solve this mystery. And we can't sit on them any longer. We both have to go to the police. Today. Right now."

Wanda's face grew tight. "Why would we want to do that?"

"So they can find Charlotte's killer."

"But that's what we're doing, isn't it?"

Candy gave her a look. "We?"

The word hung between them. Wanda obviously had let the word slip, but seemed to regret it.

After an awkward moment, Candy cleared her throat. "Look, I'm glad you showed the blueprints to me," she said, trying to sound a note of reconciliation. "But I'm not a detective, and I don't work for the police. I've already been reminded of that. So you need to take that document over to the station. I'll go with you, if you want."

"And tell them what? I stole the blueprints from her office?"

"Tell them anything. Tell them Charlotte left the plans up in the archives and you discovered them up there by accident, or say you saw them sitting behind the front desk and picked them up. Or yes, just tell them the truth—you were snooping around Charlotte's office after she was killed and found them."

For an instance, a look of fear crossed Wanda's eyes. "I can't tell them that. They'll throw me in jail."

"Probably not. Yes, they'll be pretty mad at you—at both of us. But that doesn't change the situation."

"There is no situation. We're done here, *ma'am*."

And with that, Wanda Boyle marched out of the house, with James Patrick Mulroy's blueprints clutched tightly in her large fist.

# THIRTY-THREE

Candy walked onto the porch just in time to see Wanda's SUV disappearing down the dirt lane in a cloud of dust, headed back toward town.

Maggie wandered out of the kitchen and stood beside her, holding a brownie square she'd rummaged in the kitchen. She nodded at the dust cloud left by Wanda, as casually as a sea captain might acknowledge a whale off the starboard beam. "Thar she goes." She took a bite of the brownie. "So what was that all about?"

"Oh, just Wanda in one of her moods."

Maggie turned toward her, eyes wide, head nodding, obviously impressed. "Hey, way to go! Sounds like you're finally beginning to get a handle on Wanda. Took you long enough."

Candy crossed her arms thoughtfully. "Yeah, I suppose that's true. She's a hard one to figure out."

"You're telling me."

"The problem is," Candy continued, "you just don't know where you stand with her. Is she helping or hurting? Is she your friend or your enemy? Sometimes it seems like she's both at the same time. I wouldn't trust her as far as I could toss a moose."

Maggie had to hold back a snort. "I'm guessing that's not very far."

Candy smiled. "No, I guess it's not, is it? But then again, I haven't had much time to practice my moose-tossing skills lately. They're getting a little rusty."

"Well, sure, that'll happen," Maggie said without skipping a beat. "You know, I saw a moose once when I went hiking. He was really tall, with skinny legs, and he had this long face with a big nose. He kind of reminded me of my aunt Lucy."

Candy laughed. "You had an aunt Lucy?"

"Oh, yeah. She was pretty popular back in her day. They used to call her Lucy the Moosey."

"Was that a compliment or an insult?"

"You know, I'm not really sure."

Candy looked at her skeptically. "You're making this up, aren't you?"

"No, I'm not, cross my heart. Hey, I was wondering—if I found a moose at the humane society and decided to adopt it, do you think Mr. Antlers would be a good name for it?"

"Mr. Antlers? It's kinda catchy I guess."

"Yeah, I thought so too. I like Bullwinkle also, but I think that one's taken."

Candy laughed again and put her arm around her friend. "I guess it is. Come on, let's round up Wilma Mae and take you home so you can see your kids. Then I have a date with the police."

Five minutes later, with Wilma Mae settled in the backseat of the Jeep, Candy locked up the house, and they headed across the narrow peninsula toward Fowler's Corner. Postparade traffic had thinned in the last half hour or so, but traffic was still heavy due to the holiday weekend. The day was starting to warm as the sun fell into the west and the winds shifted, while out toward the east Candy saw a bank of low, hazy clouds building over the ocean. "Looks like the fog's coming in," she said to no one in particular as they drove through a thickly settled area toward Maggie's home.

Quite abruptly, Wilma Mae leaned forward and tapped Candy on the shoulder. "By the way, dear," she said sweetly, "have you found my ledger yet?"

Candy glanced back over her shoulder at the elderly woman. "No, Wilma Mae, I'm sorry, I haven't. But I've been looking for it."

"I know you have, dear," Wilma Mae said, settling back into her seat, "and you've been doing a wonderful job. I've been watching and listening to you. You've talked to so many people, and it seems to me you're getting close. I think it's right under your nose."

"It is?"

"Oh yes. I wouldn't be surprised if you find it any day now." Wilma Mae paused. "I overheard you talking to that horrid woman at the house. So I take it Charlotte Depew had Mulroy's blueprints, which showed her how to find the secret document drawer in my house."

Candy exchanged glances with Maggie, who sat beside her in the passenger seat. "You *overheard* us?" she whispered loudly to her friend.

"Wanda's voice does tend to carry," Maggie whispered back.

"Why are you whispering?" Wilma Mae asked.

"Um, no reason." Candy looked up at the rearview mirror, so she could see the elderly woman in the backseat. "Yes, well, it does seem that Charlotte had the blueprints to your shelving unit. And, yes, it does sound like she's the one who took Mr. Sedley's recipe."

Wilma Mae looked pleased with this revelation. "Well, it's about time we made some progress. It should be simple to find the ledger now, shouldn't it? It's either at her house or somewhere out at the museum, where she works. Don't you think?"

Candy nodded as she made a right-hand turn onto Maggie's road. "Yes, that's probably right."

"So Charlotte's the one who made Mr. Sedley's stew at the cook-off, isn't she?"

"Yes, that's what we think happened."

Wilma Mae was silent for a moment, considering the matter. As always, she held her purse in her lap, tightly clutching the handle with two hands. "Well, I don't know how it happened, but I'm glad she didn't win," Wilma Mae said finally. "It just wouldn't have been right—winning the cook-off with a stolen recipe, would it?"

"No, it wouldn't," Candy admitted.

Wilma Mae said nothing else the rest of the way. A few minutes later they pulled into Maggie's driveway and parked behind a shiny new Chevy pickup truck with a crew cab and a long bed. Cameron Zimmerman, the boyfriend of Amanda Tremont, Maggie's daughter, had bought the truck with money he'd inherited from his deceased mother.

As soon as Candy pulled the Jeep to a stop, Maggie jumped out and raced into the house, anxious to see her daughter. Candy was about to climb out too when Wilma Mae spoke up from the backseat again, stopping her.

"He's her grandson, you know."

"What?" Candy put her arm on the back of the passenger seat and shifted her body so she could turn halfway around to face Wilma Mae. "He's whose grandson? And who's *he?*"

"Roger. He's Daisy's grandson."

"Roger Sykes?" Candy had to think about that a minute, remembering the conversation she'd had with Wilma Mae in her kitchen a few days ago. "You mean he's the grandson of Daisy Porter-Sykes? I wondered if those two were related, but I kept forgetting to ask you about it," Candy said, referring to the mistress of Cornelius Roberts Pruitt, who had stopped the business end of a ketchup bottle with her morning dress at Moosehead Lake Lodge so many years ago.

"Oh, it's true." Wilma Mae perked up. "I

became suspicious when I saw his face at the cook-off on Saturday. He has the same high cheekbones as her, and the same profile. And his hair is nearly the same shade as hers. But it's his eyes. I wasn't completely positive at first, but then he looked me in the eyes for just a moment, and I knew right then and there. I practically went into a tizzy. It was about the time I was eating that delicious stew."

"So it was a double whammy, huh?" Candy said sympathetically. "And that's what made you faint?"

"Oh yes, I'm sure that was it. I'm very healthy for a woman my age, you know."

"Wilma Mae, I don't doubt that for a moment."

"So you'll look into it?" the elderly woman asked, pressing her.

Candy gave her assurance. "I will definitely look into it. Now, have you met Maggie's daughter and boyfriend-in-law?"

"Oh no, I haven't yet," Wilma Mae said with a shake of her head.

"Well, you're in for a treat."

# THIRTY-FOUR

They found Maggie in the kitchen with the kids, talking and laughing. Maggie had her arm thrown casually around her daughter's shoulders, while Cameron had his hands wrapped around a double-decker Italian sandwich from a takeout place up on Route 1. Candy noticed another three or four still-wrapped sandwiches on the counter. Obviously they had stopped and put in a good supply for Cam before heading home.

Cam had grown taller and even shaggier since the last time she'd seen him just a few weeks ago. His face had also changed over the past year or so. It had become leaner and more mature as the last of his boyhood years fell away and he approached adulthood.

"It's amazing how you stay so skinny, considering the way you eat." Candy gave him a quick peck on the cheek before she turned to hug Amanda. She'd come to think of both of them as her own kids.

"Whatever diet secret he has, he should bottle it and sell it. He'd make a fortune," Maggie agreed.

"I already got a fortune," Cameron said around a mouthful of cold cuts, cheese, extra onions, and Italian dressing.

"It's all the hiking and camping he does," Amanda added, brushing aside a few strands of her long dark hair. "He climbed Mount Baxter a few weeks ago."

"And there was still snow at the top!" Cameron said with genuine enthusiasm. "It was awesome."

"You're awesome, babe," Amanda told him.

"No, you are," he shot back at her, and they all laughed.

He certainly had come alive since finding out about his real birth parents, Candy mused, watching him eat and laugh with the others. He rarely used to smile, let alone laugh, except when he and Amanda were together. But now he was more social and easygoing, joining in on conversations and even expressing opinions. He seemed to have a new appreciation for life and his place in it. But his love for Amanda had never changed nor faltered.

Maggie saw Wilma Mae standing near the doorway and crossed quickly to her, pulling her into the conversation. "Wilma Mae, this is my daughter Amanda and her boyfriend Cameron Zimmerman. Amanda graduates on June 12 in the top third of her class," Maggie said proudly, "and Cam's been practically living here for the past year or so. He's been taking care of some family business. Isn't that right, Cam?"

The tall teenager gave her a thumbs-up, but he was too busy chewing to say anything.

"He's working with a famous writer, who's helping him publish a book of poetry written by his biological father," Maggie explained. "But that's a whole 'nother story."

"Oh, isn't that wonderful." Wilma Mae's face was as bright as a full moon as she shook hands with the two teenagers. "It's so nice to meet you both."

Amanda said hello to her pleasantly, and as she

shook hands with Cameron, he said earnestly, "I was very sorry to hear about Mr. Sedley. He was a nice old guy. I used to see him in the hardware store."

"Oh, thank you so much, young man. He was a dear old friend."

Cameron took another bite of his sandwich, chewing briefly before he continued. "Yeah, he loved poking around the store, checking all the shelves and bins to see what had just come in. He used to buy tools for himself, and I think he sometimes used to buy stuff for the museum, too."

"Oh yes," Wilma Mae said with a smile. "He loved volunteering out there. And he frequently made donations, though not money. Just things he felt they needed, like tools and knickknacks and such. I think he recently bought a new set of chisels for the maintenance people. He was wonderful that way. Those were his two passions—cooking and the museum."

"The lighthouse museum?" Candy asked, her interest piqued. She turned abruptly to Wilma Mae. "You never told me Mr. Sedley volunteered out there."

Wilma Mae gave her a curious look. "You never asked. Besides, I thought everyone knew. He's been doing it for years."

"But . . ." Candy turned toward Maggie, her face scrunched up in thought. "Did you know about this?"

"About what? Why, what's wrong?"

Candy drew a long face as she considered the question. "I'm not sure."

But deep down she *was* sure. It was all too coincidental. She could feel her heart beginning to beat faster. Her mouth was suddenly dry.

She turned to look at the people standing around her. They were all watching her curiously. Then her eyes met Wilma Mae's. Something the elderly woman had said stuck in her mind:

*It seems to me you're getting close. I think it's right under your nose.*

*Right under my nose.*

Her gaze dropped to the floor.

"Well, well," she said, mostly to herself.

Maggie was studying her carefully. "What's going on? Are you okay?"

Candy looked up at her best friend. "I have to go."

"Go where?"

"There's something I need to check out."

Maggie seemed to know instinctively what was going on inside her friend's head. She suddenly became very serious. "You want some help?"

"Maybe. I'll call you, okay?"

Maggie nodded as a worried look came to her face. "Okay, but . . . be careful."

"I will."

"Don't do anything crazy."

"I won't."

"You sure you don't want some company?"

Candy smiled gently, looking from Amanda to Cameron to Wilma Mae, all of whom were still giving her curious looks. She suddenly realized how much she loved them all. "No, I'll be fine. You stay with your family. And take care of Wilma Mae. I'll be back as soon as I can."

And before she could change her mind, she walked out of the house toward the Jeep, fishing her keys out of her back pocket.

# THIRTY-FIVE

As Candy drove toward town, she encountered the first probing fingers of a quickly moving fog, and by the time she turned left onto the Loop's northward leg, heading past the docks along the river and the Rusty Moose Tavern, she was enveloped by it. She switched on her lights and eased off the gas as the lines of fog trailed across the road and between the buildings, giving the town a ghostly appearance as visibility dropped to only a few thousand feet.

It wasn't uncommon for great banks of fog like this to move quickly onshore, especially in the late spring and early summer, when the air was warming but the ocean waters remained cold. As she hit a particularly thick patch of fog, she slowed even more, so she didn't miss the entrance to the parking lot at the English Point Lighthouse and Museum.

Perhaps eight to ten cars remained in the lot, their windshields becoming misted by the moist air. Candy pulled into an open slot near the head of the pathway that led to the lighthouse and shut off the engine. The day had dimmed to a brownish orange glow, created by the pale light of the descending sun filtering through the dense atmosphere.

As she climbed out of the Jeep, she was grateful she'd put on her yellow fleece pullover before she left the house that morning. Inland the air had gradually warmed through the day, but here by the coast it felt thick and damp as the fog rolled in. She could hear the low rumble of the foghorn over by the lighthouse, and the muted thunder of the ocean as the surf broke on black rocks, sending up great ragged sprays of foam that hissed as they splashed onto the shore.

Slipping her hands into the pullover's pockets, Candy turned to survey the scene around her.

An elderly couple was headed toward their car, huddled together against the dampness and chill of the late afternoon. Farther down toward the oceanfront, a few devoted adventure seekers were climbing out onto the black rocks that lined the shore, allowing the spray of the crashing waves to wash over them. But other than that, the place looked deserted. Candy supposed a few folks might still be somewhere out along the Waterfront Walk, though with the arrival of the fog they probably wouldn't be there much longer. And she might find some lingering tourists down by the lighthouse and museum.

*The museum.* That's where Candy thought she might find the last few answers she needed. As she started off along the path, she wondered if she'd be able to get inside. Was it even open this late on a holiday? It didn't matter, she decided. One way or the other, she was going to have a look around.

Wilma Mae had been right about the ledger. If Charlotte had stolen it, then most likely she'd hidden it either at her home or in her office. And everything Candy had learned lately, including the most recent clue about Mr. Sedley's volunteer work, pointed here. The connections were just too suspicious to be coincidence.

As she came over the rise and descended the path toward the lighthouse, her eyes rose along the height of the tower. Its white exterior seemed to glow ghostly in the dull gray matrix of the fog. A few visitors, indistinct shapes now, their clothing drained of color, still moved around the tower's base and the Keeper's Quarters. They all turned toward a small, squat redbrick building behind the tower as the foghorn sounded again. Housed in its own building, the foghorn could be heard at a great distance out over the waves, but its bellow was muted to anyone who stood inland, due to thick brick walls that funneled the mournful warning call seaward.

Still, the sound of the foghorn this close was enough to chase off most of the remaining tourists, who were starting to meander back to their cars, giving up on their sightseeing activities for the day.

Candy followed the path past a couple of outbuildings and a flagless flagpole, crossed the open area in front of the tower, and angled toward the museum. As she climbed the wooden steps to the small porch, she glanced back over her shoulder. She saw only the retreating backs of the other visitors as they headed toward the parking lot and their cars.

Quickly she looked in both directions. She was alone. If she was going to get inside, now was the time to do it.

A handwritten sign posted on the inside of the door window indicated that the museum was closing today at three P.M., due to the holiday. Candy glanced at her watch. It was a quarter past four. She turned the old doorknob in a faint hope it might still be open, but it was locked. She knocked as she peered in through the window, just in case someone might still be inside. But other than security lights, the museum was dark.

Candy took a few steps back, surveying the windows on either side of the door. They consisted of old glass in green-painted wood frames with what looked like original hardware, well maintained. They also looked like they were tightly locked. She'd never get in that way.

She turned, surveying the property, looking for Bob Bridges or anyone else who might let her in.

Her gaze settled on the maintenance shed. It stood off to one side of the central open area, its twin barnlike doors hinged open and secured by lengths of rope so they wouldn't flop around in the wind. From where she stood, she could see no one inside.

She cast one last look over her shoulder and stepped down off the porch. As she started toward the shed, the fog seemed to pull apart before her like unraveling strands of cotton candy. But as she neared the shed, the fog closed back in around her, moving like a living thing. She pulled the collar of the pullover together and studied the shed's interior as she approached. "Hello?" she called out, her voice sounding muted in her ears.

She reached the door and looked inside. "Hello?" she said again.

It was deserted.

She took a step inside, entering cautiously, her gaze sweeping the interior. The place was relatively neat for a maintenance shed. Workbenches stood at either end, laden with carpentry tools and various types of hardware. Ropes and extension cords were coiled in one corner, while stepladders of varying sizes leaned against each other in another. A couple of hand-propelled lawn mowers, along with clippers, trimmers, hedgers, and garden tools, were smartly arranged or placed on shelves to the right of the entrance. Along the back wall were several filing cabinets beside a small desk and chair, which sat in front of a large calendar hanging on the wall. Tasks and reminders were jotted into most of the date boxes.

There were only two small windows at either end of the shed, which accounted for the gloominess inside. But the windows were relatively clean, not swathed in cobwebs as one might expect in a place such as this, and the floor looked like it had been recently swept.

Apparently Bob Bridges was a very neat maintenance man.

Stopping a few steps inside the door, she turned quickly from one workbench to the other, and finally to the desk, her eyes scanning. She had only a faint hope she'd find what she was looking for—a set of keys, maybe one that would get her inside the Keeper's Quarters. It seemed possible Bob kept a spare set out here somewhere. She thought it was worth a quick look.

The desktop, like the shed, was kept fairly neat. Two wire baskets held paperwork, and a gray and red blotter was surprisingly free of doodles. Pens and pencils were either lined up at the top of the blotter or corralled in an old white coffee cup. A clipboard with a sheet attached rested to one side of the blotter.

She could see no keys on the desktop but doubted they'd be left out in the open. More than likely, if they were out here, they'd be kept in one of the drawers—probably the top desk drawer.

She took a few steps toward the desk, and as she did so, she heard voices outside.

Her head snapped to her left. Out the window, she saw Bob Bridges coming around the corner of the Keeper's Quarters, wearing the same uniform she'd seen him in before—a dark green shirt and pressed jeans. A faded green ball cap hid most of his sandy-colored hair, and his face was red, probably because he appeared to be arguing with his son, Robbie, who was walking along beside him.

". . . don't know what you think you're doing," she heard Bob say to his son. "You've got yourself mixed up in this thing too deep."

"Don't worry, Dad, I can handle it," Robbie replied, sounding somewhat sullen.

"I do worry about it," Bob said, "and now you've got me involved."

Candy stood frozen, uncertain of what to do. Bob and Robbie appeared to be headed right toward her and the shed. Her heart beat faster. Should she make herself known to them, or should she hide?

In the end her instincts took over. Moving quickly, she stepped lightly across the shed into the front corner, trying to meld into the shadows.

It wasn't much of a hiding place, though, and if they entered the shed, she'd surely be seen. Her mind quickly tried to formulate an excuse, so she'd have something to say if she were caught.

"It's time for you to get out of that game," Bob said, walking along the side of the shed now. "You've already lost your shirt once, and it's cost us both. Get out before it gets the best of you."

"I can't get out now," Robbie protested. "I have too much invested."

"That's the problem with these things. They grab you and don't let go. There's no way you're going to win your money back. Listen to me, son. I know how these things work."

Candy could hear Bob unhooking something on the front of the shed.

"I'm fine, Dad," Robbie protested, his voice now tinged with frustration. "I'm not in high school anymore. I'm almost twenty years old."

"You're still my son," Bob said sternly, "and you're still my responsibility."

"Is that what this is all about?" Robbie asked angrily. "Responsibility?"

Candy heard a creak of hinges as Bob closed one of the shed's doors. It slammed tightly shut.

"Don't take that tone of voice with me. You're grown up now, but I'm still your dad."

Robbie said something Candy couldn't quite make out, and then she heard him marching away. Bob called after him as he unhooked the other door from its tether and swung it closed. She heard a hurried sound and then a snap, as if a padlock had been attached to the outside door handles.

"Robbie! Robbie, listen to me!"

Bob ran after his son. Candy caught a glimpse of him out the window on the other side of the shed, hurrying up the pathway toward the parking lot, chasing after Robbie.

Candy waited in the stillness for a few minutes, allowing her heart to slow and her breathing to ease. She realized she was sweating.

*Candy, you have to stop doing this to yourself,* she thought with a shake of her head.

When she felt she'd waited long enough to make a quick, unnoticed escape, she emerged from the corner and rushed to the door, pushing on it first with one hand, then with the other.

It refused to open.

She pushed again, harder this time, with her shoulder, but no luck.

She couldn't get out.

She was locked in.

# THIRTY-SIX

She stood staring at the door in disbelief. He'd locked her in! How could he have done such a thing? She felt her face getting flush. A few fingers of panic reached into her, causing her to stiffen. She looked around, searching for another exit. But there was no other way out, she realized with a start.

She was trapped inside Bob Bridges's maintenance shed!

She couldn't believe she'd gotten herself into this jam. What was she going to do? "Just stay calm," she told herself in a low breath. "Stay calm and figure this out."

Despite her admonition to herself, she could feel her heart beating faster as the panic threatened to build, to sweep through her in an unbridled surge. But she kept it under control as she tried to decide what to do next.

For a moment she actually forgot what day it was, which caused the panic to spike, but she quickly remembered. Memorial Day. A holiday. Her head twisted toward the window on her left. The fog had settled in outside, becoming impenetrable. Any tourists who might have lingered on the property were probably all gone, driven off by the worsening weather and leaving her stranded alone on the grounds of the English Point Lighthouse. She had a chilling vision of being trapped here all night, sitting dejectedly in Bob Bridges's desk chair with her head dropped onto his tiny desk, miserably trying to get some sleep.

That wasn't a vision she liked, but it worsened further as more questions jumped into her head, making her shiver briefly, uncontrollably. What would she eat? What if she got thirsty? What would her hair look like in the morning?

More important, what would she say when they found her in here the following day? What would she say to Bob Bridges? What would she tell Doc when he asked why she hadn't called him and let him know she wasn't coming home?

*Call him. . . .*

Suddenly she reached back with her hands, urgently patting her pockets, as if they were on fire. Her cell phone! Her left hand fell upon it. It was still in the left front pocket of her jeans!

A wave of relief washed through her as her shoulders visibly sagged. She'd found a way out. She could breathe again.

She pulled the cell phone out and clutched it tightly in her hand, cherishing its feel. The hard black plastic was warm and comforting against her skin, her lifeline to the outside world. At this particular moment, she realized, there was nothing else she'd rather be holding—except perhaps a door key to get her out of this place.

But even that wouldn't work. These doors, she realized, had no interior keyholes—no real locks at all. She recalled seeing large metal handles on the front of the doors. Bob must have padlocked the handles together, so even if she had a key, she couldn't get to the lock.

She'd have to call someone to come get her out.

Flipping open the phone, she brought up the contact list and scrolled down to her home phone number. She couldn't recall if Doc had anything planned this afternoon, but he'd pick up if he was around the house. He was her best option, she decided as she pressed the button that selected the number. But before she pressed send, she hesitated.

Maybe it would be better to call Maggie instead. No doubt Doc would look very unfavorably upon Candy's current predicament and would probably give her some sort of lecture, or at the very least disapproving looks for days. Maggie was the better choice.

She quickly found Maggie's number. Her thumb hovered over the send button. But again, she hesitated.

Her gaze rose to the door, studying it for a few moments before she turned toward the small window at the far end of the shed. Outside, the light was fading, squeezed from the day by the dense fog. She walked to the window and looked out. A few lights were flickering on around the complex, activated by sensors, she guessed. They formed glowing pools of pale illumination in the murky day.

She turned and looked up at the ceiling of the shed. She hadn't even noticed before, but a single fluorescent light strip hung over her head.

"Candy," she softly chided herself with a shake of her head.

She found the light switch by the door and turned it on. The fluorescent light cast an eerie glow in the shed's interior, but she barely noticed. She was moving again.

Maybe she wasn't as trapped as she thought. Maybe she could pop open one of the windows. Or maybe she could use a crowbar to wedge open the double doors far enough apart to squeeze through.

She'd try both those avenues of escape—right after she took care of something else, something more important.

It was time to do what she'd come here to do.

It was time to check out Bob Bridges's desk.

A key to the Keeper's Quarters could still be hidden somewhere in the shed, and she decided to take a few minutes to search for it.

Crossing to the desk, she pulled open the top drawer and studied its contents. It was as neat as everything else she'd seen in here. Pens and pencils were carefully arranged in a long tray, pins and thumbtacks occupied smaller bins, boxes of paper clips and rubber bands were lined up along one side, and scissors and rulers were laid squarely next to each other. Farther back were writing pads and other office supplies, like boxes of staples and various types of Scotch and masking tape, all in their appropriate places.

Candy pulled the drawer out a little farther and slipped her hand far into the back, feeling around for a set of keys. She was careful not to disturb anything. She didn't want Bob to think someone had snooped around in here. Her fingers reached and probed, but she didn't find what she was looking for.

She closed the top drawer and checked the others just as carefully and as cautiously, working top to bottom. One drawer held envelopes and labels, another a couple of reams of paper and ink cartridges for a printer, and another neatly labeled, alphabetized, and categorized files. None of the drawers held a set of keys.

Slowly she straightened, sliding the bottom drawer closed as she rose. No luck.

She stood quietly for a moment, still clutching the cell phone in her left hand. She looked down at it, thinking. Maybe she should just give Maggie a call and get herself out of here in time for dinner. Maybe she was trying too hard to solve this mystery. Maybe it would be best to bow out now, before things got worse, and let the police do their job.

Maybe.

But she felt she was so close. Wilma Mae had felt it too. *I think it's right under your nose,* the elderly woman had said.

*Right under my nose . . .*

Again, Candy looked down. Nothing there but a cement floor. She looked left and right, along the floor on either side, her eyes shifting all the way to the walls.

Something in the far corner caught her eye.

It looked familiar.

Squinting, she took a few steps toward it, never taking her eyes off it.

It was a blue tarpaulin, just like the one Mr. Sedley had been wrapped in.

She took a few more steps toward it, crouching down as she reached out to touch it with her hand, testing its texture and thickness.

It seemed like the exact same material. In fact, it was exactly the same type of tarp.

Could this be where the first one came from—the one used to wrap up Mr. Sedley's body?

Quickly she straightened. Her gaze shifted.

There, on the workbench nearby, she saw something else she hadn't noticed before.

Fishing line.

The panic surged through her again. Here was the evidence she'd been looking for. Here were the clues to Mr. Sedley's murder—and Charlotte's.

And she was locked in!

It was time to get out.

She found Maggie's phone number again and texted five words to her: *Need help at the lighthouse.* Then she flipped the phone closed, slipped it into her pocket, and looked around.

She could sure use a crowbar.

Her eyes scanned the workbenches and shelves, searching for the right tool. She finally spotted it hanging from a pegboard above the workbench.

She started toward it, her gaze focused on it and on the tools hanging around it: awl, block plane, bow saw, caulking gun, crowbar . . .

Candy shook her head again in disbelief. Bob had *alphabetized* his tools.

The only problem was, since it came early in the alphabet, the crowbar had been hung at the top of the pegboard, out of her reach. She wondered idly how Bob, who was not a tall man, managed to get to it. He probably just climbed up on something like she'd have to, she guessed. She looked around, then bent down and noticed a wooden stool tucked underneath the workbench.

Candy pulled it out, tested it for sturdiness, and gingerly stepped up on it, reaching toward the crowbar. But it was still beyond her grasp, so she stepped right up onto the workbench itself. To steady herself, she held on to one of the side shelves as she reached toward the pegboard . . . and froze.

As she had taken hold of the shelf, she'd glanced to her left. Something thin and long, with a battered gray and red cover, had caught her eye.

*It couldn't be.*

She looked down. Positioned neatly on one of the higher shelves was a black wire tray, containing a stack of neatly arranged papers. And sitting right on top of the stack of papers was an old ledger with a gray and red cover.

*Right under your nose . . .*

Candy felt a chill go through her.

Somehow, Wilma Mae had been right.

Hesitantly, as if in slow motion, she reached out for the ledger, half-afraid it would suddenly disappear before she could touch it. Her fingers stretched out toward it as the fog outside parted, allowing a stray beam of the late afternoon sun to stream in through the window, illuminating the shed's interior in a beatific glow.

She closed her fingers on it, thumb on top, the rest of them on the back of the ledger, and lifted it toward her. Still standing on the workbench, feet slightly apart so she could maintain her balance, she held the ledger up and delicately opened the cover.

*The Journal of James Edward Sedley,* read the first line at the top of the first page. The words were written in a neat, ornate script. And underneath that, on subsequent lines, he'd written in an equally neat yet slightly less ornamented hand, *Begun at Kettle Cove in Maine, on the northern coast of Saco Bay, within sight of Richmond Island and Piney Point, on this 25th day of January, in the Year of our Lord Nineteen Hundred and Forty-Six, on the cusp of a great adventure.*

Candy let out a quick breath. She felt her eyes begin to water.

She'd finally found what she'd been looking for all this time.

It was Mr. Sedley's ledger, hidden away here in Bob Bridges's maintenance shed.

She looked up in sudden shock. Her heart thumped again in her chest, more powerfully than before. She felt her blood turn cold. She teetered unsteadily, almost tumbling from the workbench.

Someone was at the door. She could hear the padlock rattling outside. The click of the key in the lock sounded as clearly as if it'd been positioned just inches from her ear. She heard the lock slipping away from the metal door handles, heard the hinges creak as the doors were pulled open. "Who left the lights on in here?" a voice muttered as a dark figure strode into the shed.

Candy gasped.

Bob Bridges stopped in his tracks, his head swiveling toward her.

A look of complete confusion clouded his face for a few moments as he studied her, trying to figure out what he was looking at. His gaze shifted briefly to the ledger, which she still held in her hand, and then upward again as their eyes locked.

A scowl came to his face. "What are *you* doing in here?"

Candy couldn't move. She couldn't breathe. She couldn't speak.

She'd been caught red-handed!

# THIRTY-SEVEN

Bob Bridges took a few steps toward her, his face flush, his eyes hardened and accusing. "You shouldn't be in here. What do you think you're doing up there?" He leveled a finger at her. "Get down from there right now," he said angrily.

Candy instinctively jumped and let out a yelp, but she had no intention of doing as he asked. "Stay away from me, Bob," she said, holding out one hand toward him. Her heart thumped in her chest as she twisted her head back and forth, searching desperately for an escape. But there was only one way out—the shed's double doors.

And right now, Bob Bridges stood between her and freedom.

As he came toward her another few steps, she moved away from him, along the top of the workbench to her left, slipping sideways like a crab, toward a back corner of the shed. She kept her eyes on Bob, not on her footing. As she moved, she knocked over a neat stack of illustrated workbooks and nearly tripped. One of the books slid off the workbench onto the floor, landing with a slam.

Bob gave her a distressed look. "Hey, don't mess anything up!"

"Just stay away!" she yelled back at him with all

the force she could muster. "Don't come any closer. I know what you've been up to."

He gave her a quizzical look. "Now what the hell does that mean?"

"You know exactly what it means." Candy glanced back over her shoulders, looking for a weapon. She'd reached an area of the long workbench where he kept woodworking tools. She spotted a variety of blue-handled chisels, arranged according to size, hanging on the pegboard against the wall. She grabbed the longest one and brandished it like a knife. "Just back away and no one will get hurt!"

Bob stopped dead in his tracks. He held up two hands. "Hey, hey, calm down."

Candy looked around frantically. Her gaze settled on the double doors again. *If I could just get there before he does . . .*

Bob had shifted his position, shadowing her as she moved along the bench toward the back of the shed. *There might be a chance,* she thought, *if I can just slip past him.*

Moving quickly before she had a chance to reconsider, she ran back along the top of the workbench toward the other end. But about halfway along she sprang off, holding the ledger tightly against her chest with one hand and the chisel in the other. She angled her jump in the direction of the door, hoping it would cut her travel time to the outside. But she landed awkwardly, since she couldn't use her hands to balance herself properly, and it took her a few moments to recover her footing.

By the time she'd regained her balance, the compact physique of Bob Bridges was blocking her path.

And he didn't look like he was about to let her pass.

Candy pulled to a stop, her feet slipping slightly underneath her. She scrambled backwards, holding out the woodworking tool. "Just stay where you are. Remember, I have a chisel and I know how to use it."

"I know you got a damn chisel in your hands. I can see the thing pretty clearly from here," Bob growled, flicking his gaze from the weapon to her face and back again. "Don't you go hurting anyone with that thing now, especially yourself. I just sharpened it the other day."

"Well . . . that's good then. At least you know what you'll get if you take another step."

Bob's head tilted oddly, as a dog might if it heard a high-pitched sound. "Hell, I don't know what's got into you," he said in a mystified tone. "You've been coming around here the last few days, snooping around and causing trouble, and now you're breaking into the facilities, stealing things, and threatening me with my own damned chisel. What the heck do you want?"

"I just want to get out of here," Candy said. She

retreated a few more steps, until the workbench poked her in the back.

"Well, okay," Bob said. "Just take it easy now. No one's gonna hurt you."

Candy wasn't fooled. "Yeah, I bet that's what you told the others, huh, Bob?"

Again, he gave her a strange look. "Others? What are you talking about?"

"I saw the tarpaulin. Or at least one exactly like it. And the fishing line. I know all about those."

"About what?" His gaze shifted to the neatly folded tarp in the back corner, giving Candy the chance she needed to try for the door again. She scooted to her left, then her right, and dashed forward, headed around him, moving as quickly as she could. But he moved quickly too, shuffling across the floor, blocking the exit again. "Hey, you're not getting away yet."

She yelped again and retreated. "Stay back, Bob."

"Look, I'm not playing games."

"Neither am I. Let me go," she said warily, watching him in case he charged her.

"Okay, you can go," he said, "but you can't take that with you." He indicated the ledger, which she still held tightly against her. "That belongs to the museum. You'll have to leave it here."

"Leave it here?" Candy nearly shouted the words as anger mixed with the fear and panic inside her. "It's not yours. You stole it!"

At this accusation, he looked more annoyed than anything else. "Quit goofing around and put it back."

Candy clutched the ledger tighter to her chest. "I'm not goofing around. And I'm not giving it back. It doesn't belong to you."

"Of course it belongs to me." Bob sounded irritated now. "You found it in my shed, didn't you?"

"That's right. I found it in *your* shed, Bob. What are you doing with it?"

"Oh hell, I don't know." He squinted at the object. But he couldn't see its cover clearly, since she still held it tightly in her arm. "What the hell is it, anyway? It looks like some sort of book or something."

"You know perfectly well what it is. It's the ledger, Bob. The one written by Mr. Sedley."

"Sedley?" At the mention of the name, Bob's brow fell dramatically.

"That's right. He gave it to Wilma Mae Wendell for safekeeping, but you stole it from her, didn't you?"

Bob finally seemed to understand what was going on. His face went pale. "It's Old Man Sedley's?" he asked after a moment, as if the realization had only just hit him. He shifted his gaze to the ledger, studying it. Suddenly he straightened and walked forward, holding out his hand. "Here, let me have a look at that."

Candy darted off to one side again, out of his reach. "Just stay back."

"Look here now," he said, planting his feet and putting his hands on his hips. "I've had just about enough of this. Maybe you should tell me what's going on, so we both know."

Something in his tone made the fear, panic, and anger inside Candy suddenly dissipate. She still stood warily in a combative stance, and she still held the blue-handled chisel out in front of her. But she was looking more closely at Bob now. She was starting to realize that something was not as it seemed. "You mean you don't know?"

"Know what?"

"About the ledger." For some reason she couldn't explain, she held it out in front of her, so he could see its cover. "*This* ledger. It was stolen from Wilma Mae's house last week. You took it, didn't you, and hid it up there on that shelf." She pointed.

"No, I didn't," he retorted.

"But I found it there."

"Well, I don't remember putting it up there."

"Don't remember?" Candy was flabbergasted. "How could you not remember something like this? You obviously take really good care of things around here, Bob. You even arranged the tools alphabetically."

"And by category and size," Bob put in.

"Right, by category and size," Candy repeated,

though she hadn't noticed that. "So how come you don't remember putting this ledger up on that shelf?"

Bob's confusion grew. He tilted his head again and scratched thoughtfully at his chin. "Well, now, that's a darn good question."

Now Candy was confused. "What do you mean?"

"What I mean is, you're right. I know everything that's in this shed. I know exactly where I put things. I even have a map that shows where I've placed every item, and a complete inventory of all the museum's equipment. But I don't remember ever putting a ledger up on that shelf. And I certainly don't remember stealing it from Wilma Mae's house."

He paused, his face shifting, becoming more thoughtful. "But I think I know who did." He held out a hand. "May I see it?" He paused. "Please?"

Candy held it tightly a few more moments, uncertain of what to do. But something in his tone made her trust him. He seemed more curious now than threatening. "Just remember," she said, "I have a chisel."

"I remember." He still held out his hand.

Hesitantly, she extended her arm and gave him the ledger.

He took it carefully, drew it closer, and examined its cover. "If this is what I think it is . . ."

He opened to the first page and read the

inscription. Grunting softly, he flipped back through a few pages. "It is Old Man Sedley's, isn't it?" He shook his head, deep in thought. "I can't believe she actually did it."

Candy knew instantly who he was talking about. "Charlotte! She took it, didn't she?"

He looked up at her. "You know about that?"

Candy nodded. "I've heard things about Charlotte, yes. But honestly I don't know what to believe. Or who to believe. So why don't you tell me. What's going on here, Bob?"

Suddenly he seemed very weary. He closed the cover of the ledger, looked over at his desk, and crossed to it. He flopped down heavily in the office chair, set the ledger on the desktop, and rubbed at his forehead with thick fingers. "I never should've got myself mixed up with her in the first place."

"You were helping her, weren't you? That's why you stole the ledger for her?"

"Stole it?" Bob shook his head, his eyes hard again. "I keep telling you, but you're not listening. I didn't steal it." He paused, and his face drew down into a long mask of regret. "But she wanted me to."

"She did?" Candy took a few steps toward him. "She asked you to steal it?"

"More than that," Bob said. "We made a deal."

"What kind of a deal?"

When he hesitated, she spoke again, coaxing

him. "Two people are dead. You need to tell me everything you know. Then we need to go to the police."

He placed his hands on his knees and sighed. "Well, I guess you're right. It's just . . ." He paused again. "Well, there are other people involved."

"Like who?"

At that question, Bob suddenly looked ill. "Like my son Robbie."

# THIRTY-EIGHT

"It's that boy that got us into this," Bob said, a pained expression on his face. "And those damned poker games of his."

"Poker?" Candy couldn't believe what she was hearing. "Is that what this is all about?"

"Yeah. That's part of it at least. But there's a lot more."

"So why don't you tell me all about it."

He waved a hand at her. "I'm getting to it, I'm getting to it. Things have been moving so fast I haven't been able to keep track of it all myself—and now, with Old Man Sedley gone, and Charlotte too, well, the whole thing has heated up to the boiling point, hasn't it?"

"It sure has. So, did you have anything to do with either of their deaths?" Candy asked point-blank, crossing her arms.

"Me? 'Course not. Well, not directly, I guess."

"But you were involved?"

Bob gave her a piercing gaze. "Not in the way you're suggesting."

"Then what about the tarp in your shed?" Candy pointed toward the corner. "It's just like the one Mr. Sedley was wrapped up in after he was killed. And what about that fishing line on your workbench over there? Charlotte was strangled with fishing line, you know."

Bob looked horrified. "She was?" He shook his head. "I hadn't heard that."

"What about it, Bob? If you didn't kill them, who did?"

"I don't know."

"Then what *do* you know?" Candy's tone had grown demanding. She felt it was the only way to get the information she needed out of him.

And it worked. He sputtered a bit and gave her a dark look, but he started talking.

"Charlotte's the one who came to us," he said finally, reluctantly. "It was all her idea, and that's the truth." The pained look in his eyes returned. "Robbie . . . well, Robbie ran into some trouble with one of his games—several of them, actually. He was doing okay for a while, making some money at it. I warned him not to get himself in too deep, but he wouldn't listen to me. He got cocky—and reckless. He started playing in these high-stakes games over near

Bangor, run by some rich guy out of Boston—Marblehead, I think he said. The guy's name was Paul or Pete or something like that. Old-money type of thing. Anyway, Robbie got in over his head."

"How much?" Candy asked, her voice quieter now, encouraging him.

Bob hesitated before he answered. "Twenty-five thousand dollars, maybe a little more."

Candy let out a low whistle through pursed lips. "Wow."

"Yeah." Bob ran a hand through his sandy hair. "It was a shock all right. When he told me that, he might as well have hit me with a brick. I was stunned. But he's my son, you know?" He paused, averting his eyes for a few moments. He took a deep breath before he continued. "Robbie said they brought in some ringer, backed by this moneyman. So this guy strings Robbie along for a while and then cleans him out. Takes everything. 'Course, Robbie thinks he can win it back, so he goes in deeper. He lost a lot of money before he realized it was time to quit. The poor kid came to me asking for help. And I wanted to. But I didn't have it either."

"So you went to Charlotte," Candy said, jumping ahead in the story.

But Bob held up a finger. "Well, not exactly. Like I said, she came to me."

"So how'd she find out about it?"

Bob puffed out his cheeks. "Captain Mike, I guess."

"Captain Mike?"

"Yeah. I had to talk to someone about it. So one day I told him what happened. Charlotte must have overheard us talking. That's the only thing I can figure out, and it makes sense, since she was snooping around a lot, trying to find out what Wanda was doing. The next day she came to me, when I was working out here in the shed. She said she had a proposition for me."

"Let me guess. She offered to lend you the money if you stole the recipe for her."

"No, not lend." Bob shook his head. "She offered to *give* us the money, free and clear. An even trade. I steal this recipe for her from Wilma Mae's house, and she'd give us the money, no questions asked, so we could get Robbie out of trouble."

"Wow," Candy said again. "She was that desperate to get the recipe?"

"I guess so. I was pretty surprised too."

"And you agreed to do it?"

"Of course I agreed to do it. People were starting to lean on the kid, make veiled threats. Time was running out. I didn't have a choice."

Both of them were silent for a few moments as they considered Bob's predicament. Finally Candy said, "So you agreed to steal the recipe, but you said you didn't go through with it. What happened?"

It took Bob a long time to answer. "I was ready to do it. I really was. Charlotte gave me the money, and I gave it to Robbie, so he could pay off those vultures. She told me exactly when she wanted me to break into the house. I think she might have been staking out the place. She seemed to know when Wilma Mae came and went. She even had this costume she wanted me to wear—old man's clothes and a wig she'd made. She was pretty good at that sort of thing, you know."

Candy remembered. Charlotte had dressed the mannequins in the museum's new exhibit. She'd even made the wigs, she'd told Candy that day she first visited the Keeper's Quarters.

It seemed she had used her skills for another, more sinister purpose.

It also seemed like she had everything well planned out.

Bob confirmed that thought. "I think she even took photographs of Old Man Sedley when he was out here volunteering—told him it was for a brochure or something like that. That's how she got the costume and the wig so exact. Anyway, she told me if I dressed up like Mr. Sedley I could slip into Wilma Mae's house without anyone noticing. That was the plan, at least. Get in, get the recipe, and get out."

"But someone noticed," Candy said as an image of Mr. Sedley wrapped in the tarpaulin sprang into her mind. She shivered as a chill overtook her, but she shook it off.

"Yeah, I guess so," Bob said. "But they didn't notice me, 'cause I'm not the one who broke in and took the recipe. In the end, I just couldn't do it." He paused. "I thought about it a long time, but I knew deep down I didn't have it in me. I'm not a criminal, no matter how much I needed the money. So I pulled out at the last minute."

"Charlotte must have been pretty mad about that."

Bob gave her a strained look. "You have no idea. I've never seen her that mad before. She threatened me in all sorts of ways. She said she'd have me fired. She said she wanted her money back, but of course I didn't have it anymore. She even threatened to go to the police, though she was just bluffing about that. We both knew that would never happen. I told her I'd pay her back somehow."

"So if you didn't break into Wilma Mae's house, who did?"

Bob shrugged. "Charlotte did it herself, I guess. As far as I know, she dressed up in the clothes she'd made, put on the wig, and broke into the place. She told me she already knew where the recipe was located—something about a secret drawer. But I don't know nothing about that."

*The blueprints,* Candy thought.

The pieces were finally starting to fit together.

"Do you think she killed Mr. Sedley?"

Bob shook his head. "I don't know nothing about that neither."

"So what happened after she stole the recipe?" Candy asked.

"Well, you saw her that day when you were here," Bob said. "She was tense, but she was a pretty cool cookie too—especially if she's the one who killed Mr. Sedley. And she was still pretty furious at me, as you can probably guess. She said I had to pay her back in installments, which I agreed to do. For the last few days she barely spoke to me. She seemed to forget I was alive."

"Did you talk to her or see her at all yesterday? The police think she was killed sometime last night."

At that question, Bob scrunched up his face. "The police were out here earlier today, asking me the same thing. She was here in the afternoon, but she left in a rush. I had the feeling she was meeting someone."

"Did you tell the police that?"

Bob nodded. "Sure did. I also told them that she'd been pretty upset ever since the cook-off. She wanted to win that thing pretty bad. But I got the feeling there was something else going on. She became very secretive. I thought she was up to something."

"What?"

"I don't know for sure." Bob pointed at the

ledger sitting on his desk. "But I think it had something to do with that."

"The ledger?"

Bob nodded. "I saw her reading it a few days ago in her office, but I didn't know what it was back then. I just thought it was something she'd picked up in the archives. I didn't realize it belonged to Old Man Sedley."

Candy eyed the ledger. On an impulse, she crossed to it and picked it up. She opened the cover and glanced at its first few pages. "Maybe there's something else in here we've been missing. Maybe . . ."

But she never had a chance to finish.

A figure had appeared suddenly out of the fog and now stood silhouetted in the doorway.

"I'll take that," the figure said, motioning toward Candy and the ledger.

Her head twisted toward the door.

It was Roger Sykes.

And he was holding a gun, leveled right at her heart.

# THIRTY-NINE

"I see you've found it. I'd wondered where she put it. The silly woman was trying to hide it from me."

His voice was surprisingly calm as he took a few steps into the shed. The fog seemed to cling to him, as if reluctant to let him escape its grasp. He wore a black jacket, gray shirt, and dark slacks. He also wore gloves, Candy noticed.

"Why don't you set that ledger right back down on the desk," Roger instructed her, "and step away from it." He swung the gun toward Bob. "Both of you. Back over that way." He motioned toward the workbench.

When they both hesitated, stunned by his sudden appearance, his face abruptly turned dark and his eyes lashed out at them, full of ferocity. "Now!" he shouted, jabbing at them with the gun. They both jumped. Bob sprang out of his chair as if bitten by a spider, and Candy quickly shuffled sideways, dropped the ledger on the desk as Roger had instructed, and moved away.

Side by side, she and Bob backed up, toward the side workbench. Both of them held their hands up in the air, even though Roger hadn't asked them to. It seemed appropriate, and was more instinct than anything, especially when facing down the barrel of the metal gray pistol he held. They were both too shocked to speak.

Roger's face had returned to its previous calm state, his sudden burst of anger gone as quickly as it had appeared. His eyes, though, were bright and glassy, with thin pinpricks of light shining out, as if lit from within. When he was satisfied they were a safe distance away, he strode purposefully across the shed, keeping the gun loosely pointed in their direction. He stopped in front of the desk, let out a visible sound of relief, and slowly reached out toward the ledger, as if it were some great talisman he had found only after a long, arduous quest.

"So here it is at last," he said, taking it in a gloved hand. He studied its cover, then used his thumb to flip it open and read the first page. Satisfied, he closed it again and turned toward Candy and Bob.

"I'm sorry to put you though all this," he said, sounding genuinely concerned. "It wasn't supposed to be this difficult. It was a simple arrangement. I paid Charlotte—"

"You paid Charlotte?" Candy cut in.

Roger looked slightly annoyed at the interruption. His mouth twitched at the edges. "As I said, we had an arrangement. She would acquire the ledger, she would take that recipe she wanted, and then I would get the ledger, with everything else in it."

"Why, Roger?" Candy asked, her curiosity getting the better of her. "What's in that ledger that makes it so important?"

"Information," he said after considering her question for a few moments. "Valuable information."

"And that made it worth everything you've done—including murder?"

He gave her a hard look.

When he didn't answer, she went on. "You killed Charlotte, didn't you?"

In response, he reached into his jacket pocket. He pulled something out, glanced at it, and tossed it toward Bob. It hit the maintenance man in the chest. He flinched and fumbled for it but couldn't grab hold of it, and it clattered to the floor between Bob and Candy.

It was a roll of dark green fishing line.

"Does that answer your question? I borrowed that from your boyfriend," Roger said to Candy, allowing a trace of mockery to enter his voice. "Ben's a very trusting fellow, you know—and not as observant as you'd expect for a newspaper man. He never noticed it was missing from his tackle box. Of course, he's had other things on his mind this weekend—like that old man's murder . . . and, of course, *you*."

"What?" Candy wasn't sure she'd heard him correctly.

Roger almost laughed at her expression. "You heard me right. He likes you a lot, you know. He talks about you all the time—even when everyone else around him gets tired of hearing about you. But at least it was a way for me to keep up with what you've been doing around town the past few days. You've been quite active, I've heard. Interviewing that old woman. Searching for her recipe. Judging the cook-off with me. Finding the body. Getting that promotion—oh yes, I heard about that too. Ben has been a perfect gentleman at spilling all the secrets about your *investigation*. Of course, he had no idea what he was doing—or who he was spilling his secrets to," Roger added with a slight grin.

Candy gasped, suddenly angry. "You've been *using* him."

"And setting him up," Bob added, looking down at the fishing line.

"Of course I have." Roger flashed his white teeth as his grin grew. "What are friends for?"

Candy couldn't believe what she was hearing. "You betrayed him? But I thought—"

"What, that we were friends? That's what he thinks. But we never were. He was a family friend of sorts, and I met him a few times in college. The rest is a fabrication I've nurtured over the years, hoping I could tap into it someday. And it looks like today is the day."

"But why kill Charlotte?" Candy asked. "What did she ever do to you?"

Roger's face turned dark again. "She went back on our deal, that's why."

"Because she realized you betrayed her too?"

Roger glared at her. "You're smarter than you look. How did you figure that out?"

"Something Oliver told me earlier today. He said Charlotte was furious with him when she didn't win the cook-off, and confronted him. She kept saying, *He promised, he promised*. She was referring to *you,* wasn't she? *You* promised her she'd win that contest—and then you went back on your deal. You made sure she *lost,* even though she was using Mr. Sedley's recipe."

At that, Roger chuckled. "Well, yes, it's true. I thought it'd be fun to play with her a little. You know the old saying: you can't always get what you want."

"You purposely dismissed that recipe—and you placed that bowl of stew in front of Wilma Mae too, didn't you? Because you wanted to get rid of her. You didn't want her campaigning for Mr. Sedley's stew."

"I admit, it was a last-minute decision," Roger said. "I didn't completely know what I'd be facing until I arrived at the inn that morning. But it seemed a little too troubling to have Charlotte using that old man's recipe, and that old woman as a judge. I had to defuse the situation—so I improvised. Oliver helped. He told me the number of Charlotte's stew. He said it had been compromised." Roger shrugged. "It was easy."

"So you got Wilma Mae out of the way, and you made sure someone other than Charlotte won."

Roger gave her a sly smile. "From what I understand, I wasn't the only one who was trying to influence the outcome of that contest. The entire judging process was tainted—as you probably know, I'm guessing."

Candy indeed knew. She pressed on. "So why

kill Charlotte? What did she threaten to do to you?"

"Oh, she made plenty of threats," Roger said, his smile disappearing. "That woman could get her fur up when she was mad. She was incensed when she lost the contest. She threatened to destroy the ledger, so I'd never get it. She used it as leverage."

"You made another deal with her, didn't you?" Candy surmised. "What did you offer her?"

Roger let out a grunt. "What she wanted."

"And what was that?" Candy asked.

"She wanted to get out of this two-bit town, if you must know. She wanted a more prestigious job, possibly at some museum in Boston or New York. I told her I had a few connections, I'd pull a few strings for her. And, of course, I offered her more money."

"And the handover was supposed to take place at that picnic area up along the English River, wasn't it?"

"She was supposed to have the ledger with her," Roger confirmed, "but of course she didn't. She said she'd hidden it away where I'd never find it. She said she wanted double the amount we agreed on. Apparently she'd read through the ledger and knew what was in it."

"So you killed her," Bob cut in, his face twisting in anger.

"I'd just left Ben's place. I didn't bring my

fishing gear with me on the trip up here, so I borrowed some from him. I had it in the trunk. And I'd stuck the fishing line in my pocket, just in case I had to use it. Turns out it was a little messier than I thought. Good thing I was wearing gloves."

"And for what? That damned ledger?" Bob asked incredulously. He inched forward. It was clear he was having thoughts of rushing Roger, maybe trying to overtake him. But Roger waved the gun at him.

"Stay right where you are. And yes, because of the ledger. Charlotte was the one who brought it to our attention, you know. I only found out about it recently. She said she'd heard rumors about what was in it—and I'm not talking about the recipe. Apparently Old Man Sedley let a few secrets slip when he was volunteering around this place."

"Like what?" Candy asked, unable to contain herself. "What's in that ledger that's worth murdering someone?"

"If you must know," Roger said, his gaze narrowing on her, "Sedley wrote down a few things back in the forties that are very important to my family. But that's all you need to know for now. I met with Charlotte a few weeks ago, and we put our plan together. I agreed to fund the operation—and I helped her out by driving a willing participant her way."

"Robbie!" Bob burst out, suddenly seething. "You tricked my son!"

Roger turned toward him, regarding him as if he were a bellboy at a hotel. "He was very helpful," Roger confirmed. "He played right into our hands—no pun intended."

"So you brought a ringer into one of your games to clean out Robbie, and then what?" Candy asked.

"Then we waited. It was only a matter of time. Eventually, we figured, Robbie would tell Bob—"

"And Bob would tell someone around the museum, and eventually Charlotte would get involved and make him an offer," Candy finished.

"Now we're getting to it," Roger said, sounding very pleased with himself. "It was all too easy. But in the end, it wasn't easy, was it?" He looked at Bob. "You fell for it right away, just like you were supposed to, didn't you, Bob? Just like we'd planned. You were supposed to steal that ledger for us, get the money for your son, which of course came right back to me, and then go away. But you had second thoughts. And look what happened. Two people died."

"You can't pin this on me, Sykes," Bob said.

"Oh, but I can. And I will. It took me a while to figure it out myself, but there's a perfect way to do it." He pointed toward the fishing line. "The evidence is right there. And it's in your shed, Bob. The police will surmise you took the fishing line from Ben, or maybe not. I'm sure you have other rolls of fishing line around here. It doesn't matter.

The point is, you had every reason to kill Charlotte—and James Sedley. You had a motive to do what Charlotte wanted, and then you put her out of her misery. Or, at least, that's what the police will think. You did it because of the money and your son's gambling debts. Didn't you, Bob?"

The maintenance man could barely contain his anger. "You know I didn't."

"It's only fitting, you know," Roger continued, "since if you had just done your job the way you were supposed to and stolen that recipe yourself, Old Man Sedley and Charlotte might both still be alive. But somehow she screwed up the theft— veered from the plan, entered on the wrong side of the building or something stupid like that. And she got caught. And . . . well, we all know the rest, don't we?"

"You can't blame this on anyone but yourself," Candy said.

Roger turned back to look at her. "It doesn't really matter anymore, does it? What's done is done. Now it's just a matter of cleaning up some loose ends."

"Like us?" Bob asked.

"Like you," Roger confirmed. "It's fairly simple from here." He looked back out over his shoulder. "We're headed to the tower, Bob. You've got the keys, right?"

# FORTY

What happened next was so surreal Candy found herself barely believing it. After a quick look around the area to make sure they were alone, Roger marched them to the Keeper's Quarters, but first he told Bob to lock up the maintenance shed. "We don't want anyone getting suspicious about doors that are open when they shouldn't be, right, Bob?"

He held the gun on them as Bob unlocked the door to the Keeper's Quarters and relocked it once they were inside. "We don't want any interruptions, do we?" Roger said mockingly.

The museum's main display area was dimly lit, and Candy thought if they had any chance of rushing Roger, it would be now. She tried to catch Bob's eye, but he looked too stunned to be of any help. Candy twisted her head, ready to spring—but Roger was watching her, with the gun aimed toward her.

"Keep moving," he said, making sure he stayed several paces behind them. "That way." He pointed with the gun toward the hallway behind the wooden counter, and the locked door that led to the tower. "We'll need your keys one more time," Roger said.

Bob looked at him, a worried expression on his face. "We shouldn't be going up there. Visibility's not very good and—"

"We're not going up there to sightsee, Bob. Open the door."

For a few moments, Candy thought Bob might make a move. But this was no Bruce Willis movie. They weren't heroes or movie stars. They were just a couple of folks from a small town in Maine, trying to stay alive.

Bob opened the door.

"Hold on just a moment," Roger said from behind them. When Candy turned, she saw Roger standing by the long counter. He had the ledger open and was flipping back through it, his eyes searching. He soon found what he was looking for, tore out several pages, and read through them, scanning the lines James Sedley had written decades ago. When he had finished, he folded the pages over and tucked them into a jacket pocket.

He tossed the ledger onto the counter. "Okay, let's get going."

Candy had never been in the tower before, and it was thrilling in more ways than one. It was dark and silent inside, a great echoing cone looming above them. Underneath her feet was a black and white tile floor, worn with age but well kept. A glass-enclosed sign attached to a gray-painted wall informed her that nearly a million bricks had been used to build the tower. On her left were the first steps of an iron staircase, painted black and ornately decorated, twisting upward.

Her head craned back. It was like looking at the

inside of a spiraling seashell, only this was one she could stand in.

"Up," Roger instructed.

"But it's dark up there. We'll trip on the steps."

"Up!" Roger ordered again, this time in a threatening tone.

Bob held up a hand. "Wait." He crossed the tower's circular floor to the opposite wall and moved toward a panel hidden under the staircase. Roger called out to him, brandishing the gun, but Bob just pointed toward the panel. "Lights," he said.

Roger seemed to finally understand. He nodded curtly. Bob opened up the panel cover and flipped several switches.

The tower's inside was suddenly illuminated, glowing with a soft yellow color, looking much as it must have a hundred years earlier, when the lightkeepers in their dark blue wool uniforms climbed these steps with gas lanterns in their hands.

As Bob came around the foot of the steps, he let out a long breath. "There are one hundred and seventy-four steps to the top, just so you know. Six landings—twenty-nine steps in each section." And he started up.

Candy followed.

She held tightly to the railing as she climbed the thick metal stairs, which were bolted to a winding frame. They reached the first landing and continued on, moving steadily upward. As she climbed, Candy found herself growing a little dizzy, and her thighs started to feel the stress. *I bet those old lightkeepers never needed to head to the gym,* she thought idly. This was enough of a workout to keep anyone in shape.

At the third landing, they saw a small alcove, where a tall, narrow window looked out over the ocean. On a clear day, she imagined, the view from here would be magnificent. But today she stared out at a patchy seascape of mostly gray colors, although spots of blues and whites peeked through.

"Keep moving," Roger said, standing several steps behind her.

She nodded and started up again.

She could hear Bob wheezing above her now, and even Roger was breathing heavily. Candy tried as best she could to control her own breathing. She didn't want to become too winded or light-headed. She might need her wits once they reached the top.

On the fifth landing, Bob stopped to catch his breath, and Candy came up behind him, laying a hand on his shoulder. "Are you okay?"

He glanced back at her and nodded. "I climb this tower a dozen times a month. I'm used to it."

"Enough talking," Roger said, coming up behind them. "Get going."

At the sixth landing, Candy saw several old

waist-high wooden cabinets with locks on them. "This is the service landing," Bob told her. "This is where the old lightkeepers used to keep their log books, as well as tools and mineral oil when the light was still an actual flame. They used to haul up the five-gallon cans of oil using a pulley system." He pointed at the ceiling, where Candy saw a large iron hook. "The light's right above our heads," Bob said, nodding at the ceiling. With his head he indicated a nearby hatch in the circular wall. "And that's the way out onto the watch deck."

Roger climbed the last few steps behind them and motioned toward the hatch. "That's where we're going."

"Outside?" Candy asked, incredulous. "But . . ."

Roger pushed on the hatch's handle, but the door didn't open. He swung the gun toward Bob. "Unlock it."

Bob stood motionless for a few moments. It was clear he was again running various scenarios through his head. But it was also obvious he had no plan for escape. He shrugged and walked to the hatch, pulling out his keys once more. He unlocked the hatch, pushed on the handle, and opened the door.

"Out," Roger ordered.

With a last look at Candy, Bob stepped out onto the iron walkway that encircled the top of the tower, just underneath the light.

Roger turned toward Candy. "You too."

Candy gulped. She had a deep dread of where this was all headed. "What are you planning to do, Roger?"

"I told you. I have to tie up some loose ends. Now move."

Candy hesitated as Bob had, but then she too stepped toward the hatch, and passed through to the outside.

# FORTY-ONE

The first thing she noticed was the wind. It had been relatively calm at ground level, but here, nearly a hundred feet up in the air, the wind was surprisingly brisk. A wave of panic surged through her as she felt herself being pushed sideways by a particularly strong gust, and she reached for the iron railing that surrounded the watch deck.

The fog had broken apart briefly, separating around the tower. Its rounded side fell away beneath her, and she could see all the way to the ground far below. Only the crisscross matrix of the iron deck separated her from certain death.

She gasped as she looked down. From somewhere underneath her, the foghorn sounded its long, low blast.

Bob was standing nearby, clutching at the iron railing, looking ill. Candy joined him. They both turned to watch Roger emerge from the hatch.

He pulled up the collar of his jacket against the

wind and turned to face them. "So, here we are," he said, his voice rising to be heard above the rush of the wind and the thunder of the ocean. "Unfortunately, we've reached the end of our little climb. Now there's only one way down for the two of you."

"Roger, what are you doing?" Candy asked, nearly frantic.

"You both know what's next. I can't leave the two of you alive."

"But no one will believe we jumped off the tower," Candy shouted, trying to convince him to change his mind.

Roger flashed an eerie smile, showing off those white teeth, framed by the black goatee. "Of course they will. It all makes sense. Bob killed Sedley and Charlotte. And you found out he did it. He brought you up here, and you two struggled. Unfortunately, you both went over the side. See, I said it was simple. And very clean. All the loose ends are tied up in a neat package." He lowered the gun at them. "So, there we are. No more need for conversation. You both just need to do what you have to do."

"There's no way!" Bob shouted. "We're not doing it."

"Oh, but I think you are," Roger said, and he tightened his finger on the trigger.

But before he could pull it, a musical note sounded from his jacket pocket.

It was his cell phone, Candy realized. Roger looked down, distracted. And in that moment Bob rushed him.

Roger caved under the impact as Bob slammed him back against the tower's exterior wall. Bob went for the gun, and they struggled for it briefly as it fired into the air. Candy ducked, covering her head with her arms. She backed away, around the curved side of the tower, as Roger threw Bob back toward her. She grabbed the maintenance man's arm and pulled him with her, around the tower and out of Roger's line of sight.

"Are you okay?" she shouted at Bob as they stumbled together.

He nodded and pointed back over her shoulder. "That way."

His plan was clear. If they could get back around the tower and approach the hatchway from the other side, they might be able to escape down the stairs.

But Roger had the same idea. As they cautiously rounded the tower to the far side, they saw him peering out at them, guarding the hatch.

"The other way!" Candy shouted, and they hurried back the way they had come. But again, as they rounded three quarters of the tower, Roger blocked their path to freedom, his gun aimed in their direction. He fired again, missing them as they ducked back around the curved tower.

"We're trapped!" Bob shouted.

"We need to find a way to distract him so we can get to the hatch!"

"But how?" Bob asked.

It came to Candy in a flash. "The cell phone!" She pulled it out of her pocket, flipped it open, and brought up the contact list. Ben had given her Roger's number the day before, she remembered, and she had keyed it into her phone.

Clutching the small black plastic device in both her hands, she frantically tried to find his number, scrolling through the menus as her heart pounded in her chest.

"Hurry!" Bob cried, watching both directions for any sign of Roger.

Candy finally found Roger's number, brought it up, and pressed the send button.

A few moments later, they heard a musical note from their left, just around the curve of the tower.

"He's over there!" Bob yelled, and they both darted off in the opposite direction.

They could hear Roger laughing somewhere behind them. "Good call!" he shouted, his voice echoing out from the tower.

Candy and Bob moved forward slowly, rounding the tower, crouched low. Candy led, but Bob was right behind her. She kept her eyes sharpened ahead, around the vertical horizon of the tower's curve, while Bob watched back over his right shoulder in case Roger came up on them from behind.

But there was no sign of him. For the last quarter section of the tower's circumference, Candy crept forward slowly, her left shoulder hugging the tower, almost scooting along its surface.

The hatch finally came into view, and still no Roger. "Hurry!" Candy called to Bob, looking briefly back over her shoulder at him. She rushed forward, turning into the hatchway.

But Roger was waiting for them on the landing inside, his gun held up. Candy skidded to a halt in front of him.

"Well, there you are," he said. "I wondered what was taking you so long. Okay, you've had your fun. Now it's time to get to business." He motioned toward the hatch with his gun. "Back outside. Let's get this over with. And keep your hands up where I can see them. No more tricks with cell phones, shall we?"

He lifted the gun's muzzle to point it at her forehead. Candy's eyes widened as she backed away quickly, pushing Bob out behind her. "Don't shoot! We'll do anything you say!"

"That's better," Roger said as he walked out the hatch, following her. They all turned left, toward the town and the Keeper's Quarters. "I'll give you a choice of where you want to jump," Roger said, his white teeth flashing again. "This way"—he pointed down toward the left—"you'll hit concrete. That way"—he pointed off in the other direction, toward the ocean—"you'll hit rocks. Either way you won't know what hit you. It'll be fast and painless. I promise. Now, over you go."

"It won't do any good, Roger," Candy said earnestly, trying to buy time, still backing away. "They'll know it was you."

"No chance. They have no reason to suspect me. The fishing line's in Bob's shed. And everyone in town knows you've been after that recipe all week. When they find the ledger downstairs, they'll put two and two together, and figure you accused Bob of the murders, and he brought you up here to toss you off, and you both fell together." He shrugged. "It happens all the time. Now *jump!*"

As he said the last word, a small section of the tower's exterior, just behind his head, broke off and splattered on his shoulder. Candy and Bob backed away, startled. Roger shifted to see what had happened behind him, his body turning. A split second later they heard a soft whirring sound, then another, and suddenly Roger was on the ground, clutching his left shoulder. The gun had slid out of his grasp, across the watch deck. Candy dashed forward and kicked it over the side, then grabbed Bob by the shoulder, jumped over the prone and writhing Roger, and headed through the hatch and down the spiraling staircase.

She moved as swiftly as she dared without tripping, taking the steps quickly but carefully.

The landings seemed to rise up to meet her, and she counted them—*one, two, three*—as they spiraled downward, her hand playing loosely along the cold iron railing. "What happened up there?" Bob called out behind her as she heard sirens in the distance.

"I don't know. Keep moving! He might still be behind us."

But she heard nothing to indicate that he was coming down the stairs after them. For the moment, at least, he seemed to be incapacitated.

Before she knew it, they were at the bottom. She heard voices somewhere nearby, through the door that led into the museum, and suddenly Maggie was there, carrying a flashlight and moving quickly toward her. "I got your message. Are you all right?" Maggie asked, looking frantic.

"No time to talk. We have to get out of here. Roger's gone mad! He killed Charlotte!"

"I called the police!" Maggie said as she spun on a dime and headed back the way she had come, running alongside Candy. "They're on their way. Are you sure you're all right?"

Candy nodded as she ran past the counter and spotted the ledger, right where Roger had left it. She paused only a moment to snatch it up, holding it tightly with both hands as she followed Maggie and Bob out the door and onto the porch. In a tight group they hurried down the steps and ran off toward the parking lot.

"Halt! Who goes there!"

Candy yelped in surprise as half a dozen figures, partially obscured by the trailing fog and all carrying rifles, emerged from the bushes that surrounded the open area in front of the Keeper's Quarters and the lighthouse.

"Don't shoot! Don't shoot! They're with me!" Maggie shouted, throwing her arms up into the air.

All three of them came to a stop, watching as the men slowly gathered around them, lowering their weapons.

"Who are you?" Candy asked, as a familiar-looking figure materialized out of the fog.

"I called them right before I called the police," Maggie told her. "Just like you said."

It was Captain Mike. He smiled at her and winked as he chewed on a toothpick. Candy wanted to hug him.

"See," he told her as he tipped his battered old cap at her, "I told you we had your back!"

# FORTY-TWO

The following day, under an overcast sky, Candy drove northward along the Coastal Loop. She passed by the Lobster Shack, where she saw the typical long lines and packed picnic benches, and, farther on, Pruitt Manor, where she saw few signs of activity. Off to her right, the seas were choppy beyond the buildings and rocks. Ahead of her, out the windshield, dark clouds of varying shades drifted northeastward, driven up along the coast by a warm, steady wind.

Despite the threatening day, Candy had the Jeep's windows rolled all the way down, with a Fleetwood Mac song playing on the radio and her elbow hanging out the window. She loved the feeling of the wind in her face, bringing with it all the promise of summer, and she loved the freedom of being out and about today, with the sky, clouds, buildings, and landscape painting continual new images for her to enjoy.

She felt just a little guilty, though, like a kid playing hooky from school. She usually worked at the Black Forest Bakery on Tuesday mornings, and she knew Herr Georg probably needed her help, especially today. The summer tourist season had arrived, though the weather wasn't quite cooperating yet, and she imagined the bakery was swamped with locals and vacationers clamoring for his pastries, muffins, cakes, candies, and other assorted goodies. It was a great time of year for Herr Georg, as it was for all the shopkeepers and proprietors along Main Street and Ocean Avenue, who saw their profits jump with the season. Everyone in town knew the value of this influx of revenue and pitched in wherever possible to help meet the demands of the town's burgeoning population.

Maggie had certainly done her part. "Tell you

what," she'd told Candy over the phone late last night. "I'll go in and work for you tomorrow."

"You're offering to work at the Black Forest Bakery for me?"

"Sure, what's wrong with that?"

"I just want to make sure I heard you right. It's the Tuesday morning after a holiday weekend, you know—and the first weekday of the first week of the tourist season. You're aware of all that, right?"

"Well, yeah, I suppose. What's your point?"

"The patrons will descend on you like a pack of zombies," Candy said, greatly amused. "They'll be totally out of control."

"Really? They're that bad?"

"You have no idea. They'll try to eat you alive."

Maggie blew a breath of air out between her lips. "Hey, you've never seen me at Macy's on the day after Thanksgiving, have you? No zombie can compare to a woman clamoring for a cocktail dress on sale. They won't bother me."

Candy laughed. "You're sure about this?"

"Absolutely!"

"You have no idea what you're getting yourself into—but thanks," Candy said, genuinely grateful. "You don't know how much that would mean to me."

"You deserve a day off," Maggie told her. "After all, you worked all weekend, for both the newspaper and as a detective. You've got articles due to Ben. And you had to fight off a killer last night—without me, I might add! So it's the least I can do. Besides, it'll be fun. Maybe I'll take Wilma Mae with me. She can help work the counter."

"You know, that's not a bad idea. Actually, I think you two will work great together. I'll call Herr Georg and let him know you're coming."

The German baker had been gracious, as always, and concerned about Candy's well-being, given her harrowing encounter with Roger Sykes at the lighthouse.

Ben had been equally concerned, and then some. He had called her shortly after the police arrived at the tower. Apparently the news about Roger had gotten back to him fast.

"I just can't believe this," he had told her, completely devastated. "Roger, of all people. I've known him for years. I never imagined anything like this could happen. I just don't know what to say—except I'm glad you're okay. You *are* okay, right?"

For the most part, she'd told him, yes, she was okay. A little traumatized, a little bit in shock, still shaking, but generally okay.

But that had been last night. Today the shocks and the shakes were gone, and the intrusive memories of the night before were beginning to lose their sharpness, fading into something a little less terrifying. Despite her looming deadlines, she'd worked in the garden all morning, getting dirt on her knees and under her fingernails, which had helped. So had the trip to Hatch's Garden Center after lunch, where she'd picked up a few bags of manure, a couple bales of hay, some chicken feed, a jar of fresh blueberry honey, and a few plants, all of which she piled in the back of the Jeep.

She'd been driving in circles around the Loop ever since, unable to head home yet.

She needed to take care of some unfinished business.

As Candy gazed out over the rooftops of Pruitt Manor, she wondered idly how Helen Ross Pruitt was doing, and if the family matriarch would show up in Cape this coming week to open up the mansion. And she wondered what Mrs. Pruitt would think about everything that had happened in town over the past week, and what she'd think if she knew it all had started more than sixty years ago with a single bottle of ketchup, improperly handled. And that Mrs. Pruitt's own father, Cornelius, had used that bottle to set in motion a string of events that had led to the deaths of two people and the arrest of a murderer.

For Roger Sykes was indeed under lock and key. He'd still been sitting up on the watch deck, his back against the tower wall, clutching his arm, when the police found him. He'd been wounded in the shoulder—serious but not critical—and he'd lost some blood. But he'd live to stand trial.

Amidst all the chaos that had enveloped her last night on the lighthouse grounds, after she safely descended from the tower with Bob, Candy had eventually found out that it was one of Captain Mike's friends, Francis Robichaud, who had fired the critical shot. An excellent marksman, he'd aimed to wound Roger only, to remove the threat. Still, it had been a tricky shot, Captain Mike assured her.

"The fog, you know," he had told her. "We had to wait for a break."

The first shot, behind Roger's head, had been a miss on purpose, to reposition Roger and separate him from the other two. Only after Candy and Bob had backed away toward the railing, and he had a clear shot of the villain, had Francis fired again, this time hitting his mark.

Everyone in Captain Mike's entourage had been armed last night, though their weapons had conveniently disappeared before the police arrived. Candy had thanked them all personally. She'd recognized several of the faces and recalled that some of them were snowplow drivers who worked for the town—Tom Farmington and Payne Webster and Pete Barkely, in addition to Francis Robichaud. They'd all been in the Rusty Moose Tavern yesterday when she met with Captain Mike in the back booth.

And they'd probably be there again today when she stopped in.

She was still fretting about what she had to do, but she could think of no alternative. All night she'd tossed and turned, her mind running over the clues and events again and again, trying to see some other resolution. But she could think of none.

So here she was, circling downtown Cape Willington, as she'd been doing for the better part of an hour, driving around the Coastal Loop, cutting across on Main Street or River Road, and back around the Loop again.

This was the seventh time she'd passed Pruitt Manor.

Out on the point, beyond the mansion, she could see the top of Kimball Light, one of the two lighthouses in Cape Willington. It had a different design than the English Point Lighthouse. It was a little more elegant, with a sleeker shape and a taller, more rounded glass-enclosed top. It must have been built a few decades after English Point, she surmised, probably sometime in the early nineteen hundreds. It was privately owned now, so she'd never been inside. But she thought it might be fun to take a tour of it someday, perhaps even climb to the top.

Someday. But not for a while.

She stopped at the red light at Ocean Avenue, glancing over at the lawn of the Lightkeeper's Inn on her left. A little farther up the street, on the right-hand side, was the dark storefront of the

Stone & Milbury Insurance Agency. The place was shut down—there'd be no more business transacted there, at least not in the near future.

When the light turned green, she continued up along the Loop, past Town Park and the cemetery, past the Unitarian church on the left and, on the opposite side of the road, the entrance to the parking lot for the English Point Lighthouse and Museum.

Not so strangely, she had no desire to stop in there today. She'd found out everything she'd needed to know last night.

Now, like Roger, she just had to wrap up a few loose ends.

She drove farther on up the Loop, past the docks on her right and the Rusty Moose Tavern on her left. She slowed, switching on her turn signal. This time, she pulled the Jeep into a parking space in front of the tavern, turned off the engine, and sat with her hands on the steering wheel as she peered up through the windshield at the wooden building's dark brown facade and its weather-beaten sign, which swayed gently in the wind.

"Well, Candy," she said to herself, "are you going to do this or not?"

She knew the answer. She was going to do it—whether she wanted to or not.

With a determined expression on her face, she tugged on the door handle, climbed out of the Jeep, and locked the doors, leaving her purse on the floor in front of the passenger seat. She didn't expect to be staying long, and she didn't plan on buying anything inside.

She just had to put the last piece of the puzzle into place.

She'd expected the joint to be busy, but at this time of day, in the early afternoon, the tavern was sparsely populated. A few stalwart denizens clung precariously to their bar stools. Rosie, the waitress, gave her a bored wave.

Most of the tables and booths were empty. But as Candy suspected, she saw one patron seated in his favorite spot.

Captain Mike occupied the back booth, sitting alone, nursing a half-full mug of beer.

He was reading a battered old copy of a mystery novel by John D. MacDonald, squinting at it in the dim barroom light. As she approached the booth he looked up, his eyes glinting. "Ah, here you are. I was wondering if I'd see you today."

Candy slid into the booth opposite him, giving him a guarded smile. "Hi, Captain Mike. You were expecting me?"

He responded with his subtle maritimer's shrug. "I had an inkling. You are, after all, a detective."

She tilted her head and appraised him. "People keep telling me that."

"Probably because it's true." Captain Mike folded down a corner of the paperback novel, slapped it closed, and slid it off to one side. "You proved that last night. That was a mighty brave thing you did, facing down that criminal like you did."

"There was nothing brave about it," Candy confessed. "I almost got myself killed—again. And Bob Bridges too. If you and your friends hadn't showed up when you did . . . well, I probably wouldn't be sitting here today. I owe you my life, Captain Mike—which makes the reason for my visit here today much more difficult."

"Ahh. And why would that be?" he asked, taking a sip of his beer and squinting at her over the rim of the mug.

"Well, there are a few small things I still haven't been able to figure out."

"I see. Like what?"

Candy shifted in her seat. "Like who moved Mr. Sedley's body, for instance."

Captain Mike studied her. "I'm not sure I know what you mean."

"Well, parts of it don't make sense, do they? You see, according to the police, Mr. Sedley didn't die in the basement. He was killed somewhere else in the house, and his body was moved to the basement. So how did it get there? Did Charlotte move the body? Perhaps—but she wasn't a big woman. In fact, she was fairly petite. Could she have moved it by herself? Possibly. Possibly not."

Mike shrugged. "He couldn't have weighed that much. She could have dragged him down there."

Candy nodded in agreement. "She could have. But there weren't any marks on the floor, anything to indicate the body had been dragged down the stairs or from room to room. It just doesn't seem likely to me."

"So you think she had help moving the body?"

Candy evaded the question. "Then there's the issue of the tarp."

"The tarp?"

"The one Mr. Sedley's body was wrapped in," Candy clarified. "According to the police, it didn't belong to Wilma Mae. It must have been brought there by someone else—presumably the murderer. I noticed an almost identical tarp in Bob Bridges's maintenance shed out at the lighthouse yesterday. At first I thought he was the one who had killed Mr. Sedley and wrapped up the body in a similar tarp he had stashed in the back of his truck—or something like that. But that doesn't make sense either."

"Why not?"

"Well, Bob didn't kill Mr. Sedley, did he?"

"Maybe they were working together. Maybe Bob didn't do the actual killing. Maybe he just helped Charlotte move the body."

Candy shook her head. "I thought about that. But I was with Bob yesterday, in the shed and up in the tower. I looked into his eyes. I just don't believe he was involved with anything like that." Candy paused, leaned forward, and said in a voice barely above a whisper, "So do you want to tell me what *really* happened that day at Wilma Mae's house?"

"Me?" Much to her surprise, Captain Mike laughed. "What makes you think I had anything to do with it?" He quickly drained the rest of his beer mug and signaled to Rosie for another. Almost as an afterthought, he flicked a finger toward Candy. "You want one too?"

"No thanks. Anyway, it makes sense, doesn't it?"

"What does?"

"Well, you, to be honest. You're the most likely candidate. You volunteer at the museum, so you knew everyone out there, including Mr. Sedley."

"We worked different days," Captain Mike informed her.

"Okay, but you knew Charlotte pretty well, right? You two seemed to get along okay. You've probably been in Bob's maintenance shed a few times. You had access to the tarps. And you're a pretty big, strong guy—certainly capable of moving a body."

He looked her hard in the eye, and she looked right back at him.

"I've been all through it, Captain Mike, backward and forward," Candy said after a few moments. "And the way I see it, there are only two people who could have taken that tarp to the house and helped Charlotte move the body.

Robbie's one. Obviously he's been in the maintenance shed before. He could have grabbed a tarp and taken it over to Wilma Mae's house. And he certainly had the motivation. But I just don't think he could have done something like that. He's a sweet kid, although he's got a bit of a gambling problem. But I don't think he has it in him. On the other hand—"

"On the other hand," Captain Mike finished for her, "you think I do?"

Candy waited.

Captain Mike considered her logic. "There's someone else, you know. Roger Sykes could have helped her out. We know he was behind the whole thing, and we know he killed Charlotte."

"That's true," Candy agreed, "and you're right—he could have. But he didn't. Last night, when he was talking about framing Bob for the murders, he tossed a roll of fishing line at us. He was planting evidence in the shed. But Roger never mentioned the tarp. A similar one was sitting right there in the shed, in the back corner, but he didn't even look at it. It was another piece of crucial evidence he could have used to frame Bob. But he didn't. Why not? I think it's because he didn't know about the tarp—or at least he didn't know it came from Bob's maintenance shed."

"So that leaves me."

"That leaves you," Candy confirmed. "So, I

repeat my question—do you want to tell me what really happened?"

Rosie arrived with the mug, which she set down before Captain Mike. "Enjoy it," she told him.

"Like it was my last one," he replied with a wide grin. He raised the mug toward the waitress and then toward Candy, as if in salute, and took a long swig as Rosie walked off. He waited until she was back behind the counter, out of earshot, before he spoke again. "It was an accident, you know."

"Excuse me?" Candy said, not understanding.

"Old Man Sedley's death. It was an accident, pure and simple. At least, that's what Charlotte said."

Candy nodded sagely. "How did it happen?"

"Well, Sedley surprised her, you see. She couldn't get Bob or Robbie to steal the recipe for her, so she decided to do it herself. And, of course, she botched it up—let someone see her entering the building. She had on that stupid disguise, which she thought would let her snoop around unnoticed. But Sedley caught her all right, he sure did. He must have recognized her or something, because he backed up too fast and hit his head on the banister. He went down hard, or so Charlotte said. She tried to help him up, but he thought she was attacking him. Things got out of hand—and he fell down the stairs. Broke his neck. Probably died instantly."

"And that's when she called you," Candy said.

Captain Mike nodded. "She did."

"And you agreed to help her."

"I did. I'd borrowed one of Bob's tarps the day before. I just took it out of the shed—never even had a chance to tell Bob I took it from him, so he wouldn't have known. I'd planned to return it right away, but I never got the chance. When Charlotte called, well, she was pretty frantic. All worried about going to jail for the rest of her life. She begged me to help her."

"So you went over to the house."

Mike let out a brief sigh. "I did. I wanted to call the police. It was an accident, I told her. They'd understand. But she refused to let me. She said we had to hide the body."

"So you grabbed the tarp from your truck."

"I couldn't think of anything else to do," Captain Mike admitted. "I wanted to take the body out of the house, put it in the truck, and dump it somewhere in the woods behind Sedley's place. Make it look like an accident. No one would have ever known what'd really happened to him. But Charlotte almost went to pieces on me. It took all our efforts just to get the body down to the basement." He paused, and looked over at her. "She offered to pay me. She talked about a lot of money. But I told her no."

"Why?" Candy asked, tilting her head in surprise.

He looked down at the table. "Well . . . I'd rather not say."

Suddenly, seeing the look in his eyes, Candy knew. "You cared for her, didn't you?"

He still wouldn't look up at her. "Yup. Yup, maybe I did."

Candy sat back and was silent. After a few moments, she said, "Can I ask you another question?"

Captain Mike chuckled. He finally looked up. "What else do you want to know?"

"Well, last night. You knew I was digging around town, trying to find out what happened to Charlotte and Mr. Sedley. So why give me those clues yesterday like you did? And why help me last night? You knew I might figure out what really happened. And yet, you and your friends saved us—me and Bob."

"We did."

"Why?"

Captain Mike eyed her again. "Well, that's what we do in this town, Miss Holliday. We help each other out when we're in trouble. You would have done the same thing for me, wouldn't you?"

"Of course," Candy said, and she meant it.

" 'Course you would. You're a Caper. It's what we do around here. That's one reason I helped Charlotte. She needed my help. I couldn't say no to her."

Candy smiled. "Thanks," she said.

"For what?"

"For calling me a Caper."

He smiled too. "Well, you are, aren't you? Might as well admit it. And I've read your column, you know. Yup, I've read it. And, well, it's pretty damn good."

"Thanks, Captain Mike."

"Anytime, Candy."

"So." She leaned forward again and crossed her arms on the table. "One last question."

He grinned. "Last one? Promise?"

"Promise."

"Okay, shoot."

"What happens now?"

Captain Mike's expression turned serious again. "I was afraid you were gonna ask me something like that. But, of course, you're right, ain't ya? We gotta do something about this, don't we?"

"We do."

"And I suppose you have a suggestion?"

"I do. We have to go to the police and tell them exactly what happened."

"Do we now?"

"We do."

"I have another suggestion," Captain Mike said.

"And what might that be?"

"Well, you see," and he pointed out the front door with a steady finger, "I have a boat moored right out there at that dock. And I'm thinking about taking her out right about now."

Candy thought about that for a moment. "Where would you go?"

"Oh"—he waved a hand in a general eastward direction—"out that way somewhere."

"When do you think you'll be back?" Candy asked.

Captain Mike took a long swig of beer, smacked his lips, and shook his head. "I don't really know."

Candy looked toward the tavern's wall, and beyond it, as if she could see right through it, all the way past the buildings and the trees and the rocks, and out over the coastline to the sea beyond. "It looks like it's pretty rough out there today."

"I know," Captain Mike said with a satisfied look on his face, "and that's just the way I like it."

# FORTY-THREE

Four days later, on Saturday afternoon, Candy and Maggie sat at an outside table on a second-floor deck overlooking the busy wharves of the city of Portland and the Fore River beyond. They were at a popular chowder house, sipping strawberry margaritas and enjoying the unseasonably warm day. Most of the tables around them were filled with chattering guests, and Candy could hear music playing somewhere nearby. From where she sat, she could see, out on the river, an amphibious duck boat chugging upstream, giving sightseers an aquatic view of the city.

"This is nice," Maggie said, tilting her face back

to catch the sun's rays. "I'm glad we decided to do this."

"Me too," Candy agreed.

"Too bad Wilma Mae can't be here to enjoy it with us."

"Yes, it is. But I think she'll be happy. It's probably for the best."

"True, true. Still, I'm going to miss her. She's a sweet old lady. And we were becoming such good friends. Although she kept beating me at pinochle. I think she cheated."

Candy laughed. "Wilma Mae didn't cheat."

"Sure she did. I think she kept a few cards stuffed up her sleeves—or maybe down her blouse."

They both laughed at the disjointed image of prim and proper Wilma Mae Wendell cheating at cards.

They'd dropped Wilma Mae off at the Portland Jetport earlier in the day. The elderly woman was flying out to California to move in with her sister. A change in scenery was just the thing she needed, she'd decided a couple of days ago, right after Mr. Sedley's funeral on Thursday morning. Wilma Mae's sister had invited her out for a permanent visit. She'd even booked a cruise, just for the two of them. They were headed up the Pacific coast to Alaska on a fourteen-day seafaring adventure the following week, and Wilma Mae was greatly looking forward to it.

It had been a frantic forty-eight hours, getting the elderly woman packed and her house closed up. Candy and Maggie agreed to keep an eye on it for her until she decided what to do with it. But she knew she'd never live in it again.

And they knew they might never see Wilma Mae again.

"Well, at least things can start getting back to normal," Candy said, and she looked over at her friend. "Even for you. So you're going back to work, huh?"

Maggie beamed. "I sure am. I heard from Mr. Gumm yesterday. I start working at the hardware store on Monday."

"And how much do you know about hardware?" Candy asked.

Maggie beamed even broader. "Absolutely nothing! But Cameron promised to teach me everything he knows. I can't pass up a deal like that. But mostly I'm just going to run the cash register to start."

"Well, that certainly sounds exciting."

"It's not much money," Maggie said with a sigh, "but it's a start. I'll work my way back up in this town again. Just you wait and see."

"I have no doubt you will. You're pretty industrious. You'll do fine."

"Yeah, I think I landed on my feet. I learned that from Mr. Biggles—may he rest in peace. So . . . have you heard anything else from the police?"

Maggie asked curiously, taking a sip of her margarita.

"They called yesterday. They want to talk to me again early next week."

"Again?"

"Yup. Just to verify things, they said. Go over it once more. But I think they've got most of the story down."

"Are you still in hot water with them?"

Candy smiled. "Of course. I'm always in hot water with them. But they're getting used to me. I think we're starting to understand each other."

"Are they going to return the ledger to you?"

"They said they will—at some point. I don't know when, though. It might not be until after the trial."

"And did they ever find the missing pages?"

Candy shook her head. "That's the most frustrating part. I know Roger ripped something out of that ledger. I saw him do it. But when they searched him, they didn't find anything. And he's not talking. Whatever he took out of that ledger has mysteriously disappeared."

"There's no way of knowing what was written on those pages?"

"Apparently not. I asked Wilma Mae about them, and she said she couldn't remember—or just refused to. But I can't blame her. She says she's done with it. When or if I ever get the ledger back, I'm supposed to pass it along to Juanita at the diner."

"Oh, that's nice," Maggie said. "It sounds appropriate."

"It sure does, with Juanita winning the cook-off and all," Candy agreed. "One day soon everyone in town might be able to taste Mr. Sedley's lobster stew recipe, if they decide to put it on the menu."

"So life goes on in Cape Willington, Maine, doesn't it?" Maggie said philosophically.

"It does."

"Speaking of life going on, how are things with you and Ben?"

Candy made a face and shook her head. "I don't know. He's still devastated. He just can't believe Roger would murder someone. And threaten me. Ben feels responsible. And, I think, somewhat embarrassed. He says he'll make it up to me somehow."

"Hmm," Maggie said with a lascivious grin, "that sounds like fun."

Candy waggled an eyebrow at her. "Yes, it does, doesn't it?"

They were silent again for a few moments. After a while Maggie asked, "Heard any news about Captain Mike?"

Candy shook her head as she gazed out at the river. "Not a word."

"Think we'll ever see him again?"

"I have no idea."

"Well, I have a feeling he'll pop up again sometime in the future."

Candy turned to look at her. "I hope you're right. I hope he's okay. Hey, speaking of missing persons, have you heard anything about Mr. Milbury? Have they caught him yet?"

"Oh, yeah, I forgot to tell you. I got a call this morning before I left the house. They nabbed him at the Mexican border south of Bisbee, Arizona. He was trying to flee down to Guatemala or Costa Rica or someplace like that. But he didn't make it."

"And he's headed to jail?"

"Yup."

"Well, maybe he can share a cell with Roger."

And with that gratifying thought, they both turned and watched the boats cruising down the Fore River, headed past the islands of Casco Bay and out to the cold, deep sea beyond.

# EPILOGUE

Because she had to drive several hours north, Candy limited herself to one margarita, although Maggie allowed herself a second one. And they both had a bowl of clam chowder, which tasted delicious—perhaps not quite as good as Mr. Sedley's lobster stew, but still very good.

The afternoon passed by all too quickly, and as the sun slid toward the western sky, they decided it was time to head back up north to Cape Willington.

They had parked the Jeep in a garage up on Fore Street, so they headed across Commercial Street and angled up Market. As they turned a corner onto Fore Street, headed toward the parking garage, they passed a newsstand, and something caught Candy's eye. She took several steps along the sidewalk, stopped suddenly, and doubled back. "Hey, hold up a minute," she called to Maggie.

Her friend slowed and turned around. "Why, what's up?"

Candy didn't answer. She stood staring at the headline of the Portland paper, displayed on the newsstand for all to see: *Wealthy financier distances himself from brother,* the headline read. And underneath that, in smaller type, *Porter Sykes unveils plans for Portland waterfront redesign.*

Candy picked up a copy of the paper, rummaged in her purse for change to pay for it, and read the first few lines of the story:

Porter Sykes, a Boston financier and real estate magnate, as well as a member of the wealthy Sykes family of Marblehead, Mass., has announced plans for a major building and renovation project on Portland's waterfront. A fifty-four-room luxury hotel and convention complex will serve as an anchor for the project, said Sykes, of the investment firm Sykes and Dubois. Friday's unveiling event, however, was marred by the recent arrest in Cape Willington, Maine, of Mr. Sykes's younger brother, Roger, who is charged with the murder of the town's museum director.

Candy read the paragraph again, her eyes hovering over two words: *Marblehead, Mass.*

She felt a chill go through her. She'd heard something about Marblehead just a few days ago, hadn't she? What was it?

Standing on the sidewalk along Fore Street, with crowds of people passing around her, she searched her memories and, after a moment, remembered. It was something Bob Bridges had told her last Monday afternoon as they stood in the maintenance shed at the English Point Lighthouse:

*Robbie said they brought in some ringer, backed by this moneyman . . . some rich guy out of Boston—Marblehead, I think he said. The guy's name was Paul or Pete or something like that. Old-money type of thing.*

Marblehead. Old money.

And there was something else, wasn't there? Something strange Roger had said, when he'd been standing in the maintenance shed with a gun pointed at them:

*Charlotte was the one who brought it to our attention.*

*Our* attention.

Roger and Porter Sykes. Brothers.

Porter Sykes.

Why did that name seem so familiar to her?

And then it came to her in a flash: *Porter Sykes! PS!*

Candy felt her legs go weak. They threatened to give way beneath her right there on the sidewalk.

"Honey, are you all right?" Maggie said, concern in her voice as she took Candy's arm to steady her. "What's wrong. You look like you've just seen a ghost."

But again, Candy didn't answer. Her mind was working too quickly.

Porter Sykes.

PS.

An image of the inscription written in the upper left corner of the blueprints, laid out on the table in Doc's office, jumped into her mind.

The inscription on the blueprints had read, *Here are the plans. PS Make sure no one else sees this.*

*PS.* It didn't mean *postscript,* as she had thought. They were initials!

*Porter Sykes's initials!*

He must have written that note to Charlotte, signed his initials, and then added the last line: *Make sure no one else sees this.*

So Porter Sykes had given the plans to Charlotte!

But how had they known each other?

Candy had a cold feeling in the pit of her

stomach as she read down the columns of newsprint. Toward the end of the article, she found what she was looking for:

*An art and history aficionado, Porter Sykes sits on the boards of a number of museums throughout New England, including . . .*

She read the last few words as the blood pounded in her ears. In disbelief, she looked over at Maggie. "Oh no," was all she could say.

"Honey, what's wrong? What's going on?" Maggie asked, a worried expression on her face.

Candy shook her head, feeling as if she were in shock. The hairs were standing out on her arms. A feeling of dread washed over her.

"I don't know for sure," she said uneasily, "but I don't think we've heard the last from the Sykes brothers."

# RECIPES

## Lobster Stew

**Created by Executive Chef Troy Mains**
**No. 10 Water**
**The Restaurant at the Captain Stone Inn**
**Brunswick, Maine**

1 white onion, chopped
1 cup whole unsalted butter
2 stalks of celery, chopped
2 tablespoons Old Bay seasoning
1 tablespoon minced garlic
4 cups clam broth or really good lobster stock
2 pounds shucked lobster meat
1 teaspoon paprika
1 quart heavy cream
Salt and pepper to taste

In a large pot, sauté in butter the celery, onion, garlic, and spices. Once browned on medium to high heat, pour in the clam broth or stock and let reduce by half (boil down). Then add the cream to thicken, and season with salt and pepper to taste. Once thickened, add the generous amount of lobster meat and serve in a large bowl. This recipe should serve 6–8.

I also like to garnish the stew with a puff pastry

in the shape of a lobster. You can purchase a lobster cookie cutter at a cooking store to create this pastry. Cut it out of dough, brush with egg white, sprinkle with paprika for color, and bake at 400° for 7–10 minutes.

This will fancify a Maine classic.

## Lobster Veloute

**Created by Chef Jason Williams**
**The Well at Jordan's Farm**
**Cape Elizabeth, Maine**

2 quarts (serves 4)

1 lobster, about 1¼ pound, in hard shell
2 yellow onions
1 carrot
1 celery stalk
1 bay leaf
2 black peppercorn
4 ounces butter
4 ounces flour

Bring 4 quarts of water to a boil in large pot. Drop in live lobster and cook for 7 minutes. Remove and place in ice water.

Reserve cooking water.

Remove lobster meat and chop into pieces. Roast bones, return to cooking water, and add onions, carrot, celery, bay leaf, and peppercorn. Simmer for 2 hours. Strain.

In a separate large pan, melt butter and stir in flour; cook over low heat for about 3–5 minutes. Whisk in 2.5 quarts lobster stock. Bring to a simmer; continue simmering for about 20 minutes.

Serve with chopped lobster, some chopped chives, and some crusty bread. Enjoy!

## Fuel's Lobster Stew

### From Eric Agren, Owner
### Fuel Restaurant
### Lewiston, Maine

4 whole lobsters, steamed and cooled
Heavy cream (about a quart)
4 tomatoes, roughly chopped
4 cloves of garlic, crushed
4 shallots, diced
1 bunch of fresh tarragon, chopped
1 cup of Cognac

Remove all meat from the lobsters and reserve for later.

Break the shells into pieces. Use sturdy kitchen shears if necessary.

Heat canola oil in a large sauté pan over high heat.

Add the lobster shells and cook for about 5 minutes, until blistering but not burned.

Deglaze the pan with 1 cup of Cognac.

Flambé the Cognac and reduce to about 2 tablespoons.

Add the tomatoes, garlic, shallots, and tarragon.

Season with salt and white pepper.

Add cold water to the sauté pan till almost full (about 10 cups).

Bring to a boil.

Reduce the water until there is about 1 cup left in the saucepan. While reducing, squeeze the shells and other ingredients with a wooden spoon.

Reduce the heat to low.

Add the quart of heavy cream.

Bring to a low simmer. Simmer until the cream is reduced by 50 percent. Remove from heat.

Strain the liquid with a chinois, pushing the ingredients with the back of a wooden spoon, and reserve. Discard the shells and other ingredients.

Add the liquid to a saucepan on low heat.

Add the reserved lobster meat and heat through.

Serve immediately.

Serves four, although the servings are small; this is a super rich and very, very flavorful stew.

# Cod & Lobster Chowder

### Created by
### Executive Chef Mitchell Kaldrovich
### Sea Glass at Inn by the Sea
### Cape Elizabeth, Maine

6 slices of Applewood Smoked Bacon, diced

1.5 sticks of unsalted butter

2 cups of leeks halved lengthwise and thinly sliced crosswise, white part only

2 cups celery root, diced into small pieces

2 cups carrots, small diced

1 cup Spanish onion, small diced

6 each garlic cloves, minced

2 each bay leaves

¾ cup all-purpose flour

2 cups dry white wine

2 quarts lobster stock or clam broth

1 quart half-and-half, or more depending on consistency

4 each 1¼ lobsters, steamed for 2 minutes, meat sliced

2 tablespoons fresh thyme

3 tablespoons chopped parsley leaves

Lobster bodies and shells reserved for stock

6–8 portions, 4½–5 ounce each fillet of cod

1 pound golden fingerlings or new potatoes

## FOR THE CHOWDER

In a heavy saucepan at medium heat, cook the bacon until all the fat has been rendered and the bacon starts to foam (save half of this fat for the potatoes), then add the butter, garlic, leek, onion, celery root, carrots, bay leaves and cook for about 5 minutes or until the onions are translucent. Add the flour and mix well. Then add the wine and mix well. Cook for about a minute. Then add the lobster stock and lower the heat. Simmer gently for about 15 minutes or until the flour has thickened a little. Using a wooden spoon, stir constantly to prevent the vegetables from getting stuck at the bottom of the pot. Then add the half-and-half, salt, pepper, and fresh chopped thyme and parsley. Keep warm. Right before serving reheat the soup and add the pieces of lobster, seasoned with salt. Let the lobster finish cooking just for a couple of minutes.

## FOR THE POTATOES

Place the potatoes in a pot and cover with cold water and salt. Simmer slowly until the potatoes are done when pierced with a sharp knife. Strain and reserve. (This step can be done before the soup.) Before serving, cut potatoes in half, season with salt and pepper, and brown in a skillet using the reserved bacon fat and some olive oil or butter. Put in at 350°F for 5 minutes for a crispy skin.

## FOR THE COD

Pat dry the fillet of fish. Season with salt and pepper.

Heat a cast-iron skillet and add some canola oil and butter (about 1 teaspoon of each per fillet). Brown the fish for about 4 minutes (depending on the thickness of the fish). Put in a 350°F oven for another 3 minutes (only turn the fish when ready to plate).

Place about 5 ounces of the chowder in each preheated shallow bowl, place some golden potatoes around, place fish in the middle of the plate, and garnish with crispy smoked bacon and fresh chives.

## FOR THE LOBSTER STOCK

Lobster bodies and shells, wash and dry all shells (up to 6)
2 tablespoons vegetable oil
1 small onion, chopped
1 small leek, washed and sliced
1 carrot
1 bay leaf
3 each garlic cloves
3 tarragon sprigs
1 tablespoon fennel seeds
1 tablespoon tomato paste
1–2 each ripe tomato or 1 cup tomato juice
1 cup dry white wine

1 cup sherry wine
Cold water, about ¾ gallon

Heat a stockpot or heavy saucepan; add the oil and the shells and brown them on all sides for about 6–7 minutes. Add onion, leek, garlic, bay leaf, fennel seeds, carrot, and tarragon, and cook for about 5–6 minutes, constantly stirring to prevent burning. Add tomato paste and tomatoes, mix well, add wines and let evaporate the alcohol, then cover with cold water, about 1 inch above the shells, and gently simmer for 2 hours, skimming all impurities and foam that are floating. After 2 hours strain with a fine colander and put back at medium heat and reduce to half. You should have about 2 quarts of lobster stock.

Serves 6 to 8

## Center Point Publishing

600 Brooks Road ● PO Box 1
Thorndike ME 04986-0001 USA

(207) 568-3717

US & Canada:
1 800 929-9108
www.centerpointlargeprint.com